The Cowboy's Last Chance

by

Lee Ann Sontheimer Murphy

Dedication

Dedicated to my late, great friend and mentor Bennet Pomerantz. a like-minded spirit who encouraged and uplifted my life, who inspired and challenged me to reach, then exceed my goals.

Chapter One

If Vivian shut her eyes and held her nose, she could almost believe they were in Nanna's spacious living room at the Missouri farmhouse, instead of a tiny space within a long-term nursing care facility. But she couldn't manage, so the stark beige walls, the narrow hospital-style bed, and the single window overlooking an enclosed patio represented reality.

Nanna at ninety-four now resided here. Her once-vibrant brunette hair had become fully gray and although wheelchair bound, she made few complaints. After all, the farm had become more she could easily handle several years ago. Although she had stayed, the steep stairs to her bedroom had become difficult and finally impossible.

When Nanna Kate gave up driving four years ago, she no longer could make the trek to the grocery store or church or the café, so someone had to play chauffeur. Although sometimes one of Viv's many cousins did their duty, she had been too far away to drive except on the occasional weekend or holiday. When a March snowstorm made the roads between town and the farm impassable, Nanna had exhausted the contents of her fridge and pantry. Then she had fallen while going downstairs, tripping over a blanket wrapped around her to stay warm. The result had been a cracked hip and a new address at the Sunny Morning Senior Citizens

Home, a sweet-sounding name for a place Vivian would rather avoid.

Until Nanna's fall three months ago, Vivian lived in Kansas City, working as a reporter and photographer for a small suburban paper. Her hope had been to one day advance to the ranks of the *Kansas City Star* newspaper but so far, it hadn't happened. Now wasn't the best era to be involved in print journalism and once she got the call about her grandmother, Viv gave notice and moved back to Southwest Missouri.

For convenience, she bunked at the old farmhouse. Time and the interstate had combined to make the place not at all remote any longer. The two-story house had stood since the 1920s and once was a working farm out in the boonies of Southwest Missouri. Now, she could stand on the front porch and watch the vehicles zip by on the interstate. Even in the quietest hour of night, she heard the big trucks engage their compression brakes, the whine of steel-belted radials on the pavement, and the noise of engines, large and small.

A short trip down the driveway led to the outer road, then Vivian could take I-49 to town, getting off at the closest exit to the facility. It led past the local discount store, a variety of fast-food establishments, a low-price grocery store, and a big-box home improvement store. Once at the facility, she parked and steeled herself to enter. Seeing Nanna in this setting remained difficult but Vivian entered her grandmother's room. Then, she leaned down and kissed Nanna's cheek.

"Did you find a new job?" Nanna sat in the room's power recliner.

Although she could no longer reach the chair

without staff assistance, the old woman preferred it. She said it made her almost feel like she was at home. "I heard they're hiring here, for a social services director."

Vivian would rather stab herself in both eyeballs with a screwdriver. "Nanna, I don't really have the skill set for that. Besides, although it would be nice to be where you're at, I don't think it would be a good idea. Besides, I'm going to do some freelance work, especially photography."

"You take lovely pictures," her grandmother said. "At my house, I had several framed and hung on the wall. I think the one of the roses in bloom is my favorite or maybe the daffodils."

Those floral photos had been in her first years as a photographer and were more artistic photos than action shots. Years as a photojournalist in the city had changed her focus. "Thank you, Nanna. I plan to visit a few rodeos and shoot action photos there."

Vivian envisioned a book of gritty action photographs from various rodeos, some in black and white for a vintage look. Besides, she had an affection for all things rodeo and for cowboys.

"Oh, my!" Nanna exclaimed as she patted Vivian's knee. "That sounds like fun. Maybe you'll get a cowboy of your own."

"Maybe," Vivian said with a smile. Her grandmother had long wanted to see her married and settled, but Viv, although not opposed to one day having a husband, wasn't actively seeking a lifetime partner.

"When are you going to a rodeo?"

"Tonight," Vivian replied, more than a little reluctant to say. In mid-June, rodeo season was well underway and the one tonight a medium-sized event. Although the rodeo wasn't quite sixty miles to the south in Arkansas, Vivian planned to head out the minute she left the nursing home. Sometimes, if Nanna knew she wanted to go somewhere, she did everything possible to extend the visit. Today could not be one of those times.

"Well, then you should leave soon," Nanna said. "You need to allow plenty of time to get there. I don't want you speeding, and besides, you might meet a cowboy. I'll be praying."

She did her best to hide her disdain. Viv had parted ways with church and religion around the time she turned twenty-one. That had been after her parents had been killed in a home invasion, and her fiancé ended their engagement so he could move to California. Vivian couldn't wrap her mind around the idea God would allow her parents, faithful Christians, to die in such a horrific way. Where, she wondered, had been the angels to protect them? Then, just two months after she'd buried them, Arthur Covington broke up with her. The wedding had been planned for June.

The last day Vivian had sat in a pew or visited a church had been at her parents' funeral. Her Bible gathered dust before she shoved it into a drawer, then removed it to a box she dragged up to Nanna's attic. If her life depended on it, she couldn't find it without a long search.

"All right, Nanna. I'll be back in a day or so to see you."

"Drive safe," the older woman said. "And call me."

"I will." Her ride was a classic 1968 sports car, a two-door, hardtop model with the original engine. Painted a fire-engine red, the car could pick up and go.

Vivian had a need for speed. Driving fast always helped clear her mind, and she savored the rush of freedom when she hit eighty or more. Although she'd paid a lot to upgrade and restore it, the car had been her grandfather's back in the day. When she discovered it in the barn behind Nanna's house at the age of fifteen, she fell in love. Viv had begged and wheedled until Nanna gave her the car, the only possession she would ever have from the grandfather who died long before she was born.

To make good time, Vivian traveled the interstate south part of the way. At Anderson, in the last Missouri county before the state line, she exited the main road, then meandered down two-lane Highway 59 the rest of the way to Siloam Springs. Her car hugged the tight curves as she wound through the hills and held the road, even when she pushed past the speed limit. She rolled into the small town around six p.m. but parking was already at a premium. Vivian found a spot at the rodeo grounds for her classic ride underneath a shade tree in the parking area closest to the stands and hoped the space beneath it would remain. She slung her camera bandolier-style across her torso and grabbed her bag.

Although she'd worn jeans and a favorite tank top, Vivian wished she had thought about boots. Her sneakers didn't navigate over the uneven ground well, and by the time she got through the gate, her feet ached. Vivian strolled through the plethora of food stands, surprised at the variety. Some of the delicious food aromas enticed her, but others lacked appeal. She noticed many options were fried—including deep fried Oreos, chicken on a stick, fries, funnel cakes, and some kind of potato on a stick billed as tater twisters. Other options featured hamburgers, hot dogs, chili dogs, nachos, corn in a cup, walking tacos, popcorn, cotton candy, pizza on a stick, and jumbo corn dogs. She could choose a loaded baked potato, a burrito, a large turkey leg, or a barbecued brisket sandwich.

Many hours had passed since her strawberry-banana-oatmeal smoothie at breakfast, so Vivian was hungry. She stepped out of the main walkway to consider her choices. She couldn't remember the last time she'd had a chili dog, especially one topped with shredded cheese and onions. Vivian never noticed the cowboy until he stepped up beside her and spoke.

"I'd order something else if I were you." His voice resonated deep and quiet with some twang. "Those chili dogs bark back."

Vivian raised her head. He stood at least six feet tall, with a lean body. His curly hair gleamed black as a moonless midnight beneath his cowboy hat and touched his shirt collar. Since he wore jeans, a burgundy paisley Western shirt, well-worn boots with spurs, leather chaps, and a protective vest, Vivian figured he planned to complete. "What do you mean, they bark back?"

He put his right hand over the center of his abdomen. "They're likely to bring on a bellyache. I didn't figure a pretty lady like you wanted that."

"I don't," Vivian stated. His dark brown eyes met hers, deep and candid. Beneath the scruff, he turned out to be handsome. "What would you recommend?"

He laughed. "I don't eat before I ride rough stock. I won't eat until after the rodeo and probably somewhere in town. If I was going to eat here, I'd probably go for a funnel cake or maybe a turkey leg. I'm Calhoun Kelly, by the way."

"Vivian Bradburn." She offered her hand to shake. "Do you mind if I take your picture while you're competing? I'm a photographer."

Calhoun Kelly smiled.

Her heart did a flip-flop. His lips were well formed, the bottom one slightly larger than the top.

"I figured that from the camera." Calhoun chuckled. "I might be a cowboy and I've had my share of concussions, but I still have enough of my mind left to see that."

She laughed, too. If she'd been hoping to meet a good-looking cowboy, then Calhoun Kelly fit the description. "I'd hope to shout," she responded, with a laugh. "When do you ride?"

"I'm riding bulls tonight. It's the last event, and I drew next-to-last slot," he told her. "If you want to shoot pictures, you probably ought to sit on the north end of the arena and a few rows up. If you're too close, the rail and such will be in the way."

Without his suggestion, Vivian would have parked herself in the front row. "Thanks, I appreciate the advice. If you ride toward the end of the rodeo, would you share a funnel cake? I don't think I can eat an entire one myself."

"As long as you just get powdered sugar on it. I won't want any of that goopy fruit stuff poured over the top."

"Just the way I like it, too." A new friendship was born over their preference and the treat.

Once they had the funnel cake on a paper plate, Calhoun led her into the stands. They shared the hot, sweet confection and talked.

Vivian glanced around the arena, noticing the hard-packed dirt, the abundance of Western wear, and the crowds. She savored the rich flavor of the funnel cake and licked excess sugar from her fingers.

"Is this your first rodeo?" he asked.

"I've been to a few but not for years."

"Then why are you here?" Calhoun lifted one eyebrow and grinned as he shot her the question.

"I like cowboys." Vivian loved their attire, the way most swaggered, and their bravery in mounting unpredictable animals, risking injury, and death to win. "And I thought it would be a good event to shoot some pictures and see how they turned out. I'm freelancing right now, so if I can sell a few, that's even better."

He pinched off a piece of funnel cake, ate it, then licked the sugar from his fingers. "That might work. I take it you ain't from around here."

"I was raised in Missouri, not so far away. I was working in the Kansas City area for a few years, but I came back last spring."

Calhoun whistled loud and long. "That had to be a change."

"It is. But my grandmother fell and broke her hip, then had to go into a residential living center. She's all the family I have left, so I'm living in the old farmhouse. I don't want to be that far away again. Are you from Arkansas?"

"Texas. Down around Rusk and Palestine."

He pronounced the last *Pal-es-teen*, not the familiar pronunciation that ended in *stine*.

"I'm not familiar. What part of the state is that in?"

"East Texas. It's pretty country, right in the Piney Woods," Calhoun said. "There's not as many pines as I remember growing up, though. I don't have much family left myself, just my brother, Lincoln, and his family. I don't see him often in rodeo season. Granny raised all three of us, but she's been gone for ten years or so."

"Three of you?"

"We had a younger brother." His smile faded as he spoke. "Sullivan, but he passed away."

"I'm sorry." Vivian rested a hand on his, to offer comfort and show sympathy.

"Got stomped by a mean bull at a rodeo." Calhoun heaved a sigh and rubbed his face. "Couple years back. I was there."

His simple statement wrenched her heart. Vivian couldn't imagine losing a sibling and the anguish he must have experienced to watch his brother die.

"I'm so sorry," she told him, with her hand still connected. She rubbed his arm in an effort to offer comfort. "That must have been horrible. And you still ride bulls?"

He turned toward her with his dark brown eyes filled with tears. "It's something I do and do well. It's not just for the money, it's to honor his memory. Besides, I believe if it's your time, it's your time."

" 'To everything there is a season and a time to every purpose under the heavens, a time to be born and a time to die.' "

He stopped there but she recognized the passage from Ecclesiastes. The same one was read during her parents' funeral. Her chest tightened at the memory. She preferred not to remember that day. For the first time, she noticed he wore a small wooden cross on a stainless steel chain.

"I sure miss him, though." His voice dropped low

and soft as he spoke.

Vivian could relate. She still thought of her parents often, although with emotional pain. At a loss how to express that without seeming to compare losses, she ate another piece of funnel cake.

As the rodeo got underway, the announcers offered details over loudspeakers that resonated through the arena. Vivian noticed the wind had died down as a mounted color guard rode into the arena with both state and United States flags. When a young woman in a red shirt and white hat sang the national anthem, she stood with the rest and noticed Calhoun removed his hat.

When the mutton busting began with little boys clinging to sheep's backs, she laughed. "Did you ever do that?"

"Sure. It's how I started out. I need to go around to the chutes before long. If you want to stick around, would you like to go grab a bite to eat afterward?"

Her mind wanted to refuse, but he appealed to her heart. Besides being attractive, Calhoun had a solid quality she couldn't quite define. He seemed to be both tough and gentle. Vivian realized she wanted to get to know him.

"I'd like that. I'll be waiting."

A grin lit his face for a moment. "I'll be looking forward to it." He rose and started to go,

Vivian reached out and grasped his hand. "Hey, Calhoun." She tried out his name on her lips, using it for the first time. "Be careful, okay?"

He nodded. "I'll do my best, Pretty Lady."

Calhoun walked away with a stride that had a little bit of swagger.

She watched, then moved up a few rows and got

her camera ready for when he rode. If she still prayed—which she didn't—she might have been tempted to offer up a few words asking for his safety.

Chapter Two

Calhoun Kelly had no idea why he'd spoken to the pretty woman, but she had appealed to him. Since he'd never seen her around this or any rodeo before, she wasn't a buckle bunny, and he liked that. Like most rodeo cowboys, he could have his pick of the women who hung around the arenas, but he hadn't seen one he found attractive.

Buckle bunnies were rodeo groupies, seeking out a cowboy almost as a prize. Some wanted relationships, most just wanted the temporary thrill of spending time with a bronc or bull rider in a one-night connection. A few followed their favorites around the circuit. Most wore too much makeup and tight clothing that left little to the imagination. They tended to be aggressive in their quest to hook up with a cowboy. Calhoun didn't mind a little attention, but he preferred his women to be more modest and not to come on so strong.

At first, he'd thought Vivian's hair was short. When she had turned, he realized it was long because she coiled it into a bun pinned up in back. Her hair was a rich brown, not as dark as his black hair. Her eyes were hazel and her lips a soft pink. She wasn't dressed Western either, but in a pair of jeans and a tank top. When Cal saw her eyeing the chili dogs, he decided he'd offer a friendly warning. He'd suffered more than once from one of those concoctions, and he'd hate to see her take sick over one.

He half expected her to walk away without answering, but instead, she responded. Next thing he knew, they were having a conversation while sharing a funnel cake, and she asked if she could take pictures of him while he competed. Calhoun didn't mind if she did. He'd drawn Texas Terror, a tan brindle bull with a bad reputation and worse temper. If he could stay on for the full eight seconds, he would accomplish what he came to do.

Cal didn't plan to ask her to join him for a meal, but it pleased him. He had enjoyed her company more than he had anyone's in a very long time. Now, though, he needed to clear his mind and not think about her. Concentration was as important as skill when it came to bull riding. At the chutes, he paused and removed his hat long enough for Clem McSpadden's Cowboy Prayer and then one from Roy Rogers. Every rodeo began with the national anthem and the cowboy prayer, but he liked to say them again. Calhoun knew the familiar words written decades ago by heart and recited the words along with the announcer.

"Our gracious and heavenly Father, we pause in the midst of this festive occasion, mindful of the many blessings You have bestowed upon us. As cowboys, Lord, we don't ask for any special favors. We ask only that You will let us compete in this arena as in the arena of life. We don't ask that we never break a barrier, draw around a chute-fighting horse, or draw a steer that just won't lie. We don't even ask for all daylight runs. We only ask that You help us to compete in life as honest as the horses we ride and in a manner as clean and pure as the wind that blows across this great land of ours. Help us, Lord, to live our lives in such a manner that when we make that last inevitable ride to the country up there, where the grass grows lush, green and stirrup high, and the water runs cool, clear, and deep, that You, as our last judge, will tell us that our entry fees are paid. Amen."

With head still bowed, Calhoun added his own. "Dear Lord, protect me as I ride this bull. If I should stay on for eight seconds, let the glory be Yours and not mine. Keep all the riders safe in this arena and be with Linc's family down in Texas. If this bull bucks me and I'm hurt, let it not be too bad. If it's my time to die, then let me come to You with grace. Be with this pretty lady I met tonight. I feel like she might need You a whole lot. Amen."

First, Calhoun wrapped his wrists and ankles to minimize damage during the ride. He put his hat on again and gathered the rest of his gear, his bull rope with a braided leather handle and his leather glove. Although tempted to glance back at Vivian, Calhoun didn't and entered the chute. With the help of other cowboys, he climbed onto Texas Terror, who tried to pitch him off before he settled into a good position. When the chute opened, he raised his left arm high in the air and hung on as tight as he could with his right. He used the spurs to guide and control the animal, but Cal doubted the bull noticed.

Texas Terror dug at the dirt with his front hooves and kicked his hind end high into the air. Snorting and bucking, the bull did his best to unseat Calhoun.

But he gripped the bull rope tight and did his best to hold his seat.

The animal contorted and writhed.

Eight seconds wasn't long at any other time, but when he was on a bull, it seemed like forever. His body twisted in every direction as he held tight, and he knew he'd be sore later.

Calhoun always thought he would count the seconds but never did. He became too engaged in staying on. He knew sooner or later the bull would succeed, and he'd hit the dirt arena hard. No matter how much he tried to prepare, it always hurt when he landed. This time was no exception. He rolled over.

Others kept the bull away.

One of the pickup men rode close.

Cal waved him away. He found his feet and walked out of the area, grinning. He lasted eight seconds before being thrown. Before he made it very far, he heard the score—half for him based on his skill, half for the bull with two judges. The score of eighty-five was outstanding. If he kept it up tomorrow night, he'd ride as a finalist on Saturday. Calhoun headed for the stands.

Vivian met him halfway.

"What a ride!" she exclaimed. "Are you hurt? It looked like you landed hard."

Her praise gave him a burst of warm happiness.

"I did but I'm good. Looks worse than it was. Did you get some good pictures?"

She nodded. "I think so, yes."

"Let me clean up a little, then we'll head for town. Give me about ten minutes and I'll come find you."

Vivian smiled but she glanced at the arena where the action continued.

"All right, but the rodeo isn't quite over."

"My part is. I'll be back in a flash."

At his tiny travel trailer, he used water stored in the

tank for a fast shower. Then Calhoun dressed in a pair of black jeans, one of his favorite bright-red Western shirts, his best boots, and donned his favorite cowboy hat, a black felt gambler style.

When he emerged, he hustled over to the stands. When he didn't see Vivian, his heart skittered to a stop. Maybe she'd given up waiting. Then he saw her waiting behind the stands on the edge of the gravel parking area, midway to where the trailers and rigs parked.

She waved.

He met her halfway. Cal yearned to kiss her but didn't. It might be too much, too soon. "Are you hungry?" he asked. "I sure am."

Vivian nodded. "Where are we going?"

"There's a little diner in town that's open late that I like. We can get a burger or a steak or breakfast."

"Sounds good. Do you want me to drive or will you?"

"I can get the truck." He should have driven it over. He figured she drove some tight little economy car or boring sedan.

"My car is right over here so it's probably closer," Vivian pointed. "I'll bring you back after we eat, I promise."

Calhoun caved. "All right, sure. What do you drive?"

"Bright-red 1968 sports car," she told him, her mouth stretched into a wide smile as she pointed out her ride.

"Wow." Her vehicle blew him away. It was nothing close to what he'd expected, and neither was she. Cal ran a hand over the smooth finish with envy. "My truck's vintage, but it's not as awesome as your

16

car."

"Do you want to drive?" Vivian asked.

For a moment he figured she couldn't be serious.

But then she held up her key ring.

"I'd love to," Calhoun replied. "Are you sure you trust me?" Her smile combined sunshine with sweet cotton candy.

For a moment, she hesitated. Vivian didn't really know him or how he drove. With her lips pursed together into a frown. "Is there any reason I shouldn't let you?"

"None."

Vivian made a satisfied nod and tossed him the keys. "Then let's go, Calhoun."

He didn't hesitate but opened the passenger door for her, then climbed behind the steering wheel. Although the car was small, he scooted the seat back a notch so his tall, lanky frame would fit. When Cal turned the key, he heard the motor purr like a contented kitten. The radio poured out vintage country music, his favorite, and he sang along with Hank Williams for a few bars in his classic, "Setting the Woods on Fire."

She joined in the next verse, and their voices blended in harmony.

Calhoun had never sung with a woman before, and he liked it. Blending their voices brought familiarity and a sense of intimacy.

"Are we taking in all the honky tonks?" Vivian asked, referencing another verse when the song ended.

"Not a one," Calhoun replied. "I don't do honky tonks."

Something about the way she tensed in the passenger seat, shoulders tight prompted him to add, "Is that a problem?"

"I thought cowboys liked to drink beer and whiskey and get crazy. They do in most of the songs." She breathed a sigh. He couldn't tell if the fact he didn't drink was a relief or a shock.

Cal adjusted the rear view and side mirrors for his height. "That's true enough, but I don't." This might be the moment when she changed her mind, but he hoped not.

"I don't care for it, either." Vivian turned toward him, with a smile that lit her eyes. "I'm glad."

A wave of pure joy rolled through him, and he grinned. "Then let's go eat. We're here." Despite the hour, almost every table brimmed full. Calhoun inhaled the delightful aromas of good food. Once they reached a small corner booth, he handed Vivian a menu.

"Don't you need one, too?"

"Nah, I know what I want." He knew this menu by heart. "I'm having a double bacon cheeseburger with the works with a side of fries. I figured you might want to look over what they offer."

Cal waited to see if she'd opt for grilled chicken or a salad or something light.

But she closed the menu. "I'll have the same but a single, not a double. With sweet tea. Do you eat here often?"

"Every year when I'm in town for the rodeo." He made a firm nod. "I've got favorite places all around. I'll likely eat here again before this rodeo is done."

Vivian blinked twice. "I thought it was over."

He laughed.

"Tonight's performance is over by now. The rodeo goes on here for two more days, Friday and Saturday. I figured you'd stay and take more pictures."

"I planned to drive back home, but it's a long way if I return, especially the way I came." She sipped her tea from the glass, not with a straw.

"Where do you live?"

"Near Neosho, Missouri," Vivian told him. "I could have taken the interstate, but I like the two-lane roads better. The trip here took an hour and a half. I probably should have left earlier. At night, it may be two hours one way to go home."

Calhoun's spirits sank. If she left now, she probably wouldn't be back, and he wanted to become better acquainted. No woman had interested him this way until now. He'd dated, had a few girlfriends, but nothing serious ever came from those relationships. "You won't get home 'til after midnight."

Vivian sighed. "Yeah, I know. I didn't think this through, I guess."

"You could stay." The words flew from his mouth before he considered them.

She lifted one eyebrow. "With you?"

From the heat in his cheeks, he figured he blushed and hated it. "No, that wouldn't be right, Pretty Lady. There're quite a few motels around, more than there used to be because of the casino over the state line in Oklahoma. I'd be happy to pay for one if it would run you short. I've been winning so far this season, and I'm not hurting for cash." From her frown, Cal thought he must have stepped in it.

"Would that be at the same place you're staying?" she asked.

"I drag a travel trailer everywhere I go," Cal told her. "Otherwise, I might spend my earnings and then some on hotel rooms."

"Why would you pay for my room, then?" Her lips puckered, and her eyes narrowed. "I don't understand."

She sounded perplexed and maybe a bit suspicious but not angry, so Cal did his best to explain. "I like you. I'd worry if you took off home this late. Besides, I was hoping you'd be here for the rest of this rodeo."

Vivian relaxed her shoulders. "I'd like to be, Calhoun. I just worry about someone taking advantage of me."

Her notion that he would rubbed Calhoun wrong. He'd been raised to treat a woman like a lady, and his morals were rock solid. "I wouldn't do that."

Her gaze met his. "Somehow, I believe that. I can pay for my own room, though, but thank you for offering."

"*De nada,*" he replied. He intended to be a gentleman, but the way she objected made him shrug. "The offer stands, if you want it. Let's eat before the food gets cold."

The waitress put down their plates along with a bottle of ketchup and the bill.

Asking a blessing came as natural to Calhoun as breathing, so he stretched out his hands and took hers. "Dear Lord, I thank You for this food we are about to eat. Bless the hands that prepared it. Thank You for Vivian and for her company tonight. Let us be safe in all ways and healthy. Thank You for all the many things You do for us, in Jesus' name, amen."

Vivian stared. "You didn't have to do that to impress me. I don't pray, not anymore."

Cal shrugged. "I do, and it wasn't to impress you, darlin'. I ask a blessing over all my meals, alone or not." He picked up his cheeseburger and took a bite. The tender beef paired with American cheese and smoky bacon filled his mouth with flavor. He took another and then munched a crisp fry. "Good stuff."

Vivian smiled. "That's the best-tasting burger I've had in a long time. Thanks for inviting me to eat."

At least, she didn't have champagne tastes on an iced tea budget. "Glad to do it, Pretty Lady."

"Tell me what happens tomorrow night at the rodeo. Will the show be the same? Do the cowboys ride in the same order as last night?"

"About the same," Cal replied. "My scores from tonight and tomorrow will be combined. What I score on that last night will be what counts. If I'm the top scorer, then I'll bring home the prize purse. It's fair enough here but at some rodeos, the winnings can be substantial."

"Do you sign up to ride or what?" Vivian had no clue. *I probably should have researched it more before I headed down to take photos.*

Calhoun grinned. "Well, yeah. I'm a member of PBR. It stands for Professional Bull Riders. Membership gives me a heads-up what rodeos are upcoming. I decide where I want to compete and plan my season. At each rodeo where I do ride, I pay the entry fee first thing."

Vivian frowned. "Does it get expensive?"

Cal shrugged. "Sometimes, but the fees are part of what builds up the prize purses so it's worth it, if you win more than you lose."

"And you win." It wasn't a question.

"Enough to keep going, yeah."

Vivian digested the information. It might be useful

if or when she sold some rodeo photographs or wrote an article. "So, you ride after tonight, here?"

"I'll be competing here through Saturday."

She nodded. "And after Saturday night, what happens then?"

"On to the next rodeo," he told her. "I'll ride somewhere almost every weekend during the season, which starts in February and runs into fall. That adds up to thirty or forty rodeos. Later on, there're semifinals and finals, if I qualify. If I don't, then I'll go home to Texas until next year. If I'm lucky, I'll earn enough prizes to keep me financially afloat. If not, I'll work awhile when I'm back home on my brother's ranch, if nothing else."

"And that's in East Texas?"

That she remembered flattered him. "Yeah, around Rusk. My brother has a cattle ranch there, Kelly Cattle Company. He raises beef and some rough stock for rodeos but not as much rough stock since he got married."

Vivian wrinkled her nose. "Does that mean bulls like you ride?"

"Bulls and saddle bronc horses, yeah."

"That sounds interesting, I guess. During the season, you travel, right? You pull a trailer where you stay, but what about a horse?"

"Riding rough stock, I don't need to bring my horse," Calhoun replied. "I ride mostly bulls these days, so no need to bring a mount. I have a paint horse, though, back home. I raised him from a foal. His name is Johnny." Cal pulled out his phone and thumbed through it to find a picture, then displayed it. "That's him."

Vivian smiled. "He's pretty."

He laughed. "I suppose you could say that. If you're about finished, let's go find you a room for the night. Then you can drop me back off at the rodeo grounds.

She ate her last bite, wiped her lips with a napkin, and drank the rest of her tea. "Sounds like a plan. Let's go."

After riding, Calhoun was more than ready for his bed and some sleep. He faced another bull tomorrow.

Chapter Three

The idea that started Vivian on this journey had been a simple one. Drive down to Arkansas, shoot some action photos at a rodeo, then head home. If the pics turned out, Vivian thought she would try to sell them and maybe write an article about cowboys. Down the road, she had thought maybe she might write a book on the rodeo riders. She remembered well the old saying, one of her grandmother's favorites, about the best laid plans of mice and men and laughed as she drove in search of a room for the night.

Despite Nanna's offhand comment about meeting a cowboy, Vivian hadn't expected she would, but she did. She watched, then moved up a few rows and got her camera ready for when he rode. If she still prayed—which she didn't—she might have been tempted to offer up a few words asking for his safety. Watching Calhoun Kelly compete turned out to be exciting but also worrisome. Through the zoom lens of her camera, that bull seemed huge and dangerous. During the eight-second ride that seemed to last forever, fear Calhoun would be thrown, and possibly hurt, clutched her tight and hard as she watched from the stands. When he landed hard in the dirt, her breath caught and held, but when he stood then walked away, she exhaled a relieved sigh.

Something about the man intrigued her and

touched her. Calhoun happened to be stunning and handsome in a way beyond ordinary. That helped, but it wasn't all. His handsome face, his quiet manner, the way he treated her with respect and kindness, and the way he carried himself with a masculine poise and power caught her attention. Vivian thought he must be tough, tougher than an aged hickory nut and strong physically.

Tears had sprung into her eyes when he talked about his younger brother who passed away. Vivian knew loss too well but could not imagine watching as a brother died. She'd been away, living at college when her parents died, and hadn't even had the guts to glance at their bodies until they were prepared for the funeral.

Over a shared funnel cake and conversation, Vivian realized they had some similar tastes. When it came time to grab something to eat, she handed him the keys to her sports car, something she'd never done. Her former fiancé never drove the car, and she'd been the only driver since her grandfather. Calhoun drove it with skill, and at the diner, they turned out to like the same foods. The more she became familiar, the more she craved to learn more about him.

Her plan to head home tonight lacked any appeal, and when Calhoun said he'd worry about her driving at that late hour, her heart did a funny little flip. Now they were heading to find a motel room for the next two nights. If she stayed, she would be here for the rest of the rodeo.

The options narrowed down to a room at an upscale chain hotel or a clean mom-and-pop motel. Vivian chose the latter. One, it would be less expensive, and two, it wasn't far from the arena. Calhoun offered to pay, but she refused. For now, she had enough money. Although he meant well, it was too much from someone she just met. He did insist on going into the office with her.

"Calhoun! It's good to see you, kid. Need a room?" An older man with a military crewcut and ramrod straight posture cried as they entered the lobby. A Marine Corps tattoo on his left arm and the Corps flag hung over the desk indicated he must be a veteran.

"No, sir," Cal replied. "I've still got my tin can, but my friend needs a place to stay."

"Sure, we've got rooms. If it was you, I was gonna let you have one of the rooms with a spa tub, though."

"Let her have it, Rick," Calhoun stated.

Vivian smiled, glad. She wanted the spa tub.

"All right, all the more if you'll use it to soak your hurts."

"I might," Cal replied.

She paid through Saturday night and planned to head home on Sunday. Tomorrow, at an earlier hour when it wasn't so late, she would call Nanna to let her know she had stayed in Arkansas.

"Do you have suitcases I can tote in?" Calhoun asked.

"Just my camera bag and a couple of things," Vivian put her hand on his arm. For once, she could relax and let someone else do the lifting. She always carried a change of clothes in a go-bag, just in case. "If you're ready, let me run you back. You look tired."

"I'm worn out," he admitted. "I'll come over in the morning and take you to breakfast, if you'd like."

Vivian should refuse because all of this seemed too fast and soon, but she nodded. "Sure, I'd like that.

Don't worry about coming early. You need some sleep, and so do I."

At the arena, he directed her to where his trailer was parked. As he got out, he winced.

"You're hurting." Vivian wished she could make his pain go away, as easily as kissing a baby's boo-boo.

A ghost of a smile flashed across his lips, then vanished. "A little." He made another face and shifted his body. "Always do. It'll pass. Thanks for the ride over and the company. I enjoyed it. Last night was the best I've had in a while."

"Same," Vivian told him. "Good night, Calhoun. I'll see you tomorrow." At the motel, she took a long, hot shower, then crawled into bed and slept. When she woke, sunlight streamed around the edges of the window, and she sat up, mouth dry and momentarily disoriented. Then Viv remembered. She made coffee in the room's small pot and dressed for the day in her clean outfit. Later, she would pick up a few things she needed to stay a couple more days.

When an older but pristine truck pulled up and parked, Vivian checked her appearance, then opened the door. "Good morning, Calhoun."

"Morning, Pretty Lady," he replied. "I brought breakfast." He brushed her cheek with a kiss as he offered Vivian a fast-food bag and two coffees.

She accepted the food, then placed it on the tiny table by the window. "Thank you."

"I know I promised I'd take you out, but there's something I'd like to show you so I figured we could eat and head out."

Curious what he might have in mind, she decided to accept the change in plan. Right now, she had nothing pressing or better to do. "Sure." She took the lid off the cup and drank some coffee with pleasure. It tasted much better than what she'd brewed in the motel room.

Calhoun reached in the bag for sausage biscuits and hash browns. Once he shared, he bowed his head.

Since he had mentioned having the faith she lacked, Vivian didn't react. She didn't pray but paused 'til he finished. The sausage was perfect if a little spicy, but it didn't have too much of a burn, so she enjoyed it.

Once they finished eating, Calhoun glanced down at her feet. "I don't suppose you have any boots."

Curious about the question, she stared at him, then answered. "I do, at home, although they're not cowgirl boots."

"That won't help today. I know a boot shop on the way."

"But Calhoun—"

"But nothing. You need a good pair of Western boots."

Vivian planned to refuse right up until she slid on a pair of boots that fit as if they'd been made for her feet. She'd already realized how stubborn Calhoun could be and doubted he would debate it. This pair featured a cushioned insole and a rubber outer sole. Attractive in black leather with turquoise trim, the size eight boots were comfortable.

"These feel so good." Vivian strode up and down the aisle of the western-wear store. "I shouldn't spend the money, though."

"I'll buy them." Calhoun pointed to the footwear. "I'd like to see that you're well shod."

She didn't know if she should laugh or get angry.

"I'm not a horse."

"Of course not."

"These are expensive." She wouldn't pay the price, not on her budget. "I don't think you should pay for them. I don't really need them. Like I said, I have some boots at home."

Calhoun ran one hand through his curly hair and sighed. "The cost is worth it for good boots. C'mon, Vivian."

If the boots hadn't been so snug and pleasant on her feet, she would have said no. She liked the boots, though, and she liked this cowboy. Vivian caved. "All right, Calhoun. I shouldn't let you, but I am."

The turquoise on the boots matched the button-down shirt she wore over a red tank, and she admired them as they headed across the Oklahoma state line. "Where are we going?"

"Not far," Calhoun replied. "West Siloam Springs is in Oklahoma. We're headed to Natural Falls State Park to see a waterfall. It's one of the most peaceful places I've ever been. I thought you'd like it."

Reaching the seventy-seven-foot-high waterfall required hiking over a steep, narrow trail, but Vivian was game. Getting there proved more difficult than she expected. In the rougher places, Calhoun took her hand to guide her through. Once they arrived at the base of the waterfall, though, it was well worth the effort. Water cascaded from the rocks into a lovely pool at the base. Smaller springs trickled out of the rock formations. Rainbows sparkled in the sunlight that filtered through the trees, and the air seemed much cooler near the water than above. A few benches were available, and they sank onto one.

An aura of peace hung in the air, and Vivian relaxed, finding it soothing. The place exuded calm, quiet vibes. For the moment, they were alone. "Oh, Calhoun, it's beautiful. It's like something out of a fairy tale."

He grinned and put an arm around her. "I like to think it's sacred. I always come when I'm here for the rodeo."

"I can see why." Vivian hadn't brought her cameras, but she snapped some pictures using her phone. "I already want to come back."

"Then we will, sometime."

Using *we*, Calhoun sounded like he believed they had a joint future, which pleased and frightened her.

" 'The Lord hath made everything beautiful in His time.' "

Some of her contentment vanished. "That's from the Bible."

"Ecclesiastes, third chapter."

Vivian stood, moving away from his arm. "I guess I'm ready to go." Ever since she gave up on faith, Bible quotations and prayer made her uncomfortable. Once she'd believed but not after her parents died. Vivian moved so fast she tripped over her feet and almost fell.

Calhoun grabbed her arm and steadied her. "Whoa. What's the matter?"

"All this God stuff," she muttered.

His dark eyes widened, and he frowned. "You don't believe in the Lord or His son Jesus?"

She crossed her arms. "I used to but not anymore. Come on, Calhoun."

"Wait a minute, Vivian," he told her. "I don't understand. I'm not trying to convert you. I just said what I think. Faith is the foundation of my life, and I'm sorry you don't share that. Sit back down, but don't go off mad."

Vivian almost dashed back up the trail to the car, but she remembered they came in his pickup. She wouldn't have a way to leave, anyway. His quiet tone didn't offend, and maybe she'd reacted out of turn. She sat and sighed. "I'm not mad, not exactly. It's just that I can't believe anymore." A frown replaced her earlier smile, and she slumped on the bench.

Calhoun leaned toward her, the lines in his face more evident. "If you want to tell me why not, I'll listen."

"And you won't try to tell me I'm wrong?"

"I won't."

Vivian considered it. Maybe talking about her loss of faith would help. Most of the time she lived in denial. She didn't think about her parents at all. Nanna had complained about it, but she'd tuned out her voice when she did.

Calhoun gazed at her, then laid a hand over hers with a light, gentle touch.

His calm eased her, and she decided if she could talk about it to anyone, she could confide in Calhoun. "All right, I will but not here. I don't want to ruin this lovely place. I want to hang onto this peace and keep it as a memory."

"Fair enough."

Neither said much on the rugged trail back to the visitor center, but although they said little, she wasn't uneasy or upset.

Calhoun opened the passenger side door at his truck and offered his hand to help her climb inside.

"We can get some lunch if you want. We can eat in a café or get something to go, take it to a park or back to my trailer. I gotta go back to the arena sometime before tonight, but we'd have privacy. It might be a little hot, though. There's no electric or water hookups here, so no air conditioning."

Curiosity to visit his humble home, at least on the road, appealed. So did the chance to talk without anyone listening. "Let's pick up something. You choose what." Before they got food, she talked him into a quick stop at a discount store where she bought two pairs of cheap jeans, some shirts, a spare bra, some panties, socks, and a few toiletries.

After they made their purchases, Calhoun drove to a small, cinderblock building where he picked up some street tacos and soft drinks. At the arena, he navigated back through an acre of parked vehicles to where various RVs sat. His proved to be a vintage 1950s trailer, restored and well-kept. Calhoun parked and unlocked one of two doors.

Vivian took note of the place. The furnishings included a built-in couch, a small table with bench seating, and a lamp attached to the wall. To the left, counters enclosed a tiny kitchen with a stove, sink, and a few cabinets. A brief hall with a small fridge tucked into a recessed space along with a microwave led to a bedroom where a queen-size bed claimed all the space. A second door opened outside. Calhoun opened what she took to be a closet to reveal a toilet and another with a dinky shower, so small she wondered how he fit. It was compact, clean, and attractive.

"Home sweet home for the season," he said. "Not much but it works."

"I like it," Vivian told him. "It's small, sure, but it's actually homey." She noted a bookshelf above his bed with several novels including some titles by Larry McMurtry, Craig Johnson, Dean Koontz, and Tony Hillerman. An old-style percolator sat on the kitchen counter and some of his clothing hung on hooks between the doors. Bins beneath the bed contained the rest.

"Come sit down and let's eat," he told her.

They settled onto the couch. The tacos featured bits of steak, seasoned and browned inside a flour tortilla. A cilantro blend and cooked onions topped the meat. The café had provided two kinds of sauce, a tomato-based one and one made from green chilies. Both had delightful flavor, but the green was too hot for Vivian. Cal hadn't asked again, but she told him her brief, tragic story.

"Seven years ago, I was still in college, at Missouri Southern State University in Joplin, about to graduate," Vivian began. "My parents lived in the country at the time, and that spring, four men broke into their house. They killed them in a terrible, brutal stabbing. They shot them, too, as a final coup de grace."

Her throat hurt with unshed tears as she recalled. She drew a deep breath, then continued, "At first, no one knew why, but it turned out it was drug-related, and the killers, stoned out of their minds, hit the wrong house. Worse, it happened on Easter, early in the morning. I'd planned to go home for the holiday, but I didn't. I can't help but think if I had been there, I could have stopped it, somehow. Until then, Calhoun, I believed. I prayed and went to church on Sundays, but that ended with their deaths. I couldn't wrap my head around a God who would let that happen to my folks, who were good people who never hurt anyone. Their funeral was the last time I sat in a church."

Calhoun put down his lunch, frowned, and reached out his hand. "Oh, Vivian, I am so sorry. That had to be terrible, and I can't imagine."

He'd lost a brother in the arena, but he demonstrated empathy. When he grasped her hand, she let him. "My parents' deaths were the worst things that had happened to me, ever," she said. "So many people, including their pastor, told me there's a reason for everything, but I couldn't see one. I'd like to know where Jesus was when my parents died screaming on Resurrection Sunday. Where were the guardian angels? They failed them, and so they failed me. I couldn't pray anymore after that. Trying felt fake and empty, Calhoun."

Rage seared her heart and the tears that burned in her eyes were angry, not sad. Now he'd quote the Bible. She expected to tell her the same things she'd heard so many times. He would chide her for losing faith, then talk about those footprints in the sand or something. When he did, she'd be out of here. She would walk back to the motel since it wasn't far and pack up her things to go home. And, as much as she loved the boots he bought her, she'd give them back.

"Vivian, I don't know what to say. I don't have the right words, but what happened to you shouldn't have," Calhoun told her after a long pause. "I lost my folks, too, but in a bad car crash over near Dallas when I was ten. That's why Granny raised us, me and my brothers. I didn't understand either why, honey, but my heart hurts for you."

"And then you lost your younger brother. Calhoun, I can't imagine how awful that had to be."

Losing her parents had been a terrible blow, but at least, she had been an adult. Calhoun was orphaned as a child, then his brother died riding rodeo.

He nodded. "It was. What else?"

"What do you mean?"

"I just feel like there's something more."

How did he know? She'd told him that much that she might as well share the rest. "I was engaged to be married that June. But Arthur, my fiancé, decided he was moving to California. We graduated, and then he told me. He had a job, but he had to go alone. He broke off our engagement, and I gave him back the ring. It was for the best, I think. He wasn't a nice person, and he didn't support me when my parents died. He didn't even come to their funeral."

Calhoun listened. Then he stood. "I'd say you're better off without someone like that, Pretty Lady. I'm glad because if you'd married him, you wouldn't be here, and that would be a pity."

His kindness broke her. Vivian hadn't cried when she received the news of her parents' deaths. She didn't weep during the funeral or at the graveside. Instead, she buried her grief, even after her wedding was cancelled. She'd stayed with Nanna through the summer, then for a year. Afterward she'd headed for Kansas City where she had a new job and focused on that. Now, the long-repressed tears came. They poured down her cheeks.

Calhoun used two fingers to wipe away the tears, then offered his hand.

Vivian took it and rose.

Calhoun wrapped his arms around her and held her

close. "Cry it out, honey. I figure you've waited a long time to cry."

She sobbed against his chest, tucked tight into his embrace. When she had no more tears left, Vivian accepted a wet washcloth he handed her. And, although it seemed like it had been hours, less than thirty minutes had passed.

Calhoun warmed their lunch, and they ate in quiet harmony.

He was so easy to be with because Calhoun didn't judge or want her to be someone she wasn't. Instead, he accepted her just the way she was, and Vivian liked that.

During the long afternoon, she called Nanna from the motel room.

Calhoun sprawled across the bed, but he wasn't asleep.

"Hel-lo," the old woman answered the phone.

"Nanna, it's Vivian. I decided to stay a few days in Arkansas to watch the rest of this rodeo." If Nanna begged her to come home, she would, first thing Sunday morning.

Instead, her grandmother laughed. "I expect you found yourself a cowboy," she said. "What's his name?"

"Calhoun Kelly," Vivian replied with enough embarrassment that a flush heated her cheeks. "He rides bulls."

"It's a strong name. I like it, and I expect he's a good man. You wouldn't give the time of day to any other. Enjoy yourself, and call me soon, all right?"

"I will."

Now she had no reason to worry about leaving

imminently so Vivian decided she would stay. Sunday would be soon enough to figure out what to do, but already, she couldn't imagine parting with Calhoun. Somehow, he'd become important.

Chapter Four

Calhoun enjoyed the day more than any he had in years. Vivian's name suited her.

She was lively and as vivid as bright, bold colors, the ones he preferred. He called her Pretty Lady because she was, but he thought she had substance, too. Cal's heart ached for her when she explained why she no longer prayed. He recognized her loss and pain in his own. Their situations might be different, and he hadn't lost faith, but Cal knew the emptiness of a life without parents.

The pain of losing Sully remained and always would. He rode in rodeos because it was something he'd done from a young age, and he had some skill. Most seasons, he earned enough to make a living for the year, and the chance existed he might hit it big one year. At thirty-three, that seemed more unlikely, but it could happen. If not, he had a little piece of land in Texas adjacent to Lincoln's ranch.

His life, though, had become increasingly lonely. Now that Linc had married and had three stair-step kids, Cal tried not to intrude. He enjoyed being part of the family, and as an uncle, he loved those children. He didn't force his presence, though, or overwhelm his brother's family by being around all the time.

The longer he lived, the lonelier he had become. Some of his rodeo friends had already hung up their spurs and moved on to a different lifestyle. Others who remained didn't share his Christian faith, which often set Calhoun apart. Some of the riders were hard drinkers who enjoyed whiskey and beer, or maybe occasional gambling. None of that appealed. Nor did the buckle bunnies. Some guys collected them. Cal ignored them. Since he traveled from one rodeo to another from spring into fall, he didn't try to pursue a relationship. Even at home in Texas, he knew he'd be gone again before long, so it wasn't an option. Now, he wanted to see where this could go with Vivian.

Late in the afternoon, Cal got his gear ready while she watched. Bull riding always left him aching, and this morning's hike hadn't helped. He popped six ibuprofen to get ahead of the ache.

"What's wrong?" Vivian frowned as he took the pills.

"Nothing." He lived with daily discomfort. It was part of being a cowboy. "Just stiff and sore from bull riding." It would be worse after tonight but that didn't need to be mentioned. Calhoun opened the door to shake the dirt from his jeans he'd worn the night before.

"Aren't you going to wear clean jeans?"

"There's no point," he replied. "These are my bull riding jeans. I wouldn't want to rinse away my luck. I do wash them every once in a while, but they're so stained with dirt from the arena, you'd never know it. Besides, there ain't a washateria handy in every town."

The unfamiliar term caught her by surprise, and she couldn't figure it out. "What's that?"

"Texas slang for a laundromat."

Calhoun dressed, then added the protective vest. Next, he taped his wrists and knees, then gathered all his gear. Cal felt ten feet tall as he led the stroll from his tin can to the arena with Pretty Lady at his side.

More than a few stared as they passed by. Some called to him, and more than one of the barrel racing gals glared. Two of them had long tried to gain his interest, but it hadn't been there.

He grinned back at everyone, and once he'd checked in, he headed for the stands with Vivian.

"When do you ride?" she asked once they were seated.

"There're four timed events, and three of those are rough stock. Mutton busting comes first with the little ones, then calf roping, team roping, steer wrestling, and barrel racing. Then comes the rough-stock events. Bareback and saddle broncs will go first, then bull riding last. Tonight, I drew next-to-last position. Are you taking pictures?"

Vivian laughed. "I can't. The camera's back at the motel, but it's fine. I want to see you ride without distraction."

That brought a burst of joy. "Good. I'll sit here with you until it's time to go to the chutes and get ready to ride. Afterward, maybe we'll get something to eat again."

"I'd like that. Just promise me you won't get hurt."

"I'll do my best, Pretty Lady, but no guarantees."

She tucked her arm into his and put her head against his shoulder. "I'll worry then. I kind of like you."

"Yeah?" His cheeks heated with a flush at her admission. "I like you, too, Vivian. Want another funnel cake?"

"Not tonight. I'm still full."

As the rodeo began, a rider brought out the American flag so they stood, Cal with his hat off and held over his heart, as the national anthem was sung. Then the announcer offered a cowboy's prayer. Although Vivian didn't say anything, not even amen, she tightened her grip on his arm.

He clapped his hat on his head and studied her. "That's what else I should have got you today, a hat."

"You bought me boots."

"And I should've got you a cowboy hat, too. Maybe a turquoise one to match the trim on your boots. You'd look pretty in it."

"Don't you think I'm nice looking without one?" The compliment prompted her to smile.

Calhoun bent and kissed her hand. "I do, Pretty Lady, but it would be a fine sight, you in a hat."

"Maybe you can tomorrow."

"I'll plan on it." With his mind brimming over thinking about Vivian and things they might do the next day, he almost lingered in the stands too long. Calhoun hurried to the chutes to get in position for his ride, aware that every step he took emphasized the ache in his lower back and legs. He'd drawn one of the wildest bulls, a behemoth named Rowdy Rebel. Once seated, he jockeyed his position, and when the chute opened, he lifted one arm and gripped the leather handle hard.

Rowdy Rebel came out bucking, hind legs kicking up a wild rumpus that brought them higher than his head.

Cal held his seat for six seconds with the crazy animal twisting and turning in every direction, then lost his hold. He flew and knew he would hit the dirt hard. The impact jarred him from head to toe, but most of all, the shoulder he'd dislocated in April in Paducah, Texas. Sharp pain shot through it, and he winced as he struggled to his feet. Calhoun clamped one hand to it and left the arena.

A volunteer rodeo medic approached. "Hey, let's get you checked out. Dislocate that shoulder?"

If he had, the pain would be ten times worse. "Nah," Cal replied, certain he hadn't. "I did back in April. It's sore from whacking it when I got bucked. I couldn't move it if it was dislocated again." He demonstrated he could raise and stretch it out. Then he cowboyed up and moved on, never looking back. His score could wait. Right now, he wanted to get out of here and quit hurting.

Vivian rushed forward.

He held up his hands to prevent her jarring his shoulder.

"I saw you fall," she cried. "You're injured, Calhoun. Do you need to go to the ER? I can take you."

Her concern touched him, but he shook his head. "You ain't got your car, Vivian. I'll do. Just banged up my shoulder, that's all." It wasn't. His muscles ached, too, and he had a stinking headache. Calhoun was certain he hadn't cracked his head on anything, so he figured it was fatigue, maybe stress. He could wear a poker face with the best, however, and he didn't want Vivian to think he was a wuss.

She took his right hand and held it. "You look awful, Calhoun. You're pale as snow, and you're sweating. I know you're in pain. Let's get you out of here and help you feel better."

At his trailer, he removed his gear, flinching with every moment, but he managed not to groan. As soon as he had on a worn pair of jeans and a clean shirt, he grabbed his keys. "Let me run you back to your motel, honey. I don't feel much like eating right now." His stomach rolled, uneasy, and he hurt too much to have an appetite.

"Neither do I. Gather up some clothes and come back with me," she told him. "You could use a soak in that spa tub at the motel. I've got plenty of ibuprofen and some naproxen sodium you can take, too. I'll get something delivered so we can eat later when you feel better."

Nobody had tried to tend his hurts, not since Granny died. Lincoln and his family cared, but it wasn't the same. Cal couldn't remember the last time a woman he liked offered to provide some TLC, and he wanted it badly. "Nah, it's better if I get you back and then wallow in my misery alone," he tried to joke.

"You're not doing any such thing," Vivian said, blowing air between her lips in frustration. She opened a few drawers, dragged out some clean underwear and T-shirts, then grabbed a pair of flannel lounge pants. "Do you want me to drive?"

He would rather she did. "I do believe you're bossy, Pretty Lady."

"Give me the keys."

"It's a stick," he replied.

"And I can drive it." Arms folded, she set him straight.

At the motel, Cal drew on inner fortitude to climb out of the truck and walk into the room.

Once there, Vivian turned on the spa tub.

As it filled, Calhoun downed some over-the-counter pain reliever. He should've brought along the

43

arnica cream he sometimes used for the shoulder, but he'd manage without. He toted the change of clothes into the bathroom, then shut the door. Once he'd shucked off his clothing and folded them, he climbed into the water and sighed. The heat eased some of his pain, and the jets helped. He settled down for a good, long soak and almost fell asleep. If the bathroom door hadn't cracked open and he heard Vivian call his name, he would have.

"Calhoun?"

"Yeah?"

"You might want to get out before you cook your bones. If you feel like eating, I can order something."

The tub left him feeling relaxed and boneless. Although the pain had receded a bit, all he craved was sleep. The headache had gone, and he managed to put on a T-shirt and lounge pants after his bath. "Maybe later, honey. I don't suppose you have any arnica cream?"

"I don't even know what it is," Vivian replied. "But if you need it, I can go get it."

"It'll help the shoulder. It wouldn't hurt anything else, either. But you don't need to do that, and besides, everywhere is closed. I should drive back to my trailer and get some sleep." Calhoun sat on one of the two double beds to pull on his socks. Then he reached for his boots and couldn't help but groan.

"I'll go get the arnica from your place if you tell me where to find it. Stay awhile, Calhoun. Then you won't need the boots, not now."

Before he could protest, she grabbed his boots and parked them against the wall. Then, she brushed his unruly hair back from his forehead and kissed it.

It could have been a sisterly kind of kiss, but it wasn't. Her lips lingered a little long and afterward, she cupped the right side of his face in her hand, then caressed his cheek. Sweet sensations erupted at her touch and tingled down his spine. "The arnica is in the kitchen. There's a little cabinet left of the sink where I keep any meds I have. The trailer shouldn't be locked, but if it is, you have my keys. And thank you, Vivian. I'll stretch out while you're gone, then I'll go home and get out of your hair."

"Don't be silly. You're not a bother, Calhoun. Do you want anything else while I'm gone?"

"A cold root beer." He lay down on the bed, on his right side and rested his head on two pillows. Fatigue crawled over him, heavy and pervasive. "I do appreciate this, Pretty Lady."

"Anytime."

Calhoun didn't know if she drove his truck or her car. He meant to listen when she left because he would know by the engine's sound, but he shut his eyes, just for a moment, and slept. When he woke, too comfortable to move, he reclined for a few minutes. Curious if Vivian had returned, he shifted position and sat up. His muscles protested, but he wasn't as sore as he had been. The shoulder twinged a little, but the arnica would help. When he caught sight of the LED clock on the table between the two beds, he figured it must be wrong. He hadn't thought it was as early as ten o'clock. They'd left the rodeo grounds later than that. Then he caught the aroma of coffee and maybe food.

"Good morning." Vivian sat at the round table by the window, sipping coffee. "How do you feel?"

Before he answered, Calhoun scrubbed his face

45

with both hands. "Better, quite a bit. Where did the coffee come from?"

"I went down the road and picked it up along with breakfast. Are you hungry?"

His stomach rumbled.

She laughed.

"Yeah, I'm pretty empty."

"I hope you like omelets," Vivian told him. "It's a big one, with steak, cheese, onions, green peppers, mushrooms, and three eggs. I got a side order of biscuits and gravy, too."

Calhoun thought his mouth might start watering. He padded over to the table and sat across from her. "Smells good and yeah, I like anything with eggs." He opened the container and goggled. "That's huge, Pretty Lady. Want to share it?"

"Sure." Vivian handed him a plastic fork. With deft hands, she tore off the lid of the to-go box and made a plate, then divided the omelet. She did the same with the biscuits and gravy, giving him one biscuit, one sausage, and plenty of gravy. "Here's your coffee and breakfast."

He folded his hands and spoke a blessing.

Vivian paused, fork halfway to her mouth, and bowed her head.

Then he drank the black coffee and sighed with pleasure. The caffeine flowed down his throat, reviving him. When Cal tasted the food, he grinned. The eggs were fluffy, the cheese melted, and the veggies crisp, not soggy. "This is good."

"I got carryout from that same diner where we ate the other night. When I got back with the arnica and your soda, you were sacked out, so I let you sleep. I figured you needed the rest."

"I did." The blend of egg, steak, and cheese combined in a delicious way in his mouth. "I haven't slept that long since I don't know when." Calhoun craved sunshine, so he pushed open the curtains, but it appeared cloudy. "It's raining." He traced the line left by a raindrop outside on the glass with one finger.

Vivian nodded. "It started after midnight."

"It'll make the arena a muddy mess." He sighed, imagining landing in the squishy mud.

"You're planning to ride tonight?" She put down her fork and stared.

"Why wouldn't I?" Her question perplexed him.

"Your shoulder and the rain. Won't they cancel it?"

"I've seldom seen a rodeo cancelled for anything, not rain, snow, or tornado. Might pause it for a bit but never call it off. My shoulder's not so bad I can't ride. It's the last night here. I need the score if I hope to win. Rain will probably quit before evening, anyway. Are you still staying for it?"

"I am. I have an umbrella, if I need it."

Relief she wasn't leaving, not yet, made him almost giddy. "Good. I'd miss you if you took off."

Her hazel eyes met his gaze without blinking. "I'd miss you, too. Where's the next rodeo?"

"Fort Worth, at the Cowtown Coliseum," he told her. "It's an indoor arena, and they have rodeo every Friday and Saturday night."

"That's farther away than I thought it would be." Vivian frowned at the distance indicated.

"It's a fair piece, but I'll be able to spend a couple days at home on the way," he said.

Her smile faded. The idea of telling her goodbye

made him sad.

"I've got a little bitty house on my brother's spread, and I'll get to see Linc."

She hadn't finished her breakfast, but she stopped eating. "You'll be able to rest, too. That'll be good for you. You need it."

I need her more. The thought blindsided and stunned him but Cal recognized the truth. Without mulling it over, on impulse, he issued an invitation. "Come with me, Vivian. It's a whole different class of rodeo. You could get some great pictures, and that rodeo lasts just two days, not three. You could meet my brother and see my home. What do you think?"

"I don't know, Calhoun. I want to, but I should go see my grandmother, and that's in the opposite direction. Besides, where would I stay?" Her eyes sparkled as she spoke.

He figured that had to indicate some interest. "You could bunk with Lincoln and Sasha. They have several guest bedrooms. And we could head up to Missouri first. I wouldn't have to be in Fort Worth before noon on Friday, so there would be time."

Vivian blew air between her lips and ate a little more. "I'll consider it, Calhoun. I'll decide by Sunday, okay?"

"Sure, but if you want to shoot pictures there, you gotta register online." He sent up a silent prayer that she would go. Vivian was the best thing that had happened to him in a very long while, and he wanted more time with her. Sooner or later, they would have to part ways but not yet. "That reminds me. I'd better check in with my brother. I'm surprised he hasn't called."

"Uh, he did, last night." Her cheeks turned red as

Vivian confessed she'd forgotten to mention intercepting a call.

Alarm made his stomach hurt. His brother wouldn't expect anyone, especially a gal, to pick up his phone. Linc might think he'd hooked up with a bunny.

"He must be frantic, then if he called and didn't get ahold of me" After what happened to Sullivan, Linc freaked if they didn't keep in touch. "He might even be on his way up here."

"He's not," Vivian told him. "I talked to him. I hope you don't mind."

"No, I don't. I'm glad you answered it." Although he'd been surprised, now he accepted Vivian's action. Likely, the fact she talked to him had eased Lincoln's anxiety. "What did you tell him?"

She gulped down a last bite of biscuit and gravy. "I answered after he called twice. I told him you were worn out and asleep. He asked who I was, and I said I'm a friend. Was that all right?"

Linc must be either worried sick or over the moon with delight. His brother had nagged him endlessly to find a lady, but he'd resisted. "Yeah, it's fine, honey. Did he say anything else?"

"Just call him soon and he hoped he would get to meet me."

Calhoun repressed a whoop. The Lord did move in mysterious ways. Here he'd come up with the notion of inviting Vivian to come with him to Texas, but his brother had already expressed hope they would meet. He offered silent thanks and picked up his phone to make the call.

Chapter Five

Calhoun sprawled backward, pillows propped behind his back, and called his brother. It rang twice before he picked up the phone.

"It's about time I heard from you." Lincoln's East Texas drawl was more pronounced. "What in tarnation is going on?"

"Same old, same old. Riding rodeo, like always."

"First time I ever called you when a lady answered your phone," Linc said. "And told me that you were worn out and sound asleep. She refused to wake you, man, but she told me you had a rough ride last night and wrecked. You all right?"

"Sore but fine, yeah."

"She got me worried, little brother. I already told Sasha that if I didn't hear from you today or if you didn't sound right, I would head up that way."

"Bro, I'm good." Calhoun appreciated his brother's concern, but he wanted to blow it off. He didn't want Lincoln fussing over him. "Better than I've been in quite a while." Although Linc laughed, Cal knew he hadn't fooled his astute brother.

"I smell a rat, Cal. There's more to this story. Either you're hurt more than you're letting me know, or there's something with this gal. Which is it?"

"Busted." Calhoun laughed. He never could fool Linc for long. "I ain't hurt bad or anything, but I landed on my shoulder last night so it's sore as a bear. And I'm hurting like any bull rider but nothing serious."

"I figured something like that. Is it the shoulder you dislocated over at Paducah? And the woman? I hope she's not a buckle bunny."

"You ought to know better than that." Linc had to be aware how little Calhoun thought of the pushy women with their scanty clothing and desire to take a cowboy home for the night, nothing more. "Same shoulder, but it's not dislocated this time. It just hurts. And she's the farthest thing from a bunny you could find, Linc. Her name's Vivian Bradburn. She's a writer and photographer from Missouri."

"Is she pretty?"

"Very."

"Is she there?"

"Yeah, she is." Cal shot a glance at Vivian, standing before the mirror, brushing out her long hair and rolling it into a bun.

"Is she at your trailer?" After a pause, Lincoln questioned him further.

"No, we're at her motel, but it's not what you probably think. It's at Rick's place, the old Marine guy, you know? Her room has a spa tub, and she offered me the chance to soak my sore body. Besides, there're two beds. I didn't plan to stay, but I fell asleep after being in the tub. But we kept it decent."

"I wouldn't expect anything else from you."

Vivian walked over beside the bed with her hair neat and tidy. "Calhoun, the cold root beer you wanted is in the fridge. And I've got the arnica. If you want, I can rub some into your shoulder."

He glanced up and smiled. She was so attractive.

51

"I'd like that, Pretty Lady, soon as I get off the phone."

"Is that a hint?" His brother chuckled.

"Might be."

"Then I'll let you go, but hey, are you still comin' next week on the way to Fort Worth?"

"You bet, but it might be a couple days later. I might take a run up to Missouri first. Linc, do you still have room for a guest at your place?"

"I do. Does that mean—"

"Maybe," Cal interrupted. "I'll let you know for sure when I do. Take care, Linc."

"I will, and you do the same, you hear?"

Talking to Linc left him more than a little homesick, but he'd be there soon, long enough to enjoy the breezes beneath the tall pines and ride his horse. Calhoun shut his eyes for a moment, imagining his brother's place.

Vivian put his root beer on the bedside table and tiptoed away.

"I'm not asleep." He scooted over so she could sit on the bed if she wanted. "Linc said they have plenty of room, if you decide to go home with me to Texas."

"I'm still thinking about it." She stood in front of the window but turned to face him.

"Good. If you want to rub some of that cream on my shoulder, I'm game."

"Is it still hurting?" Vivian settled onto the edge of the mattress.

"Some." Calhoun shrugged, which shot pain through it. He pulled off his shirt for easy access and hid his smile when she ogled his chest.

Cal stayed buff because he had to be fit enough to compete. Behind all the mystique and excitement, bull riders were athletes, too. He also had a seven-inch scar down low on his left side.

Vivian traced it with her fingers. "What happened there?"

"Got gored when I was nineteen." He kept his tone casual, but the injury had been serious when it happened.

"By a bull?" Her voice rose up the scale.

"Yeah."

"You have a dangerous occupation." She wore a frown.

"Oh, yeah, I do." He couldn't deny that. Conversation wasn't easy as her fingers rubbed slow circles on his bad shoulder. Her touch was light enough it didn't hurt as she rubbed the arnica cream into his flesh, but he was very aware of her touch. When she finished, she handed him his undershirt, so he pulled it over his head.

She washed her hands at the sink, then returned. "Do you want anything?"

"Ibuprofen, please," he told her. "It's to keep ahead of the hurting, honey. I feel decent right now. What time is it?"

"Twelve thirty."

"That's all?" He figured it must be three or after. "I'll need to head over the arena to get ready by five at the latest. I hope the rain quits." He could hear it, pattering against the window and falling over the parking lot.

"It's really coming down," she told him. "Makes me sleepy. I've always wanted to take a nap or sleep late when it's raining, but I hardly ever get the chance."

"We've got time. I'm a bit drowsy myself, Pretty

Lady." Cal resumed his earlier position.

"You're tempting me." Vivian yawned.

"Stretch out and get a few winks," he advised. "I'll set an alarm for four." Calhoun hoped she might lie down beside him, although he knew she really shouldn't. That would be more intimate than he'd be comfortable with at this point.

She removed her shoes and lay down on the other bed. Then she pulled up the comforter. "All right, you convinced me." She removed the clip from the back of her hair and undid her bun.

For the first time, Calhoun saw her hair down, and he enjoyed the way it fell past her shoulders. He didn't figure he would sleep, just watch Vivian as she did, but it wasn't long before drowsiness claimed him. Cal dozed until the alarm he'd set on his phone blared. He'd changed both the alarm and ringtone on the first night he met Vivian to Hank Williams' classic, "Hey, Good-Lookin'." Cal woke and turned it off.

But not before Vivian sat up. She shook back her long hair. "That's your ringtone?"

"Yeah, and my alarm, too."

"Who's it for?" she asked, lips puckered into a pout.

"For you, Pretty Lady," Calhoun told her. "Only for you."

"I like it, then." Her smile returned, brighter than ever.

He watched as she rose, brushed her hair at the room's vanity, and put it up again.

Then she went into the bathroom, changed tops, and picked up her purse. "I'm ready when you are."

"Let's roll, then. There's no need to take two

vehicles, is there?"

"Not if you want another soak in that tub later."

Cal did and by the end of the night, he'd likely need it. "Yeah, if you're offering, sure."

At the rodeo grounds, rain drummed a rhythm on the roof of his trailer, and they dodged puddles as they raced to the door. Once there, Vivian settled onto the couch while he taped his joints, then changed into his rodeo outfit including spurs. The showers stopped as they emerged to head over to the arena, and the sun broke through the clouds. The air became hot and steamy.

En route, Cal stopped to find out his position and last night's ranking. Despite the tumble he'd taken, his ride scored a total sixty-two, not bad. He would ride among the ten finalists, and this time, he would be last. If he could stay on the bull for eight seconds and not make any mistakes, he could win some decent money, maybe as high as a thousand bucks or a little more, depending on his final score.

As had become their habit in just a few days, they found seats on the bleachers. This time, they held hands as they watched and waited.

"What bull do you ride tonight?"

"Badlands Bruiser."

Vivian frowned. "Do they all have names that sound mean and scary?"

"Pretty much." He didn't mention it was the same bull he had ridden the night he dislocated his shoulder in Kentucky. When it came time to head for the chutes, Calhoun touched her shoulders and turned her to face him. "Kiss me for luck." He stood.

So did she.

Cal put his arms around her and kissed her, his mouth slow and sweet on hers. It grounded him, and when he sauntered off to ride, he wasn't nervous at all.

Sometimes, his intuition warned the ride would go wrong, but tonight, he knew he'd ride well. Despite the wild antics and thrashing the bull delivered, Calhoun held his seat and maintained the right form. Most of the time, he tuned the announcer out, but he caught bits and pieces of the chatter as he lasted the full eight seconds. He landed on his feet, but he still had been splashed with mud. He returned to Vivian to hear his score for the night and cheered when he heard the final. Between his ride and Badlands Bruiser's performance, he ended up with a rare ninety.

Vivian shrieked as she hugged him, smearing mud on her jeans.

But she didn't seem to care. He took home third place, and they waited for the payout. After a change of clothes, they headed for the diner. The counter, tables, and most of the booths were full of rodeo people. Many waved a hand or called a greeting as they passed. More than once, Cal paused to shake hands or exchange a high five with another rider.

Once seated, Calhoun ordered a rib-eye steak with a side of shrimp, fries, and Texas Toast. "If you want steak, honey, order one," he told her. "If you can't eat it all, I'll help you." When the food arrived, he tasted the steak and found it perfect, cooked medium to his taste. He ate all his and the last third of hers.

Although his muscles ached and his back hurt, he rode a happiness high. He'd come out with prize money, he hadn't been hurt, and Vivian was with him. For this moment, life was grand, and he savored it.

"The rodeo's over, so what happens now?" She finished her tea and rattled ice in the empty glass.

Cal shrugged, then winced because it made his sore shoulder twinge. "Sometimes, I stay the night and head out in the morning, or sometimes, I go now. It depends on where I'm headed and how far. I generally stop for church along the way."

"If you were coming to Missouri, when would you leave?" Vivian set her glass down and traced the water ring it left with one finger.

Hope surged through him. "Are you going home with me to Texas?"

"I thought I would, if you still want me to go and if we can visit Nanna first." She raised her head and offered him a sweet smile.

Thank you, Lord. Joy filled his heart, and he grinned. "You know I do, Pretty Lady, and we will. It's late, so we'll head out tomorrow morning." Now that they had a plan, he returned to his tin can, so he could grab a few hours of sleep, then secure everything for the road.

Vivian promised she would check out early and come over to the arena.

Then they would set out in a caravan. Vivian would lead the way, and he would follow. Since he would be pulling the trailer, they would take the interstate.

On Sunday, Calhoun called his brother again. "Good morning," he said when Lincoln answered.

"What's shaking? I hope you didn't call to tell me you got banged up and are in some hospital."

"Nah, not this time," Cal said. "We'll be there probably Tuesday or Wednesday, and I am bringing

Vivian so get a room ready. That's why I called, to let you know." He could imagine Linc's face, eyes wide and mouth hung open.

"That's the gal you were with at the motel?"

"The very one."

"And you're bringing her home?"

"Yeah, I am." Calhoun tried to keep his tone casual but he wanted to whoop out loud, maybe even dance a little jig. He didn't think he could stand to part company with Vivian and now he wouldn't have to say good-bye.

"You haven't had a girlfriend in so long. I'm surprised but I'm glad. Is this a serious relationship?"

Asked point blank, Cal took a moment to answer but told the truth. "I hope so," he told his brother. "I want it to be, and I'm hoping she feels the same. I'm crazy about her."

"The very fact you're bringing her down here says a lot. What happens after that?"

"I don't know," Calhoun admitted. "Guess we'll find out."

Lincoln laughed. "I reckon you will. All right, see you when you get here. If it's gonna be past Wednesday let me know, okay? I'll smoke a brisket, and we'll get a room ready for your lady. Take care, Cal."

"I will. Thanks, bro."

"*De nada.*"

He had dosed up with ibuprofen before Vivian arrived at his tin can, bringing fast-food biscuits and coffee. "Good morning, Pretty Lady," he told her. "Thanks." The rich sausage aroma piqued his appetite.

"I figured you might be hungry," Vivian replied. "Good morning, Calhoun."

The biscuits filled his belly as they sat at his trailer's tiny table. He noticed she wore the boots he'd bought her, so she must like them. Vivian had tucked her jeans into the boots, and she wore a tunic-style, floral print blouse. He caught a whiff of her perfume, something sweet that reminded him of roses. Her long, beautiful hair was pulled back into the usual tight bun. *I need to get this gal a decent hat and maybe some Western shirts.* "How long will it take to get to your place in Missouri?"

"Two hours, maybe a little more on the interstate," Vivian stated. "I figured when we get to the farmhouse, you can pull the trailer around back between Nanna's house and the barn. We'll settle, then head over to the facility to see Nanna. Sometimes, I eat dinner with her on Sundays, but if you'd rather not, we can grab a bite somewhere else."

Cal had never eaten in a nursing home and seldom visited one. "Sure. We can eat with your grandma. I hoped we might find a church somewhere along the way."

"Do we have to?" Her expression went sour, and her lips flipped to a frown.

"I'd like to. I haven't missed church in years, even being on the road so much."

"If you can wait until evening, I'll go with you to the little church I used to attend. They have an evening service at six."

He suspected agreeing to go to church was huge, so he nodded. "Sure, that'll work."

"I'll make supper for you afterward."

"Can you cook?" Calhoun wondered as she rewarded him with a sweet smile that brightened her pretty face.

"Yes, although just for me, I often don't. What's your favorite home-cooked meal?"

"Pot roast with noodles, fried chicken and biscuits, or pan-fried pork chops. Unless I eat with Linc's family, I seldom have a homemade meal."

"You'll have one tonight."

As soon as he got the trailer hitched to the truck, they set out, winding through town to US Highway 412 which would link them to I-49 at Springdale. Vivian took the lead and he followed. At the early Sunday hour, traffic was light, and he had no trouble keeping up. Once on I-49, they zipped through the metropolitan cluster of towns in northwest Arkansas and crossed the state line into Missouri. Calhoun followed her when she exited the highway near Neosho and wound beneath it to a country road.

She drove down it and turned into a long driveway beside a two-story frame farmhouse, following it to the barn where she parked. Calhoun pulled his trailer beside her without blocking the barn doors and stopped.

Although it was obvious, she waved as she got out of the car. "We're here."

He climbed out of the truck, his back aching and knees twinging. "Nice place."

Although the adjacent fields held knee-high weeds and not cattle or horses, the pastures stretched green and vibrant in several directions. The big white house boasted a front porch with a swing and the barn, apparently empty, appeared solid. It demonstrated the potential to be a working farm again.

"It's where Nanna and Papa lived," Vivian explained. "I grew up coming here to visit. I spent every weekend I could and more time in the summer. I've been staying here since I came back from Kansas City. It will be mine, I guess, when Nanna's gone. She did a beneficiary deed that will go into effect then. None of my cousins wanted it. They either live somewhere else or have their own spreads."

Calhoun could hear the whine of steel-belted radials on the interstate, but otherwise, it was a quiet place. Honeysuckle bloomed somewhere, and the fragrance filled his nose, bringing a rush of memories. The vine had bloomed in Granny's backyard. To him, it was a lovely oasis and would make a great place to retreat to when he could.

"Will you live here, then?"

"I have been now, and I'd like to," she replied. "Maybe. If I stay here, either the freelancing has to pan out, or I'll need to get a job. Come on inside."

They entered through a back porch which led into a mud room, then into a kitchen.

At the end of the kitchen, she pointed out a bathroom.

Cal followed her through a dining room, with a bedroom to one side, then into a spacious living room. In addition to a couch, two easy chairs, an older television, lamps, and end tables, he noticed a spinet piano beneath the open staircase. The steps began next to the front door and led up three to a landing, then turned upward. Near the top, they curved again.

Vivian mounted the stairs.

So, he trailed behind. A narrow hall held four bedrooms and a bathroom at the end.

"The front bedroom was Nanna's until she couldn't manage the stairs." Vivian opened the door to a pleasant bedroom overlooking the front yard.

"Do you sleep here?" Calhoun ran one hand along intricate woodwork on the stair railing as he ascended.

Vivian shook her head and moved to the next. "I sleep in this one, but you can take your pick between the others. I'll put fresh sheets on the bed."

Although he liked the homey feel of this house, he shook his head. "I figured I'd bunk in the trailer. I don't want to be any trouble."

Vivian turned to him. "You're no trouble at all, Cowboy. I wouldn't invite you to stay if I minded. I'll be staying with your brother I've never even met, so you can sleep inside. Take the blue room across the hall."

Calhoun peeked inside and surveyed what she called the blue room. The walls were a light, bright cobalt-blue. Navy and white floral curtains framed the single window. Both rugs on the floor were shades of blue. The metal frame double bed had been painted an antique white and so had the cedar chest at the foot. "All right," he told her. "I'll go get my gear. Out of curiosity, what color is your room?"

"Pink." Vivian tossed her head and her ponytail bounced. "I liked pink as a little girl. And the other one is the yellow room. The bathroom's done in shades of green. The front bedroom was Nanna's with a peach color scheme. Nanna always wanted to try her hand at interior decorating, so after Papa retired, they redid the rooms. I need to bring up my bags, too."

"I'll get them for you. Any chance there might be coffee?"

"I'll make some. How's your shoulder?"

Cal put his right hand on it. "Not bad. My back's

hurting a bit, though, but that's every day. It's part of a bull rider's life."

"Take something for it. I'll make coffee."

They drank it on the front porch, sitting in the swing. Calhoun moved the truck and trailer, then unhooked it so he could drive his vehicle. When he finished his cup, he put it down and took her hand. "I like it here. Someday, after I hang up my spurs, I hope to buy a place something like this."

Vivian shook her head and frowned. "Don't you want a place in Texas?"

"I just want my own." He rocked the swing with one foot and sighed. "It could be in Texas or here or anywhere. I've always wanted my own spread."

"Will you raise rough stock?" Vivian caught hold of the chain that held up the porch swing.

Calhoun considered the question. "Not likely. Beef cattle, I reckon, and maybe a few horses."

"Like your paint, Johnny?"

She remembered his horse's name, which pleased him. "Yeah, probably."

"How old are you, Calhoun? If you're talking about retiring, I wondered."

"Thirty-three," he told her. "I might look older, but cowboys retire young, if they don't get crippled or killed. I figure I might have two or three good years left. Maybe less, maybe more, so I think about it." Her fingers wrapped tight around his hand.

"You don't look old, Calhoun. You're a good-looking man. I might've guessed thirty. Before you ask, I'm twenty-eight."

Five years younger, he counted. "I would have guessed younger, honey. What comes next?" As soon as he asked the question, he wondered if he meant today or down the road because he wondered about both.

"I suppose we'll head over to the Sunny Morning Senior Citizens Home before long. I talked to Nanna this morning, so she's expecting us. I'm changing clothes before we do, though."

"That works. I can drink another cup of coffee while you get ready." He would also go choose a better shirt and his best black jeans. He wanted to make a good first impression on her grandmother.

Chapter Six

Vivian poked through her closet before deciding she'd wear a dress. She chose a casual dress, blue and white, with tiny navy flowers on the fabric. The skirt dropped below her knees, and larger white flowers decorated the hem. Three small, white buttons were for show, and the dress had three-quarter length sleeves. She didn't mess with pantyhose but changed from the boots into a pair of navy flats, then hurried downstairs.

Calhoun had put on something nicer, too. He wore a snap-button, blue Western shirt with teal embroidery on the shoulders and black jeans. He'd combed his wild hair to tame it and shaved. He'd always been handsome, but now, he took her breath away. She stumbled on the last stair.

He caught her.

He smelled delicious, of musk and leather. "You clean up very nice."

His dark eyes roamed over her, and he grinned. "You're gorgeous, honey. I guess blue is the color of the day."

"It seems to be."

Calhoun bent down and kissed her, his lips brushing hers in a swift but tender kiss. "Let's go, Pretty Lady. Do you want to take my truck or your car?"

"Car," Vivian managed to say, her breath short as

her heart raced. "You can drive, though."

At the residential care center, he offered his hand as they entered, so they walked through the halls hand in hand.

If the stark institutional décor bothered him, it didn't show.

As they passed folks in wheelchairs parked along the way, Calhoun spoke to them, using simple greetings which made them smile. He picked up a fallen lap blanket for one resident and retrieved a dropped pair of glasses for another.

Vivian stopped in the office to pay for two lunch trays so they could eat with Nanna. When they reached her grandmother's room, she entered first.

Nanna sat in her wheelchair near the window.

Beyond it, a summer garden bloomed with black-eyed Susans, tiger lilies, and petunias. "Hello, Nanna."

The old woman wheeled the chair about with skill. "Hi, Vivian. I see you brought your cowboy. Introduce us."

"Nanna, this is Calhoun Kelly, from Rusk, Texas. Calhoun, this is my grandmother, Kate Quinn." Vivian extended her hand toward her grandmother, then toward Cal.

"I'm pleased to meet you," Nanna told Cal with a smile.

Calhoun knelt and took Nanna's hand. "I'm glad to make your acquaintance, Mrs. Quinn. I can see where your granddaughter gets her pretty looks."

Nanna blushed.

Vivian thought she might, too.

"You're one with a sweet tongue, I see," Nanna told Calhoun. "Just call me Nanna or Kate."

"Why aren't you in the recliner?" Vivian questioned. Nanna lacked the mobility to move from it to the wheelchair and back without assistance.

"If you're eating dinner with me, we'll eat in the dining room," Nanna replied. "And I thought maybe we could go out on the patio for a little while. I don't think it's too hot yet, and I'd like to be outside. All that is easier done in this chair than the recliner. Besides, I went down to the parlor for church this morning."

"We'll go to church this evening. I usually go to a morning service, but I don't like to miss church." Cal remained on the floor near Nanna's feet and grinned.

Nanna's eyes grew large. "Vivian's going to church? Praise the Lord."

Calhoun rose and shrugged. "She said she would, and I plan to hold her to it."

"It's just to be nice, that's all. I know Calhoun likes church and prayers and all that." To ensure her grandmother knew she hadn't had a revelation or return to faith, Vivian spoke up.

"Where are you going?"

She hesitated before answering, worried Nanna might read too much into it. "Sweet Springs. I'm not familiar with any other churches. It's no big deal, Nanna. I'm just doing a favor for a friend."

If either Calhoun or Nanna said anymore about it, she wouldn't go. She didn't have to, and she wouldn't. Sitting in a pew would be hard enough since she hadn't set foot in that church since her parents' funeral. The place might trigger memories she would rather forget. A curl of anger flamed to life within, and Vivian waited for either of them to say something so she wouldn't have to go after all.

"Ready to go outside, Nanna? It is a pretty day."

Calhoun didn't take the bait but ignored it. *He's wiser than I thought*.

"Yes, I am, young man." Nanna placed her hands on the wheels to move the chair forward.

"I'll drive." Calhoun released the brakes on the chair, then grasped the handles and rolled her toward the door. "C'mon, Pretty Lady. Let's go see the flowers."

Her irritation faded, and she let her prickly objections go. "All right." No other residents were on the patio, so it was private for now. A birdbath in one corner attracted birds, robins, house finches, and one female cardinal.

Calhoun wheeled Nanna to a shady spot near a bench, parked her, and sat. He winced and rubbed his left shoulder.

"Did you ever take anything?" Vivian settled beside him.

"No, I forgot. It's all right."

"I don't want you hurting. I've got some ibuprofen in my purse. I'll go get you some water."

He flashed a grin. "I appreciate that. Thanks."

Her heart skipped a few beats in response to that smile. Vivian returned to find Calhoun and Nanna deep in conversation. She hesitated at the edge of the patio, wondering if they were talking about her, but they weren't.

"My family's been in Texas since not long after the Civil War," he informed Nanna. "At least some of them. My great-great—well I don't know how many greats—granddaddy was a man named Barlow Washington from Kentucky. He fought for the South in the war, then headed to Texas. I'm not sure how it all happened, but he and his brothers ended up owning a ranch. His daughter, Amelia Ann Washington, was my daddy's great grandma several times removed. I've heard a lot of stories about those old days in Texas. Then one of my other great grandpas, Lucas Kelly, came over from Ireland."

"You should write it all down, Calhoun," Nanna told him. "I love family history. I started doing mine when I was just a little girl. Vivian's never been very interested in such things, though."

"It's not a lack of interest but time." On her return to the garden, Vivian handed Calhoun a bottle of water and some ibuprofen. "I think they're serving in the dining room, if you want to go eat now."

Dinner proved to be roast pork, cornbread dressing doused with gravy, buttered carrots, bread and butter, and pineapple chunks for dessert. Vivian ate it with little enthusiasm. The meal wasn't terrible, but it wasn't very good. The meat proved to be dry and overcooked. She found the gravy salty and the carrots half raw. Bread and butter meant white store bread with margarine. She didn't complain, though, because Nanna didn't have any other options.

"Well, that's right tasty," Calhoun announced after he'd cleaned his plate and winked at Vivian. "Not bad at all."

After they ate, Calhoun rolled Nanna back to her room, and when she requested to sit in her recliner, he didn't wait for the staff. He picked her up with care, asking her to put her arms around his neck, and placed her there. "It takes two or three staff members to do that," Vivian told Cal with a grin. "You're showing off,

Calhoun."

"I wasn't trying to." He shrugged. "I knew I could do it, so I did."

"Thank you, Calhoun." Nanna beamed at Vivian's cowboy.

Vivian suspected her grandmother was smitten with Calhoun. No wonder. So was she.

"You're welcome. I'm fixing to go find a soda," he replied. "Do either of you want one?"

"I'm good," Vivian told him. "Nanna's not supposed to have pop."

"I'll be back." Calhoun nodded and gave a double thumbs-up.

As soon as he departed, Nanna turned to her granddaughter. "He's a good one, Vivian. You'd better hang on to him."

"We're friends, that's all. I'm going with him to Texas, though, for a few days, home to visit his family, and then for a rodeo in Fort Worth."

"Oh, that does sound promising. I've prayed for you to find someone, Vivvie. I won't always be here, and I don't want you to live alone forever." Nanna's eyes sparkled as she reached out to take her granddaughter's hand.

The idea of spending her life with Calhoun filled Vivian with a warm, pleasant emotion. She'd only known him for a few days, but she could envision it. Still, she wasn't about to admit that, not to Nanna or anyone else, especially Calhoun. "You're jumping the gun, Nanna. I barely know him."

"And you're going to church. That makes my heart glad, honey."

"I'm going for him, not for me." Vivian ached to

scream. Nanna should know her aversion to all things religious by now. "It's my effort to be nice to him. He's been kind to me."

"It's a start." Nanna scrutinized Vivian with a keen gaze. "You haven't set foot inside that church for what is it now, six, seven years?"

"Seven." Nanna knew exactly how long it had been. She also ignored Vivian's insistence she barely knew Calhoun. "I don't want to talk about church anymore."

Nanna huffed. "All right. Tell me more about Calhoun. What does he ride?"

"He's a bull rider. The first time I watched him, it scared me to death." Vivian grinned. She couldn't help it. She wiggled in the room's one visitor chair but couldn't get comfortable.

"Did he get hurt?"

"He's been hurt many times, but it wasn't the evening we met." Vivian rose and stared through the window. "The second night, he banged up his left shoulder. He dislocated it a few months ago, and it's been sore. Last night, though, he rode so well."

"Bull riding's the most dangerous part of rodeo."

"I know, Nanna. If we do get together, I'm hoping he might quit. He told me this morning someday he'd like to own a farm and raise beef cattle."

A mischievous smile lit Nanna's face. "My place would be perfect for that."

Although she had the same thought, Vivian protested. "Nanna!"

Calhoun strolled into the room, a bottle of his favorite root beer in one hand. He sat in one of the room's chairs and sighed. Then he held the cold bottle

71

against his forehead.

"Do you have a headache?" Vivian asked before she could stop herself. She usually wasn't the kind to hover or nurture.

"A little one. It's all right. It's just from being tired. It'll pass."

"We can leave if you're ready. I need to swing by the store to get something to cook for supper, then we'll be at the house until time for church. Nanna, we'll come by tomorrow. I don't think we're leaving until later in the week."

"You kids go ahead and go," Nanna said. "I'll see you both tomorrow."

Vivian pecked her grandmother's cheek. "We'll be here."

Calhoun picked up Nanna's wrinkled, worn hand and kissed it like a gentleman.

The old woman smiled, then fanned herself with one hand as if she might swoon.

Vivian rolled her eyes, but she liked their interchange. "See you then, Nanna."

At the car, he handed her the keys.

She lifted her eyebrows in silent inquiry.

He laughed. "I figure you know how to get around, Pretty Lady. I'm not familiar."

Vivian headed to the small store that had always been her favorite. She loved the friendly atmosphere at the home-owned, old-fashioned market. She selected a small chuck roast, a package of thick egg noodles, and fixings to make biscuits. When she saw the root beer brand he favored, she grabbed a two-liter.

At the checkout, Calhoun pulled out his wallet. "I've got this." He handed some bills to the cashier.

"But…"

"No buts," he told her. At the house, Calhoun flopped into the old rump-sprung recliner that had been her grandfather's and closed his eyes. "I think I'll have a short nap, if you don't mind."

"Make yourself at home. I'll get this roast ready and play around in the kitchen." Although Vivian had left home last Thursday, the time seemed longer. She adored this old house and had learned to cook here. Slipping out of her shoes, she browned the roast and put it in the oven, then stirred up some biscuits she would bake when they returned. She found a jar of peanut butter, so she made a batch of cookies, complete with the crisscross fork marks.

At four thirty, she went upstairs and freshened up, then came downstairs to wake Calhoun. Vivian paused. Sound asleep, he appeared younger. His dark eyelashes lay against his cheek. She brushed her fingers across his face, then called his name.

The third time, he roused. "What is it?"

"It's almost five so if you want to go to church, we need to get around and go. I was tempted to let you sleep, but I know you want to go."

"I do." He brought the chair forward and scrubbed his face with both hands. "All right. Thanks, honey."

"Sure." While he combed his hair and did whatever else necessary, Vivian added the noodles to the roaster and turned the oven to low. "Do you want me to drive?"

"No, I figured on taking the truck. You navigate me there."

Vivian smiled. "It's not very far." The simple white frame church that dated to the early 1900s sat beneath tall trees along a country road that lay between the interstate and the old highway. Vivian had attended services here for as long as she could remember, skipping up the sidewalk holding her parents' hands. She had gone to Sunday School here and vacation Bible school, too. Vivian was baptized here when she was ten. Once, she had figured she would be married here. Her parents had been and so had Nanna.

Calhoun rolled the truck to a stop and parked on the gravel.

She had knots in her stomach. Memories of the last time she'd been here hit hard as she remembered her parents' matching caskets parked in the main aisle, the floral arrangements that made the church smell like springtime, and the familiar faces of the congregation, dark with sorrow.

Calhoun offered his arm as they mounted the steps.

She took it, grateful for the support. "I don't know if I can do this," she mumbled.

He halted. "Honey, if you're not sure, we can skip it."

"But you want to go to church."

"I need it, same as I need air to breathe," he stated. "Church grounds me and gives me a foundation for the week. I do want to be here, but if it's too much, I understand."

This from the man who still rode bulls when his younger brother died doing the same. He'd never said what arena in which town, but Vivian suspected he still competed there. She would attend church for Calhoun. The service would only last an hour, maybe a bit longer. "Let's go inside before I change my mind."

"Did you really believe, before your folks died?" he asked.

After a long sigh, she nodded. "I did, Calhoun, but after, I just couldn't believe a loving God could let them be murdered in such a brutal way."

"You know what one of my favorite verses is?"

"No."

"Philippians 4:13—'*I can do all things through Christ which strengthens me.*' You've got this, Pretty Lady."

"I hope."

In the vestibule, the cradle roll remained painted on one wall, and she saw her name there. She might have bolted, but they linked arms as they entered the sanctuary.

Lavinia Longwell stared, then smiled. "Vivian! It's been so long since I've seen you! I don't know when anyone last did. I heard you were back. How's Kate doing in that nursing home?"

"Nanna's fine," Vivian replied.

"And who's this handsome fellow?"

"I'm Calhoun Kelly, ma'am."

Vivian tried to hide her smile since Cal saved her the trouble of answering.

Before they slid into a pew, four other people greeted her and asked questions.

Vivian ignored them, and when the first song began, she said a silent thanks, if not to God, to someone. She fumbled for a hymnal, but Calhoun didn't need one.

He sang out in a rich tenor voice, never missing a single word or note as those gathered sang the familiar "Amazing Grace."

Vivian didn't sing. She couldn't, not around a lump in her throat and an ache in her chest. If Calhoun noticed, he didn't say anything but sometimes sent a smile in her direction. He sang the other two opening songs, all old standards she knew well, "Just A Closer Walk With Thee" and "Power In The Blood." By that hymn, she managed to sing a little, self-conscious and awkward.

When the pastor took the pulpit, many church members opened their Bibles.

"You didn't bring your Bible," she whispered to Calhoun.

He pulled one of those small New Testaments, the kind often given out free at school or other places, from his pocket. "I always carry this one. My mama gave it to me when I was saved."

Vivian stared into space as she tuned out the sermon. Calhoun held her right hand throughout the service, keeping his Bible in the other. She couldn't have told him one single thing that was said or named a verse.

When the collection plate came around, he dropped a twenty into it and passed it down the pew.

When the last song began, she forgot to breathe. "On Eagles' Wings" had long been a favorite until she had requested it be sung for her folks' funeral. She hadn't heard it since, and as the music flowed over her, she wept. By the time the refrain was sung for the third time, she wept and pulled her hand free. Vivian dashed outside and headed for the truck. She leaned against the bed and sobbed. Around her, the cicadas hummed as Cal caught up.

"Hey, don't cry. Come here, honey." He rested his hands on her shoulders. He turned her around to face him and folded her into his arms.

She leaned against him, glad for his support, and did her best not to keep weeping. His quiet presence calmed her, and she stopped but lingered for a few more sweet moments. "I'm sorry. It was the song. It's one I chose for my parents' funeral."

"I figured. We played the same for Sullivan. You okay now?"

"Yes, thank you. Are you hungry?"

"Starving to death. That lunch over at the nursing home was rank. Gave me a little bit of indigestion."

Vivian laughed as he opened the passenger door and helped her into the truck. "Then why did you tell my grandmother how good it was?"

His eyes danced, and he laughed. "Nanna has to eat there, so I figured it wouldn't be nice to talk bad about the food."

"Thank you."

"*De nada.* Let's go back to the farmhouse and have some supper, then. Whatever you're cooking smelled good before we left."

As they ate the pot roast and noodles at home, she savored the rich, pleasant flavor. The noodles melted on her tongue, complimented by the well-seasoned beef. Calhoun said nothing more about church. He didn't ask her if she liked it or if she wanted to return. Instead, he praised her cooking and ate until he swore he couldn't manage another bite.

After announcing he was tired, Calhoun headed to bed.

Vivian took a long bath in the old clawfoot tub and contemplated the day. For seven years, she'd been alone and lonely. No matter how busy she'd been with work in Kansas City, despite her friends and coworkers, and even with Nanna, she'd felt detached. Everyday routines carried her through the days, and at night, she'd often wished for companionship. The few men she'd dated didn't provide the company she craved, and her friends couldn't fill the emptiness. When she returned home from Kansas City, although her cousins offered a welcome and seemed glad to see her, Vivian felt like she no longer belonged, not like she once did.

Tonight, though, Calhoun's presence comforted her. Knowing he was down the hall, asleep by now, filled her with contented joy. If she called his name, then he would wake and come to see what she needed. In the morning, he would be there, his brown eyes alight with a vibrant spirit.

It didn't matter how short a time she'd known him, she thought. He'd become a friend. In fact, Calhoun might be the best friend she had ever had. And maybe, just maybe, Calhoun might be something more.

Chapter Seven

Calhoun's plan to head home for a short visit before taking on the Fort Worth rodeo almost fell apart before it got underway. On Monday morning, they ate breakfast, scrambled eggs, and bacon with more of Vivian's perfect biscuits. If he kept eating this delicious fare, he'd get fat. They headed over to the residential care facility for another visit with Nanna.

She greeted them but insisted she always played bingo at ten a.m. and all but shoved them toward the door.

Back at the farmhouse, a place Calhoun had grown to love during the short time he'd been there, he picked up his keys from the kitchen counter.

Vivian appeared in the doorway with her hands on her hips and glared. "What are you doing?"

"I'm about to put your car in the barn, so it'll be out of the weather and safe," he replied. "Then I suppose we'll hit the road."

"I thought I'd drive it and follow you." Vivian glowered, her stance rigid.

"There's no need for that, Pretty Lady." Cal had expected she would willingly leave it behind.

"If I leave it, what will I do for a vehicle when we're gone?"

"You won't need one." He grinned as he pushed back a lock of hair falling loose from her ponytail.

Vivian crossed her arms. "How will I get from one place to another?"

"I'll take you anywhere you need or want to go."

Her lips twisted. "That could work, I suppose. But if I'm at a motel and you're at the arena…"

"I'll leave the trailer at Linc's place," Calhoun explained "We'll get a room somewhere close to the stockyards and the Cowtown Coliseum. Did you sign up to take pictures?"

"I did," she replied. "I'm confused. Maybe I didn't ask you enough questions. I'm not sure I totally understand what we're about to do. So, we're going to Texas where you can visit your brother, and I'm staying at his house."

"Right." Calhoun sighed, struggling to remain both calm and patient.

"Then we're going to Fort Worth where you'll ride bulls, but you're not taking the trailer."

"That's it." He nodded as he ruffled a hand over his hair.

Vivian drew a deep breath. "What happens after that?"

Here's where it gets complicated. "We go back to Linc's and get the trailer, if that's what we decide. Then, either I can bring you back up here, or you can go with me to Prescott, Arizona, over the Fourth of July."

"What's in Prescott?" Her frown faded although she wasn't smiling.

So far, she hadn't flat out refused so he still hoped and crossed his fingers. "It's the world's oldest rodeo, and it's a big deal. It's part of their Frontier Days shindig. I'm already signed up to ride, so I'll be there, but I'd like it if you want to come along."

"Wouldn't I need my car after Fort Worth?" She folded her arms, tapped one foot, and stared.

"Not if you're with me."

"And where would I sleep?"

Calhoun's spirits sank. He hadn't thought so far ahead, and his tin can had one bed and one bedroom. "You could have the bed, and I'd sleep on the couch, since it folds out into a bed. Or, if you'd rather, I'd rent more motel rooms. I'm getting spoiled, but they're more comfortable."

When she didn't say anything for what seemed like a very long minute, he figured she might be done with the trip and finished with him. If so, he'd head on out now, forget about the side trips he'd planned for Vivian along the way, and cut his losses. It would hurt, sure, but not as much if it happened later.

"Go ahead and park the car in the barn." A smile played across her lips. "I'll grab my suitcase and my camera bag. I'm going to Texas, and I'll go with you to Fort Worth. I might have to think a little longer about Arizona."

Cal whooped and pulled her in close for a kiss. His mouth latched onto hers with powerful happiness and need. After the kiss, he cradled her for a moment. "All right, honey." Feeling ten feet tall, he danced and whirled across the yard. For now, his persistent aches didn't bother him a bit. In short order, he got her car secured in the barn. Then he hooked up the trailer to his truck and pointed it down the driveway. As soon as she joined him, they would hit the road. Calhoun didn't think he'd been this excited about going anywhere in years, if ever.

He fueled up on the south edge of town, said a

quick prayer, then headed down the highway. Vintage country music blasted from the speakers.

Vivian scooted over beside him, her denim clad leg against his. Fifteen minutes into the trip, she peered into the glove box. "Where's the map?"

"Map?" he asked, confused.

"Don't you have one of those paper fold-up maps?"

Calhoun guffawed. "I haven't seen one of those in years, honey. Besides, I don't need one. I know the way home and just about every major road from the Ozarks to the plains to the Ark-La-Tex by heart."

Vivian stared and tossed her head so her ponytail bounced. "Seriously?"

"Totally. I don't use GPS on the phone, either. The one time I tried. I ended up driving in circles at a highway interchange in Colorado."

Arms crossed, she gazed at him. "Then how will we navigate?"

"I told you." He removed his hat, ran a hand over his hair, then put it back on. "I'm familiar. You'll follow along on your phone if you want, but I'm going old school. I'll tell you where we're at, how far to our next location, and all of it. It might be fun."

"All right. It might be, at that." Vivian sighed. "Sure, I'll try it."

After that, they settled into a comfortable harmony. Sometimes, he sang along with the tunes playing over the speakers and sometimes she did. On some songs, their voices blended.

"Why'd you ditch the cowboy hat?" Vivian asked.

She had noticed he traded it for a baseball team hat. "I don't usually wear it when I'm driving very far," Cal explained. "It's in the trailer, tucked away. The brim sometimes makes it hard for my peripheral vision. I wear a cap instead. Besides, it keeps people from recognizing me most of the time."

"Oh, okay. You have fans?"

Calhoun hadn't expected her to be skeptical, but he nodded. "A few, Pretty Lady, a few."

They barreled through northwest Arkansas and shot through the Bobby Hopper Tunnel fast enough to make Vivian squeal. She dug her fingers into his leg, and Cal figured if she had been a praying woman, she would have offered one up. "Scared?"

"Maybe a little. All the lights in the tunnel messed with my head."

"We're through it now."

She leaned her head against his shoulder. "I'm glad. I have a question, though.

"Shoot."

"Isn't it going to be late when we get to Texas? I looked it up on my phone, and it's farther than I thought."

Calhoun had a surprise, one he thought she would like. He hadn't meant to tell her yet, but since she asked, he did. "We're not going to Rusk tonight, Pretty Lady. We'll stop at Rich Mountain, and we'll spend the night. We can either park the trailer at the campground or stay at the Queen Wilhelmina Inn. I travel the rodeo circuit all season, but I don't get much vacation, so I thought we'd take a night and spend it there."

"Is it scenic?"

"Very. I think you'll like it, and your camera will love the place."

Vivian wore a quirky little smile.

Maybe she didn't hate the idea.

"Will we eat lunch there?"

"Nah, we'll grab something at Fort Smith. It's still another hour and half, maybe two hours from there. I ain't gonna let you starve, Vivian." Since he was pulling the trailer, Cal couldn't go through a drive-through or take up half the parking lot at a restaurant, so he headed for a truck stop. The large travel plaza on the south edge of Fort Smith seemed to be the best shot at a quick lunch.

"We're eating here?" Vivian asked as she turned her head from side to side as he parked. "This looks interesting. I've never been to a truck plaza before."

"Never?"

"Not that I remember, no. They always seem so big and busy. Those huge trucks intimidate me."

"They don't bother me. Let's get something quick and head on down to Mena. It's going to be another couple of hours before we're at the Queen Wilhelmina."

Vivian chose a turkey and Swiss wrap.

He grabbed a burger along with a pair of sodas, standard convenience store fare. They ate in the truck and got back on the road. Calhoun anticipated her reaction to the Ouachita Mountains. Although not as tall as the Appalachians or as majestic as the Rockies, they ranked high on Cal's list of favorites. To him, they were impressive, even more than the Ozark Mountains around Branson, Missouri. Like at the spring he'd taken her to, he found peace here. Although the Queen Wilhelmina State Park and the lodge drew tourists, there were never crowds like in Colorado Springs or Pigeon Forge. Rodeo fired his blood, but sometimes, he needed time away from the arenas, the crowds, and the constant danger. Nature delivered that. In places like this, he could and did recharge body and soul.

Not until they approached Waldron did the scenery begin to change as they entered the Ouachitas.

Vivian sat straighter and glanced around. "Wow! It's prettier than I ever imagined, and they really are mountains." Vivian turned her head as she gazed at both sides of the road.

"Of course, they are." Calhoun laughed. "Just wait, though. The drive up to Rich Mountain and the views from the Queen Wilhelmina are even more awesome. Plus, it will be way cooler up there, even in the summer."

"I like that." Vivian smiled as she gazed at the scenery. "Calhoun, this is going to be so nice."

"That's the idea, Pretty Lady." At Mena, they wound through the small town to take Highway 88 up the mountain.

Vivian scooted across the seat to gaze through the window.

The road climbed steadily upward, with many curves, some of them tight. He always had to watch the trailer so he wouldn't sling it around the truck or too far to the side.

She chattered, her eyes bright and smile wide as she gasped at some of the more scenic views.

When they reached the first of several off the road vistas, Cal pulled in to park. Awestruck as always, he removed his hat and quoted from Isiah: " 'How beautiful upon the mountains are the feet of him who brings good news, who publishes peace, who brings good news of happiness, who publishes salvation, who says to Zion, 'your God reigns.' "

"This is amazing. Oh, it's so beautiful." Vivian clasped her hands together and smiled.

He noticed she didn't respond to the verse, and that was fine. She didn't have to although he wished she would. "If you want to take some pictures, get your camera."

She grabbed her bag and unloaded her camera. With deft fingers, she changed to a zoom lens and stepped out of the truck.

He watched as she strode to the edge and started clicking photos, twisting the camera at different angles. She wore a smile bigger than the vista that stretched out before them, and he grinned. He liked seeing her happy, but his nerves twitched with sudden anxiety when she stepped closer to the edge of the lookout.

Despite an ache in his back and a hitch in his knee, he stood beside her as she tripped over a stray rock and teetered. If she went over the edge, nothing would stop a tumble. Before she could pitch down the side of the mountain, he grabbed her. "Easy there, honey, or you'll be halfway down the mountainside." His heart pounded hard and fast.

Vivian grasped Calhoun as she shook from head to foot. "That scared me."

"Took ten years off my life," Cal replied with a huge sigh. "I'm too fond of you to watch you fall and get hurt."

Or worse. If she took a header down the mountainside, it could be the last thing she did.

"Now you know how I feel when I watch you ride bulls," Vivian admitted. She hadn't removed her hands from his shoulders, and he savored it. "I haven't seen you ride saddle broncs yet, but if you do, I'll be just as anxious."

Although Calhoun didn't want her to worry about him, he liked the fact she did because it meant she cared. He'd used the word *fond* which was probably a mistake. People were fond of their favorite aunt or a particular color or a special food. *Fond* wasn't strong enough for what he had begun to feel for Vivian, but he wasn't quite ready to use the *L* word. "You shouldn't fret over me," he stated, pleased but embarrassed enough to blush. "I don't plan to get hurt, honey."

"You already have, Calhoun." Her forehead creased.

She still hadn't let go, and neither had he. "Not much since you've known me. I'll be all right, Pretty Lady."

Her arms tightened around him, and she looked so lovely gazing up at him that he kissed her. She tasted sweeter than the root beer they'd been drinking, and her lips fused to his, eager and willing to share the kiss. Calhoun used his mouth to cherish her lips and show by his actions what he wasn't ready to say in words. If he didn't stop, he wouldn't want to, so he pulled back after a few tender moments. "We'd better get going. I have a reservation for the campground."

Vivian nodded. "That works for me. I'll stay where you do."

Calhoun doubted she realized it, but he heard the echo of Ruth's words from the Bible, *for where thou goest, I will go*. "We'll figure it out when we get there." Cal held her hand and led her back to his truck, careful with each step because he found her precious.

The Queen Wilhelmina Inn, the third of that name

to stand in the same spot crowned the top of Rich Mountain with a royal presence. Calhoun could only imagine how majestic the first one had been, back in 1898. Panoramic views spread in all directions.

"Oh, my." Vivian stared at the place, eyes round and mouth open.

"It's impressive. It's fine but not fancy. We'll eat supper there, if nothing else. Let's get the trailer parked, and we'll decide what to do next." Once he'd registered and got the tin can backed into the assigned space, he took care of the water and electric hookups.

Vivian sat on the adjacent picnic table, gazing at the mountains, lips parted wide.

Each site featured a fire pit and a table. Cal joined her at the picnic table and folded his long legs to sit. "What do you think, honey?"

"I love it here. You don't mind if I stay here with you?"

"No, I'd like it fine." He noticed she was wearing her new boots and smiled. "Let's go get something to eat. Want to walk or should I drive?"

"Let's walk if you'll lock our stuff in the camper or truck. It's nice on Rich Mountain, so much cooler, and I'd like to stretch my legs."

"Then we'll take a stroll," Calhoun replied. Maybe it would work the kinks out of his bum knee.

At the inn, Vivian grinned as soon as they stepped into the lobby. The open space contained a freestanding stone fireplace and many windows. They visited the gift shop, read about the history of the inn from the original hotel in 1898 to the current version, and sat in comfortable rockers on the wraparound porch on the south side. The wind that teased around them was light and cool, a refreshing change from the late June heat. A panoramic view stretched out before them, with mountains forested in green.

"I've heard you can see twenty miles from here," Calhoun noted as they rocked with easy rhythm. Being idle wasn't something he often enjoyed, but today he basked in it. The pleasant place salved something within him and so did Vivian's company.

"I believe it," she told him. "It's breathtaking."

"It's not too late to get a room." He'd asked before and this would be the last time. Cal had to make sure Vivian would be happy.

"I'm fine in the trailer." As she spoke, she took his hand and held it in hers.

He liked the weight and warmth of it.

"I'll stay with you in the trailer sometime, right?" Vivian asked. "I might as well get used to it."

"I suppose so." Her suggestion made him happy enough to grin. Maybe it wasn't the best option for two unmarried people, but he would never cross a line with her, and she apparently knew it. Sharing the twenty-four-foot space might be cramped, but it would work. "After here, we'll be at Linc's, then at a hotel or motel in Fort Worth. It won't be until Prescott we'll be back in the trailer and then only if we want. Does that mean you're coming to Arizona?" Hope fluttered in his chest like a butterfly darting from one flower to another.

"I thought I would," Vivian said, her tone casual although her smile beamed bright. "I've never been to Arizona, and there ought to be some great photo opportunities. Besides, I like spending time with you."

"Same." If he read her right, judging by the lilt in her voice and sparkle in her eyes, she might have similar feelings to his.

They lingered on the porch until it was time for an early supper, then headed into the Queen's Restaurant. Calhoun could have chosen a burger or steak, but when he saw catfish on the menu, he ordered it.

So did Vivian.

"I haven't had fish for a long time," he commented as they munched the crisp, tasty fillets. "It's tasty, but nothing's as good as that roast you fixed. I miss home-cooked food."

"I can cook whatever you want, Calhoun. You have a stove in the trailer."

"Yeah, but I've seldom used it. I'm not much at cooking, Pretty Lady. I've fried a few burgers, made a grilled cheese sandwich or two, cooked a little bacon and some eggs, but that's about it. Maybe warmed up some ravioli or slapped together a bologna sandwich. If you want to use that stove, I'd love it. While we're at Linc's place, my little house has a kitchen, too, but I think he's planning to barbecue when we arrive."

"How many days will we be there?"

He counted, using his fingers for reference. "If we leave tomorrow, we'll get there Tuesday and leave on Friday so that's four days. Two full ones, Wednesday, and Thursday."

"Then there should be time for me to cook. You'll have to tell me what you want to eat, though." She reached across the table and took his hand in hers.

"Biscuits," he stated without hesitation. "Those were the finest biscuits I ever put in my mouth, honey."

"Nanna taught me to make those. I like to cook, but it's not much fun for one person."

"Well, I'll give you plenty of opportunity to have

fun, then." He would, too.

After they ate, they lingered on the porch again 'til almost dark, then meandered back to the trailer. By then, his knee hurt and his back ached, so he popped a few ibuprofen tablets. Calhoun tried to convince her to sleep in the bed.

But she rejected the idea. "You're too tall to get comfortable on this couch."

"It folds out into a bed, honey. I'd rather give you the bigger, more comfortable spot."

"No way. I'm a lot shorter than you are, and I don't even need it folded out. Give me a pillow for my head and a blanket, then I'm good."

"Are you sure?" He lifted one eyebrow.

"Positive." She bobbed her head to emphasize.

"Bathroom's closer to the bedroom."

"I'll manage, Calhoun." She laughed.

She sent a look his way that made him ache for another kiss, but he resisted. "You can call me Cal if you like." He grinned at his suggestion.

"Cal. Okay, maybe sometimes. I like Calhoun, though. It fits you."

It did. He couldn't imagine being called anything else like Randy or Rowdy, Steve or Sam, or Will. He dug out a spare pillow and a blanket. "I'm gonna read a bit so good night. If you need anything, just holler."

"I will. Good night, Cal." She stepped closer and brushed her lips against his.

He put on shorts and a T-shirt for bed before preparing to dive into a book. Calhoun couldn't focus. His mind brimmed full of many diverse thoughts. Going home, this thing with Vivian, the rodeo in Fort Worth, and the rest of the season filled his thoughts.

The ibuprofen dulled the pain, but he still couldn't sleep. Cal rose, trying to be quiet, and slipped out through the rear door of the trailer. When he peeked, he saw Vivian appeared sound asleep.

At almost twenty-seven hundred feet above sea level, the night air carried a chill, and he wished he'd slipped into pants instead of shorts. Calhoun walked past the firepit to the picnic table, then sat on top, feet on the bench seat. Above him, the stars glittered. From the nearby forest, night sounds reached his ears, and he relaxed. He savored the place and the relative quiet. Cal imagined what it would be like if Vivian accompanied him on more of the circuit after Forth Worth. If she didn't, he would miss her.

Not for the first time, he considered hanging up his spurs after this season. In the real world, thirty-three wasn't old, but in rodeo, it could be. He considered all his past injuries and thanked God he hadn't been permanently damaged. A life on a quiet farm or ranch would be a good one, he thought, and couldn't stop recalling Nanna's farm in Missouri.

"Calhoun?" Vivian's voice echoed through the night.

"I'm right here." He waved a hand so she'd spot him.

"Are you all right? I noticed you weren't in bed."

He could get used to her sweet concern. "I'm good. Just couldn't sleep, so I came outside for a bit. Look at the stars, honey; they're magnificent."

She climbed on the picnic table and leaned against him. Vivian turned her face toward the heavens and gasped at the night sky.

He put an arm around her.

"Oh, my, that's beautiful."

He noticed how her eyes sparkled with wonder, brighter and prettier than the stars.

The night sky was lovely and so was she. They sat in tandem, their spirits in communion, and Calhoun wished this moment could last forever.

Chapter Eight

In the morning, she woke to thick fog outside the windows and a distinct chill in the air. For a moment, Vivian couldn't remember her location. When she did, she sat up and plugged in the coffeemaker. As the coffee brewed, she dressed, pulling on a favorite pair of faded jeans and a long-sleeved blouse. She thrust her feet into the new boots and wiggled them. They fit and felt so good. A quick check of the cabinets and fridge revealed nothing she could turn into breakfast, so she poured a cup of coffee and settled down to drink it. She heard the shower, and when Calhoun emerged, damp, dressed in a simple T-shirt and jeans, she poured him a cup of coffee. "It's foggy outside." She handed him a cup.

"Thanks for the java." He took a sip. "It's not fog, though. We're in the clouds. We're at the top of a mountain, the second tallest in Arkansas. If I'm not mistaken, it's like this about every morning."

She peered through the window above the sink. "I guess that gives new meaning to having our heads in the clouds."

"I suppose it does. Do you want to have breakfast over at the inn? I figured we'd wait to leave until the clouds are gone. I don't fancy pulling the trailer around those curves when I can't see barely past my hand."

"Fair enough." She grabbed her purse when he

picked up his keys. After eating pancakes with real maple syrup and thick bacon, sunshine burned through the cloud cover.

They traveled down the mountain, back to Mena, and headed south on the two-lane highway.

"When will we get to Rusk?" she asked after the first thirty minutes. After all, he had promised to provide information as they traveled, old-school style.

"The Kelly Cattle Company, Linc's place, is a little west, past Maydelle. The property backs up to the Neches River. Rusk is about four, four and a half hours from Rich Mountain, then maybe fifteen minutes more to the ranch. I figured on grabbing lunch in Shreve."

"Shreve?" She faced him, frowning at the unfamiliar name.

"Shreveport, Louisiana, on the Red River." Calhoun laughed. "I like it. There's a lotta history there. Come September, I'll ride in the Red River Parish Fair and Rodeo at Coushatta. It's about an hour south of Shreveport."

September seemed distant, and Vivian wondered if she would still be with Calhoun. Right now, she couldn't imagine she wouldn't be. "How long 'til Shreveport? Isn't it close to Bossier City? I had an uncle who was stationed at Barksdale Air Force Base there." Vivian stretched her feet out as far as she could and slipped out of her shoes for comfort.

Calhoun nodded. "Right across the Red River, and it's three hours from here to Shreveport. Once we're out of the mountains, we'll be in the Ark-La-Tex, and it'll be flat country."

He tossed out names like she should know what they meant. "What's the Ark-La-Tex?"

"Arkansas, Louisiana, Texas," Cal explained. "It's the corner of the world where the three states meet. It's different than the rest of the state. There's still oil in the region, honey. Once upon a time, some of the richest oil deposits in the country were down around there. Some say they still are."

Vivian listened. He made the simple highway seem almost exciting, and the time passed quickly. A steady stream of vintage country poured from the speaker, but the artists they heard found their fame in the 1950s. Johnny Horton, Johnny Cash, Jim Reeves, Claude King, Webb Pierce, and Kitty Wells, that old possum, George Jones, Hank Williams, and some early Elvis.

Calhoun sang along with almost every song.

When she knew the lyrics, she sang along. "You must really like Johnny Horton," she commented when the sixth different song by Horton played.

"Pretty Lady, he was a hometown boy."

"What hometown?" She scooted closer.

"Horton called Rusk home, too. His folks are buried there, so is at least one of his sisters. He graduated from Gallatin, which is just a few miles from Rusk. Besides, he was one of the artists who got famous on *The Louisiana Hayride* in Shreveport. It was second only to *The Grand Old Opry* in its day."

"I've heard of it. Nanna's talked about it, and she has several of Horton's albums. Until riding with you, I really didn't know his songs except "Battle of New Orleans", "Sink The Bismarck", and "North To Alaska"."

His fingers tapped out the rhythm from the last song she listed. "Those are the big hits, but I like a lot of his lesser-known music the best. He's buried east of

Bossier City in Haughton, and someday, I'll show you his house in Shreveport."

Calhoun changed CDs to one with songs she didn't know that featured just Horton and a guitar. "These songs are just Johnny making music at home, I swear I heard a canary in the background and maybe a clock chime the hour. These were some of his demos. He later recorded several of the songs. Although, some he never did. I like the simplicity of these tunes." Cal explained.

So did she. Horton's voice held a rich quality, but it was genuine. His accent reminded her of Cal's. From what she remembered, Horton had been a nice-looking man. Although, she thought he'd died young, in some tragedy.

The mountains were behind them before they reached Texarkana, a city half in Texas and half in Arkansas.

Calhoun didn't stop until they rolled through the small town of Fouke, Arkansas.

Vivian counted three convenience stores, two on one side of the highway, and one across. Her eyes bugged out when she realized that one of them featured an entry door with a fierce monster customers had to walk through to go inside. The name of the place was Monster Mart.

Cal noticed where she indicated and laughed. "I'm fixing to get some fuel and make a pit stop. There's not much else between here and Shreveport. Do you want me to stop over there or pick a regular store?" He pointed toward the creature outside one of the places.

"An ordinary convenience store is fine. Why the big, ugly monster?

"Honey, we're in Fouke, Arkansas. I don't suppose

you ever heard of the Boggy Creek Monster?"

"No." She crinkled her nose at the question.

"Well, it's a local Bigfoot creature. People have been seeing it, they say, for decades. I remember a movie about it back in the 1970s or something. Fouke doesn't have any other claim to fame, so they play up the monster bit."

"I don't like scary creatures or horror movies or any of that." She shuddered as she spoke, arms tight around her torso.

"Good. Neither do I."

They exchanged smiles as he pulled in to get fuel. Ten minutes later, they were on their way again. South of Fouke, she saw oil pumps at work, a first for Vivian.

"Those are nodding donkeys. See the way they move." Cal shared.

Vivian grinned like a kid on her first vacation. Although she'd traveled a little, her journeys hadn't ever taken her in this direction. Vivian had been across most of Missouri, over in Illinois, up to Nebraska, and on a few trips elsewhere. She'd been to California, to Washington DC, and to Denver. In northwest Arkansas, places like Eureka Springs and Fayetteville were familiar.

This represented her first foray into the Deep South, and so far, Vivian liked it. It wasn't what she expected, at least not thus far. Part of it was the way Calhoun presented it. His stories and bits of local color made it intriguing. She'd loved the waterfall they had visited, and Rich Mountain would always rank as a special place. Someday, Vivian would like to return, with Calhoun, and stay in the inn.

She liked him a great deal, but his front-and-center

style of faith sometimes irked her. It wasn't him at fault, not really, and she knew it. She had a knee-jerk response to anything religious. Once, she'd believed, too, but all that had changed. Each time they ate, he asked a blessing. Sometimes, Calhoun popped out Bible verses from memory. Now, a song she remembered well, an old hymn sung by George Jones and many other artists came from the speaker. The familiar words washed over her, and the notion that troubled souls could find peace touched her so much she began to cry.

Caught up in singing along, Cal didn't notice until the song ended. He whirled his head toward her. "What's the matter? Vivian, what's wrong?"

"It's the song." Tears rained down her face.

He reached for a tissue from the box in the center console of his truck and offered her one. "Don't you like it?" He frowned.

They were passing through the tiny town of Hosston, Louisiana, after crossing the state line a few miles back. She didn't answer, unable to string together the words to explain.

Cal pulled into a branch library parking lot. "Honey, tell me what's wrong. What about "Old Brush Arbor" upset you?"

Vivian buried her face in both hands and sobbed. Even in her current state, she expected Calhoun to put his hand on her back for comfort.

Instead, he opened the truck door and climbed out and shut the door.

The noise reverberated and she cried harder. Maybe he wasn't as nice as she thought, and she'd driven him away with tears.

He opened the passenger door and turned her

around to face him. "Don't cry like that, Pretty Lady." His voice became low and tender. "Tell me why you're so upset."

"I wish I could find a peaceful harbor." Vivian spoke through her sobs. "Nanna has that old record, and it's one of her favorites. It reminded me of when I still had faith. Sometimes, I miss going to church, Calhoun. I loved God and Jesus so very much. I thought they would keep me and my loved ones safe, but instead my parents were murdered in *my* home. That old song made me remember going to church and how I looked forward to Sundays and singing in the pews. I want that back, Cal. I want my parents back. It's silly after seven years, but I do. Why did God fail me? I don't understand."

Calhoun lifted her from the truck.

She stood before him as he snuggled her in his arms.

"Aw, honey, love never fails, and neither does the Lord. I don't know why your parents died. I don't know why He saw fit to take mine in a car wreck when I was ten years old. But it says in Romans that all things work together for those who love God, who are called to his purpose. I hang onto that. I did the same when Sullivan died not five feet from me in the arena. If I didn't have faith, I couldn't stand any of that. I'd curl up in a ball and die."

"How can you, though?" His certainty and faith wasn't something she could understand.

"How can I not?" Cal replied, in a softer tone. "I sure wish you could, honey. Someday, you'll need God enough to cry out to him, and he'll answer your prayer. I believe that."

She didn't, but his words provided a vague comfort. "I wish I could." His wiry arms offered sanctuary, a harbor of sorts, so she basked in them, savoring his strength and his care. Vivian loved how he smelled; fresh-air clean with undertones of some woodsy cologne with musk. Her faith had died with her folks, but Calhoun gave her hope, not in the Lord but in him. "You make me feel better, somehow."

"I'm glad, honey. Now quit crying. We'll be in Shreve in half an hour, grab a little something to eat, and head for home. In about two hours, we'll be there. Lincoln's smoking a brisket, so there'll be a big meal at suppertime."

"I need to wash my face." Meeting his family made her self-conscious. Her hair must be in tangles, coming out of the ponytail. "I probably look a fright."

"You can fix yourself when we stop." Cal planted a swift kiss on her lips, then helped her into the seat.

They were on the road before she dug out a tissue from her purse to wipe away stray tears.

Once they reached Shreveport, they stopped for some fried chicken and Calhoun's root beer. While he ordered, Vivian found the restroom and washed her face. She took down her hair, combed it, and put it up with a clip. She found him at a table with their order.

After he asked the blessing, taking her hands in his, they dived into the crispy chicken with coleslaw and honey-butter biscuits.

"These are good." She broke off another bite of biscuit and popped it in her mouth. "I like the seasoning on this crisp chicken, too."

"The biscuits aren't as delicious as yours." Calhoun buttered another half and ate it.

Still unsettled by the hymn, Vivian nodded. Sometimes, it felt like she'd known him a long time, but she realized a full week hadn't passed since they met. She first saw him last Thursday, the first night of the Springdale Rodeo, and this was Tuesday. *Maybe I'm crazy. I've known this man five days, and I've gone traveling with him to Texas, even promised to go to Arizona.*

Another still, small voice in her head whispered, *when it's right, it's right. This* is *right.* Vivian wanted to believe it was.

After they headed west from Shreveport on Highway 79, his cell rang.

She couldn't help but smile at his ringtone, the old Hank Williams tune "Hey, Good Lookin'" since Cal said he had changed it after they met.

His phone rode in a holder stuck to the dash so he punched the speaker button. "Hello, Nail. What's shaking?"

"Not very much. I'm heading to Fort Worth at the end of the week. What about you? Did you do any good at Springdale?"

"I won a little. I'm on my way home for a few days, then we'll go to Fort Worth, too."

"We? Did you find a traveling partner?"

"You might say so. Vivian, tell my friend Rusty, the one I call Nail for short, hello, Pretty Lady."

"Hi." Calhoun put her on the spot. "I'm Vivian." Rusty pierced their ears with a long whistle.

"Well, I'll be. Tell me she's not a bunny, though."

"Farthest thing from one. I expect you'll meet her in Fort Worth."

"I'll be looking forward to it. That's why I called to

see if you'll be there. Going to Prescott for the Fourth?"

"I am."

"Good deal! I'll talk at you later, man. Stay safe."

"Do the same," Calhoun replied.

"I guess that's a friend from the rodeo." Saying hello to someone she didn't know left her feeling awkward.

"Yeah, a good one. We go way back. I don't have many buddies left on the circuit. I know most of the ones who compete regularly, but since I don't party or go to the bars, I'm often the odd one out. Nail and another guy, Bill, who we call Pecos, are the main ones."

"Why did this guy and your brother ask if I'm a bunny?"

"They're talkin' about buckle bunnies, honey. That's a woman who comes around the events all dressed up, wanting a cowboy for one night. They're not real cowgirls, usually not even country gals. They're women who have a thing for a cowboy. They tend to get around, but some men like them. Not me. I like a real woman, like you, Pretty Lady. You'll likely see some buckle bunnies sooner or later."

Vivian wasn't sure she wanted to, especially if the bunny had her sights aimed at Calhoun. She scooted in close and laid her head against his shoulder.

"Tired, baby?" He turned and kissed her cheek.

"A bit."

"Take a little nap, if you want."

Confusion outweighed her fatigue. All the unfamiliar terms like buckle bunny, circuit, and more were things to learn. Anxiety about meeting Calhoun's family crept in, and she wondered if they would welcome her like family or treat her like a guest. Maybe he brought women home often, she thought, and that possibility rankled. Vivian didn't want to be one of many. He didn't seem like the kind of man who would, but she didn't know. She shut her eyes and tried to rest but couldn't. "Calhoun, if I asked you to take me home, would you?"

He swerved, crossed the center line for a split second, and recovered control. "Do you *want* to go home?"

Calhoun's extreme reaction surprised her so Vivian considered the question and didn't. "No, but I just wondered if I did, would you take me?"

"Honey, I'll do whatever you want. Just tell me what makes you happy. I figured you'd know that. What's wrong?"

Vivian shouldn't have asked that question, but she tried to answer his. "I don't know. Nothing, really."

"Are you still upset because of that song?" He pulled off his ball cap and ran a hand through his hair.

"Maybe a little." She sat straighter and sighed.

"Vivian, are you having doubts about going home with me and to more rodeos?" Calhoun tossed the hat on the dash.

"I am, and I'm not." She folded her arms across her chest.

With a sigh, Calhoun turned into the driveway of an old farmhouse and parked. "You're not making any sense, Pretty Lady. Do you still want to come to the ranch and meet my family?"

Outside what appeared to be a deserted home, she shrugged.

He shifted position to face her. "What?"

She did, more than anything. "I do, but I'm afraid." Vivian twisted her fingers together.

His grin vanished, and his face shifted into a grim expression. "Tell me what you're scared about."

Vivian put one trembling hand on his leg and released a long sigh. "I want this so much, Calhoun, that it scares me because it's happening so fast. A week ago, I didn't even know you, and now we're here together, heading to Texas. We're almost there. I took you to meet Nanna and to the old farmhouse. She adores you, and the homeplace fits you. I've experienced more with you in five days than I did in two years with my former fiancé. I haven't dated much since him, and I wasn't looking, but here you are, and here I am. What frightens me is that I don't want to be anywhere else except with you."

He said nothing for a long minute, then began to shake. He put his head against the steering wheel and laughed until he coughed, then choked.

"It's not funny. She shifted position and sat, arms crossed across her chest.

Calhoun reined in his mirth and raised his head. "No, it's not, honey. But I'm glad, oh, so glad. I thought for a minute you were done with me and wanted to head home. That would have broken this old cowboy's heart into a million pieces, but I would have done it, if that was what you wanted. If it's right between us, then a day, a week, a month, or a lifetime doesn't matter. I'm laughing because I'm happy, you silly woman. Is there anything else on your mind, or can we get on down the road?"

Whether or not she would admit it, she'd already given him a piece of her heart. He hadn't done anything to cause her anger. A combination of the song, his casual attitude they were a couple, and fear they might not work out had fueled it. His words eased some of her anxiety. "Let's go," she said in a lighter tone. "I hear there's a fatted calf in the form of brisket waiting to welcome you home." A week ago, she wouldn't have made a Biblical reference, but she did, and it didn't sting as much as she thought it would.

"Sounds good, Pretty Lady."

Calhoun leaned in for a kiss filled with both hunger and sweetness.

Vivian locked her arms around his neck and gave back the kiss. She yearned to see where this relationship would go and wanted to meet his folks. Calhoun in his natural habitat could prove interesting. This cowboy, this journey, and the kiss felt like a beginning, one she wanted to embrace.

Chapter Nine

As his tires hitting the pavement sang the song of the highway, Cal heard the refrain as an echo of "a day, a week, a month, a lifetime." He had every hope for future possibilities, and he thought maybe Vivian did, too. As the highway wound closer to Rusk, Calhoun anticipated his homecoming with pleasure. He hadn't been home since he'd left to start rodeo season in March. With Vivian beside him, he savored it more than ever. Her earlier tears over the song hadn't worried him as much as her question about whether he'd take her home. Cal figured her reaction to the hymn might mean the Lord touched her heart. He hoped so. For a few moments, he thought she'd changed her mind about him, and that had hurt. Since it turned out that she hadn't, his spirits soared, and he sang along to the classic country tunes he loved.

Loblolly pines stood tall on both sides of the road. A few hardwoods, mostly elm and ash, were scattered among them. Calhoun rolled down the window, hoping he'd catch the scent of pine...although it was doubtful.

"The evergreens are beautiful," Vivian commented.

"It's why they call this part of East Texas The Piney Woods," he offered. "Now I know I'm almost home." The familiar road and the tall pines were a balm for his soul. If time permitted, he wanted to show her Rusk, his hometown. Home was on the Kelly Cattle

Company ranch now, but that was Lincoln's spread. His childhood home where he'd lived as a kid on Butler Street wasn't far off the highway, but Calhoun wasn't sure he wanted to drive past it. The last time he did, it was in sorry shape, which made him sad.

After his parents died, though, the three boys had moved in with their grandparents over on Lone Oak Street. The rambling, two-story frame house had more than enough room for the Kelly kids and had been home. Even now, if Cal thought about his childhood, he recalled Granny's house. After she died, soon after Sullivan did, Lincoln and Calhoun agreed to sell it. Linc sunk the money into the ranch. Although he'd offered half, Cal didn't take it. He hadn't wanted it and didn't feel that he needed it.

Granny's former home wasn't far from the footbridge in Rusk or the courthouse square. If they lacked time today, maybe they could spend a morning or afternoon seeing the sights in Rusk. The Texas State Railroad ran a train from Rusk over to Palestine, and Calhoun would like to take Vivian on one of the excursions.

His cell rang, and he used one finger to answer on speakerphone. "It's Calhoun," he stated without bothering to read the Caller ID display.

"Where in tarnation are you, kid?" Lincoln's voice rang loudly in the pickup cab. "I hadn't heard from you for a couple days and wanted to make sure you're still coming. I have the biggest brisket I could find on the smoker, and Sasha's made a bunch of stuff to go with it. We laid in root beer for you, too."

"We're almost to Rusk." Cal laughed. "We'll be at your place in half an hour or less. Dragging this tin can along behind the truck slows me down a bit."

"A turtle could walk it faster," his brother teased. "I'll see you when you get here. Tell Vivian we have her room ready. Sasha went down to put fresh sheets on your bed at the little house. The boys are going crazy waiting for their uncle to get here."

"Tell them I'll be there soon. Thank you, Linc."

"*De nada,* bro."

Highway 79 merged with 84 as they rode into Rusk. At the familiar junction of 84 and US 69, Calhoun glanced around, excited. To Vivian, it probably appeared the same as any small town in East Texas or anywhere else, but this place had once been the center of his world. "Welcome to Rusk, Pretty Lady!" he exclaimed. "If you need to pick up anything or have a pit stop, let me know, and we'll do it. Otherwise, it's on to Linc's place."

"I'm good." Vivian snuggled beside him. "It's a pretty little town, Calhoun. What's the population?"

"Less than six thousand, I think."

"How old are your nephews?"

"Seven, five, and three. They're at cute ages. They're curious as little monkeys. Do you like kids?" He kept his tone casual, but he wanted to hear the answer. If this relationship moved forward, someday he planned to have a family.

"I suppose. I haven't been around many," Vivian admitted. "Since I was an only child, I haven't been around any children except some of my cousins' kids, because Nanna is their great-grandma. What are their names?"

"Cooper, Caleb, and Chance," Cal replied. "Chance is named for Sullivan. On the rodeo circuit, he rode as Chance Sullivan, because all his life everybody always said Sully liked to take a chance. He was born the year Sully died. Cooper remembers my brother a little, but I don't think Caleb does."

Sometimes, he wished his brother and sister-in-law hadn't named their youngest Chance. What Calhoun didn't tell Vivian was that Sullivan's family nickname had been Last Chance since he was the youngest, just like his namesake. When Sully died in the arena, boots on cowboy fashion, the nickname hadn't been funny anymore.

"Hey, you zoned out."

That jerked him back to the present. Cal didn't notice he'd stopped talking, lost in memories "Sorry, I was just thinking."

She brushed one hand against his cheek. "You look sad."

"I was remembering my brother. Coming home is a good thing, but it stirs up some stuff I'd rather not think about."

"Lincoln is older, and he was younger, right?"

Her hand dropped down to his arm, and she stroked it, slow and comforting. "Yeah, Linc's five years older, and Sully was six years younger than me. Mama always said I was the monkey in the middle," Cal spoke with a small smile and a long sigh.

"That's cute." Vivian giggled.

"I suppose." He'd driven on auto pilot while woolgathering, and they were almost to Maydelle. Cal would be at Linc's, the closest place he had to a permanent home, within ten minutes. He could have driven the rest of the way blindfolded, down 84 to the farm-to-market-road turnoff, then a mile and a half to the dirt road that trailed to Lincoln's place. White pipe fencing fronted the road along with a tall open gate. A sign to the left proclaimed it to be The Kelly Cattle Company. Although he slowed, aware of pulling the trailer behind, dust still plumed behind them as he turned into the long drive.

To the right, Angus cattle were pastured behind barbed wire with a large pond. Beyond that, a larger field stood tall in hay that would be cut next month. Two large barns and several corrals stood between the pasture and the tree line.

The two-story frame house sat beneath tall pines with a long front lawn sweeping toward the road. Behind it about two hundred feet, the smaller structure he called home could be seen.

Three small figures waved from the porch of the main house.

Calhoun slowed, then stopped as the kids rushed to the truck. Laughing, he stepped out, and they swarmed him. Cooper, who now came to his waist, hugged him. Caleb threw his arms around Cal's knees and almost swamped him. Chance held up his arms. "Pick me up, Unca Cal."

He swooped the boy into his arms, and when the kid wrapped his arms around his neck, it moved him so much he could have cried. "You're growing like weeds, every last one of you." Cal put some fake enthusiasm in his voice to hide his emotion. "You act like you're happy to see your old uncle."

"Welcome home," Cooper cried, still hugging him. "We missed you."

"Yeah? I missed you, too. Pretty Lady, get out here and meet these rascals."

Vivian climbed from the pickup, giggling.

The kids fell silent.

"Vivian, this is Cooper, he's the oldest, then Caleb, and the little guy clinging to me like a possum is Chance. Boys, this is my friend, Vivian. Treat her nice, okay? I promised her you don't bite."

Cooper nodded. He ran a hand over his unruly hair and approached Vivian with a modified cowboy swagger. "I'm pleased to meet you, ma'am." He offered his hand to shake.

Cal grinned. He liked the kid's polite manners and style. Cooper had the makings of a fine little cowboy.

****

"Thank you. It's nice to meet you, too. I've heard a lot about you. Your uncle Cal had good things to say about all of you boys." Vivian took his hand as she smiled.

Caleb followed his brother's lead and shook hands. Chance launched himself from Calhoun onto Vivian. She caught him, eyes wide with surprise, then laughed.

"Try not to knock over Calhoun's friend, boys." A woman with red hair skewed up on top of her head with a clip and a face bright with freckles stepped onto the porch. She wore a wide grin and grabbed Calhoun for a neck hug. "Glad you're here, Cal. Linc's been fussing all day, wondering if you'd make it. He smoked a huge brisket, and it's in the oven now, keeping warm. Come on in. You can move that trailer down by your place later."

"Howdy, Sasha," Cal drawled. "This is Vivian Blackburn."

"Hi." Vivian suddenly felt bashful, the stranger among the family, and took a couple steps back.

"Thank you for letting me stay at your house while I'm here with Calhoun."

"You're more than welcome." Sasha laughed as she opened the door so Vivian could trail her inside. "We're glad to have you. Grab her bags, Cal, and I'll show her the room."

Sasha's warm welcome for Vivian pleased Cal and he grabbed her bags, happy to oblige. He would have done so anyway.

"I'll help tote her stuff, honey."

The man who sailed through the open front door had to be Calhoun's brother.

"Go ahead, take Vivian inside. It's hot out here."

Vivian glanced at Cal, seeking silent approval.

He nodded. "Go ahead with Sasha, Pretty Lady. We'll get your things."

She reached back into the truck for her purse. When she paused, wrinkling her forehead she waited while Calhoun came back to deliver a light, brief kiss. When she smiled, he did, too.

"It's all good, Vivian. I'll be in there in a minute."

Vivian cupped her right hand against his cheek. "Okay."

****

Linc bounded down the steps as the two women and three kids headed inside. He grasped Cal in a bear hug, then punched his shoulder. "Glad to see you, bro. I'm glad you're here. You're lookin' good. Feelin' all right?"

"Other than the usual aches and pains, yeah." He was glad Linc had chosen his good shoulder, not the sore one, to thump.

"How long can you stay?"

113

"Until Friday. We'll leave late that morning for Fort Worth."

"Vivian's going with you?" Lincoln asked with a wide grin.

Calhoun hoped he wasn't blushing like a teenager. "Yeah, then on to Prescott, too. After that, I don't know."

Lincoln studied his brother's features. "You look happy, Calhoun, happier than I've seen you in a long time."

Cal shrugged. "I am, Linc. Let's get her stuff inside before she pitches a fit. She's particular about her cameras and such."

Lincoln toted Vivian's two bags.

Cal carried her equipment. He followed Linc into the spacious house and upstairs. His brother led him to the back guest bedroom, the one across from the bathroom. Cal recalled the room, with old-fashioned wallpaper that featured giant blooming roses. It was large, with windows on two sides, and a four-poster bed. A chest of drawers stood beside the bed with a vintage hurricane lamp on top. A low cedar chest rested at the foot of the bed. A small dresser and chair sat beside the window that overlooked the back. Cal gazed out and noted he could see his place from there.

Vivian sat on the edge of the bed with her hands folded in her lap.

"Where do you want your camera stuff?"

"I guess on top of the chest. The suitcases can go against the wall for now. I'll take a few minutes to settle in, Calhoun."

"That's fine. I thought I'd drive the trailer and park it by my house, then carry my stuff in. Where are the boys? I figured they could go with me."

"In the playroom, downstairs," Sasha spoke from the doorway. "I'll go tell them. We won't eat for another hour or two."

He turned to Vivian. "If you want to go with Sasha, you can. I figured you might need a little time and space, though. Maybe rest a bit. We've traveled a lot the last few days, and there's more ahead."

Vivian stood, released her ponytail from the holder, and shook out her hair. "I'll stay at the house, Calhoun. Your family's made me feel welcome, even though you never introduced me to your brother. I really should call Nanna, too."

Lincoln laughed as he put down the last bag and approached Vivian with his right hand extended. "He's got no more manners sometimes than a hound dog. I'm Lincoln Kelly, the kid's older brother. I'm glad you're here."

She grasped his hand and shook it. "I'm Vivian. Thanks. I've never been to Texas before, but so far, I like it."

Calhoun grinned and headed for the hall.

"Come here a minute." Vivian held up one hand, then leaned close for a hug. "I can tell you're hurting. Do you want some ibuprofen?"

Her discernment startled and pleased him. He didn't think anyone could tell, but his knee had been aching for hours. It often hurt after a long drive, and he also had a headache. The last thing he'd want would be for Lincoln to notice he was in pain and fuss. Since Sully died, his older brother worried about Calhoun too much. Calhoun tucked a loose strand of hair behind her ear. "Later, Pretty Lady. I'm good for now."

"Come downstairs when you're ready. There's no hurry," Sasha stated.

Vivian's smile was her reply.

Calhoun retrieved all three boys from the playroom, a large room filled with trucks, trains, a bookshelf, toy six shooters and rifles, cap guns, building blocks, and a brimming toy chest. Cal loaded the kids into his truck and pulled down the tin can to his house. The small structure had been built in earlier decades for the ranch foreman. Once he unhitched the trailer, he emptied the water tanks and parked it in a shady spot.

When he unlocked the door, Calhoun expected the musty smell of an empty house but instead, the pleasant aroma of lemons wafted out. No cobwebs hung from the ceiling. When he peered into the ancient harvest-gold fridge, he saw his favorite brand of root beer, bottled water, a dozen eggs, butter, milk, a package of bacon, some bologna and cheese, and some hot sauce lined the shelves. The open cupboard held a can of coffee, a loaf of bread, a bag of chips, and some microwave popcorn. If he wanted a snack, he wouldn't have to trudge to the main house. "I see your mom's been here," he commented to the kids.

"I helped her. She came down and cleaned up the day you told Daddy you were coming home." Cooper grinned and revealed a missing tooth.

"Thank you. I'll tell her the same. I appreciate it." Sasha's thoughtful act humbled Calhoun.

With Cooper and Caleb's help, he brought in clothes and other items including his rodeo gear.

"Let's go, Unca Cal. It should be close to supper time, and there's cake." Caleb tugged at his hand.

"Kids." Cooper rolled his eyes upward. "The cake's a surprise, Caleb."

"I didn't hear a thing." Cal laughed. He flopped down on the ancient loveseat in the tiny living room and rubbed his knee, wishing he'd taken Vivian's offer for a pain reliever. If the boys weren't present, he'd probably dig out the arnica and rub it on, but he didn't want any fuss. "We'll go back to your house. Should we walk or drive?"

"Drive!" the boys shouted in unison.

"Okay, who wants the wheel? I think it's Chance's turn." Long ago, he remembered his dad letting him and Lincoln *drive*. Calhoun had let both Cooper and Caleb do the same. Now it was Chance's turn. Driving meant letting the child sit on his lap and put his hands on the wheel to steer. Even a little kid could usually manage to keep a vehicle in a straight line. If they veered a bit, Cal would correct the steering. His feet worked the clutch, brake, and accelerator.

Chance giggled as he steered.

So did his brothers.

Calhoun grinned. He remembered the simple, unrestrained joy of childhood when life was sweet and tragedy distant. His innocence ended when his parents, gone to Christmas shop in Dallas, had been killed when an eighteen-wheeler veered into their lane. He'd never forgotten hearing the telephone ring late at night at Granny's house, where they were spending the night, or the low voices as his grandparents received the bad news. Sullivan's death had impacted Linc's boys but in a smaller way. Only Cooper really remembered him and still sometimes acted like his youngest uncle was still traveling the rodeo circuit. Sometimes, in low moments, Cal pretended the same.

Once at the house, the boys pounded through the rooms, whooping and hollering.

Calhoun followed, inhaling the delicious aromas in the air. He found Linc and Vivian in the living room.

She sat in the swivel rocker that had belonged to Granny beside Linc in his rump-sprung recliner. Their voices had ceased when they heard the boys.

He picked up on an awkward vibe. He suspected they'd been talking about him and prayed it was positive.

"Hey, Pretty Lady." Calhoun entered the room. "Miss me?" It was a silly question, since he'd been gone no more than an hour, hour and a half at most.

But she nodded. "Yes, I did."

Her smile brightened his heart.

"Supper's ready to go on the table," Lincoln announced. "Let's go eat."

"I'm ready." Calhoun offered Vivian his hand. They walked together into the dining room.

The family gathered around the large round table. The table was set with Granny's good willowware dishes. Cal took a place next to Vivian.

The others took their seats.

Lincoln reached for Sasha's hand, and once everyone at the table connected, he bowed his head. "Dear Heavenly Father, we thank you this day for this meal that we'll share as a family. I thank you that my brother is home from the circuit, and that he brought Miss Vivian. I thank you for each and every one of my family and for this good food. I ask your blessing in our lives every day and pray that we all stay safe every day in every way. Amen."

After the prayer, Vivian slid some ibuprofen tablets into Calhoun's hand and winked.

He nodded his thanks and put them in his mouth before anyone noticed. Cal washed the caplets down with root beer from the glass at his place. The brisket was tender and delicious with a rich smoke taste. Several flavors of barbecue sauce were served on the side, along with Sasha's homemade potato salad and baked beans, hot rolls, and corn. Except for the meal Vivian had cooked, he hadn't had home cooking since early spring. He ate more than he should have and groaned, full. "Those were some fine eats. Thank you." He directed his compliments to both Sasha and his brother.

"There's still cake," Cooper announced. "Can I bring it, Mama, can I?"

"If you're careful and don't drop it." Sasha cleared away their dirty dishes.

The boy carried a bakery sheet cake to the table.

When Calhoun saw it, he grinned. The edges were trimmed in green, like grass, but the main surface had been covered with crushed cookies to depict an arena, with corral fences fashioned from fondant. In the center, a cowboy sat on a bull, one arm upraised and the other holding a rope. The figure wore a black cowboy hat, like the one he wore to compete. *Welcome home, Calhoun* read the fancy script in bright red icing. He'd never seen or imagined such a cake. The thought behind it touched him beyond words. "I love it! Where did you find something like that?"

Sasha named a regional supermarket chain. "The boys saw it when we ordered Cooper's birthday cake. They agreed then we had to get it for you, Cal. So, we did. It's chocolate underneath all the icing, your favorite."

"Let's get a picture before we cut it," he suggested.

Although Vivian's cameras were upstairs, she snapped a photo with her phone.

It tasted delicious and good, but the real sweetness was the love his family demonstrated. He savored that and beneath the table, he gripped one of Vivian's hands. " 'My cup runneth over,' " Cal said, quoting the Twenty-Third Psalm. "Thank y'all, so very much."

For now, this was as much home as anywhere, and he was here.

Chapter Ten

Two hours earlier
After the past few days, which had been good but
emotionally intense, Vivian had been uncertain about
meeting Calhoun's family. Maybe they would like her,
but maybe they wouldn't. Taking a few minutes alone
in the bedroom, Vivian reflected how she ended up
here.

In less than a week, she'd met Cal and they'd
become close in a different way than she had ever
experienced. From the rodeo nights in Arkansas, the
quick trip home to check on Nanna, the wonderful
interlude on Rich Mountain, and the trek to Texas, she
realized she wanted to be with Calhoun. Despite a few
shake-ups, Vivian knew she cared for Calhoun Kelly.

She envied his family. Although he'd also lost his
parents and his brother Sullivan, he had these amazing
people. Vivian had Nanna and some cousins. She loved
her cousins, but they weren't close. If she saw them, it
was a quick meal out, a shared holiday, or a funeral. In
recent years she lacked any time to spend with them,
and until now, she hadn't regretted it.

From the moment his nephews swarmed her, those
little boys stole a piece of her heart. Cal's sister-in-law
and brother welcomed her as if she was kinfolk. Her
room was lovely, big, and comfortable, although part of
her wished she could stay with Calhoun. In those few

days, she knew him well enough to tell when he hurt, when he favored his knee, or when he was upset. When he kissed her in front of his folks, she understood his gesture meant something. He had claimed her, in front of them all.

Once alone, she kicked off her shoes and called Nanna.

"Hel-lo," her grandmother answered across the miles. "It's good to hear from you, Vivvie."

"I'm in Texas." She described her trip to Nanna, shared about Rich Mountain, and listened to her grandmother brag about winning bingo at the facility. "After we leave here, I'm going with Calhoun to Fort Worth, then to Prescott, Arizona, over the Fourth of July. Or I am unless you want me to come back. If you do, I will."

Vivian held her breath. She meant it and would return if Nanna asked, but she wanted to go with Cal. She craved spending time together but she also wanted to explore what they might have together.

"You go and have fun," Nanna said. "I've got a dozen other grandchildren and a few great grandkids. Some of them are coming for the fireworks at the facility. I'll be fine, just like I was when you were up in Kansas City. I like your Calhoun."

"So do I," she admitted. "I'll call you soon. Call me if you want, if you need me for anything, promise?"

"I do, child. I'm glad you're out there living life, going places, and seeing things. It's wonderful."

Vivian doubted she had time for a shower, but she changed into a light-pink, peasant-style dress, casual but pretty. Cal's homecoming seemed to be cause for celebration, so she wanted to look festive. When she descended the stairs, she wondered if she would need a trail of breadcrumbs, but she found Lincoln in the living room.

He had a marked resemblance to Calhoun, although Lincoln wasn't quite as tall, and he had a stockier built. His hair was as dark as Cal's, but he wore it cropped short, and his eyes were blue, not dark. Vivian wondered if Sullivan had resembled his brothers. She wouldn't ask, but maybe she'd see a photo somewhere.

"Come in and have a seat," Lincoln invited.

"I thought I'd see if Sasha needed any help in the kitchen." Vivian settled onto the edge of a swivel rocker.

"She's got it under control, and you've been on the road all day. Cal will be back with the boys before long. I'm glad you came. He's never brought a friend before and certainly not a lady." Lincoln offered a smile.

That surprised her. She didn't expect that he'd brought a string of girlfriends home, but Vivian would have thought he'd at least brought a friend, someone like Nail on the phone, or the other one he'd mentioned, Bill. Uncertain of how to respond, she smiled and flipped her ponytail over one shoulder.

"Has he been okay? I worry about him getting hurt. Bull riding's a dangerous occupation. I know he's got a few aches and pains, like anyone who's ridden rodeo for very long does. He said the other day he hurt his shoulder again?" Lincoln fidgeted with his fingers and frowned.

If Linc hadn't sounded truly concerned, she wouldn't have answered. Vivian wasn't sure she liked the inquisition and wondered why he didn't ask his brother directly. "He landed on it, and it was sore but it seems to be all right now. His knee bothers him a good bit, and I know he hurts sometimes. I worry, too."

"You care about him." Lincoln's frown eased, and he smiled a little.

Although it wasn't a question, she replied as if it had been. "I do, Lincoln. I wouldn't be here or going on with him on the circuit if I didn't."

"Good. I'm always concerned about Calhoun. He tends to be a loner, and he's more complicated than it probably seems. I don't figure you know but we had a younger brother, and he died a few years ago. He got killed in the arena, and Cal was there. It damaged him, I think."

"I know. He told me about Sullivan."

Lincoln's eyes grew large as he leaned forward.

"Wow. He never talks about it because he blames himself."

"Why?" Calhoun hadn't told her that.

"That's Cal's story." Linc sighed, then ran a hand through his hair. "It's a long one. I don't think it was his fault, but he does. I've prayed he'd quit rodeo before he gets hurt bad or worse, but so far, he won't. He'll always have a home here. He's part owner of this ranch."

She hadn't known that, either, but she nodded. It was another piece of the puzzle named Calhoun Kelly. "He says he might retire in a couple of years."

"Yeah? That's more than he's told me. That's good to know. I don't mean to put you on the spot, but I love my brother, so I gotta ask one more question." Lincoln leaned forward, arms on his knees.

"Go ahead." She smothered a sigh and tucked a

stray strand of hair back behind her ear.

"Is this a summer fling or something more?" He gazed at Vivian as he asked the question.

Anger flamed through Vivian as she glared at Lincoln. For Cal's sake, she swallowed some hot words. "What do you take me for?"

Lincoln raised one hand. "Peace. I don't mean to insult you, and it's not my business. I know that. It's just that he's happy. I haven't seen him like this since Sully died."

"It's not some cheap game I'm playing." Her voice sharpened like a well-honed knife. "You're right, and it's not your concern, but I'll tell you this, only because I can see he matters to you. I've never felt like this for anyone before. I don't know where it will go, but it's not some fling. And for the record, I'm not a buckle bunny."

In another few seconds, she would stand up, march out of here, and find Calhoun. She'd tell him what had happened and explain she wanted to leave. There had been more than one motel in Rusk, so they could find another place to stay. Or they could camp somewhere between here and Fort Worth. Vivian braced herself, dreading the next comment.

Lincoln grinned, then laughed, a happy booming sound. "I can see you're not, Vivian. Cal said you weren't, and I believe him. I'm sorry if I've offended you or pried into your business too much. But you're good for him, and even though I made you mad, I can see you really do care. That means the world to me. He needs plenty of TLC."

Her rage faded, and she sighed, deflated. "I *was* mad but I understand now. Let's be friends, Lincoln. I

125

don't think Cal would like it if we fussed."

"He wouldn't. I can see he matters to both of us. It might be in different ways but we're on the same page." Lincoln sat back with his posture relaxed.

She offered him a smile. "We are. Tell me how you smoke your brisket."

"Simple Texas style, with a little salt and pepper, a touch of garlic powder, and that's it." Linc grinned as he shared his method. "Then I slow smoke it with hickory until it's picked up the flavor. Sasha likes to finish it in the oven, but I make sure the temperature isn't too hot, so it doesn't dry out."

"I'm looking forward to tasting it." She racked her brain for more small talk.

With the boys gone with their uncle, silence echoed through the old house. Somewhere Vivian caught the faint sound of country music on a radio and guessed Sasha listened as she cooked. She heard Calhoun's truck pull up in front.

The boys whooped as they dashed inside.

He followed them. "Hey, Pretty Lady, did you miss me?" Calhoun burst into the room.

"I did." She kept her seat although she longed to rush to him for a hug and settled for a smile. His presence loomed large and welcome to Vivian. Although he wasn't limping and didn't seem to favor it, Vivian figured his knee still hurt. His answering grin didn't reach his eyes. "Let's go eat."

At the table, she slipped a few ibuprofen tablets into her hand, and during the blessing, she transferred them to him.

He winked and swallowed them.

Every dish, from the brisket to the baked beans, the

corn, hot rolls, and potato salad, was tasty. As they ate, this family talked about any and everything. Vivian couldn't remember a time when her folks had been this chatty at the supper table or any time. Nanna had been more likely to carry on a conversation, but this went beyond that. Everyone from the youngest to Lincoln tossed in something about their day, complimented the food, or asked questions.

"I didn't see any rough stock," Calhoun commented. "Are you still raising some?"

Lincoln blotted his lips with a paper napkin. "Nah, I decided to give it up, so I sold what I had. The beef cattle are more than enough, and we have the horses, yours included. I do a little road grading for the county, and when school starts, Sasha's going to be a paraprofessional at the middle school. She'll help kids with reading."

Cal frowned. "If money's tight…"

"It's not," Linc interrupted. "You're already a partner, and you've sunk a good chunk of change into the place. We're still in the black. I just want to make sure we stay that way."

"I have savings," Calhoun stated. "All you ever got to do is ask."

Vivian listened, impressed with Cal's generosity. She rested her hand on his knee beneath the table.

"I know, kid. And, I will, if that time ever comes."

Cake had been mentioned so Vivian expected a simple one or maybe one baked in a rectangular cake pan.

But instead, Cooper carried out a bakery cake.

When she saw the decorations, she smiled. The scene depicted a bull rider in the arena. Fancy script had a welcome-home message for Calhoun. Although she'd already noted the open affection in this home, that silly cake moved her almost to tears.

After the meal, Sasha refused her offer to help clean up. "The boys can help me, and I have a dishwasher. Go relax and spend some time with Calhoun. Once the kitchen's done, we'll watch something on television, and you're welcome to join us."

The living room featured a fireplace with an ornate mantel, but she hadn't seen a TV. That turned out to be because the next room was the family room, a smaller den with a big-screen television and comfortable furniture. A matching plaid couch and loveseat provided seating along with a couple of worn but serviceable armchairs. Instead of classic children's movies, they gathered to watch old episodes of 1960s westerns like *Bonanza* and *Gunsmoke.*

"I prefer *Longmire* or even *Yellowstone,*" Lincoln told them. "But both have too many adult themes and violence for little kids. So, we watch the old stuff with them, and after they go to bed, we might watch one of the others. If you'd rather do something else, you can."

"It's too hot to sit on the porch." Calhoun flashed his sweet grin." I'd go down to the river if I wasn't so tired, but this is fine. Vivian?"

"It's all right with me." She hadn't seen the older shows in years, not since her grandpa used to watch reruns on cable television.

Calhoun settled down on the floor in front of her.

She kneaded his shoulders and sighed. "Relax, cowboy. Your muscles are like concrete."

"I'm good." He protested, but he shifted closer.

"You could be better," she crooned. "Want a massage?" He swiveled his head around to gaze up at her. "If you know how, sure."

"I have many talents." She placed both hands on his tight shoulders and kneaded them, the same way she would bread dough. With her thumbs, she dug deep into his flesh, working out kinks.

He moaned.

"Does what I'm doing hurt?" Vivian rested her hands on his shoulders.

Calhoun shook his head and turned to look back. "No, feels good. Please don't quit."

"I won't." Vivian massaged, rubbed, and caressed, sometimes with force, until his taut muscles were limp.

He sighed. Calhoun leaned back against her knees. "I'm about to fall asleep, honey."

"If you do, it's okay." She planted a kiss on the back of his neck and gave her hands a rest.

Within minutes, he dozed, resting against her, with his breathing slow and even.

Vivian savored the domestic setting, the cozy family room, the television with wholesome fare, and the comfortable furniture. Combined, those things delivered a contentment she liked.

After two episodes of *Bonanza,* Sasha rounded up the boys for a bath, then bedtime.

Linc changed the program over to a Western movie, *Silverado.*

It began with gunfire, but Calhoun didn't stir, just snored lightly.

"He's really out." Lincoln sounded amused.

"He's tired," Vivian explained. "I'll wake him so he can go to bed. He'll need to be awake to walk to his place."

"It's fine if he doesn't," Linc returned. "He's the one who wanted to bunk out there. I've told him a hundred times he can have a room here at the house. There's plenty."

"Calhoun." Vivian shook his shoulder with a gentle touch. "Hey, wake up."

It took several times, but he roused, leaned forward, and then pulled himself onto the couch beside her. "I guess I went to sleep."

"You did. Maybe you'd better head to your place before you get too drowsy."

Cal laughed and squinted at the clock. "It's too early. If I was bull riding, I probably wouldn't have even gone yet."

"Does it matter we're not at an arena?" She stretched her hands which had become almost numb from her efforts.

"Probably not," he said with a yawn. "Scoot over and let me stretch out."

The loveseat was short, but he managed, knees bent, to curl into position, and rested his head in her lap.

Vivian stroked back his hair, delighting in the abundant, soft curls.

"You're going put me back to sleep, doing that," he murmured.

"Bro, we'll throw a blanket over you and leave you," Linc stated.

"That's all right. I don't care. I'm too comfortable to move right now."

So was Vivian. She remained long after the movie ended until past the time when Linc and Sasha retired for the night. Fatigue won out, however, and she slipped Calhoun's head onto a sofa pillow. Then she found a light, waffle weave blanket on one end of the couch and spread it over him. She said his name several times, but when he didn't stir, Vivian kissed his cheek and went upstairs.

Once there, she took a long time to go to sleep, and she almost returned downstairs. Vivian wished she could concentrate on reading or that she dared listen to music on her phone. She didn't because she feared it might wake the sleeping family. When she did drift off, she dreamed, but it wasn't pleasant. Images floated into her mind of a man, younger than Calhoun or Lincoln, who resembled them but appeared thinner. His hair was longer, too, since it reached his shoulders and wasn't quite as curly as Cal's. His nose was different, and his face narrower. He wore Western garments, a fancy shirt embroidered with cactus and cowboy boots, green and brown against black fabric. His bolo tie boasted a miniature eagle, wings spread in flight.

In the dream, he stood beside her bed. His eyes were not dark like Calhoun's or blue like Lincoln's but grey as morning mist. "Hey," he spoke in greeting.

His voice carried the same Southern yet Western cadence as Calhoun's.

"Hey, you gotta listen to me, lady. It's important."

It had to be Sullivan, she thought, although she'd yet to see a photograph of the missing brother. "What?"

"Don't let him do what I did," he cried, his voice intense but cryptic. "I was a danged fool, and it wasn't his fault. If it was anybody's but mine, it was Satan's Hellion. Tell Calhoun he's not to blame, and tell him don't make the same mistake."

It had become a nightmare, but she wasn't sure she

was asleep. "What mistake?"

"He'll know. I shouldn't have ridden that night, and the bull was loco. It won't be for a while yet, anyhow, and he might not listen, but I don't want him put in the ground like I was. Ain't all it's cracked up to be, being dead. I'd rather still be alive."

"Who are you?" she whispered. Her throat was so dry it hurt. Fear gripped her hard, and she tried to shake off the dream.

"Tell Calhoun Last Chance said howdy. He'll know."

The cowboy touched her hand with fingers so cold Vivian shivered.

Vivian rocketed off the bed, hand clamped over her lips so she wouldn't scream and rouse the house. He stared straight at her, then vanished as if he'd never been there.

It wasn't a dream. On the verge of a panic attack, Vivan struggled to draw a deep breath. *I don't think that was a dream.*

Whatever it had been, dream, vision, or visitation from the dead, the odd experience rattled her. Uneasiness kept her eyes wide open, and she didn't sleep again. Vivian tried, but her brain replayed the encounter repeatedly. The harder she tried to convince herself it was no more than a dream, the more she believed it was. But she couldn't tell Calhoun some vague, mysterious message. He'd think she was crazy, and if he didn't, telling him she dreamed of his dead brother would upset him.

As the first light of dawn banished away the night, she dozed a little, enough to leave her thick-headed when she woke. Vivian slipped across the hall to the bathroom and took a swift shower, praying no one else would wake or want to use the room until she finished. With her hair wrapped in a towel and wearing a robe she found hanging behind the door, she darted back into the bedroom.

She combed her hair and braided it wet, then pulled on jeans and chose a bright-colored blouse. Maybe it would provide some cheer and banish the uneasiness left by the dream. In the light of day, Vivian decided it had to be a dream. The encounter couldn't be anything else, and it meant nothing. For now, she wouldn't talk about the experience to Calhoun.

Vivian ached to see him, hoping his smile would ground her and bring her back to earth.

She went to find him, ready to see what this new day would bring.

Chapter Eleven

Calhoun slumped in a chair at the dining room table, drinking his first cup of coffee. He'd fallen asleep in the den and woke with an awful crick in his neck. He thought he remembered lying with his head resting on Vivian's lap, but he had risen alone. Someone had tucked a pillow under his head and thrown a blanket over him. Cal suspected Vivian.

"Good morning." Lincoln joined him at the table. "Did you ever go to bed?"

"Apparently not. I woke up on the loveseat. I gotta go grab a shower and put on clean clothes, but I needed coffee first." Cal rubbed his face with both hands.

"Do you have plans today?" Lincoln cradled his coffee mug as he spoke.

"I'd like to ride Johnny sometime while I'm here." Cal stretched and rubbed his sore neck. He loved his paint horse, and riding for pleasure wasn't anything close to competing. It was better "Other than that, unless you've got some other ideas, I'd like to go fishing, either down at the river or over at the state park in Rusk. I haven't had a chance to wet a line in a long time. Wanna go with?"

Linc tossed down the rest of his coffee. "As long as we don't take the boys. I love them, but if they go, all I'll get done is keeping them away from and out of the water. Are you taking Vivian?"

"I am if she wants to go. I haven't seen her yet this morning." And, dang it, he missed her and wished she would join them at the table.

"She's coming down the stairs now, Unca Cal." Cooper dashed into the dining room, feet skidding on the hardwood floor. "Can we have some of your cake for breakfast?"

"Don't ask me. That kind of stuff is up to your daddy here." Cal wouldn't touch that question.

"You'll have to ask Mama." Linc laughed.

Sasha entered the dining room with the coffeepot and a few extra cups. "Anyone want a refill? And the answer on cake is *no*. It's likely to give you a tummyache this morning. You can have a piece with supper. Go on to the kitchen. You can eat cereal."

The boys protested, but they obeyed.

Vivian walked into the room, her long hair in a braid down her back.

Calhoun had never seen it down before and was surprised to see the length fell past her waist. Maybe it was the brilliant red shirt she wore, but she seemed pale. He stood as she approached.

She smiled. "Good morning, Calhoun."

She wore the cowboy boots he'd bought her, which delighted him. "Good morning, Pretty Lady. Would you like some coffee?" He grabbed one of the empty cups.

"I'd love some, thanks." She halted when she reached the table.

Calhoun rose to pull out a chair.

She put her arms around his neck and kissed him.

Surprised but pleased, he inhaled her fragrance. Vivian smelled of roses and balsam shampoo. Calhoun turned down his sister-in-law's offer to make pancakes

135

or waffles or scrambled eggs with bacon. "I've been wearing these clothes since yesterday morning. I'm heading to my place to shower and change. I'll grab something to eat there. Thanks for cleaning up and stocking the fridge."

"*De nada,*" Sasha replied. "Vivian?"

"I'll go with Cal, if he doesn't mind. I'd like to see his place." Vivian tossed her head, and her braid swung from side to side.

It was exactly what he hoped she would say, but Calhoun sipped coffee and didn't mention that. No reason to jinx a good thing. "Sure, Pretty Lady, you're always welcome to run with me. How do you feel about going fishing?"

"I like being outside, the wind, the water, and the sun." Vivian put down her cup and smiled. "I'm not very good at catching any fish, though. Grandpa always said I spent too much time woolgathering or picking flowers. Why? Are you fishing today?" Her eyes sparkled.

He thought she might like the idea. "I thought I would. Lincoln, too, if you can stand his company. We should've been out there already, but maybe the fish are still biting. You'd better not wear your boots, honey. They'll get wet and muddy, maybe ruined."

"I've got athletic shoes. Should I go change them?" She rose.

"Do it when we come back to get Linc. Let's go." Cal pulled his keys from his pocket and offered his hand.

Although a haze shimmered in the distance warning it would be hot, he savored the early morning as they stepped outside. The sky seemed a deeper blue than usual. No more than a few white puffy clouds floated overhead. A light breeze drifted across his face as he climbed into the truck.

Vivian moved beside him for the short trip to his place.

Thankful it was clean, he brought her inside. "Here's my humble digs." Calhoun tossed his keys on the small dining table, then cleared the change from his pockets.

Vivian glanced around, then settled onto the loveseat. "It's small but nice. It's a little more like home than your trailer but not by much."

"How so?" Cal framed the question as he surveyed his domain.

"I see a few pictures, Calhoun, some books, and a few movies, but otherwise it could be a motel room."

He shrugged. "It's just a place where I stay, not home. I haven't really had a home in years unless you count Linc's. Guess I don't really need one." Calhoun knew he did, though. Lincoln and Sasha had made that old house into a cozy home. Her grandmother's farmhouse had offered that comfortable atmosphere. He spent no more than a few months of the year here, so it hadn't seemed necessary here.

Vivian met his gaze and returned it with a hard stare. "Yes, you do, Cowboy. Everyone needs somewhere to call home. Your brother said last night he's told you that you can stay with them. Why don't you?"

Everything boiled to one question. "I want to give them their space, Pretty Lady, not intrude."

"They're family. I don't think they'd see it as an intrusion." Vivian tucked her feet beneath her as she spoke.

To avoid any more talk, he made a show of sniffing his armpits and made a face. "I need to go shower 'cause I stink."

Vivian laughed. "Then I'll make breakfast so we can eat."

"Sounds good, honey. I won't be long." He gathered up towels and clean clothes, then headed for the bathroom. Cal stripped and stepped into the shower. The water rushed against his face as he soaped up and scrubbed. He lingered long enough to let the hot shower ease the crick in his neck, then exited. He dried off and dressed. The enticing fragrance of bacon wafted into the bedroom, and he followed the aroma. "Smells good." The small table was set with silverware and napkins. "What'd you fix?"

"Bacon, fried eggs, and toast. I made coffee, too, if you want more."

"I do, thanks." He could and did drink coffee morning, noon, or at midnight. It fueled him more often than not on the circuit.

Vivian poured a cup, then handed him a plate and sat across from him.

He bowed his head to ask the blessing and noticed she did the same. Calhoun prayed silently, then dug in as soon as he said, "Amen." Vivian had fried the bacon to a perfect crisp. Although she hadn't asked how he wanted his eggs, she'd cooked them over easy, his favorite. The toast wasn't too light or dark. He thought her coffee tasted better than Sasha's, although he'd never complain.

"Where are we fishing?" Vivian tossed back the rest of her coffee.

"Down at the Neches River. The ranch extends to it, but we'll have to go over to the wildlife refuge off Highway 79 for the best spot, and I doubt we'll catch much. We're getting a late start, and it's going to be hot."

Her mouth dropped open. "If this is late, what's early? It's barely eight o'clock."

"Five would have been better." Cal laughed. "When it's hot, the fish will go as deep as they can or hole up. It'll still be fun, though."

Vivian finished a slice of bacon. "I hope so. Did you sleep all right last night?"

"Yeah, 'til I woke up with a stiff neck." Cal tilted his head. "The shower helped, though. Did I fall asleep on you, or did I dream that?"

"You did, first sitting on the floor leaning on my knees, then when I woke you, you got on the loveseat and lay down with your head in my lap."

Cal wished he remembered that part. The last thing he recalled had been a massage. "I hope I wasn't a pain."

She reached across the table and smacked his right arm. "You weren't, Calhoun. You seemed worn out."

"I was. I sleep better when someone's around than not." He stretched his fingers to touch hers.

"Everywhere but here, I'll be close at hand." She smiled over the rim of her coffee cup.

"I'm counting on that, honey. I'd best get the fishing gear before Linc comes knocking at the door." If he didn't rise, he would want to linger, so he stood.

"I'll clean up the dishes while you do." Vivian stacked their empty plates and silverware.

"You don't have to, Pretty Lady."

"I'd rather it be done." She filled the sink with hot, soapy water and began scrubbing.

A walk-in closet off the single bedroom held the fishing equipment along with a variety of junk he hadn't bothered to toss. Calhoun dug out several rods and reels, figuring his brother would bring his own, and found his tackle box. The metal container dated to the 1950s and had been his dad's, before that Grandpa's. Two trays held a wide variety of bobbers, hooks, lures, weights, and more. The space beneath held some pliers, a spool of fishing line, and a couple stringers. For Vivian, he picked out a rod and reel, one he'd used as a teenager. His own choice was a step up from the rig he handed Viv. He also brought along an old cane fishing pole. Cal changed into rubber boots and picked up his .22 rimfire rifle. He carried it all out and stowed it behind the pickup seat.

Vivian emerged, wearing an odd expression. She climbed into the truck without a word.

"You okay?" Her mood had shifted from earlier when she'd been chattering and vivacious, so he wondered why.

She tried to smile and failed. "I'm fine. I saw a photograph in a frame with you, Lincoln, and a younger guy. Was that Sullivan?"

Calhoun knew the photo. It was one of the few he'd kept of his younger brother. It had been taken at a rodeo the month before Sully died. "Yeah, it was. I guess you hadn't seen any pictures of him before." He and Linc had stood with the kid in the middle, arms around him. They all wore grins. Talking about Last Chance was enough to give Calhoun indigestion. He rubbed his stomach with one hand. "Yeah, it's him."

"He was…" She hesitated.

He wondered what she wanted to say.

"…young, he was so young."

Cal thought she held back something, but if so, Vivian wasn't saying, and he didn't want to spoil the day by asking. He released a long, slow breath. "Yeah, he was that. I miss him, Vivian."

"I'm sure you do." She scooted close and touched his face. "Where'd he get that eagle bolo tie? I've never seen one like it."

"He ordered it somewhere," Cal didn't recall the place. "It was his favorite, though. We buried it on him."

She gasped, but when she didn't ask anything more, he dropped it. Talking about his late brother wasn't his favorite subject. He grieved for him, and guilt gnawed at his heart, certain he should have saved the kid.

At the main house, Vivian changed her boots for shoes, and they picked up Lincoln.

Sasha offered to make sandwiches.

But Cal figured they would be back by lunchtime. They headed to the river. Although by mid-morning temperatures rose into the low nineties, Calhoun enjoyed the sunshine that filtered through the trees onto his shoulders. The rich loam and water smell of the river pleased his nose, and here, at least, he felt at home. As the flow and gurgle of the river echoed as it passed, Cal relaxed.

Lincoln had insisted on packing three folding camp chairs, each tucked into a portable sleeve.

He hadn't thought it necessary, but now, due to his bum knee, Calhoun was glad to have a seat. He still could stand and cast a line or walk up down the bank as he wanted or needed, and he could sit, too. Cal set up two of the chairs in a level spot close to the water.

Vivian carried the fishing rod he'd assigned her.

He toted the rest. After placing his tackle box on the ground, he opened it and considered what lures to use.

"I brought worms and some dough bait," Lincoln called from upstream. "I didn't know if you wanted to fish for bass or catfish."

"Both are tasty," Cal replied. "Enough catfish for a fish fry would be awesome, though. I don't know if they're biting enough for a mess of them or not."

"If not, there's plenty in the deep freeze," Linc informed. "Fishing at night would probably be better now that it's getting hot."

Between the three of them, they caught two fish big enough to keep and two to throw back to grow. At first, the catfish hit the homemade bait, but by eleven, they'd become more somnolent. Calhoun figured the fish were done biting, but he hated to leave. He glanced over at Vivian, who had come close to reeling in a monster size catfish but lost it at the last moment.

"You look content." Her lips curved into a smile.

"I am. I'd rather be here, just sitting, doing a bit of fishing, than in the arena with all the people, noise, and tension," he replied. "It's quiet here, and I like it. It's good for my soul. I don't have to worry about when I ride or how I'll do or if I'll get hurt this time. I'm parked in one place for a couple of days, and it feels good. Got my ever-loving baby sitting next to me."

"That sounds familiar," Vivian said.

"I imagine you heard the song while we were

driving. It's from Johnny Horton's song, "Down That River Road." If I had an ever-loving baby, it's you."

Her smile widened, and she didn't dispute it. He had feared she might protest.

"If you like this life better, why do you rodeo?" Vivian pursed her lips together as she asked the hard question.

"It's all I know how to do." Calhoun paused to collect his thoughts and find words to answer. "Well, that, and raise cattle, maybe. I've rodeoed since I was a kid."

"I remember you told me. Mutton busting, right?" Vivian grinned as she recalled the conversation.

"Yeah, when I was little," Cal replied. "Later, I did some roping and steer wrestling, then settled onto saddle broncs and bulls. I just ride bulls now and will until I retire. Honey, other than a few piddling jobs, I haven't worked as an adult."

"At Nanna's farmhouse, you talked about retiring and raising cattle, maybe some rough stock." Vivian leaned forward in the chair, almost tipping it.

"That's what I want to do a little bit down the road." He could do it now, he supposed, after this season, but his future stretched out blank and unknown. That farm up in Missouri appealed to him. So did Vivian. "Besides, I ride bulls now for Chance."

"Your little nephew?" Her forehead knotted.

"No, for Sullivan. Chance was his nickname. He often rode as Chance Sullivan because we used to call him Last Chance."

"I remember that you told me he rode as Chance. I don't remember that you called him Last Chance." Her voice wavered as she spoke.

Maybe it was the heat or the way the shadows moved across her face, but she seemed pale. Despite the heat, Cal could have remained on the river for hours, but he thought Vivian might be ready to go. "Do you want to stay longer, or are you about ready to wrap it up? They hadn't brought anything to eat, and he'd forgotten to bring bottled water. He realized she hadn't needed to pee, and if she did, it wouldn't be as easy as it was for him and Lincoln. Calhoun stood and reeled in his fishing line.

"I'm ready to go whenever you are." Vivian rose and folded her chair. "The mosquitoes are eating me up, and I think chiggers bit my ankles. They itch like fire."

He saw she had a few welts, but he hadn't been bitten at all. "I suppose that's because you're sweet. Give me your rod and I'll start packing up." She did as he asked, but he noticed her smile had vanished. In fifteen minutes, he had everything in the truck.

Lincoln put his gear away when it was time to leave.

So they headed back. They arrived in time to join Linc's family for lunch with—brisket sandwiches, some potato chips, pickle spears, and leftover baked beans. It tasted as fine to Calhoun as it did the night before, but he noticed Vivian lacked the same appetite.

The fish they'd caught were in a pail of water outside, ready to be cleaned. Cal and Linc planned to do that as soon as lunch was over. Then he wanted to spend some time with his horse, maybe saddle up, and ride a little. Lincoln had a few horses of his own, so Calhoun figured he'd invite Vivian to ride if she wanted.

"I've got a terrible headache. I thought I'd go

upstairs, take something for it, and try to nap." She rubbed her forehead with three fingers and winced.

Calhoun frowned. "I'm sorry, honey. Is there anything I can do?"

"No, I'll be fine, Cowboy. If I rest now, the headache will be history by supper time. I want to enjoy that fish fry." She had taken her purse, dug out some pain relievers, then washed them down with iced tea.

He brushed back a few strands of hair back that had escaped from her braid with his big hand. "You're not sick, are you?"

"No, it's just a headache." Vivian tried to smile. "Don't worry. I'm okay, and it'll pass. Go ride Johnny."

"I'd like that, Pretty Lady. I thought maybe we'd take a ride from Rusk to Palestine on the Texas State Railroad maybe tomorrow. Now, you get upstairs and feel better, you hear?"

"Yes, sir." Vivian mimed a salute. "I'll see you at supper, if not before. Just be careful."

"I will." He stepped close and put his mouth over hers in a gentle kiss. Three words *I love you* popped into his head, and he almost said them but didn't. Calhoun cared about this woman more than anyone he ever dated, but if he told her he loved her, she'd respond. If she shared his feelings, that would be good, but with it would come expectations he wasn't sure he could live up to yet. And if she didn't feel the same, then he'd be crushed. He didn't want to be *just friends* with Vivian.

Cal watched her mount the stairs, then headed outside to clean the fish. His two oldest nephews trailed after him while Sasha put Chance down for his nap.

They sat at a picnic table a few yards from Linc's house, scaled the fish, gutted, and fileted them. They had enough for a fish fry, and if Sasha thought they needed more, she could pull some from the freezer. Once they'd delivered the fish to the kitchen, they left the boys with Sasha. Calhoun headed for the farthest field where his paint horse waited.

More than his long-time mount, Johnny was also a friend. Calhoun quit taking the horse on the rodeo circuit when he stopped roping, but he had a fondness for the animal. So had Sully. Thinking about his brother made him sad. Even after three years, sometimes Cal couldn't believe he'd never laugh with Sullivan again or tease him or compete in the same rodeo. He missed him, and somehow, that ache always cut deeper here at the ranch.

Once he led Johnny back to the barn and saddled him, he took off for a long ride across the property. Sometimes he loped and sometimes he galloped, loving having a horse beneath him again. Calhoun enjoyed the wind in his face as he talked to the animal.

He told Johnny about Vivian, how he felt or thought he might, and what he hoped for in the future. At almost six o'clock, he took his horse back to the barn, unsaddled him, brushed him, and put him in the corral.

Calhoun headed to Linc's house, hoping her headache was gone, eager to see her smile. He was, as Granny would have said, smitten.

Chapter Twelve

The headache was genuine, but Vivian would have sucked it up and never said a thing if she hadn't been rattled. She dismissed her vivid dream from last night as just that—a dream—until she saw a photograph of Calhoun's youngest brother. She recognized the young man who had visited her. Although she considered telling Cal, she didn't, concerned he might think she was a little loco or get upset. She pushed the experience from her mind, but then, as they fished, he told her he rode for Chance. Since that was his youngest nephew's name, she figured it was for the child, but Cal corrected her, telling her his brother, Sullivan, had ridden as Chance Sullivan, and that his nickname was Last Chance.

"Tell him Last Chance says 'howdy.' He'll know."

Vivian heard the echo of that statement from the dream. To be fair, Cal had mentioned his brother rode as Chance Sullivan. But he had not told her that the family had nicknamed Sully "Last Chance" as the youngest or explained they had quit using the label after he died.

Now, she questioned whether it had been a dream, a vision, or a visitation. Whatever it was, it held a warning. Phrases she recalled included cryptic things, *Don't let him do what I did*, *It wasn't his fault*, *Satan's Hellion*, *Tell him don't make the same mistake*, and *I don't want him put in the ground like I was*. Considered together or separately, each one disturbed her. The clincher was the part about the eagle bolo tie. She'd asked about it, hoping Cal might say he had one, too, or that they were common. Instead, he told her it had been buried with his brother.

Worry gnawed at her gut with sharp teeth until her stomach ached. Her head pounded, and as she waited for the ibuprofen to kick in, Vivian wet a washcloth, then lay across the bed with it on her forehead. She willed that a dreamless sleep would come, but she couldn't relax. After trying for an hour, she grabbed her phone and called the only person who might not think she was crazy.

Nanna answered on the second ring.

Vivian poured out the story. In the past, Nanna had shared a few strange experiences she'd had, and she listened now. "What do you think? Was it a dream or real?"

"Sounds real to me, Vivvie," Nanna replied. "You couldn't make up how he looked or that thing about the eagle tie. You didn't have any way to know the family called him Last Chance, either."

Some of her tension slacked off, and her stomach eased. "Then I haven't lost my mind. But do you think it means Calhoun is in danger?"

"It could be, but then it might just be a worried brother reaching out."

Vivian kept her tone matter of fact, as if they weren't discussing a nocturnal visit from a dead man.

"Love lives beyond death, you know," Nanna proclaimed.

Vivian didn't believe it. Her parents had never

reached out, but she wasn't going to argue. "Maybe," she conceded. "It just makes me worry, the parts about Cal not making the same mistake Sullivan did. If it's nonsense, that's good, but what if it's not?"

"You won't know unless you find out what mistake Cal's younger brother made," Nanna stated.

"I can't ask Calhoun that!" Vivian almost dropped the phone as she protested.

"You may have to, Vivian, in case it is a warning."

"I don't want anything to happen to him, Nanna! I couldn't stand it if he got hurt. I can't even think about if something worse happened." Her headache slammed back, harder than ever, and she rubbed her forehead.

"Do you love him?"

Nanna's question cut through everything else, a knack she possessed for getting to the heart of things. Vivian cared very much about Calhoun but love? "I don't know, Nanna. I think I might, but I'm afraid." Vivian twisted her fingers together as she spoke.

"Of what?"

"Everything," Vivian whispered. "I'm scared he might not feel the same way. I'm afraid of losing him, even though I don't really have him—not as more than a friend."

" 'There is no fear in love.' " Nanna made the statement with certainty.

"Says who?"

Nanna laughed. "It's in the Bible, Vivian, First John, 4:18."

Despite her concerns, that logic made her angry. Her grandmother had some nerve, quoting the Good Book. "Nanna, you know how I feel about God and church and faith now."

"And you know how I feel," her grandmother replied. "And Calhoun, too."

Vivian decided to ignore that. If she didn't, she'd be mad, and she didn't want to be angry. "What do I do?" Her sigh echoed in the quiet room.

"Try to find out what mistake Sullivan made, if he did. Figure out why Calhoun blames himself," Nanna suggested. "Then wait and see what happens. I'd tell you to pray, but I don't think you will."

"I won't." At least, Nanna acknowledged the reality.

"Then do what you can. And, honey, if you do love him…tell him."

"Maybe someday. Thank you, Nanna." Vivian ached to do that very thing, but what if he said he didn't feel the same? That declaration would have to wait.

"Anytime, child. Take care."

Whether it was the ibuprofen, talking to her grandmother, or fatigue, Vivian slept after that. When she woke, daylight remained, but judging by the shadows on the wall, she guessed the time was early evening. Drowsy, she realized her headache had gone, and her stomach was calm as she sat.

"Hey, Pretty Lady." Calhoun rested in the chair by the window. "How do you feel?"

"Better." Startled, her heart beat faster for a few moments.

"I'm glad. I was a little bit worried about you." He shifted to the edge of the bed, facing her. His fingers caressed her cheek.

He smelled of wind and horse, with a faint aroma of fish, but she didn't care. Calhoun was here, he was whole and safe. Affection welled up, and Vivian launched herself toward him, her arms circling him in a tight hug. Vivian clung to Calhoun as he kissed her. It was a slow, sweet, smooch, and Vivian enjoyed it.

"Guess you're glad to see me," he commented after he let go.

"I am. I missed you." Vivian had his shirt fisted in her hand and didn't let go.

"I wasn't more than a few hours, honey."

"It was too long." Right now, she didn't want Calhoun out of her sight.

"I'm here now, but I probably stink."

"You do, but I don't care." Vivian let go and laughed.

He sniffed at his shirt and frowned. "I mind, though, and probably my brother's family will. I'm gonna go home, grab a quick shower, and come back to eat. Meet me downstairs?"

"Sure." Familiar words from a Hank Williams tune rushed through her mind as she changed into a pretty floral print skirt and a black T-shirt. Vivian sang as she fixed her hair, although she didn't do more than undo her braid, brush it into a ponytail, and put it up with a clip. Vivian wasn't much for makeup, but she added burgundy lipstick and used a bit of powder so her face wouldn't shine. She spritzed on some rose fragrance, then headed downstairs.

She'd been quick, but Calhoun waited at the bottom of the stairs as she descended, watching. Vivian put a little sashay into her step and saw the warm appreciation in his eyes. She throttled back her desire to hug him again and smiled. "You clean up nice." Vivian eyed his plain light-green pocket T-shirt, faded jeans, and the man under the clothing.

"You're beautiful," Calhoun replied. "I think Sasha has everything on the table." They strolled together into the dining room.

A platter of fried catfish rested in the center, flanked with a bowl of fried potatoes, another of corn, and a basket of hush puppies.

He pulled out a chair, seated Vivian, then sat beside her. As soon as he did, the Kellys linked hands.

"It's Cooper's turn to ask a blessing," Lincoln said.

The seven-year-old boy bowed his head, both serious and cute. Vivian followed suit.

"Dear Jesus," the child began. "Thank you for this food and for the cake we still have. Bless all my family here. Let us be safe and not sick. Thank you that my Unca Cal is here and please watch over him when he rides bulls. Thank you for bringing Vivian here and bless her, too. Amen."

"Amen," the family chorused.

Vivian came close to joining them but caught herself. It had been a reflex, she thought, nothing more. After the delicious meal and more than a few fishing stories, Vivian offered to clean up and wash the dishes.

Sasha agreed and stepped back from the chore.

Calhoun said he'd help. The two of them made short work clearing the table, putting away the few leftovers, and washing the dishes.

Although the kitchen included a dishwasher, Vivian did it the old-fashioned way, using the kitchen sink. It was how Nanna had taught her and what she preferred.

Cal dried the clean dishes after receiving them from Vivian, then placed them in the drainer. He also put most of them away, being familiar with the kitchen.

Their shared task brought contentment, and she hummed.

When they finished, Sasha and Lincoln had set up card games in the dining room and asked if they wanted to play. Both Vivian and Calhoun sat in on several rounds of Old Maid, then switched to Uno.

"How many more rodeos do you have this year?" Linc asked after the kids had headed upstairs for bath time and bed.

Calhoun rested his chin on one hand. "Seven, right now. More if I advance to any championships, which I hope I do. Less, if I cut out of any of them. Why?"

"I'd like to come see you compete at least once." Lincoln leaned forward from where he sat. "I haven't for a long time. If it was close enough, maybe we could bring the kids. I think they'd like it."

"I imagine so. Next, they'll want to ride, too." He almost wished they wouldn't, though, because then he'd never have to worry about them getting hurt.

"What's the closest?

Vivian waited to hear the answer, too.

"Let me list them." Cal dug out his phone. "I have them all on my calendar. This weekend, it's Fort Worth, then Prescott, Arizona, over the Fourth of July. After that, I thought Vivian and I would run up to Missouri so she can visit her grandma and maybe spend a few days. Then it's on to Wahoo, Nebraska, the third weekend of July, then down to Lawton, Oklahoma, for the last. In August, I'll ride in Sallisaw—that's also Oklahoma, then over Labor Day weekend at Elk City, Oklahoma. I get a break, then and thought I'd probably come here if you don't mind, then I'll ride at Coushatta, Louisiana. That's probably the closest. It's not two hours from here, so it'd be an easy drive for you. It's not too far. After that, my schedule's open."

"You make me tired listening to that list." Linc laughed. "You're welcome at home, anytime, you know that, and so is Vivian. Coushatta would be perfect, I think. We'll plan on that one."

"It'll depend on my standings after that," Calhoun explained. "Although, unless I advance in the rankings, it wouldn't hurt my feelings much to call it a season."

"Are you going with him, Vivian?" Sasha rested her hands on her husband's shoulders, her T-shirt damp from the boys' baths.

Vivian hoped she would be and glanced at Calhoun. "He hasn't asked me past Prescott. So, I don't know."

Calhoun turned toward her, his brown eyes bright and alive. "I'd like it if you would, Pretty Lady. Will you?"

With no job, no real ties but to Nanna, and the desire to go with him a powerful force, Vivian nodded. "I will, as long as we can pop up to see my grandmother sometimes."

"I believe I mentioned that we would." He grinned, then winked.

"You did, so yes, I am." Happiness soared within like a bird taking wing, and she savored the feeling.

He threw back his head and hollered out loud, a wordless cry of delight. Cal reached for her hand and kissed it. "Good deal. I'm glad, Vivian."

Her heart pounded in her chest with excitement. She'd made the decision and would go. Calhoun had proved to be the best friend she'd had in years. They had developed a closeness she had not experienced with any other man, not even her former fiancé who she now preferred to call "old what's his name." Arthur had never demonstrated as much care or concern as Calhoun ever had. He'd broken off their engagement in the wake of her parents' murder. She knew Cal would have never done such a thing.

This relationship began with her desire to take photographs, and she'd chosen rodeo, never dreaming she would meet Calhoun or that she would attend more than one. Nanna had hoped she'd meet a cowboy, but Vivian never thought she would.

"I'm glad you'll be with him," Lincoln stated. "I'll worry less, knowing you're around."

Vivian couldn't stop a two-thousand-pound bull from doing damage or make sure Cal didn't ride when he shouldn't, but she would be there at his side. She could offer support and kindness. She cared and maybe more. Perhaps she could find out what mistake, if any, his brother had made and manage to keep Cal from making the same one. *I don't want him put in the ground like I was,* echoed the words from her encounter with Sullivan. Neither did she.

"You shouldn't worry at all," Calhoun told his brother with a grin.

"Yeah, but I do," Lincoln returned. His forehead sported a worry line down the center. "Big brothers can't help that."

The words fell flat because Vivian figured it evoked the lost brother, the youngest. An uncomfortable silence fell, and the only sound was Lincoln, shuffling the Uno cards. "Anybody want to play another round?

"Nah, I'm tired. I think I'll turn in before long."

Cal yawned and raised his arms to stretch.

Vivian sighed with relief. She was more than ready for bed, too.

Linc yawned. "Sounds good. Are you staying here or down at your house?"

"At my place, I guess." Calhoun pushed back his chair to stand.

"Bro, you're welcome to stay here." Linc tucked the cards back into the box.

"I wish you would. You'd be closer." Vivian offered her opinion.

Calhoun heaved a sigh, then grinned. "It's not like I'm very far away, anyway, but all right, I won't fight both of you. As long as I can have a bed, not a short love seat."

"There are two more bedrooms to pick from," Lincoln stated. "I think you'll rest better, Cal."

"Likely so," he answered. "I thought maybe we'd take a train ride tomorrow."

"All of us or just you and Vivian?" Lincoln yawned again and stood.

"All of us if you want to go. I figured the kids would like it."

"They would, but why don't you and Vivian go? We can all go another time, Cal." Sasha stated.

"I'd love that," Vivian told Cal. She didn't mind if his family went, too, but she would treasure the outing with Calhoun.

"Then we'll do it. You're gonna love it." A slow grin lit Calhoun's face.

"Better get tickets online tonight to make sure it's not sold out," Lincoln suggested. "Come over to my office, and you can buy them."

****

Before he climbed the stairs to retire, Calhoun retrieved clean clothes and his toiletries from the smaller house. He booked tickets for two on the railroad. Their trip would leave Rusk at eleven, and the four-hour round trip would have them home in time for supper.

"Sleep well, cowboy," Vivian uttered from the top of the steps.

"I'll see you in the morning, honey." He brushed a kiss against her lips.

If he'd had an iron handy, Calhoun would have pressed his light-blue and dark-brown striped Western shirt, with pearl snaps. He paired it with a chestnut leather vest and a pair of his favorite boots. He slept better in the main house but woke early so he showered before anyone else rose. He carried the boots in one hand and went downstairs in stocking feet, thinking he'd put on the coffee. Once in the kitchen, he rustled up a cast iron skillet and started bacon frying. Bacon and eggs were one of the few dishes he could and did cook.

Although he enjoyed the early morning quiet, he craved some tunes, so he turned on the radio to a classic country station and let vintage gold fill the kitchen with sound. He kept the volume low and sometimes sang along to songs he knew well. Cal sang along with Dwight Yoakum to the classic hit, "Guitars, Cadillacs," and didn't notice Vivian had entered the kitchen until her voice blended with his. As the song ended, his voice trailed away as he turned. He found Vivian as pretty as the morning, dressed in a blouse with shades of blue ranging from light turquoise at the top to navy at the waist.

"What's the only thing that keeps you hanging on?" she asked. "You don't have a guitar or a Cadillac."

"The Lord. Without faith, I'd never manage. Second to that, my family, and now, you do." Her forehead wrinkled with the faint frown she always got when someone mentioned God or Jesus.

But she didn't protest. "Coffee might help." She poured a cup. She hovered the pot over his cup and when he nodded, she refilled it.

Cal wanted to quote some Scripture and tell her how faith had kept him from losing his mind or taking his life after Sully died. His brother's death had been his fault. God might have forgiven him long ago, but Calhoun couldn't let it go. He carried that burden and probably always would. Without Jesus, he'd never manage that. He ached to help her find the path back to her Savior to restore the joy she said she once had and revive it.

He didn't, though. Her resistance was strong. He'd seen it too often not to tread with care. The wrong words now or a strong push might send her running in the other direction. If they could ever have a future together, it would be one in faith. Calhoun believed a lasting relationship could happen and prayed it did. For now, he grinned. "Bacon should do the trick. How do you want your eggs?"

"Over easy is fine. Do you want me to make biscuits? I will if you do." Her smile brightened his morning.

"Toast is fine today. I love your biscuits, but we've got places to go and trains to ride."

"Then show me the toaster, and I'll find the

butter." Vivian opened the fridge and took out a tub, then rooted through the silverware drawer for a table knife.

By the time Linc's bunch came downstairs, breakfast was served. The day officially got underway, and Calhoun anticipated the time to spend with Vivian, hours of promise and possibility.

Chapter Thirteen

At the Texas State Railroad station, Vivian linked her arm through Calhoun's as they headed inside to board the train. He'd already purchased the tickets, and she found the station built from rock picturesque. Other than the steam train at amusement park Silver Dollar City, she'd never ridden a train. She'd brought one camera and shot several photos, delighted with the opportunity.

A vintage engine with several cars attached waited on tracks outside the station. Cal had chosen steam over diesel, and they were in a first-class car. Once boarded, they took their seats in booth-type seating. Like most people, she'd been to a few places and traveled a little, but most of the time it had been to ordinary destinations, amusement parks, museums, historic sites, and shopping centers. Her farthest and most exciting travel memory was a trip to the top of Pikes Peak with her parents when she was thirteen. Calhoun had taken her to a beautiful hidden waterfall, to the top of Arkansas's second highest mountain to a castle in the clouds, and now on a train. And she loved it.

"You wore your boots." He wore a wide grin.

"They're comfortable." Vivian stretched out her right foot and admired the boot. They were attractive, too. "I really like them."

"Still need to get you a hat to go with them."

She'd never worn a cowboy hat or thought she would, but she decided she might. "Maybe."

"We'll see about finding one in Fort Worth." He reached for her hand.

The doors of the train closed as the conductor issued the classic cry of "all aboard" stretching out the syllables. A steam whistle blew twice and sent delightful shivers down her back.

Calhoun belted out a few lines from an old Johnny Horton tune, "Coal Smoke, Valve Oil, And Steam." "Most people aren't familiar with it, but it's about trains."

"I guessed that much. Maybe you should sing."

He placed his hands flat on the table between them and grinned. "I do sing, Pretty Lady."

Vivian giggled. "I meant as a career, like Johnny Horton."

"It'd be as much traveling or more than rodeo, so I don't think so. I don't have it in me, honey. Besides, I'm not that great of a singer."

"You sound fine to me." Vivian adored his voice, rough and true. She liked his Texas accent and admired how he knew so many songs by heart.

"Then I'll sing to you, and I'll sing in church and everywhere but on a stage." He wore such an earnest expression that she ached to kiss him. "Look out the windows, sugar. You don't want to miss this."

Vivian settled back and watched the passing scenery. The majestic loblolly pines stretched to the sky as they passed through portions of the Fairchild State Forest. Twice, she caught site of an elusive deer, one with a fawn at its side. Squirrels climbed the hardwoods, and birds flitted through the trees. The conductor narrated as they traveled down the tracks, offering up tidbits of history and a few stories. Sometimes train-themed songs played from hidden speakers. Part of the time, Vivian listened, but often the passing countryside captured her attention. They passed over so many bridges she lost count.

During the four-hour journey, two to Palestine and two back, Calhoun ordered snacks to share and his favorite root beer.

The day passed quickly, and Vivian couldn't believe it was almost five-thirty when they climbed back into his pickup. She took her usual place beside him. "I had a wonderful time, Calhoun. We go to awesome places and see fantastic things. I love it!"

"I'm glad you had fun, honey. Do you want to grab a bite to eat before we go back to the ranch?" He donned sunglasses.

"Sure, as long as Sasha's not expecting us for supper." Vivan dug her own shades from her purse and put them on.

"Linc and Sasha took the boys over to visit her folks in Longview." He pulled onto the road leading into Rusk and increased his speed. "We can eat in town or go buy some steaks or something at the store. You'd have to cook, though."

"I don't mind." Vivian considered several possible recipes she could make.

"We'll have steak in Fort Worth tomorrow," he stated. "Mexican or barbecue?"

"What do you like best?" She caught his hand and twined her fingers through his.

"Honey, I like both." His grip tightened as he gazed at her without blinking.

"Mexican, then, because your brother barbecued for us." Her taste buds craved some spicy heat.

The small, homey atmosphere of the restaurant appealed and so did the delightful aroma of meat, cheese, and spices that greeted them. Calhoun led her to a table for two, guiding her with one hand resting on her lower back, then pulled out a chair.

As soon as they were seated, a server appeared with a basket of tortilla chips and a bowl of salsa.

Vivian dipped a chip into the mixture and smiled. It tasted homemade, spicy yet sweet with a touch of cilantro. She studied the extensive menu. Everything sounded delicious. "What are you ordering?"

"Tamales and chili gravy with refried beans on the side." He pointed to the meal on the menu.

After some deliberation, she ordered burritos *tipicos* with rice but took a taste of his. The tamales were superb.

After supper, they walked hand in hand along the footbridge, located in a park not far from the downtown square.

"It's supposed to be the longest footbridge in the U.S.," Cal stated as they meandered along it, pausing to look at a tree or just gaze at the park. "It's been here since 1861, but it's been rebuilt at least twice. In 1861, my family was fighting the Civil War, or so they say. Granny knew. I wish now I'd paid more attention."

Somnolent and stuffed after the delicious meal, Vivian leaned against his shoulder. "You probably know more than I do. Nanna's always tried to tell me family history, but I never listened. Now, I suppose I should. I think we had some ancestors on both sides of the Civil War, if I remember the stories."

"You ought to write it down, Pretty Lady." Calhoun brushed his lips against her hair.

"I should. Have you?" Until now, Vivian hadn't had much interest, but he inspired her.

"Sullivan did," he replied. "He was into all that old stuff. He and our cousin Lottie loved family history. They listened to Granny's tales and researched right up 'til he died. Lottie's got some old pictures and stuff. One of these days, I'll ask her to make copies for me."

His casual mention of his brother prompted her to ask, "Where was his last rodeo?"

Calhoun sighed long and deep. "Dodge City, Kansas. We were both competing there. I ain't been back since. I don't have the heart for it."

Vivian yearned to ask more, but his sad expression stopped her. "Is he buried here?"

He nodded. "Same cemetery as Johnny Horton's folks but in the newer section. I should go by and pay my respects, but we leave tomorrow. I'll do it next time. I wish you could've known him."

She resisted the urge to tell him that she might have met him. "I do, too." His anguished expression tore at her heart, and she decided not to say anything more.

"Someday, I'll tell you what happened, honey," Calhoun promised, his voice so low it was almost a whisper.

Vivian put her arm around his waist, and he did the same. They stood in tandem, arms about each other. Somewhere, she heard crickets and cicadas singing an evening song. In the distance, steel-belted tires hummed, and closer, she caught the voices of kids, calling and laughing at play. Right now, words weren't required.

"Let's head home," he told her fifteen or twenty minutes later. "I need to get my gear packed and so do you."

"I know. We're not taking your trailer, are we?"

"No. There's not really any place to park it near the Cowtown Coliseum. We've got a room at a hotel not far away, in the historic Stockyards District. I booked it on Linc's computer. It's got two beds, but if you want your own room, I'll take care of it."

"I think we can trust ourselves, Cowboy. I promise not to do anything wicked with you." His arm around her waist and warm breath against her cheek made her long for intimacy, but she knew he wouldn't, and she shouldn't. She meant to be flippant.

He answered her with a smile. "I know, honey. I imagine some folks will figure we're doing more than sharing a room, but we know the reality and so does God."

Rather than protest, on this she agreed. "That's true. Do you want to split the cost, Calhoun? I can." For now, she could. Down the road, it might be an issue, but she wasn't planning to tell him that.

"I got it, honey. I've won a lot of prize purses in the last couple of years and saved most. I pay for insurance, too, in case I get hurt. If I should be killed, then Linc's my beneficiary."

She shivered. Nanna would say a goose walked over her grave, and it refreshed that cryptic midnight message. "Don't say things like that, Calhoun, not ever."

His arm around her tightened. "I don't figure I will be, Pretty Lady, but it's worth having. The point is, I've got a fair bit of money in the bank, and I've been blessed with winning, so I can pay your way. If you want to pay for a meal occasionally or something, that's fine, too."

"All right." Vivian would. Right now, he appeared as tired as she felt. "C'mon. We both need some rest before we head to Fort Worth, you most of all."

At home, the family had gathered around the dining room table, finishing off the bull-rider cake.

Cooper stopped before he forked his first bite. "Hey, Unca Cal, you want some of your cake?"

Only a little remained. "Nah, I'm good. Go ahead, kid and enjoy it. I'm gonna take the truck down to get my gear packed up, then park here so Vivian can add hers."

His nephews insisted on helping, so Vivian watched as he and the three boys loaded up his bull-riding gear, his duffle bags with clothes, toiletries, and other stuff into the bed of his truck.

Cal left plenty of room for Vivian's things. Since the skies were clear and no rain was predicted, he left the bed cover open.

"Put my camera stuff behind the seat, please," she called. During their visit, she'd taken many photos and not all were Calhoun. She'd taken pictures of the boys with Cal's horse, playing in the yard, and watching their uncle do a little trick riding. Vivian managed a few shots with Linc and Cal plus a couple of Linc with Sasha.

Sasha whisked the boys away for their baths because it was past their bedtime.

Vivian should be packing but she lingered, wanting to be with Calhoun.

Lincoln pulled two cold root beers from the fridge, not three.

Vivian took the hint and dashed upstairs to fill her suitcase as the brothers retired to the back porch. They would leave soon, but part of her hated to go. She enjoyed the time with Calhoun's family. They supported him, and she'd learned he carried more baggage than she had imagined.

****

"Come sit on the back porch for a little bit. It hardly seems like I've had much time to talk with you, brother." Lincoln handed Cal a soda.

"I've been here since Tuesday." Calhoun opened the screen door and stepped outside.

Linc followed. "It's been busy, though, with the kids and Vivian. I like her, and I'm glad you brought her along."

"Me, too." Calhoun meant that. Vivian mattered to him. She'd become the salt to his pepper, and he couldn't imagine living without her.

They settled into the Adirondack chairs in back.

Cal sipped his root beer. From the wrinkle in Lincoln's forehead, he suspected this wasn't just a casual conversation but guessed his brother had something weighing on his mind. It likely had to do with rodeo, and he prayed it wasn't about Sullivan.

"Calhoun, it'll be four years in August since Sullivan died," Linc began and sighed. "You gotta let it go. He's gone, bro."

Cal wished he could stick his fingers in both ears and chant to drown him out. He didn't want to hear whatever this was. "I can't," he responded. "It was my fault. He shouldn't have died."

"That's nonsense, and you know it." Lincoln's voice cracked like a whip. "You didn't have any way to see what would happen."

"I should've listened to him." Calhoun put down his root beer. It'd gone sour in his mouth and churned in his gut.

"Have you talked to Vivian about Sully?" Lincoln tipped his head back and drank a long swallow.

Calhoun's shoulders hitched. "I told her he died, a little more, but not the whole story."

"You ought to tell her," Lincoln said in a serious tone.

Calhoun'd rather fight a den of rattlesnakes with his bare hands. He worried Vivian might loathe him when she learned the truth about his brother's death. "Can't."

"It's more like won't." Linc finished his root beer.

A flashback played across Cal's mind, torturing him, and in that moment, he was back in Dodge City.

In the first week of August, the heat had hung heavy over the flat Kansas prairie. They pulled into Dodge late Monday because unlike most rodeos, this one started on Tuesday and ran through Sunday night. It took place at the same time as a local festival, but the purses were high, so they came, Calhoun and his brother, the one everyone called Last Chance.

Sully rode the first night in the extreme bull-riding competition. Proud of him for qualifying, Calhoun didn't ride, but he had been there to cheer the kid to victory. They traveled together with Cal's tin-can trailer, a tight fit for two grown men, but it worked. Chance had been off his feed since Saturday, a rare thing because he usually ate everything that wasn't nailed down.

"You okay?" Calhoun asked him after they had the trailer set up. "You haven't said two words, and you haven't eaten. We can go get a burger or something if you want."

His brother held his abdomen with both hands. "I'm not hungry. My stomach hurts. I think I tore something when I came off the bull Saturday night in Oklahoma."

"You probably ate too many corn dogs." Cal dismissed the idea.

Chance met his gaze "It ain't that. Feels different, Cal."

"If it's not better after you ride, we'll get it checked out. I bet it'll pass, though. It's just a stomachache."

Wearing his favorite Western shirt, Chance still complained about his gut on Tuesday, right up until time to ride bulls. He'd shown Calhoun his bruised belly. "It hurts more when I get up from sitting or move around. It's likely to kill me when I ride that ornery bull. Maybe I ought to withdraw."

"Sounds like the kid might have torn an abdominal muscle. I did last year, and that's the way it hurt me." Their pal Rusty added his opinion, based on experience.

"Did you go to a doc?" Calhoun asked, not really paying much attention.

"I did. He told me to rest up and go easy for a few weeks, so I did. It quit bothering me after that." Rusty nodded.

The kid touched his stomach and winced. "Hurts worse when I touch it."

Calhoun was raised to be tough, so he expected no less from his kid brother. "Cowboy up, Last Chance. If it still hurts after you ride, we're heading home anyhow. You can take it easy then."

The full evening sun highlighted Sullivan as he came out of the chute on Satan's Hellion, a two-thousand-pound Plummer, a mixed breed bull of half-longhorn, half Brahma. He raised his right hand high, but as the bull contorted and snorted, wilder than most, the animal careened out of control. Chance bounced like a rag doll, clinging tight to the rope.

Calhoun saw his brother clutch his belly with both hands, letting go of the rope, before the bull bucked him.

Sullivan flew from the animal and landed hard but struggled to his feet. The bull, still kicking, nailed him with his rear feet and threw him into the arena fence with force.

As the crowd fell silent and the announcer's tones became hushed, Sullivan Kelly, known as Last Chance, landed hard and never moved again.

Although the cause of death was head trauma, the doctor who signed the death certificate noted the victim demonstrated evidence of an abdominal muscle tear. He listed it as secondary cause of death.

Calhoun knew then his brother's death was his fault. He told him to ride when he should have taken him to the hospital. If Cal had, Last Chance would still be alive.

Remembering made him sick to his stomach, and Cal stood. He made it to the edge of the porch, bent double, and puked. The spatter hit the ground below. He brought up everything he'd eaten and heaved until his abdominal muscles ached. Calhoun prayed Lincoln wouldn't touch him. Right now, he wouldn't be able to stand it. "Sorry for that display," Calhoun apologized, from the edge of the porch.

"I'm sorry I brought it on." Linc's tone was quiet as an old-fashioned library. "I didn't mean to make you upset. I just wanted to see you move forward. I truly think Vivian can help."

Fear tightened his chest. If she heard the whole story, she might want to move on and not look back. "I don't want her to know."

Lincoln put one hand on his shoulder. "She knows enough to hear what happened. I told her it's your story to tell, but you're not to blame."

"I still think I am. I failed him, Linc." Guilt twisted his stomach until it hurt more.

"You loved him, just like I did. Bull riders get hurt, and sometimes, they die. He knew the risks, and so do we. I wish you'd think about hanging up your spurs, Calhoun. I don't want to bury another brother." Lincoln lowered his hand to Calhoun's back and patted it.

The last colors of the sunset fired the sky to the west with vivid oranges, contrasting black, and brilliant red. An old saying Granny taught them came to mind, *Red sky at night, sailor's delight.*

"Tomorrow ought to be a pretty day." Cal ignored what his brother said. "I should go to bed. We don't have to head out too soon, but I want to be up early so I have plenty of time to say goodbye to all of you, especially the boys."

"I wish you wouldn't shut me out." Lincoln dropped his hand.

Cal stepped away. He faced Lincoln with a pasted-on grin, fake as a Halloween mask. "I only do when you talk about him."

Behind them, the screen door twanged as it opened.

"Calhoun?" Vivian's voice floated toward him, soft and melodious.

"I'm here." Cal turned. She stood on the porch, in a T-shirt style, light-gray nightgown embellished with tiny pink roses. The garment hung to her knees. Her feet were bare.

"Are you all right?" Vivian asked.

Lincoln patted his shoulder one more time. "I'm heading inside. I'll see you in the morning. Sleep well."

"Good night," Cal told his brother, then faced Vivian. "I'm good, honey."

"I came down to get a bottle of water and heard someone throwing up. Are you sick?" She came a few steps closer.

He shook his head. "I'll be fine once my stomach settles, but I'm not sick. We were talking about Sullivan, and I got upset, that's all." He longed for her to hug him, but he probably reeked of vomit. He wouldn't kiss her, not now.

"I saw some peppermint tea bags in one of the cabinets," Vivian told him. "Let me make you a cup. It'll ease your tummy."

For a long moment, he considered rejecting her offer and stomping across the yard to vent his emotions. She gazed at him with those pretty hazel eyes, and he knew he wouldn't. "That sounds good, Pretty Lady. All right. Thanks."

"Any time, Cowboy," she responded.

The tea did help, and as they sat at the kitchen table, she gave him quiet and space. Vivian didn't chatter or ask him to explain why he'd been upset. She was there, and that was more than enough.

Chapter Fourteen

With Rusk and his family in the rearview mirror, Calhoun was in what her Nanna would call a mood. He didn't act angry, just quiet. Although a steady stream of country gold sang from the truck speakers, he didn't sing along or say much. By the time they were halfway to Fort Worth, Vivian wanted to know why. "What are you thinking about?" She cuddled close in the truck seat.

Cal gazed at her, serious faced with no hint of a smile. "Nothing, everything."

She rolled her eyes. "That tells me a lot. Is something wrong?"

"No, honey. Lincoln and I were talking about Sully last night. He brought him up, and it stirred memories I'd rather forget. Leaving home always makes me a little sad, too. I'll get past it. By the time we get to Fort Worth, I'll be looking forward to riding tonight."

"Do you ride both nights?" Vivian scooted a little closer, encouraged by his conversation.

"I signed up to, so yeah. This rodeo is in the historic stockyards district and the hotel is close. On Saturday afternoon, we can watch a real-life cattle drive, and there's plenty to see. We'll get some of the best steaks you've ever eaten, too."

At least she had him talking, an improvement over the miles of his silence. Vivian longed to ask about

Sullivan, but she figured if she did, he would stop speaking again.

Light rain splattered the windshield.

"Will you compete if it's raining?"

"Rodeos don't cancel for rain or much of anything, but it won't matter. The Cowtown Coliseum is an indoor arena, the first one ever built, and the oldest in the United States."

The route they drove skirted south of Dallas to miss the worst traffic. Calhoun had insisted they leave Rusk by eight thirty, earlier than he'd first suggested, but Vivian understood why when they hit Fort Worth. Although it wasn't quite eleven, the noon rush had begun. Although she'd lived in the Kansas City metro area for several years, she'd never adjusted to urban rush hour traffic. Vehicles of every description sped around them, rode their bumper, passed on both the left and right.

Cal never wavered. He kept the truck at the speed limit and was familiar enough with exits to take the right ones. The rain quit before very long.

Despite the traffic, he sang along with a few tunes but fell silent when a Horton song, "Streets of Dodge," played.

With minimal guitar, Johnny Horton's voice carried a plaintive quality, poignant enough to send a shiver down her back.

Cal shut off the music. It reminded him too much of Sully, in Dodge City, where his brother died.

Sitting next to Calhoun, Vivian felt his muscles tense. "What is it?"

He removed one hand from the wheel and pushed back his unruly curls, then blew air through his nose.

"Dodge City is where Sullivan died, where he met his fate. I used to love that song, but now, it breaks my heart."

The truck drifted slightly to the left, and the harsh horn from a passing semi-truck blasted loudly. Vivian cringed.

Calhoun swerved back into their lane.

Vivian held her breath as he maneuvered the pickup across three lanes to barrel down an exit ramp at top speed. She clutched the edge of the seat, with her right hand, terrified they would be in a collision at any moment.

Once they reached the outer road, he pulled into the first fast-food place to the right and parked.

She couldn't tell if they were still in Dallas or if they'd entered Fort Worth. The urban sprawl ran together, and the heavy traffic whizzed past. A single tear trailed down his cheek, so Vivian reached up and wiped it away. "Calhoun?"

"I'm sorry, honey." He leaned his head against the steering wheel.

She put her hand against his hair, wanting to offer comfort but uncertain what she could say. "You're grieving. I understand, Cal, I do." Vivian teased her fingers through his curls.

He raised his head and turned a ravaged face. "You can't. It's not just I lost him, but it was my fault he died."

An icy chill fluttered through her. In her strange encounter with his brother, she heard Sullivan say Cal took the blame. Within the dream, his brother also said it wasn't his fault. "How could that be?"

His features were anguished, eyes bright with tears

and mouth set in a hard line. "He complained he had a stomachache, a bad one. I told him it was nothing, he probably ate too much, but he thought he'd hurt himself the night before. He thought about withdrawing from the rodeo, but I told him to ride. Even after Rusty, you know, Nail, our buddy, said Chance probably tore a stomach muscle, I told him to compete. I said if he still was hurting after, we'd head for home, and he could rest up. He said…"

Calhoun's voice cracked like shattered glass, and he swallowed hard. "He said riding that bull would likely kill him, and it did. I shouldn't have told him to ride, Vivian. I ought to have taken him to a doctor or something. He had torn a gut muscle, the doc said after the autopsy. He died from massive head injuries, but the torn muscle got listed as a secondary cause. Sullivan rode because I told him to, so I carry that on my conscience. I killed him, honey, and I struggle to live with that. Linc thought I should tell you, but I didn't want to. I figure you'd hate me, knowing I pushed my kid brother to his death."

Vivian put a hand on his back and rubbed it in circles. "I'll never hate you, and you didn't. Lincoln said it wasn't your fault."

Calhoun shook his head. "He wasn't there."

Vivian had to tell him about the dream or whatever it was now. "Do you remember when I got rattled seeing Sullivan's picture at your place? And when I asked you about that eagle bolo tie?"

Cal narrowed his eyes and stared. "Yeah. So what?"

"I hadn't seen a picture of him before that, but I dreamed about him the first night I spent at Lincoln's house. I recognized him." The words came hard because Vivian wasn't sure he'd believe her and worried it might make him angry. "In the dream, he wore that eagle bolo tie, and he told me it wasn't your fault."

"Honey…" Another tear slid down Cal's face, then another.

She put a finger to his lips. "Hush and let me tell it. He said if it was anyone's fault, it was his and Satan's Hellion's, but not yours. He said don't make the same mistake he did, and then said tell you, Last Chance says howdy. I didn't even know you called him that, not 'til afterward."

When he didn't respond, she wanted to take it all back. Vivian wished she hadn't told him. Now he'd probably rage or maybe take her back to Missouri after this rodeo and say farewell. As the silence stretched out for more than a minute, she wanted to bolt from the truck. Maybe she could find a bus station and catch a Greyhound home. He'd worried she might hate him, but now maybe he had no use for her. Vivian scooted toward the passenger seat and moved a little away from Cal.

Calhoun stretched out his right hand and rested it on her knee. "Honey, I don't know what to say except I believe you." His voice croaked with emotion. "We buried him with that tie, and I didn't tell you we called him Last Chance. If anybody could turn up after being dead to jump into a pretty gal's dream, it'd be Sully. I don't know what it means, but maybe I can wrap my head around the idea that it wasn't my doing. Probably not today, likely not tomorrow, but someday, maybe."

Relief poured over her, like water down a parched

throat. She ached to weep, but more than that, she needed to touch him and hold him close. "I hope so. I don't want you to keep beating yourself up about something you couldn't help, Calhoun."

A tiny sliver of a smile spread over his lips. "C'mere, Pretty Lady." He put an arm around her but with the tight quarters in the truck cab, it didn't work. Cal opened his door and stepped out, then beckoned for her to join him.

She slid across the bench seat and stood in the parking lot.

He pulled her into his arms and held her close.

Vivian rested her head against his chest and savored the moment.

"I don't know why you bother with me. But I'm really glad you do." He tightened his embrace.

Because I think I love you. Vivian didn't share the thought but held back. It might be too much on the heels of this already emotional morning, and she wasn't totally sure she did. "You're worth it. I'm pretty fond of you, Cowboy." The sound of his heartbeat comforted her, and Vivian enjoyed the feel of his chambray shirt against her cheek.

"Likewise. Do you want to grab some lunch or just head for the hotel? I think they'll let us check in early. When I booked it, I told them I'm here to ride rodeo." He brushed back a loose strand of hair from her face.

"I'm not a bit hungry after that huge breakfast Sasha made, so let's check in." Vivian smoothed her unruly hair.

His grin returned. "Sounds like a plan. Let's go."

They skirted the edges of the historic stockyard district, but Vivian knew she'd see it later. For now, she was glad she'd told him about her dream, but one question still haunted her, especially since Calhoun ignored it. What mistake had Sullivan made he didn't want his brother to repeat? Riding bulls? Riding sick? What? She had no idea and wanted to know but refrained from asking. Cal's emotions had been slashed open, and now wasn't the time to add another cut. She'd either figure it out or ask later.

She expected a traditional, plain motel like the one where she'd stayed in Arkansas, but instead, he'd reserved their room at a chain all-suite hotel. Located at the corner of Main and Twenty-Third Street within the district, it stood five stories tall, featured fantastic views of the stockyards, provided free breakfast, had laundry facilities, and offered a rooftop bar serving food. The room boasted a small living area with a couch and desk, two queen-sized beds, a table for two, and a spacious bath with a walk-in shower. From the window, Vivian could see the Fort Worth skyline in the distance.

"Is it all right?" Cal carried in their luggage. He stood behind her at the window and nuzzled her neck.

"It's wonderful," she replied. "No spa tub, though."

"I'll manage, Pretty Lady."

They walked down the street holding hands to get hamburger steaks at a place Calhoun liked. The historic district reminded her of old-fashioned downtowns, but this area bustled with tourists and cowboys.

A window display of ladies' cowgirl hats caught Cal's eye, and he paused. "I'll buy you one. Which one do you like?"

As she deliberated between a dark-blue style with a denim ribbon around the brim and a brown wool one decorated with turquoise beads on the hatband, someone called Cal's name and approached.

The blonde teetered on stiletto heeled sandals, wore cutoff denim shorts covering very little and a red calico print top, tied to display her bare midriff. Her eyes were heavy with several shades of eye shadow, long, fake eyelashes, and barn-red lipstick. Her platinum hair had been teased high into a bouffant style and horse-shaped earrings dangled almost to her shoulders.

"Calhoun Kelly, bull rider!" The woman reached toward Cal as if she planned to hug him.

Cal took a step back and pulled Vivian close. "I don't believe I know you."

"Oh, but I know you! You're a bull riding star! Are you competing at The Cowtown Coliseum tonight? If so, I'll be there with all my gal pals. I want your autograph, and if you're not doing anything after, I'll buy you a drink at Billy Bob's, sugar. Maybe we can get to know each other well. My name's Candy Collins, and they tell me I'm sweeter than any candy." She giggled as she spoke.

Vivian steamed. Jealousy reared up within, and if it wasn't for the fact Calhoun showed no interest, Vivian would have been tempted to shove the other woman. She ached to position her fingers into a claw position.

"No, thanks," Cal told her. "I don't drink, and I'm not interested."

Candy Collins lifted a hand and touched Cal's cheek with a five-inch-long nail painted red to match her mouth. "Don't be that way, sugar britches. Don't play hard to get with Candy. If you don't drink, we'll dance, and then maybe we'll share a night together. I promise you it'll be the ride of your life."

Vivian twined her arm through his. She parted her lips, ready to say something to make the ridiculous woman move away.

"It's not happening." Calhoun responded with speed. I'm sure you can find a cowboy who'll take you up on your offer, but it won't be me. My lady and I have plans of our own, so move on, okay."

Her red lips pursed into a pout. "Your loss, bull rider." She sashayed away on her heels.

Vivian stared after her. "What was that all about?"

"That, honey, was a buckle bunny. They never have appealed to me, so you don't have to worry."

"I wasn't." But she had been. "Does that happen a lot?"

Cal shrugged. "More around these bigger rodeos, but yeah, quite a bit. I just tell them *no,* and keep moving. Now, do you want a hat?"

Vivian might have refused, but she would like one. She ached to fit into his world, and it seemed a hat was a necessary accessory. If she would be traveling with him, she'd need one. If nothing else, it might keep the sun out of her face. "Yes. I like the blue one."

They entered the store, and she savored the aroma of rich leather and new clothing.

At the checkout, Cal paid for the hat.

But Vivian bought several things, too. She chose a sleeveless denim dress with embroidered roses on the shoulders, a wine-colored ladies' Western blouse with pearl snaps, and a T-shirt that said, *Bull Riders Do It Best.* She hadn't brought many clothes and would need to wash some at the hotel, so a few additions to her wardrobe were welcome.

On the way to the front, he picked up one more

item—a small, dainty silver cross with a heart enclosing the cross. "Will you let me get this, too?"

"It's beautiful," Vivian told him. "But you know I don't believe anymore."

"Yeah, honey, I know, but I do. I believe it'll keep you safe, so will you humor this old cowboy?" Calhoun wore a tiny smile as he asked.

She touched the wooden cross he always wore and nodded. "I will because it's pretty. If you're waiting for me to decide to go back to God, you'll have a long wait."

"Maybe and maybe not," Calhoun spoke in a serious tone "Someday, you might decide you need Him after all, and then you might pray."

If she answered, they would fight, and she didn't want to argue. Vivian let him clasp it around her neck, and she liked the feel of it on her throat. It mattered because he bought it, she thought, and that's why she liked it. She wore the new hat.

Cal carried the bag with her purchases.

At a small grill, they ordered hamburger steaks with fries, Texas Toast, and a side salad. The steak was huge, but delicious.

Calhoun finished his portion and patted his belly. "I won't eat again 'til after the rodeo. We've got a few hours 'til I need to head over to the Coliseum. Do you want to walk around more or rest a little?"

She noticed he'd favored his knee a little. "We can go back to the room, Cal. We'll be here tomorrow, too, right?"

"Yeah, we won't leave until Sunday. It's a long way out to Arizona, but we'll travel slow." Once at the hotel, he sprawled across the bed and slept.

While he dozed, she called Nanna. "I'm in Fort Worth. We're staying in a hotel in the historic stockyards district. Calhoun rides tonight and tomorrow at the Cowtown Coliseum. That's really the name!"

Nanna laughed. "I've heard of it, Vivvie. In fact, I was there once, long years ago. It's been around for more than a hundred years. Your grandpapa took me to see Elvis sing there not long after we were first married."

"I didn't know you'd been to Texas or Fort Worth." Sometimes, Nanna amazed her.

"I imagine there's plenty you don't know, child. We were on vacation. I loved Elvis, as you know, and so your grandpa bought tickets so we could see him perform. He was wonderful, so much more so in person. He sang 'Heartbreak Hotel' along with other songs."

"I'll tell Calhoun. He'll think it's awesome." So did Vivian.

"How is he doing? I hope you're coming up soon. I miss you, and I'd like to see your cowboy again." Nanna's voice rang strong over the phone.

"Cal says after Prescott we'll come up. That's over the Fourth of July. Then we'll stay a little while in Missouri before heading to Nebraska, I think." Vivian wasn't sure, but she would go where Calhoun traveled as long as he wanted.

"Tell him to be careful. I worry about him, you know. Tell him I pray for him every night."

"He'll appreciate that, I'm sure." Vivian couldn't keep a faint snark from her voice and rolled her eyes at the mention of prayer.

"I imagine so. Don't knock it too hard, Vivvie. One

of these days, you might find yourself turning back to God again." Her grandmother laughed a little.

"You sound like Calhoun. He bought me a cross necklace, and I'm wearing it, because he gave it to me, no other reason." She fingered the chain as she spoke.

"I'm glad. Did you ever tell him you love him?"

"No." She wasn't totally sure she did. Care, yes, but love? Maybe.

"You really should. If something should happen to Calhoun, and you never told him…"

"Don't say things like that!" Vivian cried. "Nothing is going to happen! I couldn't stand it if it did!"

First Calhoun, now Nanna mentioned the same. It would be more than she could bear if anything awful happened to him. Added to the vague warning from a dream, she grew so uneasy that her nerves jangled.

"Life's too short not to tell someone you love them," Nanna told her. " 'Take therefore no thought for the morrow: for the morrow shall take thought for the things of itself. Sufficient unto the day is the evil thereof.' "

"That's from Matthew." She might not read the Bible these days, but she hadn't forgotten what she'd learned. She just refused to believe any of it.

"Right! Matthew 6:34. It means, don't worry, child."

"I will, though." Caring about Cal meant she'd be concerned every time he got on a bull—especially after hearing about his brother's death.

Nanna chattered about her daily bingo game, shared what flowers were in bloom on the facility's front porch, and what she'd had for lunch.

Vivian ended the call and since Calhoun slept, she read until four, when she woke him with a gentle kiss. *Sleeping Beauty in reverse.*

Before the rodeo, he put on his gear, but first he taped his joints and added an elastic knee brace. He took some ibuprofen and donned one of his fanciest Western shirts to ride. Vivian laughed, watching Cal button his dirty bull-riding jeans. "I can wash those, you know."

"Might wash away the luck," he teased. "Bull riders don't wash the jeans they compete wearing. I told you so once already."

"I'm doing some laundry tomorrow here, so if you change your mind, let me know." Vivian twirled to show off her outfit. She wore her black jeans, the new T-shirt, her boots, and her cowboy hat. To accommodate it, she wore her hair down her back in a single braid.

Calhoun grinned. "You look pretty."

"Thank you. You look fine yourself, Calhoun." His compliments brought a warm rush.

"If you're ready, let's go, honey. I want to get signed in and pay my entry money, then sit with you for a while. Got your camera?"

"I do tonight." Although she set out with the idea of taking rodeo photographs, she hadn't shot as many as planned. Most of the shots were of Cal, and she still hoped to sell a few. Vivian had been so caught up in love she seldom picked up the camera.

Calhoun's dark eyes glowed, and he wore a sweet smile.

She kissed him.

He gave it back with tenderness.

Maybe Nanna had called it right, she thought, maybe she did love him. Deep inside, she knew that she did.

Chapter Fifteen

The first four bull riders scratched with none lasting eight seconds, and the fifth disqualified when he touched the bull with his free arm.

Calhoun rode next. Despite air-conditioning, the temperature inside the indoor venue soared with the place packed to the rafters. In the arena, beneath the lights, Cal sweated enough to take off his hat to wipe sweat from his forehead. He glanced toward Vivian's seat.

She waved.

Because bull riders were slated to go early, right after "God Bless The USA," the usual prayers, and the national anthem, he hadn't been able to sit with Vivian for more than a few minutes. Before he left, Calhoun pointed out the giant screen where she could watch replays of his ride above the announcer's booth, flanked by the American and Texas flags. On his way to the chutes, he glimpsed the buckle bunny they encountered earlier.

She pointed a finger and scowled, then said something to her friends who tittered.

Cal didn't care. The buckle bunny wasn't worth the effort or attention. Calhoun focused on the bull as he settled onto the animal named Tommy Torpedo. After saying a silent prayer and touching his cross, he did his best to filter out the music, the announcer's voice, the cheers and jeers from the crowd, and his thoughts. He tightened his hold on the rope and raised his left arm.

When the chute opened, the bull blasted from it with force, hooves flying in every direction.

But he held fast. When he came off the bull, he knew from the wild applause he'd made eight seconds. Cal sought Vivian.

She grinned, giving him a thumbs-up. Once out of the arena, he lingered long enough to watch his ride replay and hear his score, which was a solid eighty-three. Relieved and elated, he headed for the stands, but a redheaded cowboy stepped into his path.

"Whoa, pardner. I been looking out for you, Cal."

It was his buddy, Rusty, the one they all called Nail. "Come on up and meet my lady." Calhoun shook the other cowboy's hand with a vigorous gesture.

"Glad to! Good to see you, dude. You're looking better than you have in a while."

He might as well say since Sully died because that's what he meant. "I spent a couple days at home with Linc and the family. That always does me good. So does Vivian."

As they climbed to the seats, Cal opened his arms and caught Vivian when she flew toward him. He savored holding her close.

"That was a fantastic ride, Calhoun. I was on the edge of my seat, and I got some awesome shots." Vivian gazed at him with a bright smile.

He kissed her, unable to resist that pretty, upturned face. "I lasted eight seconds and got a good score. Honey, this is my pal, Rusty. Nail, this is Vivian Bradburn."

"We swapped howdys on the phone," Rusty

reminded. "You're prettier in person."

"And she's mine." Cal slapped his friend across the back. He hadn't meant to say it aloud, but Cal wasn't joking. He didn't want his friend to think for a single moment Vivian was available. Calhoun kept his arm around her.

"I won't trespass." Nail held up his hands in mock surrender. "I know better. Better get back in your seats before someone else takes them. I gotta get to the arena. I'm riding saddle broncs tonight. I don't suppose you're going to Billy Bob's afterward?"

"Not me," Calhoun replied. "Not my scene. We're eating steak before we head back to the hotel. Want to meet up for lunch tomorrow?"

Rusty nodded. "I'd like that, sure. Text me, all right?"

"I will. Bill here?" Cal made a mental note to remember.

"Nope, but he'll be in Prescott. I'll see you tomorrow, Cal." Rusty waved as he descended toward the chutes and arena.

Vivian remained snuggled close.

Calhoun draped his left arm across her shoulders. "Do you want to stay a while or go eat now?"

"Whatever you'd like. I'm good either way." She offered him a smile.

Maybe it was the contrast to the few days spent in quiet locations, the old farmhouse in Missouri, the top of Rich Mountain, and his brother's ranch, but the packed indoor arena smothered him. More than three thousand people under one roof, the loud, never-ending noise, the heat, and the combined smells of livestock, people, and everything from various colognes to old-fashioned sweat threatened to overwhelm Cal. He hungered for fresh, clean air, a breath of wind, and hushed sounds. The initial rush of a good ride and high score faded and left anxiety behind. "Let's go." He extended his right hand.

Vivian removed the long lens from her camera and packed her gear into the bag she'd carried instead of a purse. She looped it over one shoulder and took his offered hand. They made slow progress through the arena. People he knew and people he'd never met offered congratulations. Some gave advice and others praise. The return walk back to Cal's pickup seemed like miles, and by the time they reached it, his knee ached. A dull headache nagged.

At one of the oldest steakhouses in the stockyards district, he led Vivian to a booth, glad of the privacy. He ordered T-bone steaks for both, with side salads and garlic mashed potatoes.

Vivian raised her eyebrows when she noted the price listed on the menu. "You could buy the whole cow for that, Cowboy."

Cal almost forgot about his knee and headache. "Not quite, honey. Hush and enjoy." He asked a heartfelt blessing. Calhoun couldn't help but be proud he'd ridden the full eight seconds, happy he'd done so without injury, and pleased with his score.

The steak was perfect, tender, and cooked medium rare, the way he preferred. He savored the garlic mashed potatoes. Salad was something he could eat or do without, but he ate almost the entire portion. Calhoun enjoyed the company most of all. He washed down the meal with root beer, and he noticed Vivian did, too.

"Looks like I've converted you." Cal watched her expression change from delight to a frown and realized she probably mistook his meaning. *She's so sensitive about the Lord and prayer.* Her rejection of faith was the one flaw in their relationship. He'd begun to think he wanted her for the long haul, but his beliefs were at his core. Cal couldn't change that or upend his faith. If Vivian couldn't bend, then he worried it might cause friction in the future or cause dissention, which might someday sink their relationship. That was the last thing he wanted. "Pretty Lady, I'm talking about root beer and nothing else. I noticed you're drinking some, too." He held up his glass to make his point clear.

Her scowl vanished. "It's not bad, Calhoun. I'm usually more of an iced tea girl, but I like the taste. What's Billy Bob's? Your friend and the buckle bunny both mentioned it."

"It's Billy Bob's Texas. World's largest honky-tonk, but I avoid it. It's huge, crazy, and trouble waiting to happen. I suppose people who like to drink and party think it's fun, but not me. You don't want to go, do you?"

"Never. I just wondered." She winked.

Back at the hotel, Calhoun changed out of his gear, left his dirty clothes stacked in the small sitting area, and took a long, hot shower. After putting on sweatpants and a T-shirt, he dosed himself with ibuprofen and got into bed. Yawning, Calhoun climbed into one of the beds and watched a few minutes of a movie he'd never seen. Before Vivian returned from her shower, he drifted into sleep.

In the morning, he woke and realized it was late. Sunshine peeked around the edges of the drapes, which were still drawn, and he smelled coffee from the in-room pot, but Vivian wasn't there. Calhoun stumbled out of bed, visited the bathroom, and drank the last cup of coffee. It was tolerable but far from good. He considered calling her cell phone but didn't.

When Vivian returned, she carried bags of clean clothing. The scent of laundry detergent wafted into the room. She put the clothes down on the couch and smiled. "Hi, Calhoun."

"Good morning, Pretty Lady. I wondered where you were." He'd worried she'd taken off—although that was unreasonable, and he didn't see any reason why she would.

"I decided to do the wash early and get it over with. I washed your stuff, too."

Until then he hadn't noticed his stack of rodeo clothing had diminished. His bull riding jeans were gone. "You washed my jeans?"

"I did, Cowboy. They could stand up on their own, with all that dirt caked into them. I was afraid next they might walk across the room or do a two-step."

"I guess they might have. Just don't ever put my hat on the bed." Too late for not washing the jeans because Vivian had. Cal didn't have a good reason to gripe, so he laughed, but he meant it about the hat.

"Why not?" She wrinkled her nose.

"Serious bad luck, honey. What's for breakfast?"

"It's almost lunchtime, Calhoun." Vivian sat at the small table across from him.

He couldn't believe it, but the clock between the beds confirmed the time. "I never sleep this late. No wonder I'm hungry."

"We'll go eat." She twined her fingers around his

192

wrist. "They had breakfast downstairs, but I think it's over. It wasn't much. All they offered was cereal, juice, granola bars, and fruit."

"That ain't breakfast," he drawled. "That's grazing."

They ate lunch, then did a little more sightseeing. At four, Calhoun made sure she saw the daily cattle drive as it passed through the streets of the stockyard district. The sight always gave him a thrill, more so because he knew his ancestors had trailed cattle from down around Laredo north to Kansas back in the day. The round trip had taken months and had to have been more difficult than he could imagine.

"I'm descended from cowboys who did this for real. Lincoln's got the old papers and family trees. I don't remember all their names except for the first cowboy in our family to hit Texas, Barlow Washington. He had more sand than I ever will, I'm sure." Calhoun shared his family history, something he seldom did.

"That's the one you said was a Confederate, then came to Texas after the war?"

"Yeah, that's him." Calhoun nodded.

"How did he end up with a descendant named Lincoln, then?" Vivian frowned as she referenced the sixteenth president of the United States.

This woman made him laugh, and he liked that. "Honey, it's been over one hundred fifty years, so I suppose any negativity faded a long time ago. Besides, he's not named for old Abe but for the car."

Vivian gaped. "You're kidding."

"Nope, my dad always wanted a Lincoln and never did get one, so he named his first son after the car he wanted. I'm lucky I wasn't named Ford or Chevy or something."

"I suppose you are." Vivian shook her head.

"Before you ask, Calhoun and Sullivan are both family names," he explained. "I always fancied if I ever have a son, I'd like to name him Barlow or Washington, maybe."

After that, they headed back so he could get ready to ride. The clean jeans felt strange, but he liked the way they felt, too. At the Cowtown Coliseum, he parted ways with Vivian. Tonight, she left her camera behind so she could focus on his ride without looking through a lens. He rode in the second flight tonight and drew a bull with a bad reputation named Wicked Warlock. Cal hung on, despite his rosin-slicked hands for the full eight seconds before the bull pitched him off, and he landed hard.

Worse than that, the animal lowered his head and rammed his left thigh.

The bull didn't gore him, but the impact hurt and he knew it would bruise. Still, mostly to reassure Vivian, he raised one hand and lifted his fingers in a *V* for victory sign. Cal's score of seventy-eight was solid enough but he winced watching the replay.

Vivian didn't wait for him to climb up to the seats but met him outside the chute. "That looked like it hurt. Are you all right? Did he hurt you?"

Her eyes scanned over his body, probably looking for blood.

"Nah, honey, he didn't. Just slammed me hard. It'll bruise, but it's okay." It hurt more than he wanted to admit.

"What if you tore a muscle?"

Her question evoked Sully, and Cal had a feeling

she very well realized it.

"I didn't. It doesn't hurt enough for that. I'm ready to go, though, if you are.

"You scared me, Cowboy. I was so worried you were hurt. Are you sure you're okay?" Vivian hugged tight, arena dirt, sweat, and all. "What if you won money?"

Calhoun sighed. He needed to stay and see. He got injured, but it wasn't life threatening. By tomorrow, the spot that hurt like the dickens would be bruised, and he might limp a little, favoring it. At least he wasn't six feet under like Sullivan. "We'll stay and find out. C'mon, honey. Let's find a seat."

As they started in that direction, Rusty showed up. "Great ride, but you're banged up."

"I'll do," Cal replied through gritted teeth. "It'll heal by the time I ride in Prescott."

"You leaving?" Rusty raised his eyebrows.

"Gotta wait to see if I take home any bucks." Calhoun sighed.

A dozen more people inquired about his injuries on the way. The last one was a buckle bunny, this one a fiery redhead with hair so bright it had to come from a henna bottle. Her name was Dovie. He'd never welcomed her attentions, but it didn't stop her from approaching or ignoring the fact Cal had one arm around Vivian.

"Cal! That looked awful! Oh, you poor thing. I've got a heating pad back at the motel, if you want to come over to use it. I'm bunking with Tee, but there's enough room if you wanted to stay the night so I could take care of you."

"He'll get all the tender, loving care he needs from

me, so turn around and get lost." Vivian wrapped one arm around his waist.

"Cal, if this woman's bothering you, I'll get rid of her. I'll take her to fist city if you want." The buckle bunny glared at Vivian, ready to rumble.

"Dovie, this is my Lady." Calhoun stated. "Try that and I'll call security. I don't believe in hitting women, but if you touch my gal, I won't be responsible for what happens next."

She parked her hands on her hips, huffed, then walked away.

Vivian put her other arm around his waist so they held each other. "I don't like buckle bunnies, Calhoun."

That brought a smile but so had her fierce words to Dovie. "Neither do I. Let's sit."

He placed high enough in the standings to win decent money. Once Cal collected his fifteen hundred dollars, they left. By then, his thigh hurt enough he wasn't sure if he wanted to eat, but they hadn't since lunch.

Vivian suggested takeout, and so they picked up a pizza on the way to the room.

He approved her choice of sausage, black olive, onion, and mushroom and ate a couple of pieces as they shared the meal at the table in the room. "I wish this room had a spa tub," he commented. "Or even just a tub so I could soak this. There won't be one tomorrow night, either."

"Where are we staying next?" Vivian reached for a second slice.

"Amarillo," he told her. "It's a good sixteen hours from here to Prescott, and I'd rather not do that in one hook. Albuquerque's closer to halfway, but it's still hours to get there. We're not in a huge hurry, as long as we get there before the rodeo starts. So, I'm thinking to take three days. The trip is five or so hours to Amarillo, then six to Gallup. From Gallup, it's another four and a half to Prescott."

"Three days on the road?" Vivian sighed and rubbed the back of her neck.

"And that much or more when we head to Missouri. But we'll probably go a different route, and there won't be any rush at all."

Vivian finished a slice of pizza and packed up what remained to put in the room's mini fridge. "How do you know there's not a tub tomorrow night?"

"It's a budget motel. I already booked it." He rubbed his thigh.

"We can change it. I can make another reservation, if you want."

Calhoun loved the way she wanted to make sure he had every comfort. Although left to himself, he tended to be stoic to the point of near martyrdom. Part of his attitude was due to Sullivan's death and his role in it, but being tough was also the cowboy way. The old-fashioned code they all lived by included honesty, loyalty, and courage. Cal never let pain slow his roll and given a choice, he would always ride through. He took life as it came and didn't gripe. If tonight he couldn't soak in a warm bath, so be it. "It's fine," he told her. "I'll survive."

She reached across the couch where they sat and grasped his hand, twining her fingers around his. "You'd better, Calhoun. I'd never forgive you if you didn't."

"I'm glad you care, Pretty Lady," Cal said.

"Nobody but my brother's family has for a long time. It's been awful lonely."

Vivian's sparkling hazel eyes stared deep into his.

"It won't ever be again, Cowboy, not when I'm around. I'm almost fond enough of you to pray God keeps you safe."

Vivian might be joking, but Calhoun hoped she meant it on some level. "Maybe one of these days you will, honey. I'm sure I could use plenty of prayer."

Vivian touched the cross he'd bought her with her free hand.

Calhoun believed on some level she wanted her faith back. Sometimes he wished they could hold hands and pray together, so she could experience the joy he gained from his Christian walk. Calhoun held his counsel, though, and said nothing more. He knew how easily she got spooked about anything religious.

He drifted to sleep on the couch, her hand in his, but she woke him after she'd showered. Calhoun let the hot water pound against his leg. When he emerged, he found Vivian sound asleep. His drowsiness had vanished, and he stood for a long time, gazing out over the stockyards district, thinking.

He sent up prayers for the pain to ease in his back and knees, for the bruise not to be as deep or sore as he suspected—for Vivian, for her Nanna, and for Lincoln's family. Cal asked for safety in bull riding, direction for the future, and thanked God for the many blessings he received. He counted Vivian among those, and although he still failed to understand why God had taken his younger brother, he had to believe it was part of a plan.

It was his time. Cal reflected on Ecclesiastes.

Those verses had brought comfort when his parents died, shared by his grandmother. They did the same after Sully's death, and he knew that Scripture by heart.

" 'To everything there is a season,' " he whispered the prayer now. " 'And a time to every purpose under the heavens.' " If his time to die came in an arena, then it would. He didn't want it, but he would accept it. If it was his time to love, he would embrace it.

The song based on those verses echoed in his head. They'd played the song, "Turn, Turn, Turn," at Last Chance's funeral, one of three he'd chosen with Linc. Remembering the song relaxed him enough to become sleepy, so he crawled into bed, found a comfortable position, pulled up the sheet, tried to sleep, but he failed. His mind refused to shut down.

Tomorrow would bring a new dawn and day. They'd set forth for another destination, and the Lord would lead him in the right direction, one way or another. First, though, he'd find a church and breakfast, not necessarily in that order.

Chapter Sixteen

Although Vivian had grown up in church, her idea of Sunday mornings in recent years involved sleeping late, breakfast or brunch out, and maybe shopping. She liked it when the stores were less crowded. Sometimes, she might visit a park and, in the afternoon, she often saw a movie. Vivian enjoyed slow days because she didn't have to do anything. Even when she had worked as a reporter, most Sundays offered many events she had to cover. Left to decide, she wouldn't warm a pew, but since it mattered to Calhoun, she would if that's what he wanted. She rose early, around six-thirty, and so did he.

She noticed he favored the injured leg a little and he moved stiff. She had learned that was normal for the day after bull riding. "Is it very sore?"

Calhoun waggled his hand back and forth. "A little. The bruise is starting to show. I like your dress, honey. It's cute."

She'd decided to wear her new denim dress with embroidered roses. It matched her boots, and although casual, it was dressy enough for church.

Cal wore a good button-down shirt, one without pearl snaps or Western styling. He sipped his cup of in-room coffee. "If everything's packed, I'll start toting it to the truck."

"Get one of those luggage carts so it'll be one trip.

Do we have time for breakfast before church?" Vivian paused as she brushed her hair into a high ponytail.

His face lit up. "Sure. There's a pancake house in Weatherford about a half hour from here. This early, it shouldn't be too busy. I heard about a church there, but services aren't until ten thirty, so there's time. If we hit the road afterward, we'll roll into Amarillo about supper time. I wasn't sure if you'd want to go to church."

Vivian sighed. "I don't, but you do. I know it means a lot to you, so I'll do it. Nanna will be happy."

At the pancake house, some tables were already full, but they found one. He ordered two eggs over easy, grilled ham, hash browns, and pancakes.

Vivian opted for pancakes with a side of sausage. When he bowed his head for a blessing, she followed suit. When he finished, this time she responded, "Amen."

The coffee was strong but good, and the food delicious. They finished in time to make services at a small, stone church downtown. The cornerstone dated it to 1894. Although larger, the traditional sanctuary reminded her of the church where she'd been raised. Although Vivian expected to be bored enough to daydream, the music grabbed her attention, and she straightened her posture in the pew. At the front, she glimpsed an acoustic guitar, an electric one, an upright slap bass, drums, a keyboard, and two vocalists. When they began to play, the rockabilly rhythm piqued her interest. Sometimes, she knew the words and could sing, picking up the beat, but when she didn't, she clapped her hands in time to the music. The last one was one Donna Fargo made famous back in Nanna's day, "You Can't Be A Beacon If Your Light Don't Shine." She sang loud and proud on that one, an old favorite.

The music lifted her spirits, if not her soul, and she settled beside Calhoun, happy. He held her hand tight during the sermon. Vivian didn't listen to much of the preacher's words, lost in the music and memories. Afterward, they walked to the truck, parked on the street.

He kissed her as he helped her into the seat. "Thank you, Pretty Lady." He folded the fingers of his left hand to caress her cheek.

"For what?" Vivian covered his hand with her own.

"Going with me to church. I know it's not something you want to do, but I like having you with me. I've sat in many a pew alone. It's nicer with you."

Shame the devil but she'd tell him the truth. "I did like the music."

Once he was behind the wheel, he grinned. "It was awesome. Ready to hit the road? We got about five hours 'til Amarillo."

"I'm ready. Did you want to get a soda pop first?" She could use something cold and sweet after singing. Her lips were dry so she applied some balm from her purse.

"I would." Calhoun wheeled into the next convenience store and picked up drinks.

He headed north toward Wichita Falls, then took US 287 onto Amarillo. At first, they listened to classic country until Calhoun turned off the stereo. "I thought we'd take a break and just talk. What will you do with those forty eleven pictures you've been taking?"

She rested her hand on his thigh, the one that

wasn't bruised. "I might see if some of the rodeo and Western magazines are interested in buying any. I started out with the idea I might do a photography book about rodeo. I still might. The best ones of you I'm keeping, and I thought I might have a couple enlarged and framed for Linc."

"Are they all of me?" He glanced away from the wheel long enough to grin.

"No, silly. A lot, yes, but I've taken other shots, too." Vivian giggled.

"How come I haven't seen any of them yet?"

She shrugged. "I haven't downloaded or processed them yet. I'll do that when we get back to Missouri, and you can look at all of them. I thought you could pick one for Nanna. She'd love to have one to hang in her room."

"Sure, I can. I'd like to see the ones you've taken, though. Someday, when I retire from rodeo, I'd like to put them in an album or make a scrapbook or something."

"I'd be happy to help with it when you do." If she was still around, which Vivian hoped she would be.

Calhoun grinned. "I'd like it, Pretty Lady. I probably need all the help you want to give me."

She handed him his root beer so he could take a long swig. Vivian leaned against him, content. The topography of the land had changed and reminded her of some of the Westerns she'd seen. "The sky looks bigger out here."

"It does and bluer. Look at all the clouds." Cal peered through the windshield and from beneath the brim of his cap.

Puffy white cumulus clouds dotted the sky, and

Vivian remembered a game she once played with her cousins. "Calhoun, did you ever look at clouds and see shapes? I used to play a game where we did that when I was little." Remembering brought back pleasant memories.

"Sure, we did," he replied. "Lincoln and I did that a lot, especially if we were out fishing or something. Granny always vowed on the day Elvis Presley died she saw his face in the clouds. Of course, she didn't get a picture, so I don't know, but she swore she did."

"Let's play now. Look at that one, over to the southwest. Doesn't it look like a dog?"

Cal craned his head to look. "Maybe. It might be a coyote. I can't tell. Now, to the north, that one looks like a horse. Reminds me of my paint, Johnny, and that old song, "'Ghost Riders in the Sky.'"

"I see it!" she cried with delight. For the next half hour, the sky and clouds entertained them. Vivian saw a fish, an angel, and an elephant.

Cal spotted a guitar, a bull, and a hand.

She laughed a lot and so did he. With him, she never felt awkward or that she had to watch what she said or did. Vivian had with Arthur Covington, always wary she might misspeak or do something he would mock. He'd often criticized her choice of clothing or made fun of something she liked. Being with Cal was as comfortable as faded, well-seasoned blue jeans. He listened without judging, and he shared his thoughts.

Around four o'clock, his phone rang. Cal answered it on speaker. "Hey, bro, what's up?"

"Just wondering where you are," Lincoln replied.

"Somewhere between Wichita Falls and Amarillo. We're stopping for the night there, then heading to

Gallup, then finally to Prescott."

"You okay?" Lincoln barked the question.

"Yeah, I'm awfully sore and gonna have a big ol' bruise on my leg, but I'm good. Why?" Calhoun exchanged a glance with Vivian.

Lincoln's long sigh echoed clear over the phone. "I saw some online footage of the rodeo last night at the Cowtown Coliseum. You made a fine ride, but I saw when the bull head butted you, so I was concerned."

"It scared Viv, too. She worried I'd been gored or tore a muscle." Calhoun drummed his fingers on the steering wheel.

"I ran down to the chutes to meet him, to see if he was hurt." Vivian scooted closer to Calhoun.

"I'm glad he wasn't. Are y'all having fun yet?" Lincoln combined relief with sarcasm.

Calhoun laughed. "Most of the time. We stopped for church this morning in Weatherford. We're not in too much of a hurry to get to Prescott. We've got time."

"Take time to heal up a little. Better get some witch hazel for that bruise. Granny swore by it." Linc offered free advice.

Witch hazel? Vivian wasn't familiar but if it would help, they would get some along with more arnica cream. She had another plan, too—one they discussed the previous night. As soon as the phone call ended, she would try to make it happen.

"Will do, bro. I'll call when we get to Prescott, maybe before."

After the call, Vivian drew a breath. "Calhoun, is it too late to unbook the budget motel?"

"I don't know. Probably not. Why?"

"Because there's a nicer hotel that has a spa tub. I

looked it up on my phone. If we're in no hurry to get to Gallup or Prescott, maybe we could stay two nights. That way you can get some rest and soak that bruise." As she spoke, Vivian rested her hand on his knee.

He exhaled a long sigh. "That would be sweet, Pretty Lady. Probably would help my knee and back, too."

"Is your back hurting?" She figured it was but had to ask.

Cal shrugged. "Some. Give me my phone and I'll call to see if I can cancel without being charged." Five minutes later, he'd undone the reservation without penalty.

Vivian smiled and used her smart phone to book the room she'd been considering. The deluxe queen room boasted two beds, a tiny kitchenette, and a spa tub. A complimentary breakfast was available every morning as a perk. "Done! We've got two nights." Vivian shifted position and lifted her right hand to high-five Calhoun.

"That's wonderful. I'll have to undo Gallup, too. I haven't booked anything in Prescott yet." He slapped her palm, then focused on the steering wheel.

"Let me." Her fingers sped over the phone keys. Doing this for Calhoun made her happy. "We'd better stop at discount store to get that...what was it? Witch hazel."

"I'm planning on it, honey." He sent her a sideways grin.

Amarillo sat in the Texas panhandle, surrounded by both flat grasslands and a few rock-strewn mountains. The city was also on the edge of the desert. Vivian knew it was the site of the Palo Duro Canyon but not, as Cal explained, just north of the *Llano Escado*. She had never been this far west, and the scenery delighted her. It reminded her of old cowboy movies she had seen. Amarillo, however, was a large city with a population of around two hundred thousand, although it lacked the urban sprawl of the Dallas-Fort Worth metro-plex.

If they hadn't arrived when they did, Vivian would have offered to drive. Calhoun seemed tired, and she could tell, by the occasional grimace, he must be hurting. Instead, she pointed out the first discount retailer she saw and dashed inside after he parked. In addition to witch hazel, which turned out to be a liquid topical medicine, she picked up more arnica cream, root beer, and ibuprofen. Since the store also sold groceries and their hotel room had a kitchenette, Vivian picked out a pair of butterflied pork chops, an envelope of instant mashed potatoes, an onion, a few mushrooms, and gravy fixings. She also grabbed a bag of salad and some dressing. Vivian climbed back into the truck. "I hurried!"

Calhoun sat, slumped over the wheel but roused when she spoke. "No problem. I almost dozed off. I'm worn out. What's all that?"

"I bought some things for supper. I got pork chops. Isn't that one of your favorites?"

His weary face brightened with a smile. "Sure is, honey. Thank you. I was trying to figure out if we should grab some fast food or what. This will be better."

Once they were settled in the spacious room, Calhoun removed his boots and downed some ibuprofen. "I'd go soak in that tub but if I do, I won't be worth a flip, and I want to eat before I crash. I'll stretch out on this loveseat. If I fall asleep, wake me up when it's ready."

"I will." Vivian kissed him on the forehead. "Get some rest."

He closed his eyes and before she found a skillet, Calhoun snored.

She sautéed the veggies and set them aside, then braised the meat. She put a lid over the skillet, then put together the salad in a bowl from one of the cabinets. Once the chops were done, she made the gravy and returned the vegetables to the pan, topping each chop. While it simmered, she unpacked a few things from her suitcase and took a quick shower. She put up her damp hair with a clip before waking Cal.

Asleep, he appeared younger and less haggard. The sharp lines which fatigue cut into his face had eased. Although they'd only been back on the road a few days and he'd ridden in one rodeo, the outward signs of peace he'd gained at home had vanished. At his brother's place, he'd been relaxed and didn't seem to be in as much pain. Bull riding took a heavy toll on his body, and most of the bull riders were younger than Calhoun. A few were older, and he'd told her about a rare few who competed past forty. Those were exceptions.

When she saw that bull ram him, Vivian had been terrified, certain he'd been hurt more than a bad bruise. He'd been lucky, though, but next time, he might not be as fortunate. She had seen his scars.

Calhoun talked about his past injuries as if they'd been nothing, but some of them had landed him in the hospital.

Linc wanted him to retire.

She did, too. That dream or whatever it had been with his younger brother haunted her, especially the remembered words, *"I don't want him put in the ground like I was. Ain't all it's cracked up to be, being dead. I'd rather still be alive."* Vivian still wasn't sure if it was meant as a warning, but she took it as one.

Imagining Calhoun bleeding, or broken, thinking of him pale and prone in a hospital bed made her uneasy. Once again, she thought of that old saying that a goose walked over her grave as her skin prickled with dread. In that moment, she realized the truth—she loved Calhoun Kelly. Nanna thought she ought to tell him, and she should. *But what if he didn't love her the same way?* Maybe it was pure friendship. Oh, he kissed her sometimes, and she gloried in it, but maybe she read more into it than existed. If she told him she loved him and he didn't feel the same, she'd be devastated. Besides, he probably wanted a woman who still believed in God and prayed. It would be better for the moment not to tell him, no matter what Nanna thought. Maybe he'd tell her first. "Calhoun," she said and leaned over him. "Hey, supper's ready."

He mumbled something she didn't catch but didn't rouse. She tried again, repeating his name. Vivian smoothed back his hair from his face, and when that didn't make any difference, she kissed his forehead. "Come on, darling, wake up." She'd never used endearments before but it did the trick.

His lovely dark eyes opened, and he blinked, then smiled. "Hey Pretty Lady." He sat up on the loveseat and groaned a little. "Something smells good."

"I fixed smothered pork chops, mashed potatoes,

and a salad. Are you hungry?" She brushed an unruly lock of his hair back from his forehead.

"I'm starving. Let me go wash up and then let's eat." He rose and vanished into the bathroom.

Vivian found bowls for the salad and plated the rest, delivering it all to the small table. She used the china found in the cupboard and poured him a glass of root beer over ice.

He returned with slow, stiff motions and sat. Cal reached for her hands and bowed his head. "Blessed are you, Lord, maker of heaven and earth, our Father. Thank you for your loving care and kindness. Bless this food and let us be strong in body and grow in your love. Thank you for this day we've shared and this place. Touch me with your healing grace and give us both strength in every way, amen."

"Amen." Vivian repeated the final word because Cal expected it.

He tasted the pork chops and smiled. "Mm, that's delicious, honey. I can't tell you how much I appreciate this. If you weren't with me, I'd be eating a greasy burger or a cold bologna sandwich in a basic motel, hoping there weren't any bedbugs or roaches."

"Have you experienced bugs in a motel room?" She shuddered.

"Once or twice." Calhoun shrugged.

"That gives me the creepy-crawlies. What did you do?"

"Asked for my money back and slept in the truck. That's one reason why I drag a trailer most places. At least I know it's clean. This place is nice, though. I'm getting spoiled to having some extra comforts."

He deserved it. "You still have the long drives,

though. Doesn't that get old?"

"I pick the rodeos. I try to keep them closer than this. It depends on how much I want to compete somewhere. Some bull riders fly since we don't travel with a horse."

"Why don't you?" Flying seemed more efficient, both faster and easier.

"Too much aggravation. If you fly, you gotta get someone to pick you up at some airport or rent a car. I've known guys who end up sleeping on the floor at the terminal, waiting for their flight. Besides, I don't like to fly."

That surprised her. She'd never minded. She'd flown on what few trips she'd made—once to New York City, another time to Chicago, and once to Atlanta. "Why not?"

He dived into his salad before he replied. "Call me old-fashioned, but I like solid ground under my feet. I'd rather drive than fly through the clouds. Maybe I've heard about too many plane crashes or something."

"Cars wreck, too." As he should well know since his parents died in an accident.

"True but when I'm driving, I'm in control." Cal finished his last bit of salad and picked up his knife to cut the chop.

A revelation hit Vivian. Cal feared flying. Funny, because he climbed onto raging, snorting bulls weighing thousands of pounds and rode, knowing he faced possible injury or death but he wouldn't get on an airplane. The chops were tender and Vivian savored the taste but like most cooks, she wasn't impressed with her own cooking. Anything prepared by someone else always tasted better, but Calhoun finished everything, including the last scrap of salad.

Vivian cleaned up the kitchen, enjoying the domestic moment.

Cal soaked in the tub. He emerged after a long time wearing cotton athletic shorts and a T-shirt.

Until now, Vivian had seldom seen him wear shorts. His legs were muscular, but her admiration faded when she saw the bruise on his outer left thigh. It was huge, as large as her hand if not bigger, and nasty black surrounded by purple. "Oh, Calhoun!" She winced because it looked much worse than she'd imagined.

"It's sore." He glanced up. "Hurts a lot. Will you help me with the witch hazel and arnica?"

Vivian dried her hands and came to him. "Sure."

He sat in a chair.

She dabbed on the witch hazel, then rubbed in the arnica cream with gentle fingers.

Even so, he winced.

She frowned. "It's warm to the touch."

"Happens sometimes. It'll be all right in a few days. By the time I ride in Prescott, it'll be a lot better."

"I hope so, Cowboy." She finished, wiped her fingers clean, and rose.

Although he grimaced when he stood, Calhoun took her in his arms and kissed her.

Beneath the tenderness, his mouth fired her passion, but they both kept it in check. Vivian relished the solid feel of his body and inhaled his clean scent with pleasure. "What's next?"

"I'm gonna dose up with ibuprofen, and in the morning, we'll be tourists and go sightseeing. Would you like that?"

She would and pulled a blanket over him after he stretched out. "That sounds like fun. Good night, Cowboy." Once he slept, she would have called her grandmother, but it was late, so she didn't.

She lay down, but her mind refused to stop whirling in every direction. Sometimes Vivian questioned her presence on the road with Calhoun. She cared about him, very much, but Vivian had no idea what would happen next or what the future might hold. With her mind full and heart brimming with emotion, it took a long time before she slept, too.

Chapter Seventeen

Most of the time when he traveled from one rodeo to another, Calhoun didn't play tourist. After more than a dozen years on the circuit, he'd seen most major attractions. Like Johnny Cash once sang, he'd been everywhere. He'd never visited the major cities, like New York or Los Angeles, but he had no desire to go, either. The places he favored were off the beaten path, like the waterfall in Arkansas or Rich Mountain. Until now, Amarillo had been no more than a place where he had driven through or ridden, but with Vivian, it became something more.

Without her, he would have laid up in a motel and tried to heal, but Cal figured she didn't want to sit around a hotel room, no matter how nice, staring at the walls. They drove out to see the Cadillac Ranch where forty cars had been placed nose down in the dirt. Although people could bring spray paint and add to the graffiti already in place, they didn't. Calhoun would have liked to have painted a heart with their initials. It would have been something permanent to reflect his growing feelings.

After that, he took her out to the Palo Duro Canyon, the second largest canyon in the nation, second only to the Grand Canyon. They loitered in the visitor center and gift shop but didn't go down into the canyon. He pointed out the Lighthouse, a landmark rock, one of many rocks called hoodoos. After touring the canyon, Calhoun took her to the Route 66 Historic District. They wandered up and down the throughfare, then shared a huge nacho platter in the town's oldest restaurant.

On the way back to the hotel, they picked up a few groceries, so Vivian could make dinner. The options were limited since the kitchenette had two electric burners but no oven. Calhoun hankered for chicken and dumplings. With the ingredients, they headed back to the hotel after buying swim trunks for Cal and a one-piece bathing suit for Vivian.

"Now we can go swimming!" She held up the suit to admire as he drove back to the hotel.

"It's too hot," Calhoun protested.

"It's an indoor pool, Cowboy. It'll be fun."

Before dinner, they went for a swim together—a first. Although her swimsuit was modest, he gawked with admiration. *Vivian has a nice shape.* Cal refused to let his thoughts stray any farther. Swim trunks felt awkward to Cal, especially since he hadn't owned any since his teenage years.

Once in the pool, though, he liked it. The cool water eased the deep ache around his bruise. He'd forgotten how weightless he felt in water, and he swam, an old skill he hadn't lost.

Vivian paddled around a little, then sat on the edge, dangling and kicking her feet in the water.

Cal dived a few times, cannonballing into the water as she laughed. In the early afternoon, they had the pool to themselves until a family appeared with floaties and towels in hand. Sightseeing and swimming wore him out so once they returned to the room, he put on dry clothes and flopped on the bed barefoot.

Vivian tuned in the radio to vintage country and curled up in one corner of the couch to call her grandmother.

He drifted off to sleep, listening to the tunes and the soft sound of her voice. He didn't sleep well, not at all. Dreams haunted him. *At first, he was competing. Dreaming about that wasn't uncommon, but this time was different because Sullivan watched, standing in the arena. Cal craned his head for a closer look, and Sully lost his seat, tumbling to the dirt. With the wind knocked out of him, Last Chance couldn't speak.*

Sully sauntered over and stood above him, "Calhoun. Hound Dog, you gotta hear me. It wasn't your fault. I know the Pretty Lady told you, but you still don't believe it. You can't make the same mistake I did, you hear? You don't want to end up like me, brother. It ain't gonna happen yet, but it will come September, I think."

Within the dream, his brother looked ten feet tall and wore a Western shirt patterned after the Texas flag. The family had laid Sullivan to rest wearing it.

Cal made a noise to protest and did once he'd caught his breath. "You didn't make a mistake, Last Chance. I did but not you."

"Nope, you got that backwards. I was too stubborn and didn't quit when I ought to have. You got to listen. If you won't listen to me, then hear him." Sully stepped back with a laugh.

Another man, familiar but one he didn't think he knew, stood beside his brother. He was tall and lean with a sharp-featured, yet handsome, face. His eyes narrowed as he stared, and Calhoun got the impression he was tougher, stronger, and braver than he had ever been.

"I reckon you should listen," the man said in a drawl flavored with a touch of Kentucky. "Kid, you're one of mine, removed by long years but still family. Last Chance is telling you true. I'd rather not meet up with you 'til it's your true time. That gal loves you, like my Rachel loves me. If you won't listen for you, hear us for her."

He woke with a sharp cry to find Vivian standing beside the bed, forehead knotted. Cal shifted his position and sat up, pillows against his back. His heart pounded, and he had to draw deep to breathe.

"What's wrong?" Vivian leaned over him.

Calhoun scrubbed his face with both hands. "I had a dream, that's all. Spooked me."

Vivian sat on the side of the bed facing him. "Tell me."

"Granny always said not to tell a dream unless you eat first, or it might come true." Cal put a hand on his chest, willing his heart to slow.

Vivian rose and brought him a sandwich cookie. "I can fix that."

He ate it in two bites, swallowed hard. "I dreamed I was riding a bull, and Sullivan was there, watching. Then he talked to me, telling me the same things he told you, it wasn't my fault, and said not to make the same mistake he did. He told me not to end up dead like him."

Saying it aloud alarmed him. He didn't mention the kid had also said it would happen, probably in September. It would concern Vivian, and he had no clue what it meant if anything.

217

"You're upset." She grasped his hands with hers.

"Yeah, I am." The dream disturbed him deeply. "He was wearing the shirt we buried him in, and that's not all. Another man was there, told me I was his, separated over many years, but to listen to him. Last Chance called me Hound Dog, too. No one else ever did, honey."

Her brow wrinkled. "Who do you think the other guy could be?"

Calhoun tried to place the face. The man appeared familiar, and then he realized. He had to be their patriarch, Barlow Washington. His wife had been named Rachel, and he'd seen the old photo that hung in Lincoln's office. Calhoun grabbed his phone and called his brother. He moved to the loveseat and sank onto it.

"Surely you're not in Prescott so soon," Lincoln said when he answered.

"Nah, we're in Amarillo, spending two nights here. Vivian found us a nice hotel. No, the reason I called is to ask if you'd take a picture of ol' Barlow's photo, the one hanging on the wall in your office, and text it to me."

"Well, sure, Cal, I can but why?"

Here came the hard part. Lincoln might think the truth sounded crazy but he couldn't think up any plausible lies. He could say Vivian wanted to see the old picture, but she could have viewed the photo when they were at the ranch. They would be back there, eventually, too. He inhaled a deep breath and held it. "I had a dream, and I think he was in it."

"*Barlow* was in it?"

"Yeah, I think so. If I see the picture again, I'll be sure." Calhoun kept his tone even.

"Do you feel all right? Did you take a hit on the head?" Lincoln's voice shifted to a deep growl.

"No, I didn't. Never mind. I shouldn't have asked." Calhoun huffed out a frustrated sigh.

"I'll send it; that's not a biggie. It just seems like a weird thing to ask and a strange person to dream about, that's all."

In for a penny, in for a pound. He had to tell his brother the rest of it. "Last Chance was in the dream, too."

"Yeah, once in a while I dream about Sullivan, Cal." Lincoln's voice dropped low.

"This was different." When Linc didn't say anything, Calhoun rubbed his right hand over his hair. "Vivian's also dreamed about him. I'm not out of my head, Linc."

"Can I talk to her for a minute?"

"Sure, you're on speaker, and she's right here." He handed the cell phone to Vivian.

"Hi, Lincoln."

"Hey, Vivian. I gotta ask—how's my brother?"

She exchanged a glance with Cal. "Sore but he's good, Linc. If you're trying to ask if he's delusional, he's not. I dreamed about your younger brother when I was at your house. I was afraid to tell Calhoun because he might think I was crazy, or that it would upset him, but I finally did."

"This is strange," Lincoln told her. "How did you know it was Sully since you never met him?"

"I didn't until the next day when I saw a picture at Calhoun's house. He was wearing an eagle bolo tie in it—same as in my dream."

"We buried him with that on." Linc's voice

cracked and broke.

"And until then, after I told Calhoun he said he was Last Chance, I didn't know it was a nickname." Vivian twisted the fingers of her free hand.

"What did he say, if anything?" Calhoun took back his phone and fielded the question. "It seems he told us both the same, what happened wasn't my fault, but he says I can't make the same mistake he did."

"What was that?"

"We don't know, but I wish we did. I think it's important." Vivian leaned close to add her opinion to the conversation.

"Why?" Linc's voice cracked over the miles.

"Because he says if I do, I could end up like him—dead." Cal's words brought an abrupt silence, and the stark word hung in the air. A long minute passed in silence.

"And what did Barlow have to say?" Linc sighed after the question.

"Said I ought to listen to Sully and that he didn't want to meet up with me until it was my true time, whatever that means." Cal spit the truth out like bitter peanuts in a rapid spew.

"Quit for the season," Lincoln cried, speaking the words with force. "Come home, Calhoun. Don't take the chance something might happen. This is scaring the socks off me."

A rush of cold shot through Cal, and he shivered.

Vivian shuddered and rubbed her arms.

Can't be cold —must be the air conditioning. We'd better turn it up before we freeze. "Does that mean you've decided I haven't lost my mind?" Cal asked, voice dry as a drought.

"I suppose. The thing is, Cal, thank God I haven't dreamed anything like that. I've had some bad feelings. I worry more about you riding this season than usual. What was it Granny called that?"

"Premonition." Calhoun remembered it very well. Granny had tried to talk his parents out of their ill-fated shopping trip to Dallas.

His folks had laughed off the warning, but they never came home.

Vivian rose and stirred something on the stove. Chicken and dumplings. She was making the dish for supper.

From the tense set of her shoulders, he could tell this conversation had upset her, too.

"I'm not kidding," Lincoln stated. "Give it up, at least this year. It's not worth dying over. I don't think I could bear to bury another brother."

Temptation beckoned. Quitting would be simple. He'd lose the entry fees he'd paid, but it wouldn't matter. He could head home to the ranch and hope that Vivian would join him. If she wanted, they could travel back to Missouri. She'd like that, Cal figured, and so would Nanna. Giving up bull riding would give him time to heal, and maybe he wouldn't hurt as much, or so often. Calhoun considered it, then realized it would never work. "I can't do it, Linc. If I did that, it would mean I'm not trusting the Lord, and I do. If it's God's will that I ride and survive, then I will. If it's not, then who am I to hide from God? Maybe it's a trial. Look at Job. I can't yield to temptation if it's not the right thing to do, and it's not. I'll see the season through, then come home like I always do. Maybe after that I'll hang up my spurs. I don't know."

221

"Cal…"

"I really believe I'll be fine." Lord, but he hoped he would be. Deep within, Calhoun wasn't as certain, but he tried to ease his brother's fears. "'I will say of the Lord, 'He is my refuge and fortress, my God in him will I trust.' Pray for me, all right?" He pulled the words from Psalm 91, an old favorite.

"I do, every day. Tell me again, how many more rodeos?" Lincoln's voice had a rough tone.

"Counting Prescott, seven. Coushatta is the last one. It's not two hours from your house. That's the one you said you'd bring the family to watch.

"I'll be glad when the season's over, more than ever."

"So will I. Text me that picture of Barlow." Calhoun rose from the loveseat.

"I'll send it. Take care, Calhoun." His brother's admonition resonated.

"I'll do my best. Talk to you later." In a short time, his phone jingled as a message appeared. The photograph of Barlow Washington was just as he remembered, and without any doubt, it was the man from his dream. "Hey, Vivian, come see Barlow," he said as he realized she stood at the window, arms wrapped around her torso. Judging by the quiet snuffling sounds, she was crying. "Honey, what's wrong?"

"I'm worried sick." She whirled to face him. Tears streamed down her cheeks unchecked.

He crossed the carpet to her and opened his arms.

She launched into them.

He cradled her close. "Don't be. I'll be fine." Cal nuzzled her neck with his lips.

"I don't know that, and neither do you." She leaned against his shoulder, hid her face, and sobbed.

"Honey, don't cry." He'd never been good with anyone's tears, hers most of all. He never knew what to say, which made him feel useless and hopeless.

Vivian pulled back, out of the embrace. She gazed into his eyes. "Calhoun, there's something I need to tell you. I don't know if you'll like it or not, but I have to say it."

His spirits plunged. She probably wanted to go back to Missouri, and he'd take her but he'd miss Prescott. Cal couldn't blame her, not really. Supernatural visions and ghostly visitations were over the top, especially for a woman who had lost her faith. Without her, he'd revert to being lonely. Most of the time, Calhoun lacked any friends or family in the stands to cheer him on or to care. "All right, Pretty Lady. Tell me." He steeled himself to take the blow and not show how much it mattered.

She tilted her face up toward him. "Calhoun, I love you. You can't imagine how much I love you. The idea of you being hurt or k-k-killed scares me. It would break my heart, Calhoun. You're everything to me."

Within his chest, his heart trembled and stopped. His breath caught and held as he stared at her. The words he had never dared to dream she would ever say flowed over him. Like a bird that'd flown into a window, her vow stunned him and left him speechless. Her gaze never wavered from his face, but when he didn't answer, he saw fresh tears form. "Why on earth would you think I wouldn't like that?" A knot clogged his throat, and his words emerged in a croak. "Honey, I love you, too. I hadn't said so in case you didn't feel the same, but I do. Oh, Vivian…"

She hushed him with her mouth, with a long kiss that combined tenderness with longing.

After the kiss, he cuddled her close. "I'll be all right, honey, I promise."

"You have to be," she replied, her voice fierce. "How's your bruise?"

"What bruise?" he asked with a smile. Joy outweighed any pain in this moment. "It hurts some, but it'll do. "Please quit crying now."

"They're tears of happiness, Cowboy." She delivered butterfly kisses all over his face from chin to forehead.

Calhoun wiped them away with his knuckles and kissed her cheeks, then her mouth. " 'I am my beloved's, and my beloved is mine'," he told her, quoting from the songs of Solomon.

Vivian stroked the outline of his lips with a single finger. She responded to his quote with another familiar one. " 'Entreat me not to leave thee or return from following after thee, for whither thou goest, I will go.' "

Cal rejoiced to hear her say those words and that she loved him. That seemed both blessing and miracle. Cal sent up a silent prayer of thanks, and he completed the verses in response. " 'And where thou lodgest, I will lodge, Thy people shall be my people and Thy God, my God'."

Calhoun stopped short of the part about if naught but death would part them. To speak about dying might make it so, and he didn't want to think about it. Whether he had years remaining in this life or only until September, he would savor every moment with Vivian.

When they sat to eat together to eat, their hearts

were in harmony. The rich chicken and dumplings she made were the best he'd ever eaten, and he told her so.

Vivian smiled at the compliment. "If we ever got married, I'd make sure you were well fed."

"I'd like it fine." His heart swelled with joy. They spoke about wedding possibilities, but neither made any commitments.

After the meal, the good food resting easy in Cal's belly, they sat together against the pillows on her bed and turned on the television. He wasn't one to watch much TV, but they found an old Western movie he liked, *3:10 To Yuma* with Russell Crowe. Holding hands, they watched, although his mind was more on the woman beside him than on outlaw Ben Wade.

After a good, hot soak in the spa tub and a fresh application of witch hazel to his bruise, Calhoun kissed Vivian goodnight. He retreated to his own bed, so happy and too keyed up to sleep. His mind spun with the possibilities and thoughts about the future. He couldn't forget the strange dream, either, or stop pondering what it meant. Cal took it as a warning, although he didn't really believe he would die in the arena in September. *Thy will be done,* he thought, echoing the Lord's prayer.

In case he might be wrong, however, Calhoun decided he could take actions. He could change his life insurance to change his beneficiary from Lincoln to Vivian. He and Vivian could get married.

The idea popped into his head, and once he got past the shock, Calhoun decided it would be perfect. Over the meal, although he hadn't officially asked the question, they had discussed a possible wedding sometime after the season ended, and maybe in

Missouri so Nanna could be part of it or in Texas so his family could participate. Vivian had talked about a Christmas season wedding, which he liked. Cal now realized they had no reason to wait.

If they wed and the worst happened, then they would have time spent together. Calhoun loved her, and if they were married, they could share a bed. He wouldn't fret anymore about how it looked for them to have the same room, and Vivian would be off limits to any cowboy who might take a fancy to her. Buckle bunnies would be discouraged when he displayed a ring on his left hand. If he finished the season in one piece and above ground, they could throw a party to celebrate their marriage.. Then they could settle into a shared life, whether it would be in Texas or Missouri.

The more he thought about it, the more certain Cal became, so he made plans when he should have been sleeping. He would get rings in Gallup he decided, but they wouldn't spend the night there. They would head on to Flagstaff and get a hotel. From Flagstaff to Prescott had less miles and would be shorter. They could get married in Prescott. A search about Arizona marriage laws revealed no necessary waiting period, so they could get the license at the Yavapai County Courthouse. If he could track down his pal Bill, he would. Bill remained an ordained Baptist minister so maybe he could officiate. If not, they'd find someone who could perform the ceremony.

The Prescott event, Frontier Days and the World's Oldest Rodeo, would last for several days, which was time enough to get hitched. All he had to do was ask Vivian, and he never doubted that she would say yes.

Calhoun devised a plan, but the details kept him

up, mind spinning in many directions. He couldn't ignore the tragic destiny which might loom at the end of the season.

Chapter Eighteen

Calhoun didn't tell her he'd changed their plans until they were already on the interstate heading west. He figured waiting provided less chance she might object. "We're gonna spend the night in Flagstaff." Cal shifted his focus from the Internet for a moment. "We'll still stop in Gallup, but we'll get a place to stay in Flagstaff. It's Arizona so it's closer to Prescott."

Vivian didn't mind. "Whatever you want to do is fine. You're familiar with the region, and I'm not."

"You'll love Flagstaff. The city sits in the largest Ponderosa Pines Forest anywhere, and it's beautiful. I always thought if I'd been on a wagon train back in the olden days, and we reached Flagstaff, I would have stayed right there." Cal smiled. "You can see the San Francisco Peaks in the distance. There's a sweet old-fashioned motel near downtown. A guy who used to rodeo with me owns it. We can stay there before we head on out to Prescott."

"Sounds good. What about breakfast? I'm hungry."

Calhoun grinned. He could use a bite to eat, too. "I figured we'll stop in Gallup. We'll eat, and there's a mall. I know you said you might need some more clothes so there's time if you want to shop. Then we'll head on to Flagstaff.

"Then it's a plan." Vivian felt like Cinderella after the ball or Snow White waking to the prince's kiss. For now, her fears about bull riding retreated. She resolved not to worry about the possibility of injury but to focus on their future. "I would like to shop for a few more things."

"What about a dress?"

"Maybe." Vivian shrugged. She didn't wear dresses often, but maybe she would start.

After a late breakfast including chicken biscuits, hash browns, and coffee, they hit the mall. She loved walking hand in hand through the retail space, gawking and gazing until they entered one of the large department stores.

"I need to see a man about a dog." Calhoun excused himself.

Vivian browsed through the racks. She picked out a pair of forest-green slacks, two cute blouses, and then studied the dresses. She had the denim one she had bought, but she liked some of these styles. Maybe she had weddings on the brain after last night, but Vivian spotted a white sleeveless dress she adored. The garment was both modest and pretty, with a high scoop neck. Panels of lace alternated with white cotton for a mid-calf length. She tried it on, and it fit like a dream. Vivian added it to the pile of clothing she planned to buy. Since boots wouldn't look right with the dress, she picked a pair of low-heeled white sandals to match.

After waiting forever at a checkout kiosk, Vivian paid for her purchases and wandered the store. She entertained herself with the silly notion of having Calhoun paged. She imagined the message: "Would one tall, handsome cowboy report to his lady?"

Calhoun appeared, carrying several bags of his own.

"What did you buy?" Vivian tried to peek into his sacks with curiosity what he'd chosen.

"Ask me no questions, and I'll tell you no lies." His bright grin emerged and lit his face.

Sometimes he displayed a sweet, sassy Southern charm that she adored. "You're in a good mood." As she adjusted her purse strap higher on her arm, she smiled.

Calhoun kissed her, right there in the store. "Of course. I've got a beautiful woman who loves me. What else do you want to look at?"

"I found everything I need." She lifted her bags to demonstrate. "I even picked out a dress."

"Then let's get on down the road, Pretty Lady."

They rolled into Flagstaff in the early afternoon. Vivian found it as lovely as Cal described. Green, stately ponderosa pines rose high into the skies, breathtaking in their size and beauty. Vivian gazed at the mountains with awe. She might be from the Ozarks, but those were hills compared to these actual mountains. The Ozarks were pretty, too, but these evoked awe. As they headed into the small city, she liked it and Cal navigated without hesitation. "Are you familiar with this town?"

"I've been here several times before." Cal nodded. "They have a rodeo in June. I didn't ride in it this year. That's a good thing because it was around the same time I met you in Arkansas."

"Meeting you was meant to be." For the rest of her life, Vivian would be glad she'd gone to the rodeo to shoot some pictures. If she hadn't, she wouldn't know Calhoun Kelly existed.

"Synchronicity." He winked with a wide grin.

Flagstaff operated on Mountain Time, not Central, so it ran an hour behind what they were accustomed to living. Right now, it was too early to check into the motel. Neither was hungry, so they stopped at a park. Pines towered over the shaded paths, playground areas, picnic tables, and benches. They sat on a comfortable park bench under the trees.

Calhoun trailed his arm across the seat behind her.

Vivian leaned against him. Sunlight filtered through the evergreens and made lacy shadows on the ground. The aroma of pine filled the air and Vivian savored the cooler temperatures. She liked the place and loved his company.

"You look happy." Calhoun kissed her forehead.

She tilted her face toward him. "I am."

"Me, too. Hey, honey, you know how we talked about a wedding last night?"

"Yes. I was thinking maybe December unless we want to get married sooner." Butterflies fluttered in her tummy, and her heart danced. She just hoped he hadn't changed his mind.

He wore a serious look as he faced her. "I think we should, Pretty Lady."

"Get married sooner rather than later?" Vivian liked that idea very much. "A fall wedding, then? Like October or November?"

Cal grinned as he leaned for another kiss.

She inhaled his personal scent, woodsy and clean and familiar, then sighed with pleasure.

"I was thinking maybe in a couple of days when we get to Prescott." He kissed her again, then continued. "We can have a big, fancy do if you want later, but I'd like to make it official right away. What about it? Will you marry me, Vivian?"

"Definitely, Calhoun." Vivian would get hitched with a moment's notice, without any hesitation. "What about Nanna, though, and your family?"

"Do you think they'll be mad if we don't wait?" Cal wore a slight frown.

Nanna will be so happy that she wouldn't get angry. "Nanna won't mind. I don't think your family would either. We can celebrate with them later."

"Then let's do it." Calhoun wrapped his fingers around hers and caressed them.

"Calhoun, you won't believe what I bought earlier." Thinking of the garment tucked behind the seat in his pickup evoked a tiny, almost Mona Lisa smile.

"What?" He kissed her knuckles.

"I bought a lovely white dress, trimmed with lace." Vivian chuckled.

"Is that right?"

She nodded. "I wasn't thinking about it as a wedding dress but it's perfect."

"Do I get to see it?" He cradled her close.

"No way. Not until the wedding day. That's tradition." Vivian stroked his cheek.

"You're right." Calhoun grinned. "I bought some new duds, too, for such an occasion and rings. Now, I didn't buy diamonds or an engagement ring. If you want them, I will, but I like what I picked out. It ain't like we're planning a long engagement."

"As long as I have you, I can do without diamonds. What kind of rings?" She stretched out her left hand and tried to imagine a ring on her finger.

"Matching silver rings with an Irish braid design. After all, I am a Kelly."

In a few days, she would be one, too. Vivian remembered doodling on notebooks and in the margins of her homework the names of boys she liked in junior high. If she had one now, she would write Vivian Kelly, Mrs. Vivian Kelly, and Mrs. Calhoun Kelly all over it. As a little girl, she dreamed of walking down the aisle on her daddy's arm in a hoop-skirted white gown and a long veil. Vivian had imagined a multiple-tiered wedding cake and dancing with a faceless, nameless groom. Now, she didn't care about fancy trappings. She had a dress she liked and a groom she loved. As long as they said their vows and it was legal, the other details didn't matter. "Do you have any ideas about a place in Prescott for the wedding?" Vivian leaned against Calhoun.

"I don't know," Calhoun admitted. "First, we'll get our marriage license at the Yavapai County Courthouse and go from there. I know you haven't met him yet, but my friend, Bill Swanson, is a licensed, ordained, preacher. I think he'll be in Prescott riding, because he does rodeo these days. If I can get a hold of him, I hope he'll marry us. He might know a place, or someone surely will."

"Is this for real, Calhoun?" Her joy bubbled over as she giggled.

"Real as it gets, honey. Are you about ready to find some lunch?"

"If you are, sure."

When he offered her his hand to rise, he winced.

Vivian noticed his expression and frowned. "How's your back?"

"Tolerable." Calhoun stretched as he stood and made a face. "Bruise is still sore, but it's better, too. I'm too darn happy to let it bother me much."

They ate patty melts with fries at a diner downtown, then headed for the motel. Adjacent to the main business loop, the single-story structure had been built in a U-shape. Parking was outside the rooms, and each of the doors was painted light-blue. Cal stopped the truck in front of the office. "Come in with me so you can meet Chester. That's short for Winchester, Chet Winchester."

Inside the small office, the man who greeted them couldn't be much older than forty, but he walked with both a limp and a cane. When he recognized Calhoun, he whooped out loud and came around the desk to slap him on the back. "Ain't seen you in too long, Hound Dog. Who's the pretty gal?"

"This is Vivian. We're getting married in Prescott." Cal wore a wide grin. Chester was the first friend he'd told.

"I'm pleased to meet you." Vivian extended a hand to shake.

"Likewise. You can stay here, on the house." Chet told her with a wide grin. "Consider it a wedding present."

"I can't do that," Cal protested. "I'll pay."

"No, sir, you won't. How long are you staying?" Chet pushed a room key across the desk.

"Just tonight, then it's on to Prescott." Cal looped one arm across Vivian's shoulders.

"Competing in the World's Oldest Rodeo, are you?" Chester shook his head.

"You bet I am." Calhoun nodded.

Chester brought out a register for Cal to sign. Cal wrote his name with a flourish and picked up the key.

Vivian walked around, looking at the rodeo memorabilia on the walls.

She peered at one for a closer look. "Is the bronc rider Lincoln?"

"Yeah, it's my brother." Calhoun moved beside her to look.

"I didn't know he rode, too." Her fingertips brushed the frame.

"Saddle broncs. He'd quit before Sully died and after he got married. Sasha wasn't too fond of the rodeo."

Chester shook his head. "Never would have dreamed Linc would give it up."

"He did." Calhoun flashed a smile. "Now he doesn't even raise rough stock. Got three boys, too."

"Aw, good for him," Chester commented. "Sometimes I wish I'd quit before I got banged up and crippled. Maybe then Marie wouldn't have left me, and I'd be raising kids, not running a cheap motel."

Vivian wanted to say something kind but had no idea what words might make a difference, so she followed Calhoun with the key.

The double room was compact but clean. Once they toted their luggage into the room, Cal flopped onto the bed with a huge sigh.

"Why did he call you Hound Dog?" Vivian asked. "Because Sullivan did?"

"A lot of people did, but Sully started it." Cal settled into place. "Last Chance said it was because of my eyes, big and brown like an old hound. I'd rather be called a hound than some other nicknames I could have. Nobody much calls me that anymore, though."

"I can see the resemblance." Vivian gazed into his

face, focused on his eyes. "I always thought they were more like chocolate, though. Are you taking a nap?"

"Maybe. It's kind of late for it, though. I might just rest my eyes."

That meant he would doze within five minutes. "Sleep if you want. I thought I'd call Nanna. Can I tell her we're getting married?"

"Of course. Tell her we'll get married again in Missouri if she wants. We'll visit her soon as I'm done in Prescott. We should get there a week from Saturday."

"How long will we stay?" Vivian paused with her phone in her hand, glad she would see Nanna.

"I don't know, a week and maybe more if I decide not to go to Nebraska. That's supposed to be the third weekend of July but I could change my mind. I'd rather spend time with my wife." His voice slurred with sleep. Every time he competed, it upped the chance to could be hurt or die.

"I like the sound of that, Cowboy. If we don't go to Nebraska, then what's next?" She opened the calendar app on her phone and waited to add the information.

"Lawton, Oklahoma, on the last weekend in July, then Sallisaw the first week of August. If I don't go to Nebraska, we can go home to Rusk for a little bit, too." Calhoun yawned, then opened his eyes for a moment. "I'd like that. If you're telling your grandma, I'd better let Linc know."

"Call him later this evening. You're not awake enough right now." Vivian grinned.

"Okay, I will, honey. Love you." He closed his eyes again with a sigh.

She leaned over and brushed his lips in a brief kiss.

"I love you, too."

Although she knew Nanna might be in the dining room at this hour, Vivian called anyway.

Nanna answered. "Hel-lo."

"Hi, Nanna, it's me. I told him."

The elderly woman chortled. "Good for you! What did Calhoun say?"

Vivian tucked her phone tighter against her ear and curled up on the other bed. "He loves me, too, Nanna, and we're getting married!"

"Oh, child, that's the best news I've heard in a long time. When?"

"In a few days when we get to Prescott. Calhoun doesn't want to wait, and neither do I. I always hoped you would be at my wedding, but he says we can wait to get married in Missouri if you want." She crossed her fingers, hoping Nanna would say *no*.

"Don't be silly, Vivian. We can celebrate when you're here, but there's no need to wait. I've always said when you know, you know." Nanna paused to laugh. "How is Calhoun?"

"He's good. He got a huge bruise on his last bull ride in Fort Worth. Right now, he's asleep. He had a terrible dream, kind of like the one I had, with his brother telling him not to make the same mistakes, and one of his ancestors was in the same dream, too." Vivian drew a deep breath before she continued. "It shook him up. Lincoln got upset, too, after Cal told him. Linc's afraid he'll get injured or killed. He wants him to quit for the season, but Calhoun says he's going to finish. Every time he rides a bull, I'm terrified. That's why I told him, Nanna, because I was so worried."

"Are you still?" Nanna's quiet voice rose with the question.

Vivian considered the question. "I'm so happy he loves me, too, and that we're getting married. I'm still concerned, but I believe it's all going to be fine."

It must. Because it has to be.

"I know you won't, but I'll pray for Calhoun," Nanna replied. "And take pictures, Vivvie. I want to see how pretty you will be as a bride. Where are you tonight?"

"Flagstaff, Arizona, and it's beautiful here. Huge pine trees, mountains, and cooler air." Vivian rose and stood so she could admire the scenery she described.

"Enjoy it. Call me after you're married, will you? And take care of your cowboy. He needs it."

He did and maybe Vivian shouldn't read something sinister in Nanna's plan to pray. In the rush and excitement of their shared love, Vivian had almost forgotten some of her concerns about Calhoun. Some of the anxiety crept back into her heart. She required a happily ever after, not a short marriage ending in widowhood. Vivian thought about Chester, who ran the motel. His pronounced limp and dependence on a cane reminded her how dangerous rodeo could be. She blinked back tears and hoped they weren't evident in her voice. "I will, Nanna. I love you, and I'll see you next week, probably."

"I'll be here."

Vivian gazed through the window. Giant ponderosa pines raised their green branches to the sky. As her worry returned, she sought to regain her calm. It didn't diminish the love she had for Calhoun, but it cast shadows. Once, like her grandmother, she would have prayed, but her soul had run dry. Vivian couldn't summon up the words or the right attitude. Instead, she conjured the words to favorite poems, including one by Elizabeth Barrett Browning with the words, *I love thee with a love I seemed to love with my lost saints*. It fit her mood and situation.

Cal shifted position and rolled over. He landed on his bruised thigh because he groaned.

Vivian should rouse him. They hadn't eaten supper yet, and if he slept too long, he might not rest well tonight. But, despite any discomfort, his sleeping face had such peace, she wouldn't wake him.

Instead, she worked with some of the photos she'd taken, downloaded them to her laptop, and edited them. Vivian looked up email addresses for a few Western and rodeo-themed magazines, wrote cut lines, and submitted her work. Maybe they would use them, maybe not, but she'd made the effort.

For supper, she ordered a family-size box of chicken tenders with fries, Texas toast, and soft drinks to be delivered. Once the food arrived, in the absence of any table or chairs, she placed it on the desk. Vivian knelt beside the bed and let her fingers tease through Calhoun's wild curls. "Hey. Wake up, supper's ready."

He stirred, mumbled, and blinked. "Hey, Pretty Lady. What time is it?"

"Almost seven. I ordered in, so there's food if you're hungry." She pushed back a stray lock of his hair.

"Oh, yeah, I am. I didn't plan to fall asleep. Why didn't you wake me?"

"You needed the rest, Cowboy. I talked to Nanna while you napped. She's happy for us." Nanna's joy increased Vivian's.

"She okay with us getting hitched out here?" Seated on the edge of the bed, he rubbed his face with both hands. He remained in the same spot to eat.

"Yes, she said take pictures, though."

"We will. Let's eat and then I'll give Linc a call." He groped for his phone on the table between the beds to check for any messages.

"Want some ibuprofen first?" Vivian offered.

"I'll take it after, then shower, so I'll sleep well. We don't have to leave too early. We're not quite two hours away from Prescott."

Vivian sat cross-legged on the floor to eat.

He shook his head as he glanced at her position. "If I got down like that, I'd likely never get back up. Thanks, honey, for ordering something for supper. I really didn't want to drag back out and find a restaurant."

"Me, either. I wish there had been a kitchenette. I could have cooked instead."

He waved one hand. "It's okay, honey. I love your cooking, but I'm eating more often and better than I usually do on the road. If you weren't with me, then I'd probably already be in Prescott, in my trailer. Probably wouldn't have eaten at all, but I'd be reading."

"I like to read. When I saw the books at your trailer, I was glad. I read more than I watch television." Vivian didn't have any books with her, but she could read on her phone if she wanted.

"When I'm out on the circuit, I fall asleep half the time trying to read, but I do enjoy it."

"I always thought someday I might try to write a novel," Vivian confided. It was a long-time ambition, but she'd never told anyone about her dream.

"You should. Maybe once we're settled, at least for the winter, you can give it a try."

She liked the possibility. "Will you ride bulls next year, Calhoun?" Vivian would prefer to make a permanent home.

"Maybe." He grabbed one more chicken tender. "I haven't decided yet. It just depends. Will you come with me again if I do?"

"Of course." Vivian didn't have to think about it. She would. "Remember, I did say where you go, I will go. I meant it."

He reached for her hand and took it. Calhoun kissed it, then sighed. "If I do ride another year, maybe we'll look into getting a bigger trailer. It would be more of a pain to haul around but extra space would be nice."

"It would, Cowboy." Vivian started to tell him she'd be just happy to stay either in Texas or Missouri, but before she could speak, his cell phone rang.

He released her hand to answer the call. "It's my brother. I'm glad he called. We have a lot to tell him."

His grin lifted her spirits, and she pushed away her worries for now.

Chapter Nineteen

His gut reaction might be silly, but anytime his brother called unexpectedly, Calhoun tensed. He remembered too well the phone call about his parents' accident. He didn't anticipate anything as tragic, but in the past, he'd taken a few calls he'd rather have not. Once, Cooper had fallen, busted his head open, and needed stitches. Another time, Sasha had been involved in a fender bender and broke her wrist. When Granny died, Cal had been on the rodeo circuit when word came. Other than that, Lincoln wasn't very spontaneous. He hoped it was a positive call. Maybe the good news about the wedding would head off any lectures or pleas to come home before the season ended. "Hey, Lincoln, what's shaking?"

"Hey yourself, bro. How would you like some company out there in Prescott?"

Cal grinned. "I'd like it fine, especially when you find out what I'm going to do. How's that gonna happen, though?"

"Sasha's folks want to take her and the kids to Galveston over the Fourth to the beach. I'm welcome to go, too, but you know me. I'm not a beach kind of guy. I'd be bored out of my mind and get sunburned, so I was thinking maybe I could fly out, so I can watch you ride. If you don't mind, Cal."

Calhoun resisted the urge to holler with delight.

He'd wished his brother could be at his wedding. Cal recalled one of his favorite Scriptures, Romans 8:28. *And we know that all things work together for* good *to them that love God, to them who are the called according to his purpose.* "I'd love it, Lincoln, and not just to see me ride. I was fixing to call and tell you the news. We're getting married in Prescott." Cal held his breath.

Lincoln cut loose with a Rebel yell.

His brother's cry would have hurt Cal's ears if the call wasn't on speaker.

"Hallelujah! Calhoun, that's the best news you could give me. Congratulations! You know I'll be there. What day?"

"Probably Friday or Saturday," Cal replied. Delight rippled through his chest. If he'd been a girl, he would have giggled. "We'll get a license after we get there. I need to track down my friend, Bill, and see if he'll do the honors."

"Pecos Bill?"

"Yeah, that's the one. Would you be my best man?"

"Absolutely, kid. Vivian? Are you there?" Linc's voice boomed loud.

"Where else would I be?" she answered, giggling.

"Do you have a maid or matron of honor to stand with you?"

"I don't, but all I need is Calhoun as the groom." She hadn't even thought about having an attendant.

"Sasha will want to come, too. The boys can go to the beach with their Granny and Pop, and we'll come to Prescott. What do you think?"

Calhoun swallowed hard around a knot in his

throat. "I think that would be fine, if Sasha wants to do it."

"I'll ask. Hey, babe, come here quick!" Lincoln hollered at his wife.

He also had the call on speaker because Cal heard her say, "What's the matter?"

"Not a thing, but our Cal's getting married in Prescott. Do you want to go to the beach, or come with me? Vivian needs a matron of honor."

Sasha squealed. "Count me in! Congratulations, you two! I've been praying for this. Yes, I'll be there. We both will."

They discussed details. Linc would book a flight, and Cal would let them know when the wedding would take place. Although he wished his nephews could be present, too, it wasn't practical. They would enjoy beach time with their grandparents. Lincoln and Sasha wouldn't have to get them to behave on the flight. Afterward, Calhoun turned toward Vivian. "It's okay with you, isn't it?"

"More than! I'm glad we'll have family there." From her seat on the floor, Vivian leaned her head against his knees.

It pleased Calhoun she already called his folks *family*, but he regretted Vivian wouldn't have anyone there from her side. "If you think Nanna's up to it, I'll buy her a ticket, and she could fly out. Maybe one of your cousins could come with her."

"She couldn't, Calhoun, not anymore. Her traveling days are long over." Vivian gazed at him, tears in her eyes. "It's all right, though. We'll take lots of pictures or maybe even a video. When we get to Missouri, we can wear our wedding clothing to show her."

"We sure can. Maybe we can buy a little cake or something to share." Cal glanced down at his bride-to-be.

"She'd like that, and so would I." Vivian offered him a smile.

"It's all coming together. It's meant to be because it's His will." Calhoun grinned.

Vivian didn't echo his belief, but he hadn't expected she would. He prayed every day she would find her lost faith, but until she did, he promised himself not to push, or he might drive her farther away from God.

In the morning, they had no reason to hurry. After a delicious breakfast at a café where he introduced her to his favorite egg dish, huevos rancheros, they headed west, then meandered south toward Prescott on historic Arizona 89. The route took them from the mountains and pine forests near Flagstaff to the Oak Creek Canyon, then the Verde Valley where the topography shifted to rock formations and canyons. They arrived in Prescott around noon, and the small city of less than fifty thousand bustled. "A lot of people are coming in for Frontier Days and the rodeo," Cal commented as they descended into the valley. "It's a pretty place."

"I feel like I'm in living in the Old West." Vivian took in all the sights and scenery. She couldn't stop grinning. "I like all the rocks and mountains. Some of them are so colorful."

"Wait 'til you see Whiskey Row." Cal launched into one of his mini history lessons. "Prescott was a gold-rush town, way back. After the gold played out, they mined for silver. All the saloons were on Whiskey

Row, and after it burned in 1900, they rebuilt it."

He paused to point out a historical marker and a few of the sights. "There are still some old-fashioned saloons but also candy shoppes and galleries. The courthouse where we'll get our marriage license is across from Whiskey Row, and the hotel is about a half mile away."

They had booked a mini-suite room at the same chain they'd used in Fort Worth. This time, however, anticipating the wedding, they opted for a king-sized bed. The room was also furnished with a couch and chair. Cal volunteered to sleep on the sofa until after the wedding, but Vivian said she could toss a coin to decide.

They had lunch at the oldest saloon on the block, one that dated to the 1870s. Inside, it had the look and feel of an Old West watering hole, with a mahogany bar backed by a mirror, historical photos and artifacts on the walls, and a staircase to the second floor. They learned back in the old days, the Earp brothers and Doc Holliday frequented the place. Several movies had been made there, and when their food came, a prime rib sandwich with au jus dip for Vivian and a hefty half-pound burger for Cal, everything tasted delicious.

She had one of her cameras around her neck on a strap, so Vivian shot some photos of the older section of Prescott. She found it charming and loved the old Western feeling it evoked.

Afterward they explored nearby businesses, bought some chocolate and peanut butter fudge, then enjoyed them on a bench outside the courthouse.

"Do you want to get the license today or first thing in the morning?" Vivian asked.

"Tomorrow. It's almost check-in time, and my knee could use a rest." He massaged it as he spoke.

"How's your bruise?" Her forehead creased with a frown.

"Not quite as sore but it looks awful. It'll be fine."

Before they checked in, they picked up po' boy sandwiches at a deli and some soft drinks so they wouldn't have to venture out until morning. The room proved more spacious than the one in Fort Worth, and the sofa folded out into a bed. Neither would have to scrunch on the couch. Vivian hung up her dress, still in a garment bag from the store, in the closet. She didn't want it to wrinkle or for Calhoun to see it.

Cal also put away his new duds. They ate the sandwiches for supper, and he enjoyed the crisp pickles along with the meat, cheese, and bun. Cal watched Vivian order flowers using her phone. He settled into the armchair and called Rusty. "Hey, I'm in Prescott. Are you here yet?"

Rusty laughed. "Yeah, parked over behind the arena. I'll be ready to compete. Are you riding in the parade?"

"I ride bulls, man. So no, I don't have a horse here." Cal rolled his eyes. His pard should be aware. "When is it?"

"Saturday morning at nine. You should come and bring your lady."

"I will if we can, but I've got plans." Calhoun sighed with pleasure as he settled into the seat. Sitting relieved most of his back pain.

"What's more important than the parade?" Rusty's slow drawl notched up a level.

Cal savored a brief anticipation before sharing the

news. "A wedding. We're getting married. I don't know for sure when or where, but we're getting the license tomorrow."

"Whoo-hoo," Nail cried. "She's got you roped and branded. Good for Vivian! Can I come? You'll need two witnesses when you get the license so I'll bring whoever I can find."

"Sure! Pecos Bill around anywhere?"

"You bet. I just saw him not a half hour ago. Why?"

"I hoped he might do the honors at the wedding. If you see him, tell him to call me pronto." If his friend could officiate, it would be wonderful.

"Will do. Hey, Cal, I know a little church where you can get married, if you don't have a place yet. My cousin Sue lives here. She's the pastor's wife. It's just a little old church outside of town. Do you want me to call her?"

Calhoun sent a silent prayer of thanks upward. "I do, thank you, Nail. I appreciate it."

"*De nada,*" Rusty replied. "I'll let you know."

Calhoun checked in with the rodeo to confirm the schedule. He wouldn't ride until Saturday night, around eight thirty. *I'll be a married man by then.*

Linc called. "We'll be there around four thirty on Friday, give or take. We'll fly from Dallas, have a layover in Denver, and then arrive. Where are you staying? I thought I'd book a room at the same place, as long as it's not a fleapit."

"No, it's nice, really comfortable. Do you want me to pick you up?" Calhoun noticed Vivian's attention remained on the florist website.

"Nah, but thanks. I arranged to rent a car. I gotta

have wheels to get around. We'll come find you. I hope they'll have a room left to reserve. I'll give you a ring when we land."

"Good deal. I'm glad you're coming, Linc." Cal shut his eyes in silent thanks as each detail resolved.

Pecos Bill called next. "I'll be honored to perform the ceremony, Calhoun. I talked to Rusty, and he's checking on a church. Soon as you know, tell me the time and place for sure, and I'll be there. Man, I am so happy for you."

"Thank you. This means a lot to me, Bill." He dozed, sitting in the chair for a few minutes after that. When his phone rang, it jolted him awake.

"The church is yours on Saturday," Rusty said. "Anytime from between nine and two. I've got the key, and my cousin will meet us there. Sue plays the piano, so she can provide the music."

Once again, everything was coming together. Cal knew it was the guiding hand of the Lord. "Let me ask my fiancée what time." He turned to Vivian. "Hey, honey, what time do you want to get married? Rusty found a church for us to borrow, anytime between nine and two on Saturday. I ride that night but not 'til after eight."

"How about ten o'clock? That gives us time to get ready and be there." She glanced up from her laptop with a smile.

"Sure. Do you want some music? Nail's cousin will play piano if you want."

"We have to have the wedding march. So yes, that's perfect."

He relayed the information to Rusty. After Calhoun ended the call, he smiled at Vivian. "We have the preacher, the church, and the music. What about the flowers and cake?"

"I ordered a bouquet we can pick up tomorrow. How do you feel about pink?" She displayed a photo on her phone.

"I don't mind it, honey." The color didn't matter at all. What did was he would marry this amazing woman.

"That's good because I ordered you a pink boutonniere that matches the bouquet. I got one for your brother, too, and a smaller bouquet for Sasha." Vivian held up her phone and thumbed through photos.

"That's great. We have everything but the license —and we'll get it tomorrow. And a cake."

"All right. I spotted a bakery downtown. Maybe we can go in and pick one up." She gazed at him.

"We'll do it, Pretty Lady." Cal winked above a huge grin.

In the morning, Vivian wore the dress she'd worn to church the first time she accompanied him.

Calhoun donned his best black jeans and one of his good Western dress shirts. They headed out early to the Yavapai County Courthouse. Calhoun plunked down the marriage license fee. Both displayed their driver's licenses as proof of age and for identification. The process took less than fifteen minutes, including the instructions from the clerk to return the completed license after the ceremony.

Calhoun took his bride-to-be out for breakfast, then they picked up the wedding flowers. They would keep fresh in the small fridge at the hotel, and so would the two-layer vanilla round cake they chose at a local shop. At the bakery, he asked the attendant to write their names and the word *forever* on top.

"The wedding's at ten in the morning." Cal updated Lincoln with the details.

"Sounds like a plan. I booked a room at the place you're staying. I'll call when we arrive. I'll treat us all to dinner out. We can figure out a restaurant later."

To pass the time until Linc and Sasha arrived, Calhoun took Vivian to Watson Lake. The combination of water and standing granite rocks together provided a breathtaking view. He also drove her to the rodeo grounds and arena. After that, Calhoun followed Nail's directions to find the small, traditional frame church where they would be wed.

Vivian clapped her hands together when she saw it. "It's pretty. It reminds me of the church I attended growing up. I want to get married here."

"I like it, too." He'd wanted to be married in a church and was glad it worked out that they would. They shared a light lunch then headed back to the room to relax. Cal perused the license more than once to confirm the reality. He was getting married.

It was around five before Lincoln called. "We're here and we're heading to your room."

His brother had traveled to watch him ride bulls before but not often since Linc married and less frequently since Sullivan died. Before that, Linc made it to as many rodeos as he could. Once he reached the room, Calhoun hugged his brother with real affection, as Sasha embraced Vivian, gushing congratulations.

The women retreated to the couch to talk weddings.

Cal couldn't help but eavesdrop.

"Do you have your something old, something new, something borrowed, and something blue?" Sasha asked.

"I suppose. I hadn't even thought about it. I bought a new dress. I'll wear this necklace Calhoun bought in Fort Worth. Hopefully, that counts as old enough. Other than that, I don't know." Vivian displayed the cross within a heart he'd bought her.

"What about borrowed or blue?" Sasha dug in her purse.

Calhoun grinned and nudged his brother. "Wonder what she'll pull out of her bag."

"Knowing my wife, just about anything." Lincoln smirked.

"We'll find out." Calhoun cocked his ears to listen.

"I don't know." Vivian shrugged and tugged at her ponytail.

Sasha grinned. "I do. I brought Granny's blue-and-white cameo brooch for you to wear. I also have the small satin purse I carried for our wedding that you can borrow."

"Sounds perfect!" Vivian's eyes lit up. "I can't believe it, but I think we have everything in order for the wedding. What are you wearing?"

"I packed a navy dress I sometimes wear for church. It has a pink spray of flowers on the skirt, though. Will it work?"

"Sure. My flowers are pink—light-pink roses and carnations, a few dark-pink stargazer lilies, and baby's breath. I have two boutonnieres, one for the groom and one for the best man. I also got a smaller bouquet for you."

Sasha nodded. "Wait, what about a cake?"

"Picked one up this morning." Vivian led Sasha to the fridge and opened the box to show the confection.

Cal got distracted eavesdropping. He enjoyed listening to Vivian's delight, so much he failed to hear Linc call his name twice. When he did, he focused on his brother. "What?"

"I asked you if you wanted to bunk with me tonight." Lincoln chuckled. "Tradition says you can't see the bride until the wedding, so Sasha thought she could stay with Vivian, and you could sleep in our room. What do you think?"

Calhoun almost refused. He wanted Vivian close, and he'd miss her, even though it was for a single night. Still, tradition mattered so he nodded. "Okay with me. Let me ask my bride-to-be. Hey, Vivian? What do you think if Sasha stays with you, and I'm downstairs with Linc, for the night before the wedding?"

"Sure, let's do it. I want all the good luck we can find." Vivian smiled at him. "That way I can get fixed up for the wedding without you seeing me until we're at the church."

Following the custom made sense, but Calhoun would hate the absence. "I'll miss you, though."

"It'll be for twelve hours or less." Linc rolled his eyes. "You can manage."

"I suppose I can." Calhoun laughed and knew he could, but he didn't plan to like it.

For dinner, Linc located a steakhouse not too far away, and the four dined on tender, ribeye steaks seared to perfection.

With the rodeo in town, customers packed the place.

Several people called out to Cal, and one buckle bunny winked in his direction. He ignored her.

"What do you want for a wedding present?"

Lincoln finished the last bites of his delectable steak. "We didn't want to buy something you don't want or need. You're the only brother I've got left, and I want to make it special."

"You and Sasha being with me is all the gift necessary." Calhoun laid down his steak knife. Linc's offer to get a gift touched him almost to tears. "We don't need a coffee pot or toaster or towels. You're here, and that's what matters."

"Kid, I want to get something. If not now, later." His brother shook his head. "If you want anything of Mom's or Granny's, say the word."

"The fact you offered is enough. If I think of some heirloom, I'll ask, okay?" Calhoun didn't want a bunch of gifts, just a life with Vivian.

"Then I have a serious question for you—are you fixed okay for money?" Linc ran one hand through his hair. "I'm not trying to stick my nose in where it shouldn't be, but I know all the hotels cost more than hauling your trailer, and there are two of you now. I guess what I'm trying to say is, if you need some dough, just ask me. We're doing all right, and after I take some cattle to market in the fall, we'll be even better. You sunk a bunch of your money into the ranch, and I've never paid you a dime.

Love for his brother filled him. Calhoun had put money into the ranch and never complained. He'd always tried to make sure Linc knew he'd pitch in anytime extra funds were needed. "Linc, I never expected you to pay me from the ranch profits. Most I hoped was a place to live if I ever quit the circuit." Calhoun paused to clear his throat. "I've banked most of my rodeo winnings all these years. I dip into the money when I need it, but there's more than enough. I'm a long way from being broke."

Lincoln reached across the table and clasped Calhoun's hand. "Good to know, brother. We'd love it if you decided to build your own house on the ranch someday. Even if you don't, you're always welcome to stay any time. It's your home as much as mine."

Tears filled Calhoun's eyes. "Linc, I know, and it means the world to me. With gas prices, it doesn't cost that much more to book a room than dragging the tin can. I try to pay for each season out of the purses I win without using my savings. I'm better than breaking even. If I ever need money, I'll ask—if you promise to do the same."

Lincoln stared as a slow grin spread across his face. He punched Calhoun on his back. "Will do. Cal. If you've got bucks, why do you keep bull riding? It's hard on your body, man."

Explaining should be simple but wouldn't be. He wasn't about to tell his brother he did it to make up for Sullivan, because that would open a conversation he didn't want to have the night before his wedding. "It's all I know how to do." Like he'd told Vivian, he hadn't really ever held a job. "Yeah it's rough on me, but sometimes it's glorious. I'll tell you something I haven't yet. I'm seriously thinking I'll retire from the circuit after this year. I'm old for a bull rider, and I figure I've had my shot."

"Thank you, Jesus!" Lincoln lifted both hands high the way he did to praise God in church.

"I'm still gonna finish this season, though," Calhoun added.

Some of the brilliance vanished from his brother's

smile.

Cal sighed and continued. "Let's talk about tomorrow and the rest of my life. I'm ready to settle down with Vivian."

That was the future he wanted and the one he planned if God was willing.

Chapter Twenty

Vivian woke on her wedding day missing Calhoun. Since they'd met, they hadn't spent much time apart. She ached to sneak downstairs, knock on the door, and steal a kiss but didn't. Sasha convinced her to take advantage of a complimentary breakfast adjacent to the lobby, but she was too excited to eat much. After a long shower, she dried her long hair and laid out her wedding dress.

"Are you wearing a veil?" Sasha had donned her blue dress with floral embroidery on the skirt.

"I didn't buy one so no. Maybe I should have." The last-minute question brought anxiety, and Vivian chewed on a fingernail as she wondered if she'd forgotten any vital details.

"No, you're not a veil person." Sasha scrutinized Vivian's face. "How will you wear your hair?"

"I'll pull it back and put it up with a claw clip." Vivian ran a brush through her long locks. "It's the way I usually wear it."

"How about half up and half down?" Sasha pulled out a set of hot curlers. "I'm good with hair. What if I pull it back from your face, do a couple little braids on the sides, then curl the rest to fall down your back?"

Vivian tried to imagine it and couldn't. "Maybe. If I don't like it, can we take it down?"

"Sure, but you'll love it. And we'll take a rose

from your bouquet to pin over one ear." Sasha mimed placing a flower in her own hair.

Vivian had said she'd wear flowers and would. "All right, I'll wear the rose. I'll see if I like the other style." By nine, Vivian transformed into a bride. Her dress fit nicely, and Granny's cameo brooch complimented it. She loved what Sasha had done with her hair, including the flower. Viv slipped her feet into the new sandals. "How do I look?"

"Beautiful. What about makeup?"

"I usually don't wear any." Vivian wrinkled her nose. She had never worn many cosmetics and didn't want to walk down the aisle made up like a Hollywood star.

"How about just a little face powder so you're not shiny and a touch of lipstick?" Sasha mimed opening a compact and applying powder.

"I don't know." The last thing she wanted would be to resemble a buckle bunny. "If I don't like it, can I wipe it off?"

"Sure." Sasha laughed. "Don't worry. I'll use a light hand." Sasha powdered Vivian's cheeks and forehead, then added a deep-rose lipstick.

It accented her bouquet and proved to be the perfect touch. "Will you take a picture of me?" Vivian viewed her reflection. "I laid out one of my cameras."

"Of course. I'll take lots of pictures. I might not be a photographer like you, but I can use a camera. I was on the yearbook staff in high school and on the campus newspaper in college." Sasha picked up the camera. She snapped a few random shots, then took Vivian's photo.

Vivian nodded with approval. "Let's go to the church."

"You can't see Calhoun until you walk down the aisle." Sasha winked and touched up Vivian's cheek.

"I can and I will." She had to see him, and she would. "That's just superstition.

Once they arrived at the church, after Sasha backtracked around the ongoing rodeo parade, Vivian couldn't wait to see Calhoun. His truck sat outside and her heart fluttered.

He was here, and they were about to be married. Joy filled her, and she restrained from running into the building to find him. Calhoun met her in the vestibule, handsomer than ever in his black jeans, a light-blue Paisley Western shirt, and a black Western-cut blazer, embroidered around the lapels.

He stood tall in his dress boots and grinned when he saw her. "You're beautiful, honey. Prettiest bride ever."

"You make a good-looking groom, Calhoun." Vivian's hands shook as she pinned his boutonniere in place. "If there's time, Sasha will take some pictures."

A mature woman with steel-gray hair wearing a bright smile came out of the sanctuary. "I'm Sue Willis. I'll be playing the piano for your wedding. I'm Rusty's cousin, and he's here. My son can video the wedding on his phone if you want."

"Yes, thank you so much." Nanna would love it. Vivian posed alone, standing before one of the stained-glass windows, then with Calhoun.

Sasha shot photos of Cal alone, then pictures of the wedding party.

Sue took a few, so Sasha could appear in the photos. By the time they finished, Rusty and several other rodeo people had arrived. They settled into the pews, mostly in the back, and out of respect removed their Western hats.

Pecos Bill came out, greeting them. "I'm ready whenever y'all are. I should have asked sooner but I plan to use the traditional vows unless you want something else."

"Traditional is fine." Vivian buried her face in her bouquet, inhaling the sweet scent.

"Then let's get started." Pecos Bill headed into the church.

No one present could walk the bride down the aisle so they dispensed with the custom. Vivian retreated with Sasha to the back.

Sue played the wedding march.

Sasha walked down the aisle with measured steps.

Vivian followed.

At the altar, Calhoun waited with Lincoln beside him.

He'd turned paler than Vivian had ever seen, but his lips curved in a small smile.

Vivian's eyes were only on her groom, and when she reached him, she faced Calhoun. Without waiting for direction, Calhoun took her hands in his.

"We're gathered here on this fine morning to join this man, Calhoun Kelly, and this woman, Vivian Blackburn, together in holy matrimony." Bill's voice had a strong Texas twang. "Is there anyone here who objects?" He glanced around the sanctuary, but no one spoke. "No? Well, that's good. Let's get right to it. Vivian, do you take this man as your husband, to have and to hold from this day forward, for better and for worse, for richer and for poorer, in sickness and in health, to love and to cherish, until death do you part?"

Calhoun's dark eyes gazed into hers without blinking.

"I do." Vivian spoke the words in a soft voice not far above a whisper.

Bill repeated the same vow for Cal changing *husband* to *wife*.

Calhoun spoke, his voice deeper than usual, "I do." Cal cleared his throat. "Pretty Lady, I'll love you forever and ever. I'll provide for you and be at your side through anything life throws our way. I bless the day that I met you, and I thank God for you. I love you, honey."

Until then, Vivian hadn't cried but tears spilled down her cheeks. His declaration of love moved her. She ached to say something moving, like Cal had, but the words fumbled in her mouth. "Calhoun, I love you, too. Don't ever leave me. Where you go, I will go, always."

"Do you have the rings?" Bill asked.

Lincoln pulled them from his pocket and extended them toward Calhoun.

"Vivian, take the ring and put it on Cal's finger and say, with this ring, I thee wed," Bill instructed.

She slid the simple silver ring onto Calhoun's left hand and repeated the words. Lost in his eyes and drowning in love, Vivian didn't hear Calhoun say the same, but she held out her hand so he could slip the matching ring onto her left hand.

"I now pronounce you man and wife." Bill's huge grin sparkled. "What God has joined, let no man—or woman—put asunder. Meet Mr. and Mrs. Calhoun Kelly. You may kiss your pretty little bride, Calhoun."

Sasha and Lincoln clapped.

The gathered cowboys cheered and waved their hats.

Calhoun stepped forward to take Vivian into his arms. He leaned down and kissed her, his mouth searching and sweet. His lips lingered on hers. When he stopped, Cal cupped her face in his hands. "You make me the happiest I've ever been, Vivian. I love you, wife." He swept her up into his arms and carried her down the aisle.

Vivian fussed and protested. "Stop, you'll hurt your back. Darling, don't."

"I'm fine." Calhoun set her down in the vestibule.

Vivian grabbed the lapels of his coat and kissed him back. "You'd better be!"

After each guest shook Calhoun's hand or hugged the bride, they departed. Most would ride tonight and didn't have time to spare.

"What now, groom?" Lincoln asked. "It's a bit early for lunch, but we might want to go soon with all the crowds."

"Early is a good idea. I'm competing tonight so I'll want to rest a bit this afternoon."

He sent a warm look in Vivian's direction, and she blushed. He might want to rest, but first, they would become one. The idea sent sweet shivers through her body. "Let's go change before we eat. "I'm wearing white, and I'm sure to get something on the dress. We can grab the cake, too, and take it with us, wherever we go." She rode with Calhoun back to their room.

Once there, he shut the door. Calhoun shucked out of his finery. "Woman, let me love you."

"What about Lincoln and Sasha?"

"They'll wait because I don't mean to hurry."

Vivian gloried in his touch and gave back the love he shared.

Afterward, Vivian wore jeans and her favorite *Bull Riders Do It Best* T-shirt when they headed downstairs to meet Lincoln and Sasha. Cal held her hand on the way, and she basked in the lingering sweetness from making love.

"Let's go eat," Lincoln said when he let them into the hotel room he shared with Sasha "I'm nearly starved, waiting. What do y'all want?"

"Mexican!" Vivian named one of her favorites.

Cal offered his suggestion. "Burgers or barbecue."

Sasha laughed. "The first disagreement!"

"It's not worth a fight. I'll be happy with anything." Calhoun put one arm around Vivian. He kissed her tenderly. "I'll eat whatever my bride wants."

Mexican turned out to be the choice. They found a family-owned place away from the major thoroughfares. They brought along the wedding cake. Once the staff realized they were newlyweds, they were offered a back dining area. It offered privacy to cut the cake without an audience.

"These are the best tamales I've ever had." Sasha devoured her portion.

Vivian ate but although Mexican ranked as one of her favorite cuisines, she paid little attention to the taste. She couldn't stop touching Calhoun even while they dined.

"Street tacos are tasty. Honey, how's your taco salad?" Calhoun asked with a smile.

"Delicious." Vivian laughed. "It's our wedding day. I'll always remember it."

"July first." Calhoun named the day and grinned.

"We'll celebrate this day for fifty years."

"Or more!" Vivian added. "Let's be happy, Cal." If he started any talk about those cryptic dream messages on their wedding day, she would become angry.

Sasha used Vivian's camera to take cake pictures.

"I'm glad you're capturing the moment," Calhoun said. "Vivian hasn't been taking as many pictures lately. I don't have a clue why not. Maybe she realized I'm uglier than homemade sin."

"You're not!" Vivian cried. "I've been distracted. Don't worry, I'll shoot photos until you feel like the paparazzi are after you."

He laughed. "I doubt it, Pretty Lady. C'mon, Sasha, let's get this picture taken. I'm ready to eat some cake."

With Calhoun's hand on hers, Vivian posed for a photo, then cut the confection. She put a bite into Cal's mouth.

After he ate it, he fed her a tiny piece.

His lips tasted of vanilla and rich buttercream, as sweet as he could often be.

Nothing remained of the small cake but crumbs when Calhoun rose. "We're going back to the hotel 'til rodeo time. Meet us at the arena. Y'all can sit with Vivian. I'll be there 'til time to go down to the chutes."

Lincoln grinned. "It's a plan. What's up tomorrow? Do you ride again?"

"I don't plan to, not unless I get a perfect score or something." Cal shook his head. "I'd like to go to church, probably where we got hitched. We might go watch the rodeo tomorrow night. I'm not sure. We'll stay here another day or two. Then we're heading for Missouri so Vivian can see her nanna."

"Works for me. We'll hang around until Monday," Lincoln said. "I wouldn't mind warming a pew, either."

"We have to head home then, though, to meet the kids when my folks bring them back." Sasha removed the flower from Linc's lapel. "You're welcome to come by and stay for a few days on your way."

"Too many miles and I want to see my grandmother." Vivian linked her arm through Calhoun's. "We'll be back, soon, though."

"Once we get up to Missouri, we'll have almost three weeks until Lawton." Calhoun moved toward the exit. "We'll be back after we visit Nanna and hang out until I head to Oklahoma. After that, I have three more rides until the last one in Louisiana."

Lincoln slapped his brother on the back with a grin. "Anytime you want to come is fine. The boys will be eager to see their new auntie."

"We'll buy another cake so the boys can enjoy it." Vivian remembered the kids' love of dessert.

"Maybe we can find one with a bull rider and a bride on top," Cal joked.

At the hotel, Cal took off his boots and stretched out on the mussed bed. "Has it been a good wedding day, honey?"

She kicked off her shoes and cuddled next to him. "It's wonderful. Are you going to sleep a little?"

"If I can and you don't mind. It's been a few days since I last rode, and I want to be rested so the bull doesn't get the best of me."

"I don't mind, Calhoun. I'll lie right here beside you." Vivian rested her right hand on his back.

"Set the alarm, Pretty Lady, or we might sleep right through the rodeo." Cal yawned and settled into place.

They didn't. Calhoun rose with plenty of time to wrap his wrists and knees.

Vivian helped him and frowned at how dark his bruise remained. "Does it still hurt?"

"Some." He winced when she touched it. "Not so bad, though." He dressed for the rodeo, clean snap-button shirt, dirty jeans, protective vest, and boots with star-shaped spurs.

Vivian changed into a Western shirt with fringed trim. She wore her boots and hat, then gazed at her reflection in the mirror. "Do I look like a cowgirl? I hope I don't look like a buckle bunny."

Cal laughed. "You look like a cowboy's wife. I liked your hair down, though."

Vivian made a face. "It's not practical to wear it lose. That's why I put it up."

At the rodeo grounds, once Calhoun checked in and got his competition number, they sat with Lincoln and Sasha in the stands. Vivian kept close to her husband. Whenever she could, she leaned against him.

Calhoun delivered light kisses on her face and lips. When the crowd stood for the national anthem and prayer, he put his arm around her.

For his sake, she said "Amen" after the prayer.

The wild-horse race, an event unique to this rodeo, finished. Cal sighed and came to his feet. "Getting close to show time. I'd better head down to the chutes." He planted a full kiss on her mouth.

Vivian grabbed his vest. "Be careful, Calhoun."

"I always am."

She watched him saunter away with his loose-limbed stride, wearing his hat at a jaunty angle. Her calm lasted until she saw him mounting the bull, a wild one the announcer said was called Mexican Heartburn.

Vivian sighed as Calhoun bowed his head. He always said a prayer before giving the nod to release the bull, and she wished she still believed. If she did, she would pray, too. Her breath caught in her throat as the bull busted out of the chute, jerking with powerful force while her husband hung onto the rope, one arm lifted high in the air. If he lost his grip or touched the bull, he would be disqualified. In her head, she counted down the seconds. On six, Mexican Heartburn tossed her husband like a rag doll.

Linc grunted as Calhoun hit the dirt but bounced back to evade the rampaging bull. The beast tossed his head and clipped Cal with one horn.

Vivian clapped her right hand over her mouth so she wouldn't scream, but Calhoun stayed on his feet. *He won't score since he didn't last eight seconds, but at least he's okay, and we're done with rodeo in Prescott.*

Lincoln peered through the binoculars he'd brought. "He's bleeding."

Vivian jumped to her feet and peered harder toward the arena. "What?"

"I see blood. I think he's hurt." Linc scowled.

She didn't wait to hear more. Vivian jumped down a row of bleachers and followed the path to the chutes. She called Calhoun's name, and although he didn't answer, she saw him.

He sat on the ground surrounded by the sports medicine team.

Vivian shrieked his name again, and he glanced up. Blood streamed down his face from a cut on his right temple, two inches above his eye.

"Let my wife come through." Cal waved his hands

at the medics. "Honey, I'm okay. It's just a cut. Dang bull scraped me with his horn."

Lincoln had followed her and stepped closer. "Cal, you need stitches."

One of the team nodded. "Yeah, you're right. He needs to be stitched up and to get checked for concussion. I can send for an ambulance…"

Cal held up one hand. "No, Vivian can take me." He wobbled to his feet and held up both hands.

Vivian approached.

"Easy, honey. I'll bleed all over you."

"I don't care." Vivian touched his right shoulder but refrained from hugging him until she knew how hurt he might be. "I don't think I can drive, though." Her heart pounded harder than a bass drum at a homecoming football game. Her lungs struggled to breathe, and her stomach ached. Vivian didn't scream; although it took effort not to yell. A wild stew of emotions bubbled within, threatening to overwhelm her as her knees trembled worse than her hands.

Lincoln accepted a gauze bandage from a medic and handed it to Calhoun. "Hold this on the cut, Cal. Where's the truck?"

Calhoun held the pad to his bleeding head. "It's not too far. Where's Sasha?"

"She's going back to the hotel. I'll drive." Lincoln turned toward Vivian. "Give me the keys."

She pulled them from her purse and handed them over.

Although unfamiliar with Prescott, Lincoln piloted them to the medical center. He drove over the speed limit and frequently glanced over at Calhoun.

In the emergency department, Cal's injuries took

priority over a bellyache, a kid with a nosebleed, and a dog bite that hadn't broken the skin. Once in a cubicle, he sat still as a nurse staunched the bleeding and took his vitals.

Vivian wrung her hands together and paced the small space.

Lincoln leaned against the wall.

After what seemed like a long time, a doctor arrived. He perched on a stool and shone a light into Calhoun's eyes. "I hear you tangled with a bull out at the rodeo. Do you have a headache, any nausea, or any vision issues?"

Calhoun sat straight and tall. "No, sir, I don't. I don't have a concussion, either."

"Why don't you let me decide that?" The physician rolled his eyes.

"Because I've had enough concussions to know when I do, and when I don't." Cal stated.

After a series of questions, a check of his reflexes, and a few more questions, the doctor agreed. He used four stitches to close the wound and placed a large adhesive bandage over the cut. "I'd use staples, but I don't imagine you'll be anywhere nearby for me to remove them in a week. If you're like a lot of cowboys, you'll cut the stitches out on your own, anyway. I'd advise you not to ride again for a few days."

"I don't plan to. I'm not scheduled to compete again for a couple weeks." Cal slid from the exam table to stand.

"Excellent. I'll write a prescription for some pain medication…" The doc reached for his prescription pad and a pen.

"No, thanks. I won't take them if you do. I'm not

getting hooked on that stuff. I've seen it happen."

The doctor sighed. "All right, cowboy, you're free to go. Don't get the stitches wet if you can help it. Keep the bandage in place for a couple days. Stitches need to come out in a week. Good luck."

After settling with his insurance card, and a cash co-payment, they left. Vivian hovered close, her arm around Calhoun's waist as if he might totter or fall.

Frowning, Lincoln brought up the rear. At the hotel, he parked Calhoun's truck, offering to help Calhoun if necessary.

Sasha met them at their room. "Ouch. Looks like it hurts."

"Not much." Calhoun shrugged as if nothing happened.

"I could hardly watch." Vivian sighed and stroked Calhoun's uninjured cheek.

"I ordered some food. It'll be here soon." Sasha hugged Linc. "I figured we all need to eat something. Cheeseburgers and fries should hit the spot."

"Thanks." Vivian turned her focus to her husband. "Calhoun, let me help you out of that bloody shirt and vest. I'll wash them tomorrow."

"I should take a shower. I probably stink." He sniffed at his underarms.

"You can't get the stitches wet!" Vivian shook her head.

"I'll be careful. I'm sorry, honey. I didn't mean to get hurt on our wedding night." He delivered a cherishing kiss.

"I know." Vivian tamped down tears. "I know."

Before the food came, and while Calhoun showered, Vivian put down her head and cried the tears she'd held back earlier. She wanted to be tough and strong, but she'd been terrified from the moment she saw the blood.

By the time Calhoun emerged wearing a T-shirt and shorts, she had stopped crying. Vivian washed the tears away too. For his sake, she faked a cheerful tone. "Food's here. Let's eat."

Vivian wondered how Cal could thank God and ask a blessing over their meal until she realized his injuries could have been much worse. As long as he continued to compete, he could still get hurt and he might die. Fear clutched her stomach so tight she suffered indigestion.

Chapter Twenty-One

It had been a decade since Calhoun didn't compete in a rodeo on the Fourth of July. So many rodeos happened around the holiday that it was often called Cowboy Christmas. In the past, he hustled from one to another in a hectic rush, competing and sometimes winning. If he hadn't scratched without a score at Prescott, he might have taken home a couple thousand in prize money, but he'd ended up with stitches instead. As rodeo injuries went, it was minor, but the wound freaked Vivian out because it happened on their wedding night.

Lincoln and his wife headed home Monday, after spending a quiet Sunday in Prescott. The four of them attended services at the church where Cal and Vivian got married and shared an early lunch.

"We'll see you in three weeks," Calhoun told his brother after breakfast Monday morning. They had firmed up their plans to visit Missouri and be back in Texas before the next rodeo.

"Stay in touch before then, would you?" Linc embraced him in a bear hug.

"I will, and don't worry. I'm not competing again until after our visit." Calhoun had almost decided to cut a few more rodeos, but he said nothing and wouldn't until he could be certain.

On the Fourth, they lazed around the hotel pool

although Vivian insisted he keep his head and stiches out of the water. Since he got hurt, she had been quieter than usual. He picked up some fried chicken and brought it back to the hotel. His mama had always served fried chicken on Independence Day, and Cal enjoyed keeping the tradition. "Do you want to visit this lake to watch some fireworks tonight?" He liked the idea because he hadn't watched any for years. He'd always been at a rodeo. If he caught sight of a few rockets lighting up the sky, it had been while waiting in the chutes or in the stands.

"If you want to, we can. I don't really care." Vivian sighed as she spoke.

Her indifference bothered him. "Honey, what do you want to do?"

Curled into a corner of the couch, feet tucked beneath her, she shrugged. "I want you safe, and I want to go home."

Calhoun settled down beside her. "I'm all right, Pretty Lady. We're leaving for Missouri tomorrow. Are you homesick?" He thought maybe she missed her grandmother.

"Yes and no. But there's no rodeo at home. I won't worry so much." Her forehead creased with a frown.

"It's just a little cut." He tried to downplay his hurts.

"It needed four stitches." Her lips jutted in a pout.

This probably wasn't the time to mention he'd had many more stitches on numerous occasions. "What's the deal? You've seen me get banged up before."

"But not bleeding."

"Come here, honey." He pulled Vivian into his lap. "Don't you fret. I'm all right. Besides, I've decided this

273

will be my last year. I'll quit after this season."

She tucked her head against his shoulder and snuggled. "That's the best news I've heard, Calhoun. Do you think this head injury and stitches could be what those dreams were about? The ones where your brother said don't make the mistake he did?"

Understanding dawned. He got injured, and it brought those strange experiences to mind. *No wonder it scared her.* "I doubt it. As far as I remember, Sullivan didn't bleed. I still don't understand what he could mean. It's probably nothing to worry about."

Vivian blinked back a few tears. "When Linc said you were hurt and I saw blood running down your face, all I could think about was what Last Chance said, that he didn't want you put in the ground like he was." Her voice cracked like thin pond ice under a heavy boot. "I was scared you were badly hurt and might die."

"Aw, honey, I'm sorry that's what you thought. There's nothing to all that old hoodoo. It's nothing more than bad dreams." Calhoun wasn't so sure, but he'd say anything to reassure her.

"Do you really think so?" She wiped a tear away from her cheek.

"I really love you." He avoided a straight answer to her question. "Still love me?"

"Cowboy, I love you more every day. I don't want anything bad to happen to you." Her fingers clutched his arm.

"Pretty Lady, I love you so much, and I don't plan to let it." He delivered a light kiss on her lips.

Vivian smiled, her real smile the first time all day. "Then the only fireworks I want are right here in this room. Will you make love to me?"

"Anything to please a lady." Calhoun pulled her into his arms.

In the morning, Calhoun rose before six and considered the options. They could follow the same route they had as far as Fort Worth, but after a little research on his phone, he determined they could take I-40 to Lawton in southwestern Oklahoma, then change to I-44 which ran diagonally through Oklahoma to Missouri. Closer in, they could shift from the interstate to US Highway 60 and end up near the old farmhouse.

Vivian made coffee in the in-room pot and sipped it.

"How quickly do you want to get home, honey?" Calhoun couldn't go another cup of the feeble brew.

"As soon as we can, I suppose." Vivian ran her fingers through her long hair.

"We can do it in two days if we put in at least eight or eight-and-a-half hours on the road each day. We'd stop in Tucumcari the first night and the second roll on to the farmhouse. If we get too tired, we could always stop in Tulsa or somewhere in Oklahoma."

She touched his face with light fingers. "Are you up for that?"

Cal preferred to travel at a slower pace, but he'd burn the miles faster so Vivian could reach home. "Sure, Pretty Lady. It'll get us there. I've driven longer than that to get to a rodeo. If we get on the road early enough, we can hit Tucumcari by four o'clock."

"Let's do it. I can drive, too, you know." Vivian smiled. "If it will help."

"It might. Let's get packed and gone." His bag had been ready to go since before daylight.

Vivian dressed and shut her suitcase, then gathered

up their toiletries in a smaller case.

After a stop at a small café with decent coffee and tasty pancakes, they were on the road by seven thirty. Heading east, they faced into the rising sun, so Calhoun grabbed sunglasses from the glove box. With country gold blasting from the speakers, they made good time on the road. They stopped for lunch a little after twelve in Grants, New Mexico. After a quick sandwich and a faster pit stop, they rolled on down I-40.

Vivian insisted on taking a turn at driving.

So he switched places "No woman's ever driven this truck except you. You drove it a little back in Arkansas and now."

"Good. You didn't have a wife before." Her grin shone like sunshine.

Calhoun kissed her, swift and sweet. "True, and you're the only one I'll ever have."

"Is this our honeymoon?" Vivian glanced over at him riding shotgun.

"Honey, this is traveling to get you home. We'll take a trip somewhere else for our honeymoon."

"I like the sound of that, and I'll hold you to that promise." Her hand strayed from the wheel long enough to touch Cal's.

With Vivian at the wheel, they traveled a little slower, but he didn't complain. Calhoun appreciated the break. Multiple hours behind the wheel made his back ache, and his knee twinge. The time was after five before they reached Tucumcari. "Let's find a motel." He ached and wanted to lay down his weary head, then rest his battered body.

She peered through the windshield. "Looks like there are a lot of lodging choices for a small town."

"It's a popular place to spend the night for anyone traveling I-40 or Route 66. Maybe we should have booked ahead. I'm ready to eat and stretch out."

On their third try, they took the last room in a vintage motel dating back to the Route 66 glory days. It boasted both a king-sized bed and a claw-foot bathtub.

"I hope you don't mind the tub," the desk clerk commented. "I know most people prefer a shower."

"Not me." Calhoun anticipated a long, hot soak. "This is great."

Since they would stay one night, he carried in only things they would need. They walked to a nearby diner that offered breakfast around the clock. Cal opted for two biscuits and gravy, and Vivian chose eggs over easy with wheat toast. He polished off the double order. "Good but nowhere as good as what you make."

"You haven't tasted half the things I can cook." She laid her silverware across the plate. "Just wait until we get to the farmhouse."

"I bet you'll knock my socks off." He licked his lips, wondering what all she might prepare.

"I'm going to try."

Calhoun savored a long soak in the old-fashioned tub. Afterward, he relaxed as Vivian kneaded his tight back muscles with a back rub. Calhoun relaxed. He sighed as his stiffness eased and grinned when it led to making love. With no reason to hurry and pain free for the moment, he experienced a wonder and glory in their intimacy. "Honey, I love you. I don't know how I ever made it without you."

She kissed him. "Go to sleep, Cowboy. We've got miles to travel tomorrow."

They overslept and left later than planned with Cal

at the wheel. They could have made it back to Neosho, but he wanted to avoid a long day on the highway.

Halfway there, Vivian booked a room in Tulsa, using her phone.

Calhoun listened as she called her grandmother using speakerphone.

"Hi, Nanna!" We're on our way back."

Nanna cheered. "I'm so glad. I can't wait to see you and Calhoun."

"We'll be there soon. We'll stop tonight in Tulsa and get to the farmhouse tomorrow. Once we do, we'll be out to visit." Vivian positioned the phone toward Calhoun.

"Hey, Nanna."

"Hello, Calhoun. Now, you kids will need to rest up. Wait to come see me until Saturday. I'll be here, and I can't wait to see your wedding pictures." Nanna paused. "Go ahead and take our old bedroom at the farmhouse. It's got a bigger bed, and it's not like I'm coming home to sleep."

"You might…" Vivian began but stopped. *I know she's never coming home. I don't know why I said it.*

"We'll be there," Cal interrupted. "We'll wear our wedding duds, and we've got a video you can watch."

One of his rodeo buddies had filmed the ceremony on his phone and texted it to him.

"And we'll bring cake." Vivian would make sure they found one somewhere.

"How wonderful." Nanna clapped her hands, audible over the phone. "It will be like I was there. I wish I could have been, Vivvie."

"I know, Nanna. We love you." She ended the call and tucked the phone into her purse.

Calhoun had been to Tulsa before, and he remembered a local hamburger chain with chili, fantastic burgers and more. He downed a half-pound burger smothered in onions, fries, and ordered a cup of chili on the side.

"That was delicious." She blotted her lips with a paper napkin.

Calhoun woke during the night with intense indigestion from the onions on the burger and maybe the chili. Cal sat up, clutching his stomach. Sharp pains radiated from it, and he groaned.

Vivian roused and turned on the lamp on the nightstand. "What's the matter, Cowboy?"

"My stomach doesn't like the onions." He rubbed his midsection. "I've got a terrible bellyache, but it'll pass. Go back to sleep." Sometimes, he could eat onions without any trouble, but occasionally, they really tore up his stomach, like now. In addition to the onions on his burger, he'd added raw onions and cheese to the chili. That had been a mistake. "Can you bring me the bottle of antacid?" He swigged some down, wincing at the chalky taste.

"I hope it helps." Vivian frowned. "You look really sick."

"I'll do." He waved his left hand in the air. Cal lay back down, still holding his stomach.

Vivian crawled into bed and spooned around his back. She placed one hand on his abdomen and rubbed it in wide, gentle circles. "Does that help?"

"Yeah." Calhoun savored her touch. Between the medicine and the belly rub, the indigestion eased after a rough half hour. When it did, he prayed. *Thank you, Lord, that my stomach's fine now and for this woman. I love her so much. Keep her safe and turn her heart back toward you.* Cal drifted back to sleep, thinking of his brother. Sully had complained of a bellyache before his fatal ride. *Maybe this was part of the warning. Nah, it's just indigestion from those gosh danged onions.*

In the morning, Calhoun wanted to show her the Blue Whale at Catoosa, a Route 66 landmark attraction, so they left the interstate for a stop. Even traveling on the older, two-lane road, they reached Neosho before noon. Cal intended to head straight to the farmhouse.

"We need some groceries." Vivian announced as they entered the western edge of town. "We might as well get them now instead of later."

"Sure." Cal pushed the shopping basket at the market while Vivian made selections. He paid little attention to what she bought. He longed to be home for a few days, anyway. At the farmhouse, Cal carried their stuff inside.

Vivian put away their purchases, then placed clean sheets on the king-size bed in the front bedroom.

They ate sandwiches and potato chips for lunch. By then he was ready for a nap but decided instead he'd get her car out of the barn. He could tinker with it this afternoon, making sure it ran well after the idle weeks. Calhoun couldn't remember the last time he spent time under a hood without necessity, but he enjoyed the experience. Unless his truck broke down, or required an oil change, Calhoun seldom served as mechanic. As kids, Cal and his brothers had learned basic automotive skills from their dad.

Joseph Kelly had been a mechanic by trade, with hands stained black from years of hard work. In his youth, he'd ridden a little rodeo but gave up to have a family.

Although Cal was just ten when his parents died, he had already learned simple motor staples. As teens, he and his brothers tinkered with their vehicles constantly, mostly to keep them in running order. "What's for supper, wife?" he asked on his way outside.

"It's a surprise, Calhoun. I'll have it on the table around five." Vivian laughed and pulled her attention away from an ancient cookbook with a red-and-white-checked cover.

"Can't I come back inside until then?" Cal pursed his lips in a pretend pout.

"No." Vivian shook her head.

"Then I'd better stock up with a kiss." She didn't protest as he pulled her close and laid his lips on hers. In the comfortable kitchen, he wanted to linger but didn't. Now that they were married, he could kiss her as much and as often as he liked.

Calhoun strolled out to the barn with her car keys in his pocket. Except for the few days they'd spent at Lincoln's ranch, he'd been on the circuit, traveling, or competing since early spring. Leisure time suited him, and he savored the lack of need to rush. Although the weather had turned hot, the July sunshine that filtered through the trees provided a pleasant warmth on his back. Calhoun opened the wide barn doors. Vivian's sports car started on the first turn of the key, purring like a happy cat, so he backed it out beneath a shade tree. Once he opened the hood, he admired the engine. It had been kept in top condition. He added half a quart of oil and topped up the radiator. Everything else appeared to be in order. After he finished, he sat beneath the tree and called his brother. "We're back in Missouri. Vivian's cooking, and I'm monkeying with her car."

"That was a quick trip, bro." Lincoln laughed.

Calhoun shrugged. "She wanted to get home, and it's nice here at her nanna's place. I don't compete again until the twenty-eighth, so we've got about three weeks. I figure we'll be down your way before we head to Lawton."

"Works for me. The boys will be happy. They like Vivian and can't wait to call her Auntie. I might as well warn you they're begging Sasha to order a full-blown wedding cake for a surprise."

"We were going to pick up a small one. I guess it's fine. Just don't make it too big or we'll never get it eaten." Cal didn't mind, and the boys would get a kick out of it.

"I hear you. How are your stitches?"

"Fine." Cal had removed the bandage but not the stitches. He touched his head and winced. The gash remained tender, and he expected he'd have a scar. "Getting hurt on my wedding night freaked Vivian out more than I realized, but she's past the scare."

The old saying Granny often used popped from his mouth. "It'll all come out in the wash. Vivian worries, Cal, same as I do." Linc's voice shifted from light to solemn.

"Neither one of you needs to be concerned." Cal said, then added. "What will be, will be." It was another of their grandmother's frequent adages.

"I suppose it will." Lincoln fell silent in a long pause. "Still planning to hang up your spurs after this year?"

"I am. I'm not sure what I'll do, though. I've rode rodeo every season since I was a teenager."

"You'll figure it out. You can always come share the ranch. It's part yours, anyway."

"My house is too small." Calhoun laughed, half joking, half not.

"I told you you're welcome to build another one if you need to, bro."

"I'll consider it, but I think Vivian might like to stay here." Cal gazed around the back yard, then over the acres in sight. "It's a nice spread, Linc. Although right now, the fields are grown up in weeds, but the house on the property seems sound. It's a rambling old farmhouse, not far off the interstate but in the country.

"Is it hers?"

"Her grandmother's right now. Vivian said she'll inherit when Nanna's gone, which I hope isn't for a long time." A silent prayer Nanna would live for years went up. This house wasn't as large as Linc's, but it was big enough for a family. The more time he spent here, the more Calhoun leaned toward making this their home.

"Send some pictures. I'd like to see it. If you do decide to live there, we could come up sometimes."

"You don't have to wait to head this direction." From his tone, Calhoun knew Linc craved an invitation. "You can come now if you want, Lincoln. You're always welcome wherever I am, and I don't think Vivian would mind."

"Mind what?" She stood near the barn with a smile.

He hadn't noticed, being focused on the call with his brother. "If Linc and Sasha came up to visit and brought the boys."

"I'd love it! Tell Lincoln his family has a standing invitation." Vivian wiped her hands on an apron tied around her waist. "Calhoun, supper is about ready."

He seldom wore a watch, so he hadn't realized it was so late. "I'll be in in a few minutes. Is it okay if I leave your car outside?"

"Of course. Just close the barn doors, would you?" She offered a hand to help him off the ground.

Calhoun accepted it and kissed her. "Linc, I'm heading in to eat, so I'll talk to you later." He took time to close the barn doors, then headed to the house. Delicious aromas reached him as he entered the back porch. Cal washed his hands in the tiny bathroom off the kitchen and found the table in the dining room set. A platter of sliced meatloaf sat in the center, flanked by a bowl of mashed potatoes, a gravy boat brimming with brown gravy, and a dish of seasoned green beans. "Wow! It looks fantastic." He took a seat across from her and reached for her hands. Calhoun didn't miss the slight frown souring her expression as he said grace.

"Heavenly Father," he intoned, head bowed. "Thank you that we're home and in one place for a while. Thank you for this food and bless my wife's hands that prepared it. Be with our family, with Nanna, Lincoln, Sasha, and my nephews. Thank you for my wife, and we praise you. Bless us, Lord, I ask this in Jesus' name, amen." In a voice so soft he could hardly hear it, Vivian echoed, "Amen."

The meal was as tasty as it smelled. He liked the meatloaf and the way she seasoned it. The green beans were cooked with bacon, his favorite way, and the mashed potatoes were real. "I'm glad you didn't use hypocrite taters." He stirred them and swirled the gravy into them.

"What's that?" She cocked her head to hear the answer.

"Another word for instant, honey. Same as I call canned biscuits hypocrite biscuits. Thank you. Everything tastes so good." He closed his eyes and grinned as he slid a bite of meatloaf between his lips.

"There's more." Her lips formed a teasing smile.

"More what?"

"Peach pie for dessert with vanilla ice cream."

His favorite, although he couldn't remember ever sharing that fact. The crust was flaky and light, the peach filling sweet and satisfying. He liked the old house very much, but home, he decided, was wherever he might be with his wife. For now, it was here, and if he survived the rest of the season, maybe it would be forever.

Chapter Twenty-Two

Within her heart, Nanna's place was home. Vivian had been raised in a different part of the county. Her parents' house had been a modern style. The old farmhouse, however, had always been her true home in her heart. Long after her parents died and her childhood home sold, she retained an affection for this place. In the years spent working in the northern part of the state, she often wished she could be on the farm. She'd spent many a summer vacation with her grandparents and many times stayed the night. Her grandparents had been her babysitters while her parents worked. Some of her earliest memories were here, and she had always dreamed of a future in this spot.

Vivian meant what she'd told her husband, quoting Ruth. She would always go where he went. Her choice, however, would be to settle here, build a future, and raise a family. Rodeo had been how she found Calhoun. Because she loved him, she had an affection for the sport. She would admit a certain excitement fueled it, watching cowboys and cowgirls best raging animals, but competition wasn't worth injury. Her first glimpse of Calhoun's face, wet with blood, spooked her, especially after the dreams containing cryptic messages from his deceased brother. Calhoun belonged here. He fit as much as she did. At the Sunny Morning Senior Citizens Center, Nanna met them at the door in her wheelchair. She wore a brilliant smile, and at the sight of them in their wedding finery, she cried out. "You look wonderful, both of you! You're a beautiful bride, Vivian, and Calhoun, you're the most handsome groom I've seen since I wed Benjamin Quinn."

"Thank you, Nanna." Vivian leaned down to kiss the older woman's cheek. She'd done her best to style her hair the same way Sasha had for the ceremony, even tucking a rose behind one ear. They picked up a two-layer white cake to serve as another wedding cake. Vivian had prints made of their wedding photos, using the self-service kiosk at the big discount store. She enlarged her favorite into an eight by ten and bought a frame. "Where do you want to be to see the pictures and watch the video?"

"Let's go in the parlor." Nanna wheeled her chair around to face that direction. The facility boasted a spacious community room furnished with comfortable seating that the residents nicknamed the parlor. "No one's using it yet this morning, not on Saturday. Is that a cake?"

"Of course, it is." Calhoun took control of the wheelchair and parked Nanna at one of the tables in the room. "You have to eat some wedding cake with us."

"We'll wait until after dinner. You two can eat with me again."

For the aged woman, dinner was the noon meal. Vivian winked at Calhoun. Earlier, he made her day by asking if they could take Nanna out of the facility to eat. She loved the fact he wanted to, but the wheelchair made a trip to town difficult. Cal suggested fetching food instead. Nanna always loved Asian cuisine. Vivian played the wedding video for Nanna. When she watched Calhoun slip out to bring some takeout, she grinned.

"Where's your husband?" Nanna asked after they'd watched the wedding twice. "It's almost time for dinner, and they're serving chicken fried steak."

Vivian saw Calhoun coming up the sidewalk to the facility and smiled.

He carried several large bags.

"It's a surprise, Nanna, but we're not eating chicken fried steak today."

"Then what in the world are we having?" Nanna sat straighter in her wheelchair, eyes darting around the room.

Calhoun walked through the door. The rich aromas of the takeout food wafted from the bags. "Your favorite Asian dishes, Nanna. There's General Tso's Chicken, Kung Pao Shrimp, Beef and Broccoli, and Lemon Chicken, plus rice, egg rolls, and rangoons. If I forgot anything, I'll go back to the truck. I've got some paper plates, too, for easy cleanup."

"Oh, my stars! That's wonderful. I haven't had a bite of Chinese since I've been in this place. Bless you, Calhoun, and thank you." Nanna indicated he should lean down, and when he did, she put her arms around his neck, then kissed his cheek. "You've got a keeper, Vivvie," she stage whispered.

A few tears crept into Vivian's eyes. "I do, Nanna."

"Well, let's eat before they try to drag me off to the dining room." Nanna placed a napkin in her lap.

Calhoun sat and started opening the containers. "I won't let that happen, Nanna. They can't be tougher than some of the bulls I've ridden."

"Is that what happened to your head?"

Vivian had never mentioned the stitches to Nanna.

So Cal explained.

After the tasty food, they ate cake and chatted about the future.

Nanna cleared her throat. "I've got a wedding present for you and Calhoun." She handed over a brown envelope she had tucked beside her in the wheelchair. "Go ahead and open it. It's all legal, and it's done."

Vivian did and gasped when she saw the contents. "Nanna!"

"It was going to be yours, anyway," Kate Quinn replied. "Show Calhoun."

Vivian handed him the quit claim deed for the farm made out in both their names.

"I didn't want you to have to wait," Nanna said. "It's already been filed by my lawyer, Samuel Bailey. I asked him to get it ready and bring it out. He was a good friend of your papa's, and my attorney for the past forty years."

Vivian was unable to speak over a lump in her throat. "I remember. Thank you, Nanna."

Calhoun rose and knelt beside Nanna's wheelchair. He took her wrinkled hand in his. "I can't begin to tell you what this means, Nanna, but thank you."

"It's yours and Vivian's to do with what you want, but I hope you'll make it a working farm again." Nanna beamed at the handsome cowboy like a young girl in love.

Cal kissed Nanna's hand. "I'm considering raising beef cattle."

They lingered until Nanna's supper was served, then headed home. Calhoun had a thousand questions about the place, and Vivian answered as best she could. After the large lunch, neither was hungry, so they ate cold sandwiches late. After that, they sat on the front porch, rocking in the porch swing, and savored the evening breeze. It wafted the pleasant scent of honeysuckle toward the house, one of Vivian's favorites. She summoned up the courage to ask the question that mattered most. "Calhoun, will we live here?"

He put his left arm across her shoulders and kissed her. "If that's what you want, honey, yes. I like this place. I could make it a good, working farm again, and I will. We can raise beef cattle or rough stock."

Vivian tasted happiness and snuggled tight within the circle of his arms. "I would love it, Cowboy, but if you'd rather be in Texas, I'll live there."

"Nah, if we can visit Linc's family often, I'm good. We can have them come up here, too. That little house on his place isn't big enough for more than a visit. Linc says we can build if we ever want to. I have a stake in his land, but unless you want him to buy me out, I'll leave it."

"Keep it. It's an investment. I would like to raise a family, Calhoun." She reached out to grasp his hand.

"I want the same, Pretty Lady." He grinned. "You know what?"

His drawl was pure Texas. "I don't have a clue."

"We're home. A few more rodeos and I'm through." He started singing an old Johnny Horton tune, "Done Rovin'." He sang when he was happy, and when he finished the song, he offered her a smile. "I'm done rovin' down that lonesome rodeo road, honey."

"I'm glad, darlin'." She wanted to ask him to forget

the upcoming rodeos, but she knew he wouldn't agree. Vivian didn't want to argue, but even in the most joyful moments, she couldn't forget the words Sullivan said in those dreams. She shuddered with a brief frisson.

"Are you cold?" Calhoun frowned. "It's still hot."

"I'm fine. The wind got to me for a second." *Forget that nonsense and move on. It's just hoodoo and bad dreams, just like Calhoun said.* She tried to believe and failed.

Over the next two weeks, Calhoun got the old tractor out of the barn and used it. He borrowed a brush hog attachment from a neighbor and cleared the fields. With the tall weeds and undergrowth gone, the farm appeared both neat and attractive. Cal came in from the pastures sweaty, dirty, and grinning. "I'll have to do that again more than once before winter. But I don't mind. I've decided to run beef cattle, but I won't buy any until later this fall, after rodeo's done. I'll have to buy hay this year. After that, though, I'll keep some of these fields for hay. I'm glad it's sizeable with one hundred and sixty acres."

Vivian planted a kiss on his sweaty nose. In farmer mode, she found him even more adorable than usual. Vivian rearranged the house to her liking. The place had to be theirs, not a shrine to her grandparents, so she shifted furniture, changed what was kept in which cabinet, and bought new things in town. She hung different drapes in the living room and picked up several brightly colored accent rugs to brighten the hardwood floors. Although she liked the peach color in their bedroom, she decided to paint the walls a soft blue. Then she bought a new comforter to match.

When she checked her email, she squealed with

delight because one of the rodeo magazines had accepted two of her photographs, and a check would be mailed. "Hey, Cowboy," she told him over the supper table that night. "I sold some pictures of you riding bulls."

"That's awesome, Pretty Lady. You're talented, and I like having a famous wife." His slow smile became a huge grin.

"I wouldn't call it that, yet." She laughed but crossed her fingers, hoping. Her work at the newspaper in northern Missouri combined her writing and photography skills. The pictures she took now were totally different. Her true ambition was to write fiction, although she kept it close.

More than once she came downstairs to find him reading the Bible over his first cup of coffee. On Sundays, they went to services at her childhood church. Vivian enjoyed seeing folks she'd known all her life, but she still hadn't made any progress toward restoring her faith. She doubted she ever would, despite the fact it remained important to Calhoun. Vivian attended church for his sake, not her own.

On Monday, three weeks after Lincoln and Sasha left Prescott, the newlyweds rose before dawn to head south. "I traveled early like this going to rodeos. There's not much traffic, and you get there a lot earlier in the day. Sleep, honey, if you want."

Vivian dozed until they stopped for breakfast in De Queen, Arkansas, around seven. Before she fully opened her eyes, she shifted positions. "Are we there yet?"

"Not hardly, honey. We're about halfway. Want some breakfast?"

"I would love something to eat and coffee. I need coffee." She tugged on her ponytail to secure it, then put it up with a clip from her purse.

They ate sausage biscuits at a fast-food restaurant, then motored onward. On the way, they discussed whether they would take the trailer to Lawton, then on to Sallisaw.

"I don't mind if you want to bring it, but whether you do or not is up to you." She didn't consider it her decision. "I suppose it saves money."

"Pretty Lady, I can afford a few more hotel rooms before I settle down. Like I told Linc, I've saved a fair bit of my winnings over the years. Besides, it's a toss-up which costs more, hauling the trailer or renting a hotel room. By the time I figure the cost of gas to drag the tin can, it's cheaper to book a motel. That ol' tin can is cramped. Although if I shared it with anybody, I'd want it to be you."

Vivian remembered he'd once bunked in it with Sullivan. *Maybe he wants to let it go and forget the past.* "I do like my comforts, but I love you, so I'm good either way, Calhoun."

"We'll stay in hotels. We'll book ahead when we get to Linc's." He grinned and lifted her left hand to kiss it.

Although home was now the farmhouse, returning to the ranch was also a homecoming. The three boys welcomed them with whoops and hugs.

Calhoun had bought each of the kids a child-sized cowboy hat, which they loved. They put them on and wore them until Linc suggested they remove them to eat.

After supper, Calhoun's family surprised them with

a two-tier wedding cake, frosted in white buttercream decorated with icing roses. The topper featured a cowboy complete with hats and boots, with a long-haired bride, both in black silhouette.

"It's perfect!" This one might be their third wedding cake, but it was the best. Vivian got out her camera and shot photos for the scrapbook she planned to create.

Sasha took more pictures with Vivian and Calhoun.

Vivian decided she'd have to buy an album. They stayed in Calhoun's small house. Some meals she cooked, but most they shared at the main house with Lincoln's family.

The PRCA rodeo at Lawton was a multi-day event, so they headed northwest after two short days. Calhoun would ride on Friday evening, and unless he scored high, that would likely be the end in Lawton. They checked into a budget motel, since most lodging had been booked in advance for the event, one of the largest rodeos in Oklahoma.

Calhoun drove Vivian onto Fort Sill to see Geronimo's grave and to the Wichita Mountains National Wildlife Refuge to view a huge herd of buffalo grazing. He also motored to the top of Mount Scott, where a panorama of the open plains spread out below. "We're still honeymooners," he explained with his sweet grin. "We have to see some of the sights."

Vivian used her camera to record the view and the moment for posterity.

He scored a seventy-four, a decent number but not enough to advance, so they headed back to Rusk. On Sunday, they attended church with his brother's family, then sat down to a Sunday dinner with smoked turkey, rice dressing, corn on the cob, and peasant bread.

"Just three more rides to go." Cal took more turkey and another slice of the homemade bread. "Sallisaw this weekend, then we'll head home to Missouri until Labor Day weekend. That's when I ride at Elk City, and after that, there's one more in Louisiana. We'll come down again before that. Are you still planning to drive over and watch?"

"We are." Lincoln nodded as he buttered a half slice of bread. "The kids are excited. Isn't that fewer rodeos than usual?"

Vivian waited for the answer, too.

"Yeah. I'd usually have four or six more at this point. I bowed out of a couple, one in Nebraska, and another in Arkansas. I'm ready to wrap this season. I'm tired of traveling and ready to settle down on the farm. You'll have to come visit this fall to see the place."

"Come for Thanksgiving!" Vivian made the invitation on impulse. She could imagine the house filled with Calhoun's folks. She would prepare a big holiday dinner with all the traditional trimmings. Thanksgiving hadn't taken place at the farm since before Papa died. "We'd love to have you, and the weather will still be decent then."

Vivian looked forward to having no more stress over every bull ride once Cal hung up his spurs. Rodeo would be part of Calhoun's past by November.

"Let's plan on it, Linc." Sasha grinned. "The only place I've been in Missouri is Silver Dollar City. Besides, I want to see their place."

"We will, if Calhoun promises to come here for Christmas." Lincoln shot his brother a huge grin.

Cal smiled back. "We'll be here."

At Sallisaw, Calhoun scored an impressive ninety and took home several thousand dollars in cash winnings. On Saturday night, neither wanted to stay for the rodeo dance, so they headed home to Missouri. By the time they reached the house, it was after one a.m. before they arrived, and for once, Calhoun conceded they didn't have to rise early for church. Instead, they attended the informal evening service.

They had three weeks of freedom to spend at the farm. After being idle for the first few days, Calhoun got busy. He checked every foot of the fence line and repaired any breaks or sags. Sometimes, Vivian rode on the back of the tractor with him, but other days she spent decorating the house or cooking. They visited Nanna at least every other day, and Vivian took him to see some of the area sights. If Cal yearned for the arena, he didn't mention it and although Vivian delighted in playing tour guide, showing him around her home area, she longed to nest and create their permanent home. The looming return to rodeo hung over each day, dampening Vivian's spirits. She would have been content to stay here.

Because she knew he would enjoy it, Vivian planned a day at the Precious Moments Chapel near Carthage. Although Sam Butcher's angels were more cute than sacred, the focus on faith delighted Calhoun. Afterward, they dined on the best lemon chicken in the area at a local restaurant. The tart lemon combined with sweet sauce and tender poultry ranked as Vivian's favorite Asian-American dish.

On another day, Vivian drove her sporty little car over to Grand Falls so Calhoun could see the largest natural continuous free-flowing waterfall in the state.

"This is awesome." He sprawled on one of the larger rocks. "I love the sound of rushing water."

She sat beside him. "Tomorrow we'll head over to Grand Lake of the Cherokees. We'll go to Har-Ber Village, and on the way home, I'll show you my favorite spot at Twin Bridges." Memories of those places brought a smile.

"All right, honey but there's still a lot of work to do around the homeplace here."

Vivian loved how he'd taken to calling the farm *the homeplace*. "There's plenty of time for that later. All work and no play might make Calhoun a dull boy."

"Idle hands are the devil's workshop." He laughed as he spoke. "I get the point, though. I haven't forgotten I promised you a real honeymoon. I still mean to deliver. Got any ideas?"

"I don't. Being with you, Cowboy, is a honeymoon every single day." As Cal's wife, she didn't need to travel anywhere.

Calhoun planted a kiss on her lips. "Don't you think you might get tired of me sometimes?"

"Never." She locked her hands around his neck, then kissed him back.

"I'd thought we could go to Kansas City, or St. Louis, or maybe Branson, if you wanted. We could see some sights or take in some shows."

"I've seen all I want of Kansas City." Vivian wrinkled her nose and frowned at the idea of going back. "It's too far to St. Louis, and Branson is such a tourist destination. It would be so crowded."

"I've always wanted to see the Gateway Arch. I never have made it up to St. Louis.

Vivian shrugged. "Maybe later this fall or next

spring."

Grand Lake delighted Calhoun. The vast stretches of water sparkled in the sun, and the day spent at Har-Ber Village pleased them both. The reconstructed pioneer village featured a variety of exhibits, shops, rebuilt log cabins, and a path leading down to the lake, then back uphill. The grounds boasted restored buildings, including a mercantile store, a blacksmith's shop, a bank, and a doctor's office, plus many more.

The small brick chapel at the bottom of the hill facing the lake was the first thing erected on the site when Harvey Jones built the place for his wife, Berniece. The bricks had been handmade by slaves before the Civil War and moved from another site in Arkansas. Blooming roses filled multiple flowerbeds at the feet of the Christ statue. His outstretched arms overlooked the lake.

"I like this place the best so far." Calhoun sat in a pew and bowed his head to pray.

Vivian tried to dig deep to summon up a prayer but couldn't. The words wouldn't come. She remained angry at God and disappointed He hadn't saved her parents. If they hadn't died in such a horrible, brutal fashion, then she would still be a faithful believer, but their murder destroyed her faith.

Calhoun never pressed her. A few times, he had suggested one day she would need the Lord enough to pray.

Maybe so, but Vivian couldn't envision it.

Another day they trekked out to see Jolly Mill, and once, they spent the day in Neosho, visiting picturesque Big Spring Park, the history museum, the oldest national federal fish hatchery in the United States, and the Camp Crowder Museum on the community college campus.

"Camp Crowder was the real Camp Swampy." Vivian gave the history lesson this time as they viewed World War II artifacts. "Mort Walker, the cartoonist for the *Beetle Bailey* strip, was stationed here."

The days spent at the homeplace were her favorites, though, and although she looked forward to another visit with Lincoln's family, Vivian longed for the time when they would be home to stay. She wanted to begin their life together. After his last rodeo, she wouldn't worry so much.

At the end of August with two rodeos left, they headed south to Rusk. The road they traveled had become familiar, and she was glad when they arrived. This time, they would stay in Linc's house, not the smaller one.

After Coushatta, they would go home, and Vivian looked forward to that. Home was where her heart was. She wanted to savor it without worry and certainly not as a widow.

Chapter Twenty-Three

After almost a month at home in Missouri, Calhoun wore a suntan. It suited him and he relaxed more than he had all season. His time on the rodeo circuit would soon come to an end, and now that he'd made the decision, he couldn't wait to quit. Vivian wanted him to stop now and skip out on the last two rodeos, but he would honor the commitments he'd made. Besides that, Lincoln's family planned to watch his last ride in Coushatta. His nephews looked forward to it, and he thought Linc did, too. Calhoun refused to cut his family out of the experience.

He'd sold his tin can to a couple from Jacksonville who belonged to a local RV and trailer club and planned to travel in their retirement. Although the trailer had some sentimental value, Cal wasn't sorry to see it go.

School would start the Monday after Labor Day for Cooper and Caleb, so on Saturday, Vivian went with Sasha to Tyler to buy back-to-school clothing and school supplies. Since Chance was still too young for school, or to enjoy shopping, he went fishing with his dad and uncle on the Neches River. After everyone made it home, they'd gone out for hamburgers in Rusk.

None of them said anything about the cryptic dream messages from Sullivan, afraid to tempt fate.

On the last Saturday in August, the family

assembled for breakfast. Sasha made her special coffee cake and fried some sausage patties. After the meal, they would attend services at the Kelly brothers' home church in Rusk.

Caleb joined them at the table as Linc asked a blessing, and instead of taking a seat, ran to Calhoun.

He'd been crying, and Cal wondered why as he scooped the boy onto his lap. Before they could chorus "amen," the child interrupted the prayer.

"And please, God, don't let Unca Cal have a funnel," Caleb cried. "I don't want him to have a funnel."

"Who said I'd have a funnel?" Calhoun wondered what the kid might be talking about.

"I think it was Elvis, and maybe George Washington. I don't know, but they scared the fire out of me." Caleb clung to his uncle and shuddered.

Lincoln glared at his middle son and finished the blessing. "Amen. Let's eat. Caleb, stop with the nonsense, or we'll be late to church. Your aunt and uncle want to go."

"Daddy..."

"Hush and eat, son. And sit in a chair, not on your uncle's lap."

"He's fine. I don't mind if he stays." Calhoun shifted the boy from his bad knee to the other. Curious, but not concerned, he questioned the kid. "Where did you talk to Elvis and the president?"

"In my room, last night. They waked me up, whispering, and telling me stuff."

"Did they tell you that's who they were?" Cooper asked. "I didn't see anybody, and we share the same room."

"It had to be Elvis." Caleb forked a bite of coffee cake and ate it. "I know because he said, "Hound Dog," and that's one of his songs, remember?"

Cold settled in Cal's stomach when he heard the old nickname. "I do. But, what about George Washington? That seems to be a strange running partner for Elvis, a rock star, with the first president of our country."

"He said he was Barlow Washington, I think. Wouldn't that be the first president?" Caleb asked.

"Don't be a dummy." Cooper rolled his eyes. "That old guy was George. Besides, it didn't have to be George Washington. We got a great granddaddy, or something, named Washington, too. His picture hangs in Daddy's office."

Beside him, Vivian laid down her fork. Her face got a pinched look, and a single tear slid down her cheek. She appeared to be about to cry.

So was Calhoun. "Barlow Washington." He hoped his voice sounded strong and unafraid. "I know you don't remember your Uncle Sullivan, but he used to call me Hound Dog. A few rodeo folks still do."

The mood around the table darkened. Lincoln glowered.

Sasha pushed her plate away and lowered her head.

Caleb leaned back against Calhoun and raised his head. "If it wasn't George Washington, then maybe it wasn't Elvis. He did say something about Chance, but I thought he was talking about the squirt there."

"We called Sullivan Chance sometimes, or Last Chance." Lincoln's tone became as heavy as a slab of marble. "What did he tell you, son?"

"He said Hound Dog better not make the same

mistake he did. He said he doesn't want us to have to have a funnel for Unca Cal. But I didn't understand. What's wrong with a funnel? Isn't it that thing we use to pour oil into the truck, so it won't spill?"

Calhoun's mind made the leap. Not funnel, but *funeral*. His funeral. Sharp fingers of ice traveled down his back. "Yeah, that's right." He forced himself to use a casual tone although he'd lost all appetite for breakfast. "Better eat up, kid, so we can get to church."

The boy sat and ate without enthusiasm.

Vivian shoved back her chair and put a hand on her stomach. "I don't feel very well. I don't think I can go to church today, Calhoun." She dashed out of the room.

He sat still as her footsteps echoed on the stairs, and no one said a word. Cal leapt to his feet. "I better go see about her."

"Stay. I'll go." Sasha rushed out of the dining room and headed upstairs.

Lincoln stared from the head of the table. "What in tarnation?"

"I wish I knew." Calhoun shook his head. "I don't understand any of this any more than you do. It's upsetting my wife, though, and it doesn't do much for me."

"Or me." Linc sighed. "If this is for real, and it seems like it must be, what's Sully trying to tell you? It's a warning, I get that much."

"I don't know." Calhoun wished he did as he rubbed his stomach. Breakfast had soured. "I've thought about it a good bit. Maybe it's not really Sully or our ancestor, Linc. Maybe it's a trick of the devil." Calhoun didn't really believe that. It could be possible and he wished it was.

"Maybe, but I think in some crazy way, our kid brother is trying to keep you from dying." Linc fidgeted with his silverware, then picked up his coffee cup and set it down without taking a sip. "I've always said I didn't put much stock in such things. But Granny did, and I'm beginning to think there's something to this. What's it going to take for you to pay mind to it?"

All three boys looked up from their plate with widened eyes.

"Go, finish getting around for church," Linc told them, before they could fire off more questions.

Calhoun lifted his coffee cup and drank the remainder. "I'm paying mind bro. I'd be a fool if I didn't, but just because it might be a warning, it doesn't mean something will happen." He heaved a sigh, took another bite, then quit. "I've been praying. I'm still going to see the season through. I have two more rodeos—Elk City over Labor Day, then mid-month at Coushatta—and I'm done. Every time I climb onto a bull, it's in God's hands. This ain't no different."

Lincoln stared "Brother, I have faith, but it must be small compared to yours."

"Jesus said whatever we ask in prayer, we'll receive if we believe." Calhoun counted on the promise.

"I'll be praying, then." Linc reached across the table and grabbed Cal's hand. "We're coming to Coushatta to watch you ride."

Cal forced a grin he didn't feel. "I'm looking forward to it. After that, we're heading home to Missouri to start our life together."

"As long as you survive, I'm good with that."

Calhoun headed upstairs to check on his wife.

Sasha met him at the top of the steps. "Vivian says

she has a bad stomachache."

He found his wife lying on the bed, her hands clutching her middle. "Hey, honey, are you okay?" Calhoun knelt beside the bed.

"Not really." She pressed on her abdomen and groaned "My tummy really hurts, Cowboy. I don't want to go to church."

Calhoun needed to go, all the more after what Caleb said. "I'd feel better if we did, with two more rodeos coming up."

"Caleb wasn't talking about a funnel, and you know it. He meant funeral. He's just too little to understand." Vivian spit the words out with force.

"I know. Linc thinks it's a warning, but it might not be. If I don't ride, maybe I'll miss out on a blessing."

"Or maybe you'll stay alive." Vivian sobbed as tears poured down her face. "Won't you think about quitting now?"

"I can't, honey." His voice was as quiet as a church. "I'll keep the faith, like in Second Timothy. I'm praying. It would mean a lot if you would pray, too."

"You know I don't, Calhoun, and can't." She sat up and made a face. "My stomach's killing me."

Won't, not can't. It wasn't the same.

"Someday, I think you'll pray. One of these times you'll need God. He'll be there, honey. Come to church with me, please." He brushed a stray lock of hair from her face.

"If it means that much, all right, I will." She stood and thrust her feet into her shoes. "I need my purse."

Although she went, she didn't participate. Vivian said little, even when he told her stories about growing up in this church. When Calhoun introduced her to people that he'd known all his life, she forced a smile and said the right polite things but remained distant. During the hymns, she didn't sing, and he was certain she didn't hear a word of the preacher's sermon. Her hand tucked into his was cool and limp. When they left the church, Vivian moved like a sleepwalker.

"We're going to eat at a buffet up to Jacksonville. If you guys want to go, I'll buy." Lincoln issued the invitation standing halfway down the church steps.

Calhoun glanced at his wife. "Vivian, what do you think?"

"I think I'd rather go home. I still don't feel very well, but thank you, Lincoln."

"Guess we'll take a rain check" Calhoun frowned. He would have liked to go, but he couldn't, not when Vivian was sick.

"I hope you're better soon, Vivian. Take care of her, Cal." Lincoln waved and shepherded his family to his vehicle.

Once inside Cal's truck, Vivian scooted over and put her head against his shoulder. She laid her right hand flat over her belly. "I'm sorry. I know you wanted to go eat, but my stomach still hurts so bad."

"Honey, how sick are you? If you need to go to the doctor, I'll make it happen."

"I don't think any doctors are seeing patients on Sunday, Calhoun." She slid one hand beneath her shirt and rubbed her tummy.

Cal frowned. "The emergency room's always open. Should I take you over to the hospital in Palestine?"

"No, Calhoun. I'm not that ill. I'm upset, so my stomach's grumpy. It'll pass."

The fact she backtracked a little offered some reassurance. "What's the matter, honey, besides your belly?"

She shuddered against him. "I'm scared, Cowboy. Every time I forget about these vague warnings, someone dreams about Sullivan and now Barlow. I love you. I don't want to be your widow."

"I don't want you to be, either, but it won't come to that." Calhoun sighed. He hoped God heard his prayers. "Not until we're at least in our nineties, have a passel of grown-up kids, and forty-eleven grandkids."

"Do you really believe that?" Vivian clutched his arm.

"I do. I don't think the Lord will take me home just yet, not after I found a wife. Two more rodeos, and I'm done for good. Then we'll head home to Missouri. Okay?"

"All right. I wish we could go now." Vivian released his arm and stared through the windshield without another word. At the house, she changed into her nightgown, refused any dinner, and curled up in bed under a sheet.

Calhoun didn't eat, either. Worried about Vivian, he crawled beside her. He assumed his favorite position, spooned behind her with his arms wrapped around her.

Vivian slept.

Calhoun didn't. Instead, he pondered the meaning of the ongoing messages from beyond. Cal wondered if he should bow out of rodeo now. Leaving would be simple, and although it would cost him the entry fees he already paid, it would bring peace of mind to both his wife and brother. If he ended his season now, it was just three weeks early.

He decided to stick the rest of the season out. If he yielded to temptation, his decision would be from fear, not faith. Over and over, the Bible said not to fear, that fear came from the devil, and not from the Lord. Calhoun decided he had to stand steadfast in his faith. After Coushatta, he'd hang up his spurs for good. He was almost thirty-four years old, so it was time.

Vivian slept for two hours, then woke.

Cal kissed the back of her neck with light, tender lips. "Hey, honey, do you feel better?"

"I do," she murmured. "I guess I just needed some sleep and some TLC."

Relief filled him. He'd worried she might be very sick and had decided if she wasn't better, he'd insist on taking her over to the hospital in Palestine. He'd suffered appendicitis when he was sixteen. It started with an awful stomachache. He also couldn't forget that Sullivan had complained about belly pains the night he died. He'd had internal injuries, but still, the similarity bothered Cal. "I'm glad. Are you hungry?"

"I'm starving." She yawned. "I'll get up and fix something."

"No, Pretty Lady, you won't. I'll take you to town, and we'll get something, whatever you want."

They ate hamburgers followed by a hot fudge sundae, then headed back to the ranch.

He rode Johnny, his paint horse, on their last day before Elk City.

Vivian fed the horse sugar cubes, giggling as his lips brushed over her hand.

"Lincoln said I can borrow a horse trailer, and we'll haul him home when we go for good. I'll have my horse on the place." Calhoun rubbed the horse's nose.

They headed out for Elk City on Thursday for the Labor Day weekend event, although the Rodeo of Champions didn't start until Friday night. He was scheduled to ride then, and right now, Calhoun thought they might leave to come back Saturday. He had no interest in staying to watch the rodeo parade. The rodeo would continue both Saturday and Sunday nights. In addition to all the usual competitions, there would be bullfighting, man against bull, but he didn't want to watch. He could ride them, and had, every year since Sully died, but taking on a bull one-on-one, eye-to-eye in the arena wasn't something that interested him.

Their mid-scale chain hotel sat just off the interstate, about as far from Ackley Park and the rodeo grounds as it could be. Their standard room had a king-size bed, a single armchair, a desk, and a flatscreen television.

As Calhoun taped his knees and wrists, he realized this was the next-to-last time he would do this. A rush of sadness filled him, but it passed. Life with Vivian offered more than any rodeo ever would. He looked forward to becoming a cattle farmer. Cal didn't even care how well he scored tonight. Cal wanted to avoid injury. He'd made it this far and with one more ride after tonight, he hoped to survive unscathed. Once he did, all the unrest over those strange dreams would settle.

He held his seat on a bull named Raging Hurricane for seven seconds, one short of what it took to qualify. Cal waved at his buddy, the one nicknamed Nail, and his friend made tracks to him.

"Better luck next time, bud." Rusty shook his hand.

"Thanks. I'm done after Coushatta in mid-September. It'll be my last bull ride—not for the season, but for good." Until now, he hadn't told any of his rodeo friends his decision.

"Are you serious?" Rusty removed his cowboy hat to scratch his head. "I can't believe it. You didn't even quit after your brother died. Why now?"

"I'll be thirty-four years old on my next birthday." Calhoun leaned against the arena fence as he spoke. "Getting old to ride bulls, my friend. I've got a wonderful wife, and I plan on raising beef cattle in Missouri. We've got a one-hundred-sixty-acre spread to call home."

"Lucky dog." Rusty Nail slapped him across the back and laughed. "Maybe I'll have something similar someday."

"I hope you do, and hey, if you're ever in Southwest Missouri, come by. You can bunk a night or two if you want. We've got the room, and you're always welcome."

"Thanks. I'll see you at Coushatta then. If I don't, happy birthday."

Calhoun would turn thirty-four on November twenty-first, right before Thanksgiving. If everything turned out as he hoped, he would celebrate with Vivian and Linc's family. Vivian's fell in mid-December.

Right now, Thanksgiving and his birthday seemed distant.

Calhoun splurged on a late-night steak dinner before they headed back to the hotel.

"We're going home for now, right?" Vivian took down her long hair and brushed it until it was smooth.

"I figured on heading back down to the ranch.

We'll go home after Coushatta."

Her lips turned downward in a frown. "Oh, I thought since it's eleven days until you ride that we'd go home. I told Nanna we would. Your nephews start school on Tuesday, and I figured we'd be in the way."

He sighed, weary. His knee ached, and he wanted to cuddle up to his wife in bed, not argue. Cal hesitated.

Vivian's eyes narrowed. "Don't you want to go home?"

Calhoun rested his hands on her shoulders. Her muscles tensed beneath this touch. Her sharp voice cut into his peace like a well-honed knife. "I do, Pretty Lady. I just didn't think we were, but we can. It's about five hours to the homeplace and a little more than six to Rusk." Calhoun had planned to take her over to Shreveport for the day, show her Johnny Horton's former home, drive her by the auditorium where the *Louisiana Hayride* had taken place, visit Horton's grave in Haughton, and eat at a favorite restaurant, but the outing could wait. The last thing he wanted to do was quarrel, and he didn't want her to be unhappy.

"So, we are heading home?" Her fingers twisted her long locks into a braid.

Calhoun sat in the room's one chair and pulled her onto his lap. "You bet, honey. I'll call Linc in the morning to tell him. When do you want to come back, though? Will the Monday before I ride at Coushatta work? That will give us more than a week at home and a family visit for a few days before I ride."

"That'll be fine. I'm not trying to be difficult, Calhoun." Vivian rested her head against Calhoun.

"I know, Pretty Lady. We'll be done traveling soon, and we can settle down. I'm looking forward to that. Besides, I love your grandma, too. I don't want to disappoint her." He kissed Vivian's sweet mouth.

Come morning, they headed northeast, not southwest. Calhoun stopped to fill his truck before they left Elk City. They'd nibbled breakfast at the hotel. Her good humor had been restored as soon as she understood they would go home before returning to Texas.

On the way, he dialed Lincoln's number while Vivian dozed beside him in the truck.

"Hello. How was the rodeo? Do you ride again tonight?" His brother answered the first ring.

"Nope, I scratched, just made it seven seconds. Hey, little change of plans. We're heading to Missouri. Vivian wants to see Nanna, but we'll be back next Monday before Coushatta."

"All right. We'll be looking out for you. Caleb's birthday is the thirteenth. I'm sure he hopes you and Vivian will be here."

Calhoun didn't want to miss the kid's celebration. "I'll do my best. We should be."

"Good. Maybe you can catch one of the boys' soccer games. They're at practice now in town."

Soccer. He'd never played the sport, and neither had Lincoln, but Sullivan had. Cal remembered watching the kid play at the same soccer field. "I'd like that. Probably bring back some memories."

"Oh, it does. The first time was hard, remembering Sully. I know I didn't say anything, but it's been more than four years now."

Cal hadn't forgotten. He never had and never would. "I know. The anniversary was when we were in Sallisaw."

"At least, you weren't in Dodge City."

A shudder passed through Calhoun. "I haven't ridden there since and won't. I don't imagine I'll ever go through there again."

"Can't blame you for that. Bro, I'm glad you're almost done. After Coushatta, I won't worry near as much." Linc's voice cracked a little.

Calhoun took off his ball cap, then stuck it back on his head. "That's what Vivian says. We'll see you next week, Linc."

At the homeplace, Calhoun thought he would be content, but this time, he became restless. An odd heaviness weighed down his spirit for reasons he didn't understand, but he finally decided came from Caleb's talk of funnels, Elvis, and George Washington. Until now, the warnings had been vague—don't make the same mistake, stay above ground—but this last message from heaven, if that's what it was, referenced a funeral. That made it more specific and stirred up terrible memories. His parents' funeral had been a nightmare. Pop's service had been a proper send-off and Granny's a blessing. She had been ready and had asked that her favorite verse from Second Timothy be read. *For I am now ready to be offered and the time of my departure is at hand.* Sullivan's, however, had been worse than their parents', the most terrible day of Calhoun's life.

The church had been packed, as often was the case for someone young and beloved. The hymns that he and Lincoln selected still wrenched his heart when he heard them, same for the Scriptures. Calhoun had been a pallbearer, and performing that last service for his brother had taken more courage than he'd had. Without the Lord, he couldn't have done it.

Calhoun had remained after all the other mourners returned to the church for a meal and stood in the hot August sunshine. Calhoun watched as the grave was filled and smoothed. He saw the floral tributes tossed on top of the new grave. Cal had retched when the fragrance of the flowers reached his nose.

As his final rodeo and last bull ride neared, Calhoun prayed often. He wanted to survive and make a life with Vivian. The last thing he wanted would be leave her to mourn. If he died, it would hit Lincoln hard and Sasha almost as much. His three nephews wouldn't understand, and they would be hurt. Cal feared that if the worst came to pass, it would drive his wife farther away from the arms of a loving God.

Calhoun rose early on the last morning at the Missouri farmhouse. He left Vivian asleep and tiptoed downstairs. He brewed coffee and took a cup to the front porch where he watched the sun rise. From the first hint of light on the eastern horizon until the sun rose with a glorious golden beauty, turning the clouds soft pink in a calm blue sky, he prayed.

As he did, calm replaced his anxiety. His final rodeo would be fine, he decided. God was in control. In the words of the Psalm Ninety-One he found comfort. *For he shall give his angels charge over thee, to keep thee in all they ways. They shall bear thee up in their hands, lest you dash thy foot against a stone.*

Calhoun now had the strength to go to Coushatta and face whatever came to pass. A line from one of Johnny Horton's songs echoed in his mind…*there to meet his fate.* He would do exactly that.

314

Chapter Twenty-Four

Vivian woke to the sound of rain and savored it until she realized Calhoun would ride his last at the Red River Parish Fair Rodeo tonight.

Cal slept. He'd wanted to be close to his family. He opted to stay upstairs at Lincoln's house.

As his final ride neared, the more Calhoun displayed an inner calm and a peace Vivian wished she shared. Unlike her husband, her fears increased with each passing day. With the rodeo tonight, her nerves were on high alert. If Vivian didn't rise and find something to occupy her hands, she would suffer a panic attack.

She dressed in the dim early morning light and headed to the kitchen. Vivian decided to make a special breakfast for her husband. She chose the biscuits Calhoun liked so well and sausage gravy. Vivian made enough for the whole family—although she doubted the kids would take time for anything more than cereal and milk.

Since it was Friday, Cooper and Caleb had school and came downstairs early. The big yellow bus would be out front by seven thirty.

Sasha entered the kitchen with time to button them into bright-yellow raincoats before handing each kid his lunchbox. She kissed her two older sons, and watched as they dashed down the drive to wait for the bus.

"Vivian, you didn't have to get up and make breakfast."

"I don't mind." Vivian shrugged. "I'm a nervous wreck, so I needed something to do. Calhoun hasn't come down yet. Is Linc awake?"

"He's in his office, watching the weather report. I'm sure he'll be glad of a hot breakfast." Sasha eyed the bubbling gravy and sighed. "I wish I had time to eat."

"Take a minute." Vivian grabbed a biscuit, split it, and doused it with gravy. "I made so much."

"Thanks." Sasha stood at the counter and devoured her portion. "I've got to leave in a minute since I'm a paraprofessional at the elementary school this year. Linc will watch Chance today. What time do you guys leave for Coushatta?"

"Probably not until noon." Although Coushatta, Louisiana, was two hours away, they had reserved a motel room where Calhoun would get ready to ride. Afterward, if he was tired, they could sleep there. They would come back to the ranch in the morning. "When are you leaving?"

"Probably not until around four, four-thirty, after the kids are home from school. We probably won't eat until we get to Coushatta." Sasha grabbed her purse and lunchbox. "I'll see you there."

Vivian nodded. She drank a second cup of coffee but waited to eat with Cal.

Fifteen minutes later, Lincoln joined Vivian. "Good morning. Give me some coffee and a plate of biscuits and gravy. I'll take it to the table. Cal will be here any minute. I heard him on the stairs."

Vivian attempted to smile.

But when he arrived, he had little to say. He kissed

her in an absent-minded way.

"Good morning, Cowboy." She hugged him. "I hope the rain stops before tonight."

"It either will or won't. I'll still ride." He shrugged with little interest.

Vivian filled two plates and sat beside him at the dining room table. She ate most of her portion before she noticed Cal hadn't downed more than a few bites. "What's the matter? Is something wrong with the biscuits?"

"They're fine, honey." He stirred his food around and sighed. "I just don't have much appetite this morning."

"Do you feel all right?" Vivian frowned as she noticed he seemed pale.

Calhoun scrubbed his face with one open hand. "I'm just tired. I want to get this last rodeo in the books and move forward."

"I bet." Lincoln polished off the last of his gravy. "I remember when I gave rodeo up, I was glad but a little sad, too. You've competed longer than I did. Have any second thoughts?"

"Not a one." Calhoun pushed his full plate away. "I wish it was tomorrow."

Vivian cleared the table. She touched Cal's forehead. "You're warm but not hot. I don't think you have a fever."

"I doubt it." He frowned and pulled back. "Don't fuss over me, honey."

"I'm worried, Cowboy." Vivian smoothed his curly hair.

Calhoun flinched. "You don't need to be, Vivian."

Feelings hurt, she carried the dirty dishes to the

kitchen and loaded the dishwasher. She lingered for a few moments. *I need to go upstairs and pack. I also need to calm down.*

Lincoln caught her before she headed upstairs. "Is Cal okay? He's acting off."

"I agree." Vivian sighed with relief. She wasn't being paranoid. Lincoln had noticed. "You saw he didn't eat or finish his coffee."

"That's not like him. Is he sick?" Linc frowned.

"I'm afraid he might be. Some bug was making the rounds in Elk City, and there's been some early flu in Missouri. I hoped neither of us would come down with it. At least, he doesn't seem to have any fever." Vivian crossed her fingers, hoping one didn't develop.

"If he's sick and it's raining, that's a recipe for disaster." Linc sighed. "I'd try to convince him not to go, but he won't listen. Cal can be as stubborn as a goat sometimes."

Despite her concerns, Vivian laughed a little. "You're right."

Lincoln handed her his empty mug. "I gotta go see what Chance is up to in the playroom. How soon are you heading out?"

"I don't know." Vivian spread her hands wide. "I need to pack, but I think Cal has everything else loaded. We'll see you tonight at the arena."

"Be careful and take care of him, Vivian."

"I will." A rush of affection filled her heart for her brother-in-law. She didn't have a brother, but Linc had adopted her. On impulse, she hugged him.

Calhoun came inside, damp from the rain. "I'm ready to go. Let's hit the road. Linc, see you and the family later."

"Will do, bro. Is it still raining?" Linc slapped his brother on the back.

"Pouring. C'mon, honey, let's make tracks. If we leave now, I can grab a nap once we're checked into the motel."

Although it was hours earlier than planned, Vivian didn't argue. "Let me gather my stuff." She hurried and finished packing.

In Rusk, they picked up Highway 84 and followed it to Louisiana. Rain drummed a rhythm on the pickup's roof and the windshield wipers kept time to the country music echoing through the truck. Unlike most days, Calhoun didn't sing along. He said little, but Vivian hoped it was due to the heavy rain, not illness. *Maybe he's nervous about his last rodeo—after all, he's done this for probably half his life or more. It'd be natural if he's anxious even without all this premonition stuff.*

By the time they reached Mansfield, the rain slacked, then stopped. Vivian noticed the ditches brimmed full of water on both sides of the road.

When Calhoun stopped for fuel, he bought a root beer and a bottle of iced tea for her, but he drank little.

In Coushatta, the motel proved to be an older property dating to the 1950s. The room was small, and the furniture tight. Vivian had to turn sideways to walk between the bed and the desk. A shelf held an outdated television, and she noticed an absence of chairs. At the end, past the bed, a sink sat beneath a mirror. A door led into a dinky bathroom with a commode and shower-tub combination. Unless Calhoun was too tired to drive back to the ranch, Vivian didn't plan to stay here tonight. It would do as a place for him to dress in his gear and get ready. "Do you want some lunch?" Vivian asked, although it was barely noon. "I can take the truck and go get something." Vivian tossed him a towel, which he ignored, and used one to dry her damp hair.

"I'm not really hungry. If you want to grab some grub, go ahead, honey. I'll try to eat when you get back." Calhoun sprawled on his back on the bed with his eyes shut.

Vivian leaned over to kiss him. "You're awfully warm."

"I don't know how. I'm cold. Aren't you?" He shivered and rubbed his arms.

"No. What do you want? Chicken, burgers, deli sandwiches, or tacos?"

"I don't care. I'm not even sure I can eat." Calhoun rolled over and pulled the bedspread over him.

She brought back burgers from the closest place. Calhoun was asleep when she returned. Vivian ate hers and stuck his in the mini-fridge. She considered waking him but didn't. Maybe sleep would improve his mood and condition.

Calhoun woke on his own around five o'clock. He swung his legs over the side of the bed and sat up with a groan. "Got any aspirin or ibuprofen?"

"I do. What's the matter?" She drew a deep breath. *I know he's sick.*

"I got a bad headache, honey. I don't feel so good." He rubbed his face with both hands.

Vivian dug out the over-the-counter meds from her purse and brought them with his root beer from the fridge. Once he downed them, she put her hand across his forehead, and winced. "Calhoun, you're burning up."

"I feel like death warmed over. I'm aching all over,

and my nose is stuffed up." He shivered. "And I'm cold. Is that air conditioner running overtime or what?"

The ancient window unit barely worked and put out no more than slightly cool air. "I think you've got the flu, Cowboy. Didn't somebody say it's been going around?"

Calhoun shrugged. "Maybe."

"You look miserable." Vivian smoothed back his hair from his face. "Go ahead and lie back down, darling. Do I need to call someone at the rodeo or what?"

He glared. "What for?"

"To tell them you're sick and won't compete." It seemed simple.

Calhoun grasped her hand with force. "Honey, I'm still riding. I gotta."

The fevered heat of his skin concerned her. "No, you don't."

"It's not like a job where I can call in sick. Besides, it's my last rodeo. I'm hanging up my spurs after this." He grimaced as he spoke. "You ought to know bull riders don't call in when they don't feel good."

Vivian sat beside him on the edge of the bed. "I do, but I don't see why you have to ride, Calhoun. Why does it matter? It's the last time. You're sick, and you're running a fever."

"Cowboys don't quit for anything. Besides, Lincoln and the family are on their way. I can't disappoint the boys. If I can sit that bull for eight seconds, then I'm done." He held his head with both hands.

His brother had said he was stubborn. Right now, Vivian would call it bullheaded. "Cowboy, you haven't eaten hardly anything today."

His eyes glittered in his flushed face. "I promise, I'll eat afterward. Then we can go back to the ranch."

I wish we hadn't left. She wanted to talk him out of competing, but he'd made up his mind.

Calhoun needed her help to get ready for the rodeo. Once at the arena, he tottered, shaky on his feet, but he wouldn't reconsider. "I'm riding, no matter what."

Vivian's stomach churned. She couldn't imagine a good outcome. Once they found Linc's family in the stands, she stuck close to Calhoun. The boys yelled with delight and hugged Cal so hard she feared he might topple.

"Be careful, Cowboy." She put her arms around him before he left the stands.

"I always try." He brushed a swift kiss across her forehead and headed to the chutes.

"He's really sick, isn't he?" Lincoln turned to her with a knitted brow.

Vivian nodded. "He's feverish, and I think he has the flu."

"God help him." Lincoln bent his head in prayer.

Vivian almost wished she could do the same. She would if she still believed.

****

Calhoun'd known before he opened his eyes this morning he was sick. Every muscle in his body ached with dull discomfort he felt deep to the bone. For a man who lived with pain, this was different. His sensitive skin hurt. Calhoun had the beginnings of a headache that pounded within his skull. If he complained, his wife and brother would do their level best to talk him out of competing, so he said nothing. Tonight would mark his last rodeo, and he had to be there.

For one, his last ride was the culmination of a long career, and he craved that final hurrah. For another, his brother's family had traveled to watch him compete, including his three young nephews. Calhoun loved those boys as if they were his own, and he refused to let them down. Calhoun would ride, as he had for four years now, in memory of his younger brother, Sullivan. He both honored the kid's memory and paid penance. Cal carried a heavy load of guilt. Lincoln and Vivian both assured him it wasn't his fault, but he knew it had been.

Awake and miserable, coming down with a bad case of flu, Calhoun finally understood what those strange dreams or messages from Last Chance meant— why his brother had insisted he shouldn't make the same mistake he had. Until now, the warnings made no sense, but Cal understood.

Sullivan had ridden his last bull sick, his belly hurting not from overindulgence or indigestion, but with internal injuries. The kid had said that his stomach hurt and suggested maybe he shouldn't ride.

Cal, stupid in hindsight, told him to ride anyway, to suck it up and be a cowboy. If Last Chance hadn't died, Cal would have had him checked out at the hospital. If Calhoun had insisted he see a doctor instead of ride bulls, then his brother would be alive not dead.

He now believed Last Chance's message was don't ride sick, as he had, but Calhoun would. He wanted to live, more than anything, but this would square what he owed his kid brother. The cryptic communications had disturbed him more than he liked to admit, especially the most recent, the one his nephew interpreted as funnel but had been funeral. Cal had drawn into the deep well of his faith, however, and accepted that God's will would be done. He wanted to believe he'd be unscathed after tonight's ride and prayed that would be the case.

He stayed in bed longer than usual, then took a shower, hoping it would help, but it didn't. Downstairs, his wife brought him coffee and a plate of her biscuits covered with rich sausage gravy. It was one of his favorites, but today, Calhoun couldn't summon enough appetite to eat much. He didn't even finish his coffee. Cal hated the look of concern on Vivian's face but told her he was fine. She put her hand on his face, and he knew she was checking to see if he had a fever.

Fortunately, he didn't have one yet because she found his skin warm, not hot. Vivian fussed when he didn't eat much, but he put off her questions. As soon as the truck was packed with his bull riding gear and what they'd need for one night, they headed east toward Louisiana. With every mile, he felt worse but didn't complain. Although the country tunes he loved blasted from the speakers, today he didn't wasn't up to singing. Rain splattered the windshield most of the way, until Mansfield.

Cal stopped to fuel his truck and thought maybe a soda might perk him up. He couldn't manage more than a few sips of root beer. Although the rain quit, the arena would be mud instead of dust. That was bad enough, but when they reached the motel, it was a cramped fleapit. He hadn't given any thought toward lunch until Vivian mentioned they hadn't eaten. She ventured out for food, but he lay on the bed, one arm over his eyes, the sickest he had been in years. He drifted asleep but roused around five. When he sat up, he groaned. His body hurt, and the headache had become severe. He admitted his head hurt.

When Vivian handed him some aspirin, she touched his face and cringed. "You're burning up."

If he'd felt better, he would have argued and tried to fake being well, but he couldn't. Besides, he shivered with a sudden chill although she informed him the air conditioning barely worked. He didn't try to argue when she diagnosed the flu because he knew it was.

She suggested he couldn't compete.

He disagreed. "I'm riding. It's the last time. Besides, Linc and the family are halfway here. I won't let those boys down."

Eight seconds. All he had to do was make it to the arena, climb onto the back of a bull in the chute, then last eight seconds. If he could manage, no matter what his score, he would be done. Then they could head back to the ranch where he could sink into a comfortable bed. She could nurse him all she wanted. Cal wouldn't complain. Now, though, she fussed because he hadn't eaten, so he promised he would after the rodeo. He would try, at least.

He thought she'd quarrel and try harder to get him to cancel his ride, but she didn't.

Instead, Vivian helped him get ready. She taped his wrists and knees. She wrestled him into his dirty, old jeans, slid his arms into a clean Western shirt, and added the protective vest. She drove to the arena. Once there, she trailed him while he checked in, paid his entry fee, and got his number.

Calhoun would ride around eight-thirty, which seemed a long time away. He took over-the-counter pills for his fever. Calhoun ached with every slow step he made to reach his family waiting in the stands. He tried to act cheerful, but he suspected he didn't fool anyone.

Walking to the chute required every bit of strength he could summon. Cal prayed he would make it. Whether it was the flu, the fever, or the fact he hadn't eaten, Calhoun became increasingly weak. His headache grew steadily worse until his head pounded. As he climbed onto the bull, a monster animal named Chain Lightning, his head whirled. Once seated, bull rope in his hand, he realized how unsteady he'd become, but it was too late. Usually, he said a prayer before the bull burst out of the chute, but he felt too rotten to pray. Quitting wasn't an option now—he had to ride. Resigned to his fate, Calhoun lifted one arm in the air. With effort, he gave the nod.

Chain Lighting burst out of the chute with speed as Cal clung onto the rosin-slick rope as if his life depended on it. He glanced to his left and saw Last Chance. His younger brother leaned against the chutes in the Texas flag shirt they had laid him to rest wearing. The sight had to be a hallucination, but the kid smiled. Over the din of the rodeo, above the announcer's voice and the music, Cal heard his late brother's voice. "You never listen, Hound Dog. You gotta fight, Cal, and pray. You might make it. We'll be praying."

Beside him stood their sharp-featured ancestor, Barlow Washington.

Distracted and ill, Calhoun couldn't keep hold of the rope or maintain his seat on the bull. He lasted no more than three seconds before Chain Lighting bucked him into the air. Calhoun flew in slow motion. He smacked the muddy arena floor hard and landed facedown. Cal tasted mud, and his ears rang. He heard Vivian shrieking as the crowd called for him to rise. Cal struggled and turned over as the unrestrained bull lashed out with hooves flailing. Although he saw the animal's back leg coming toward him, Cal couldn't move in time, and the bull kicked him with force in the chest.

The pain hit with such intensity he thought the blow must have ripped his chest wide open. It hurt so much Calhoun feared he might be having a heart attack. Breathing became difficult, and he couldn't see. Everything around him blurred and turned to confusion. The announcer's voice echoed, but Cal couldn't make out a single word. Nothing made sense.

The sports medicine team clustered around him, talking.

But he couldn't respond. A few words broke through his consciousness: *ambulance, injury, hospital.* Calhoun wanted his wife, needing to hear her soft voice and feel her touch. He squinted hard through the agonizing pain in his chest. An ambulance's emergency lights bathed everything in an eerie red light as he was loaded onto a gurney and into the vehicle.

Vivian appeared. She clutched his hand, weeping. "Calhoun, I love you, Cowboy. Hang on, just hang on."

He struggled to say her name, but someone slapped an oxygen mask over his face before he could.

Linc stood beside her, face furrowed.

Behind them, he saw Sullivan and Barlow. He wondered if anyone else saw them, too, then the lights went out in his mind as everything went dark.

The last thing he heard was the screaming

ambulance siren as it rushed him to the hospital. *I hope I'm not about to die.* Deep down, on the last edge of consciousness, he thought he probably would.

Chapter Twenty-Five

From the stands, Vivian saw Calhoun struggle. He walked like a drunken sailor and weaved back and forth without his usual swagger. Although he climbed onto the bull, he swayed as if he might fall at any second. Seeing the bull burst from the chute, she leaped to her feet, counting the seconds in her head. If he could make it, they'd go back to the motel. In the morning, they would head home. He was in no condition to leave tonight. When the bull tossed him into the arena, Calhoun landed facedown, she shrieked and twisted her hands into tight fists.

Lincoln stood and shouted a wordless cry. Cal rolled over, and Linc clenched his hands tight. His lips moved with silent prayer.

The bull kicked.

A rear hoof struck Cal's chest.

Lincoln gave a hoarse shout. "No!"

Vivian didn't remember running, but she arrived as they loaded Calhoun into an ambulance. She shoved through the gathered crowd and grasped his hand.

Cal's lips had a bluish cast, and before he could respond, the paramedics put an oxygen mask over his face.

"Where are they taking him?" Lincoln stood at Vivian's side.

One of the paramedics turned. "The hospital in

Coushatta. But probably they'll send him to Natchitoches or Shreveport."

In tandem, Vivian and Lincoln ran to Calhoun's truck. She climbed behind the wheel and turned the key. Vivian rocketed from the parking space and careened from the rodeo grounds onto the blacktop.

Linc dug his fingernails into the dash. "Slow down or we'll wreck, Vivian. Don't go so fast!"

Vivian ignored his plea and followed the ambulance to the local medical center. Inside, she wrung her hands as they waited. Fear clawed within her chest. *I've never been this scared, ever.* She watched Linc pace the floor and counted the tiles with a strange detachment. Nothing seemed real.

Within thirty minutes, a doctor appeared. "Family of Calhoun Kelly?"

Vivian grabbed Linc's hand as they responded.

"Wife and brother," Lincoln told the physician.

"Dr. Earl Spitz, emergency physician."

If he hadn't been wearing a hospital ID, Vivian would have never guessed he could be a doctor. The short-statured man wore cargo pants with bulging pockets beneath his white lab coat and a dress shirt with a Western string tie. "How is he?" Vivian found her voice, but it trembled worse than her hands.

"He's critical. He arrived without a pulse, but we resuscitated him. Mr. Kelly has numerous injuries, including a bruised aorta, broken ribs, and collapsed lungs. He's also running a fever. Although we haven't determined the cause."

"He's sick—he has the flu." Vivian blurted the information.

Dr. Spitz nodded. "The fever is secondary to his

injuries. We've done our best to stabilize him, but he requires treatment we can't provide here. He'll be life flighted by helicopter up to Shreveport. I don't want to sugarcoat, so I'll be frank." The physician paused, then bowed his head. "If you're a praying woman, I'd talk to the Almighty. He's in danger of dying."

Vivian gasped and put one hand to her chest. A terrible grief swamped her and robbed her breath. *I can't lose him. I can't.*

"He'll be at Ochsner LSU Health, a level-one trauma center in Shreveport within fifteen minutes. They'll start treatment immediately and perform surgery to repair the bruised aorta. We've inflated his lungs and have him on oxygen." Dr. Spitz delivered the information in a level tone flavored with a slow Louisiana accent. "We need one of you to complete some paperwork."

Vivian managed, although she wasn't sure if her handwriting was legible. She had Calhoun's billfold in her purse with his insurance card. She finished as the helicopter landed. As soon as it took off, she dashed to the truck.

Lincoln snatched the keys from her hand. "I'll drive. You're too upset."

"So are you," she replied but didn't argue.

Linc called his wife as they rocketed northbound. "Hey, Cal's critical so they're sending him up to Shreve. I'm going with Vivian. Take the boys home. I'll call as soon as there are any updates. No, don't try to come." Lincoln paused and drew a deep breath. "Babe, they don't know if he'll survive. The boys don't need to hear this, not right now. Pray hard, Sasha. Get the prayer line started at church… I love you. I'll call you soon as we know anything."

The hour-long journey seemed to last a day. Lincoln piloted the truck through the night, driving as fast as possible.

Vivian slumped, numb, and paralyzed with fear. *I don't want to be a widow.* Calhoun had to live. Tonight was supposed to have been his last ride, and their true married life should have started in the morning. Right now, they ought to laughing over a good steak, not racing to see if Cal would live or die.

Lincoln seemed familiar with Shreveport and drove to the trauma center.

The news was scant. They were told Calhoun was in surgery to repair the aorta. Afterward, he would go to the intensive care unit, and they could wait for word there.

The room loomed large, and the lights had been dimmed for the night. Couches and chairs were grouped through the space. Linc lead Vivian to the farthest corner, away from any other waiting families. "Can I get you anything? Maybe a soft drink? Coffee?" Lincoln slumped against the cushions and heaved a sigh.

Vivian shook her head. "All I want is Calhoun." Her chest ached with unshed tears, but if she started crying, she didn't think she could stop. "Thank you, though."

Two hours later, a doctor entered, a mature woman in maroon scrubs. "Kelly? Who's with Calhoun Kelly?"

"That's us." Lincoln stood.

So did Vivian.

"I'm Dr. Maria Pacini." The doctor yanked the surgical cap from her salt-and-pepper hair and wiped perspiration from her forehead. "Calhoun is out of surgery. I repaired his aorta with staples. His lungs are working, but we'll keep him on oxygen as a precaution. His broken ribs have been taped. I understand he arrived at the hospital in Coushatta without a pulse." Dr. Pacini leaned closer, frowned, and softened her professional tone. "He's still in grave danger. I won't tell you anything different or raise false hopes. For his body to rest, he's in a medically induced coma in our intensive care unit. We'll keep him that way for twenty-four hours, then see if he'll wake on his own. Either way, we'll go from there."

"I want to see him. I'm his wife." Vivian had to see him, or she'd end up in an adjacent bed. Her stomach ached, and she thought she might pass out from stress.

Dr. Pacini nodded. "You both can go back to his cubicle in a moment, but you can't stay long. You're welcome to make the ICU waiting area base camp. You both can visit Calhoun for a short time each hour. We'll reassess after the twenty-four-hour period has passed. If you want to go home, then we'll call if there's any change."

"We're from Texas, so it's too far to leave. We'll be here." Lincoln cleared his throat as he spoke and fidgeted.

"I understand. I'll explain protocol and take you to Calhoun."

No one entered the unit without first buzzing the nurse on the other side of a window. Once inside, thorough handwashing was necessary. After scrubbing, Dr. Pacini led them to the small cubicle where Calhoun lay.

His face appeared paler than the white sheets on

the hospital bed. His unruly curls were pushed back from his face. Vivian gasped with the realization Calhoun had been ventilated with a tube down his throat. He wore a nasal oxygen canula and three IVs connected to his veins. Monitors displayed his respiration, pulse, heart rate, temperature, and oxygen levels. Vivian had never seen him so vulnerable. She steeled herself to approach the bed and wrap a hand around one of his. He didn't respond. "Calhoun." For his sake, Vivian struggled to use a normal tone. "Linc and I are here. I love you, Cowboy. You're going to make it. As soon as you're well enough, we'll go back to the homeplace, I promise."

"Vivian, he can't hear you," Lincoln whispered.

"He might." Dr. Pacini spoke from the doorway. "It doesn't hurt to talk to him. Some patients have told me they knew everything that happened when they were in a coma. When they described events or experiences they had no way to remember or tell a family member what was said, I believed them. After ten minutes, however, you need to return to the waiting room. You can come back every hour."

The cycle of brief visits and long periods in the waiting room became routine. By four a.m., Lincoln slept on one of the couches.

Vivian went back alone. She kissed Calhoun's forehead and smoothed his hair. His skin felt feverish. In the hour before dawn, the darkened windows reflected the room. Vivian glanced up, blinked, and looked again. She gasped and clutched her throat. A tall, young man stood behind her. He wore a shirt bright with the colors of the Texas flag. She'd seen him before in her dream. "You're Sullivan. If you've come to take him, you can't have him."

"I don't want him, Pretty Lady. I'm here hoping he's going to make it." The apparition smiled. "Back home, those three boys, one of them with my nickname, are praying their little hearts out. Up in Missouri, your grandma's praying, too. When Linc wakes up, he'll pray. Sasha's on her knees back at the ranch. Half the church folk are praying, too. Why won't you pray, Vivian? Hound Dog needs your prayers."

Groggy from lack of sleep, stressed, and worried, Vivian figured she must be hallucinating. She needed coffee and something to eat soon to keep up her strength and banish waking dreams. "I don't pray, not anymore."

"God didn't fail your folks." Last Chance shook his head. "And He didn't fail me. If you want Calhoun to live, you'd best pray."

"I can't," she whispered. "I've tried. I lost my faith."

" 'Now faith is the substance of things hoped for, the evidence of things not seen.' " Vivian recognized the Bible quote and nodded to acknowledge she'd heard.

As quickly as he'd appeared, Sullivan "Last Chance" Kelly vanished.

"I would pray if I could. It's just not in me anymore." She spoke to Calhoun.

But he showed no sign he'd heard.

Vivian returned to the waiting room, rattled and near tears.

Lincoln was awake and made room on the couch. "Did something happen? You look upset."

Vivian considered sharing her experience but

didn't. "I'm as good as I can be under the circumstances. I think I should eat something."

"We both ought to have something. It's best if we keep our strength up. If he pulls through, he's gonna need us." Lincoln nodded, and his tense expression eased a fraction.

Not *if,* but *when.*

Once the cafeteria opened, they drank coffee. Vivian managed to down part of a cinnamon roll and a little milk. Anywhere else, she would have savored it, but here, she might as well be eating dry leaves or sticks. They alternated between the waiting room and Cal's cubicle. In the late afternoon, Vivian ventured outside to call her grandmother.

"Hel-lo," Nanna's bright voice chirped like a bird. "I want you to know, Vivvie, I'm praying for you and for Calhoun. How is he?"

Vivian had been struggling to find the right words to tell the old woman what had happened. What Sullivan had said proved true. "You already know he's hurt? Did someone call you?"

"Of course not. The nicest young man, who favored Calhoun a fair bit, came by early this morning and told me. He said to pray, so I have been."

A cold chill sliced through her calm veneer. It wasn't possible, Vivian thought, couldn't be. "Who was he?"

"Last Chance." Nanna used the nickname in a calm voice. "That's what he said, then told me he was Sullivan Kelly, your husband's youngest brother."

Vivian shuddered but spoke the truth. "Nanna, he died riding a bull four years ago in August."

"Oh, I know, He told me so. If you live as long as I

have, child, you'll learn that love lives beyond death. I'd say Last Chance loves his brother very much."

Speechless for a long moment, Vivian found her voice. "Oh, Nanna, I'd like to believe, but I don't know."

Nanna snorted into the phone. "You shouldn't doubt, Vivvie. How is Calhoun?"

"I don't know. He's in a medically induced coma, Nanna." Vivian sank onto a bench and sighed.

"I'll be praying. You'd better go back to him. Call me when he wakes up."

If he wakes up, Vivian thought, but promised.

Late Saturday, the coma-inducing drip was removed. If all went well, Calhoun should wake within six to twelve hours. Although Lincoln prayed, nothing changed.

On Sunday morning, more than twenty-four hours after the medical team placed Calhoun in the coma, they removed the ventilator. Although he breathed on his own, he didn't rouse. His vitals remained stable, and since ICU beds were needed for more critical patients, the staff moved Calhoun to a single room on a different floor.

"He'll still be monitored more closely than an average patient," Dr. Pacini stated. "I'm a surgeon, so he won't be my patient now. Dr. Craig Owens, one of the hospitalists on staff, will take charge. I have every hope Calhoun will make a full recovery."

"Thank you." Vivian ached to hug the woman but refrained.

Cal's new room proved to be private, a small space with one hospital bed and a single window. As soon as staff settled him, Vivian entered with Linc behind. "At least, we can be with him all the time here."

Lincoln shrugged. "I wish I thought it made any difference. So far, he hasn't shown the slightest indication we're here."

Dr. Craig Owens arrived fifteen minutes later. He stood tall and lean, at least six foot tall without an extra ounce. His perfect posture appeared military. Although he nodded to Vivian and Linc, he said nothing as he read Cal's chart. The physician gazed over steel-rimmed bifocal glasses.

Vivian sat in the room's sole chair. "How is my husband?"

"Stable, which is a major improvement over critical. Fever's gone, but my concern centers on the fact he hasn't regained consciousness. He's breathing on his own, but I have other concerns."

Linc leaned against the windowsill. "Such as? I'm worried about my brother."

Dr. Owens hitched his shoulders. "To let his body rest, we induced a medical coma, but he should have roused by now. I'm calling it coma since he's primarily non-responsive, hasn't opened his eyes, or given any reason to think he's aware on any level."

"Is that bad?" Lincoln's frown creased his forehead. "I thought he was out of the woods. Is there still a chance he might not survive?"

Vivian cringed. Like her brother-in-law, she'd thought Calhoun was no longer in danger of dying.

"At this point, we don't know." Dr. Owens spread his hands wide. "If he opened his eyes, it would bring the chance of a good recovery to one in ten. When I tested his reflexes, he responded with very slight motor skills, which can indicate a slightly better than fifteen percent chance of recovering."

Vivian did the math. If she calculated correctly, the doctor predicted no more than a ten or fifteen percent shot at survival. *That's an eighty-five to ninety percent change he doesn't make it.* Her chest ached with unshed sobs. With a strength she didn't know she had, she drew a deep breath and found the courage to ask. "What would improve his chances?"

The doctor twisted his lips together. "If he moaned or groaned, then I would be more encouraged. A patient who makes sounds raises the percentage to thirty percent. Right now, Calhoun still has a chance. Each day, however, without change, diminishes the odds."

"Should we be worried?" Lincoln stared through the window with his back to the room.

After a thirty-second pause, Dr. Owens sighed and spread his hands wide. "If he were my family member, I would be. We'll re-evaluate in a few days. If you're church people, I suggest prayer."

Vivian covered her face with both hands. *Prayer, again. As if it would help. The same God who failed my parents isn't listening.* Her brain numbed, and she shivered. *Maybe I'm coming down with flu, too.*

Lincoln lunged toward the bed and stood over his brother.

The doctor patted his shoulder, then departed. A nurse entered moments later. She checked vitals and made notations on an electronic chart.

Vivian rose and stared through the window at the parking lot. From what Lincoln said, the Red River lay to the east with Bossier City on the opposite bank. Cross Lake was to the northwest. She couldn't see either one. The tears she'd held in check for so long rained down her face, and fear clutched her with sharp claws.

She had forgotten the nurse's presence until the woman cleared her throat. "Don't let Dr. Owens upset you. Sometimes we call him Dr. Gloom and Doom. He tells it straight, but sometimes he's too harsh."

"I'd rather know the truth. I don't believe in sugarcoating." At the moment, she almost hated the doctor for what he said, but she didn't doubt he spoke reality.

The nurse offered a small smile. "The stats he quoted are worst-case scenario. What he didn't tell you is that up to seventy-five percent of coma patients do survive, and twenty-five percent waken after ten or more days in a coma. Calhoun's still got time to come around. Talk to him. It can help."

"Thank you." Vivian grasped the shreds of hope. She returned to the bedside and touched Cal's cheek.

Lincoln stared across the hospital bed. "I can't take any more right now. I'm going to stretch my legs, Vivian. Do you want anything while I'm gone?"

"No, thanks." She ached for this nightmare to end so she could go home to Missouri with Calhoun.

"I'll rent a hotel room. We'll have someplace to go to get out of here, and we can get some sleep." Lincoln tossed the idea and gazed, waiting for her reply.

Vivian considered, then rejected the idea. "If you want one, go ahead, but I'll stay here. I need to be here when he wakes up."

The days stretched into nights, fueled by coffee and cafeteria food. Nothing tasted good to Vivian, not even the meals Lincoln brought from outside restaurants. Vivian talked to Calhoun and sometimes played country music on her phone in the hope her husband would respond. Most of the time, no matter how hard he tried, Linc failed to convince Vivian to leave the room. The rare times she agreed to take a break, she walked outside within the medical center grounds.

By Thursday, no changes had occurred in his condition. Calhoun had been in this room since Sunday, and on Friday, a week would have passed since his injury. "A feeding tube is a necessity," Dr. Owens told Vivian. "He has lost weight, and he needs sustenance if there's a chance at survival. You should consider a long-term care facility, as well. I can't recommend taking him far, but you might want to discuss whether you'd want him here or over in Texas, closer to home."

"I can't," Vivian whispered. "I can't think about it or talk about that yet." Her head whirled, and she became so dizzy she put her head between her legs to avoid fainting. For the first time, she spent a few hours at the hotel where she showered, wept until she puked, but she didn't sleep.

On Friday, Dr. Owens delivered more dire news on his daily rounds. "He's still in a coma." The doctor's blunt manner hadn't softened. "He continues to breathe on his own, but Calhoun remains in a coma because he's not responding or rousing. The patient has been in this room since Sunday, and this is the fourth day." He paused to squeeze Calhoun's hands, one at a time. He shook his head when there was no response. "He hasn't been responding to stimulus, and the facts are this—after three days, the possibility of a coma patient making a good or even moderate recovery is down to seven percent. That's a ninety-three percent chance he won't survive. If this coma continues for two weeks, the possibility for recovery falls to two percent. Today is day four, but if we count the time he spent in ICU, it's day six. After a week, half the patients in a coma will be in a vegetive state, and that's if they open their eyes, move, or make noise. He's done none of those things."

"And what's that mean in the long run?" Vivian crossed her arms as she stood at the head of Cal's bed and met his gaze. No way could she imagine her cowboy as a vegetable, lying in a coma forever. Not the Cal who caught her fancy with his grin and his wit, not the man who clung hard to outlast a bull. Sorrow cut through her the way a sharp knife sliced ripe fruit. Defiance blended with her sadness, and her tone turned sharp.

Dr. Owens stared over the glasses perched on his nose. Crimson splotched his cheeks. "His overall prognosis is poor. The longer this continues, the likelihood increases his current state will last for months or years. I'd suggest you consider the future. We can't keep him here as a patient forever, and I wouldn't recommend home care. I can ask hospital social services to come by with a list of long-term care facilities so you can start the selection process."

"No." Lincoln barked the word in a hoarse, rough tone. "No, not yet."

"Very well. I have the weekend off. Dr. James will cover for my shifts. If nothing changes—and I honestly don't expect anything will—we'll talk seriously about long-term options on Monday." Dr. Owens tone remained as level as if he discussed the weather. When neither spoke, he nodded and left the room, his soft-soled shoes whispering against the tile floor.

Heavy silence filled the room. Linc collapsed into the chair, buried his face in his hands, and wept.

Vivian shifted into denial. She refused to give up hope, so she pretended she hadn't heard a word the doctor pronounced. Vivian stood by Cal's bed. As she had done each day, she combed his hair. She leaned close and kissed his slack lips. "I love you, Calhoun. Come back to me, Cowboy. We have a lot of living to do, and I want to do it with you."

"Stop." Lincoln jumped to his feet with a shout. "Just stop. If he could hear you, if that would work, it would have by now. You've talked to him until you've nearly lost your voice. I have, too. There's nothing much else we can do, Vivian, but pray. It's in God's hands." Linc stormed out of the room.

Vivian started to follow and changed her mind. She lacked any words of comfort, and they both needed space. She held Calhoun's hands in hers, and for a second, she felt a tiny movement. Although it was probably her imagination, a small flame of hope flared. As if he spoke to her now, she remembered something Calhoun had said, more than once, one day she'd need God, and He would be there. Someday, he'd said she might need the Lord enough to pray. Sullivan, though he was dead and no more than spirit, stated Calhoun needed her prayers. Everyone else prayed. Lincoln believed no option remained but prayer. Vivian realized if a moment ever existed to get on her knees to the Lord, this was it.

If nothing changed, she would either become a widow or the wife of a man in a vegetative state. She refused to accept either reality. Vivian kissed her husband, then knelt on the hard tile hospital floor. She pressed her hands together in a once-familiar way. She closed her eyes and struggled for focus. To get her mind in the right place, she fumbled for the words of The Lord's Prayer. Her lips whispered it, and as she prayed, a sense of peace crept into her heart. Then her own words poured out from the bottom of her soul.

"Please, Lord. I've been so wrong and so far away from You. I hardened my heart and shut my ears. But I always believed most of my life, and I realize I still do. You're still there, and You've always been there. Help Calhoun. Please let him wake up. I love him so very much. He deserves a life, we want to have a family, and I promise to raise any children we have to praise Your name. I've tried to reach him, but he doesn't move or wake. I don't even know if he hears me, Lord, but touch him with Your healing."

She poured out her heart, on her knees, hands clasped together. With faith renewed, she prayed without ceasing, like a verse she recalled from the Bible. From memory, she tossed in Scriptures she recalled, as she kept praying for healing for her husband. Vivian asked that God's will be done. She begged God to forgive her hard-headedness. Calhoun would, she thought, if he lived. He would laugh with joy and quote the verses about the prodigal son.

Maybe I'm a prodigal daughter. I ought to have reread the book of Job a long time ago. I should have listened to both Calhoun and my heart.

Time lost meaning. Vivian lost track of how long she knelt and prayed. She found her faith and renewed it. A slight sound broke into her consciousness. She ignored it the first time, then paused. Vivian lifted her head and focused.

"Pretty Lady."

Calhoun's voice whispered so faint she could barely hear it.

"Vivian."

She rocketed up from her knees and rushed to his side.

His dark eyes shimmered with tears as he gazed up at her.

"Calhoun. Oh, Calhoun." Vivian wept, tears streaming down her cheeks. She covered his face with butterfly kisses and grasped his hand. Although the movement was feeble, his fingers moved against hers. "I love you, Cowboy."

"Don't...cry," he spoke with effort, but his dark brown eyes met hers without blinking.

"I've been weeping for days, but this time, it's from joy. You're going to live." A sob shifted into a laugh. "Thank you, Jesus. Thank you, Lord."

"You prayed." His lips formed a faint grin.

"I did. I love you so much. You scared me so bad I got right with the Lord." More tears rained down her face, but she didn't bother wiping them away. She held his hands in hers and kissed his fingers.

"Love you." His lips moved.

Although she could barely hear him, his ghost of a grin remained.

"Tired." Calhoun shut his beautiful eyes, but he'd awakened.

She knew he would again. Vivian sat in a chair and buried her face in her hands, sobbing with such relief her head spun.

The door to the corridor flew open as Lincoln returned. "What's wrong? What happened, Vivian? Is he…" his voice trailed off, breaking before he completed asking the question.

"He woke up, Linc. Calhoun woke up and spoke." She raised her head and met his gaze.

"Seriously?" Every bit of color drained from Linc's face.

"Yes." Vivian returned to Calhoun and cradled his hand in hers.

Lincoln tromped to the other side of the bed. "Calhoun, can you hear me?"

Cal's eyelids twitched, then opened a little. "Yeah…not deaf."

Lincoln staggered and sat. "Praise the Lord. I thought…oh, never mind. Calhoun, if I wasn't so glad you're awake, I'd want to punch you. We've been through hell this week."

Cal managed a wink.

Vivian laughed with joy. Her man was back. She tasted happiness, and her spirits shone bright. She recalled a verse she had once loved. It meant much more now. *Rejoice in the Lord, always. Again, I say rejoice.*

After a long moment, Linc grinned. "I gotta go call Sasha so she can tell the kids there won't be a funeral."

Vivian gazed at her husband. One day, they would part, but this wasn't the time. Calhoun lay prone and pale, still too weak to lift his hand, but she believed he would recover.

Anything else was unthinkable.

Chapter Twenty-Six

Everyone from his wife and family, to the medical professionals, told Calhoun he was a living miracle. After almost a week unconscious, he'd awakened after suffering serious injuries with an outlook for a full recovery. A series of MRIs revealed no brain damage, and his injuries would mend. Recovering from the bruised aorta, repaired with staples, would require two or three months to heal completely, but eventually, he would be fine. That was one miracle, he thought. The other was that his wife had gotten back on track with God. By Saturday, Calhoun could sit upright in bed. He grinned at his wife. "Are you sure I've been here for a week?"

"Totally, Cowboy. Although it seems more like a month." She grasped his left hand in hers and caressed it.

Since he'd awakened, Vivian couldn't stop touching him. If he'd been stronger, Calhoun would have climbed out of bed to kiss her. "I don't remember much." He recalled very little about the hospital, not until he woke to find Vivian kneeling in prayer.

"The doctors said that's normal." Lincoln turned away from the window. "What's the last you do remember?"

Cal drew a deep breath. Between climbing onto a rambunctious bull and opening his eyes to see Vivian praying, most of it was a crazy jumble. A few things stood out, though. He remembered looking down at himself in the back of an ambulance, his body broken and still. Then he floated high in the night sky. Calhoun remembered stars and gazing down at the Louisiana countryside. It had been beautiful with a powerful sense of a deep, abiding peace. His younger brother had been with him, he remembered, but Sullivan hadn't been smiling.

"You can't come any farther." Last Chance rode the air currents beside him and cut a flip in the air. "Calhoun, it's not your time. The family and the Pretty Lady you married need you."

"I thought you told Caleb there might be a funeral." Speaking to his dead little brother didn't seem strange at all, not now.

"There could have been and still might be. I was trying to warn you not to ride, you knot head. I'd hate for you to die too soon, like me." Sully gave a sad stare.

"I'd rather not." Calhoun wanted to live more than anything.

"Then don't."

Calhoun didn't remember making a choice, but the next thing, his spirit hurtled back toward earth. On the way, he saw familiar faces, his mom and dad, his grandparents, some he didn't recognize, and Barlow, his great-great-great grandfather. The first cowboy of the family to settle in Texas gave him a nod, as if to say he was headed in the right direction. From them, a powerful love flowed, and he imbibed it.

Sully came with him most of the way, but then he touched his shoulder. "You take it from here, Calhoun. Go home, love your wife, tell Linc I said howdy, and name that first son Barlow like you said. The original Barlow said he'd be right proud if you did."

"Why did he show up with you?" Cal knew the man was their patriarch, but he didn't understand.

"He says we're all his, his sons and grandsons. The generations don't matter. He still loves us all."

Somehow, Cal knew this would be goodbye, probably for a long time. "I love you, Last Chance."

"Back at you," the kid said. "And remember, it wasn't your fault no more than this mess was Vivian's, you hear?"

"I do. What's heaven like?" Not that he wanted to find out anytime soon, but he had to ask.

Sullivan grinned.

The expression was so true to life that Calhoun ached with grief. He missed his kid brother.

"Like life only better, the way those verses say, 'Now we see through a glass darkly.' It's awesome, man, and so is God. You'll find out when it's time. Get on back now. You gotta go, and so do I."

Calhoun plunged back into his body during surgery. A doctor, maybe more than one, and several nurses were clustered about him. He knew God directed their hands. Awareness came and pain returned, smacking him hard and fast, but he didn't complain. It meant he still lived.

From his hospital bed, Calhoun considered how to answer Lincoln's question. "I remember the rodeo and getting on the bull. After that, I doubt you'd believe me."

"Try me." Lincoln sighed. "I'm of a notion to believe a lot more than I did before all this."

Cal sketched out what he could remember.

Lincoln didn't scoff but nodded. "I believe you, bro, I do."

Vivian settled on the edge of the bed, facing Calhoun. Every time the staff caught her, they made her move, but she always returned once they left. "So do I."

"Kiss me, honey." He puckered his lips.

She leaned forward and brushed her mouth against his.

He lifted a weak hand to stroke her hair and gave her back a real kiss, the first since he got hurt. "I love you, Pretty Lady. You know what else I remember?"

"I'm almost afraid to ask." Vivian tossed back her head with a light laugh.

He laughed, too, but stopped because it hurt his ribs. "Most of the time in the coma, I could hear you, honey. I knew I'd make it because you told me so from the first night."

Vivian reached out and caressed his cheek. "The docs said you probably wouldn't, but I couldn't accept that, Calhoun. I didn't want to be a widow. On Friday, though, the doctor told us he didn't think you'd come out of the coma."

"That's when you prayed. I told you when you needed God, he'd be there, didn't I?" His dark eyes latched onto her face and held there.

"You were right," she whispered. "I got my faith back. All it took was almost losing you."

That, he thought, was nearly worth dying for, but she probably didn't want to hear his thought. Instead, he asked the question he'd wondered since he first blinked open his eyes. "When do I get to go home?"

"Not until the staples come out. And that's probably another week. Then you can leave, but you can't get back to normal for another few weeks. After that, it'll be several months before you're totally recovered." She cradled his hand between both of hers.

Lincoln fidgeted. "I figure you should come stay at the ranch when you first get out of here. When you feel up to it, you can head up to your place. We're still planning to come for Thanksgiving, if that's all right."

"Of course, it is. I want you to see the homeplace." Cal managed a grin. "Your place is as much home to me as anywhere. I'll stay with y'all for a little bit, if it's okay with Vivian."

"It is." She didn't hesitate to answer. "Your family is my family now, too. I'm good for whatever helps you get healed." Vivian bent low for a kiss.

On the last day of October, Halloween, when a hint of fall hovered in the air, Calhoun left the hospital in Shreveport. He would have preferred to walk out of the place, but the staff rolled him in a wheelchair to where Vivian waited with the truck. Cal drew on his last bit of patience as he was assisted into the passenger seat, but as soon as they had driven a short distance, he made a request. "Pull over, Pretty Lady."

Vivian did as he asked, her eyes wide. "What's the matter? Are you okay?"

Since he got hurt, she was easily rattled. Cal grinned. "Nothing, honey. I just want to drive."

"Do you? Are you sure you feel like it?" A slow smile illuminated her face.

He wasn't, but he would or die trying. He needed to get behind the wheel and go. "I do and yeah, I do." Calhoun thought she might fuss.

But she didn't. "Scoot over then, Cowboy. I'll come around to get in the truck."

Vivian understood him in a way almost no one else ever had. Oh, his brothers—both the living and the dead—always had, but not to the same depth as his wife. "I love you, honey." Cal placed his hands on the steering wheel, glad to grasp it.

She climbed into the passenger side to take her usual position beside him. "I love you, Calhoun. I think we've proved that in sickness and in health thing, so let's not go there again."

"I'll do my best. I'd rather not revisit that one, either." He drove as far as Waskom on Highway 79 and pulled to the shoulder. "Want to take the wheel?"

"Are you all right?" Vivian wrinkled her forehead.

"I am, just tired. I haven't been outside the dang hospital in more than a month. I want to enjoy the scenery."

At Linc's, he was cosseted, comforted, spoiled, and sweet-talked. After a week of being treated like an invalid, being pampered, and catered to until Calhoun couldn't stand any more, he and Vivian were ready to head back to Missouri. During those few days, he'd regained most of his strength, Cal felt better than he had in a long time.

"Stay longer if you want. My house is your house." Linc grasped his hand to shake it.

"Thanks, but I'm ready to head home." Cal ended the handshake and hugged his brother's neck. "You're coming for Thanksgiving, so I'll see you in a couple weeks."

"Three weeks to the day." Lincoln laughed. "We're coming for your birthday, bro, then staying all week."

"Good. I'm glad, Linc." Cal embraced Linc, then put an arm around Sasha. He took Vivian's hand, and they walked to the truck. By the time they got to the homeplace, it would be evening, but he didn't care, because he just wanted to be home.

Two days later, after visiting Nanna and stocking up on groceries, Calhoun sat with Vivian on the porch in the morning cool. Calhoun sipped coffee as he admired the glorious fall colors, bright oranges, vivid yellows, and deep reds. He'd turn thirty-four soon, but the age didn't seem so old now since he wouldn't be competing in any more rodeos. At least, he was here, above ground. "Honey, I'm happier than I've ever been." It was the pure truth, and he wanted her to know. "We're home to stay, the family's coming for Thanksgiving, and I feel good. No more bulls waiting to be ridden, and no more worries I'll get hurt. No funnels, either."

She laughed as they rocked in the old porch swing and took his hand. "I bet I can make you even happier." Her eyes sparkled, and she wore a mysterious little smile.

Calhoun turned toward her. "Give it your best shot." He wondered if she had arranged for Linc to bring his horse, which despite his earlier plan, he hadn't, when they visited, or if she'd decided to bring Nanna back to the farm for the holiday. Maybe she'd sold some more of the rodeo photos she'd taken of him. Or perhaps Vivian had started writing the novel she dreamed she would. Her contributor's copy of one of the magazines with a photo of him, astride a bull in the arena, had arrived while they were still in Texas.

"Cowboy, you're my husband, you're a brother, an uncle, and a good friend, but in early June, you'll be one more thing." Vivian gazed into his eyes as she spoke.

"What's that?"

Vivian put his right hand over her tummy and let it rest there. "You'll be a daddy, Calhoun. We're going to have a baby."

Her statement didn't register for a few moments or make sense, but when he understood, he shouted one of his Rebel yells, loud and proud enough to please old Barlow. Calhoun rubbed her belly with wonder. "Thank the Lord." Joy soared within him. He would be a father, and it might be a son. If so, he would name him Barlow Washington Kelly. "Our son will be a summer baby."

"Yes, if the child's born on time, probably just after Memorial Day. You do know it might be a girl, Calhoun." Vivian touched his cheek with the back of her hand.

"It could be." He remembered what Sullivan had said, that last time, and believed it would be a boy. "If it's a gal, then we'll name her Kate for your grandmother. The one thing I know is how much I'll love the kid."

Vivian smiled and put her head on his shoulder.

A thought occurred. "How do you know? Have you been to a doctor?"

"I did a home pregnancy test when you were still in the hospital." She blushed. "It was positive, so Sasha took me to her ob-gyn last week. She referred me to a doctor in Joplin."

"And you didn't tell me?"

"I wanted to share the news here...at the homeplace." Vivian kissed his neck, then his cheek.

She made the right decision. This was the best place on earth to share such happy news. "I'm glad.

354

Pretty Lady, I love you."

"Oh, Calhoun, I love you so much." Vivian's eyes danced as she rested a hand on her still-flat belly.

He kissed her then, a sweet, unhurried kiss, and they sat, swinging in peaceful harmony.

His last rodeo was behind him, but his future loomed straight-ahead. Unlike Sullivan, he survived, but Calhoun realized recovery hadn't been his last chance, but a brand-new beginning. Cal claimed the blessing, ready to live this life…with this woman, and in this place.

A word about the author…

From an early age, Lee Ann Sontheimer Murphy scribbled stories, inspired by the books she read, the family tales she heard, and even the conversations she overheard at the beauty shop where her grandmother had a weekly standing appointment.

As an author, she has published more than two dozen novels and novellas writing as Lee Ann Sontheimer Murphy, as Patrice Wayne for historical fiction and also as Liathán O'Murchadha.

She spent her early career in broadcast radio, interviewing everyone from politicians to major league baseball players and writing ad copy. In those radio years she began to write short stories and articles, some of which found publication. In 1994 she married Roy Murphy and they had three children, all now grown-up. Lee Ann spent a number of years in the newspaper field as both a journalist and editor and was widowed in 2019.

In late 2020, she hung up her editor's hat to return to writing fiction. A native of St. Joseph, Missouri, she lives and works in the rugged, mysterious, and beautiful Missouri Ozarks.

https://leeannsontheimer.blogspot.com/

Another title by this author
The Scarred Santa